Murder Aboard the Choctaw Gambler

A JANCY DEWHURST MYSTERY

MURDER ABOARD THE CHOCTAW GAMBLER

SHARON ERVIN

FIVE STAR

A part of Gale, Cengage Learning

GALE
CENGAGE Learning™

Detroit • New York • San Francisco • New Haven, Conn • Waterville, Maine • London

Copyright © 2008 by Sharon Ervin.
Five Star Publishing, a part of Gale, Cengage Learning.

Set in 11 pt. Plantin
Printed on permanent paper.

LIBRARY OF CONGRESS CATALOGING-IN-PUBLICATION DATA

Ervin, Sharon, 1941–
   Murder aboard the Choctaw Gambler / a Jancy Dewhurst
mystery / Sharon Ervin. — 1st ed.
      p. cm.
   ISBN-13: 978-1-59414-698-5 (hardcover : alk. paper)
   ISBN-10: 1-59414-698-5 (hardcover : alk. paper)
   1. Women journalists—Oklahoma—Fiction. I. Title.
PS3605.R86M87 2008
813'.6—dc22   2007047623

First Edition. First Printing: May 2008.

Published in 2008 in conjunction with Tekno Books.

Printed in the United States of America
1 2 3 4 5 6 7 12 11 10 09 08

For Bill, the trip of a lifetime

ACKNOWLEDGMENTS:

I owe special thanks to:

Former Osage County Sheriff George Wayman for candidly brainstorming theories on the homicide we both worked those many years ago;

Research Librarian Christopher Elliot, whom my research questions have yet to stump;

Oklahoma State Bureau Supervisor Tommy Graham, who still grins when he sees me coming, but takes my calls anyway;

Edward Long, the gun guru who put the Ruger in my hand, then patiently reviewed ballistics until I understood;

Nancy and Lucy, who unknowingly whacked the real Old Blue into a million pieces one spring morning when he slithered too far from home;

And Diane Piron-Gelman, Jennifer Alt, Ronda Talley, and Jane Bryant for brilliant eagle eye editing.

CHAPTER ONE

I tucked in the tail of the new silk blouse and fastened the pleated trousers, then turned to check my backside in the mirror. I felt like one of those featherbrained females whose primary concern in life is how she looks.

Usually I didn't care enough about my appearance to check the rear view. Today, however . . . well, it wasn't the prospect of investigating a homicide aboard the *Choctaw Gambler* riverboat that inspired this heightened concern. I flashed an apologetic smile at my reflection. Spending a whole day with Agent Jim Wills did. Not normally observant, Jim's dark eyes seemed to see everything about me.

I dialed the *Clarion.* "Ron Melchoir, please."

The managing editor answered on the first ring.

"Ron, there's been a murder on board the *Choctaw Gambler.* Jim Wills asked me to ride out to the scene with him."

Melchoir cleared his throat. "That's real sweet of him, Jancy."

"Okay, Melchoir, can the sarcasm."

He laughed. "Don't pitch me Arizona ocean front, Jance."

"Melchoir, it's a homicide." I resented having to defend myself to him. I was having trouble enough justifying my actions to me. "It's news. We're in the news business. It's my job. Are you telling me not to go?"

"No, I want you to go. Just don't get to mooning too much over Wills and forget what you're there for." He paused. "Call in what you've got before one." I started to hang up but

Melchoir's voice stopped me. "Jancy, I don't mind you kidding me, honey, but don't be fooling yourself with all this 'We're in the news business' crap."

I made sure he heard my audible huff and slammed the receiver down harder than I intended. Usually I didn't mind Melchoir or any of those other clowns on the paper kidding me about guys I dated, but Wills was different.

I heard a car roll into the driveway and tried to set my defenses against the butterflies winging in my stomach as I stepped to the window.

The driveway was directly below my second floor room in the big, barn-like house on Cherry Street, which I shared with four other women. My disapproving scowl softened at the sight of Jim's drab sedan with the antennas in the driveway. The clock on my bedside table showed seven-forty. Only ten minutes late. Prompt, for State Bureau of Investigation Agent Wills.

Feeling safe behind the chintz curtains, I just stood there watching—admiring—as Jim got out of the car. The butterflies in my stomach swarmed with a vengeance. My mouth got the familiar tinny taste.

Wills' close-cropped hair glistened black in the sunlight. His muscular body was neatly camouflaged—cuffed gray slacks, a stiff white shirt and a tie of geometric designs unifying the parts. The breeze whipped his navy blue blazer and I caught a glimpse of the suspenders he called *galluses*. I bit back a smile. I had a grand plan for my life. It did not include Agent Wills. Funny how I had to keep reminding myself about that, especially when he was in sight.

I was reminding myself, again, when he glanced up. I jumped back from the window, not wanting him to catch me watching.

The new tweed blazer was going to be my shield. Actually, I bought it hoping it would make me look and feel sophisticated. I slipped it on, then turned for a last glance in the mirror.

10

Would I inspire *the look* today, the sizzling twinkle that lit up his dark, dark eyes and set me tingling from tip to toe? Oh, God, I *was* turning into one of those empty-headed, man-crazy cows.

The doorbell rang. Gritting my teeth, I took a firm grip on my overcharged libido, stepped out of my room and closed the door hoping to leave that insipid me inside. As I walked to the stairs, the butterflies in my ribcage felt more like finches in a birdcage.

Meticulous nearly to a fault, Wills dressed like an advertisement for what the well-dressed man should wear. Each time we hung out, I was more aware of my usually dowdy appearance and my too-casual habits.

Dowdy came naturally, I suppose, but I had disciplined myself to disregard appearances, including my own. A news reporter couldn't allow clothing, jewelry or trappings to mask the truth of a story that might be hiding behind a façade.

But today was different. Today I wanted to pay attention and keep myself tidy.

Angela Fires, the best-looking one of my housemates, had answered the doorbell and, as usual, stood close to Jim billing and cooing and gazing coquettishly into his face. When he lifted his eyes to me at the top of the stairs, however, his subdued smile broadened and there it was: *The look,* the one that haunted my dreams and made me restless in bed at night. I flushed and my hands got clammy, a standard reaction to *the look.*

Jim had to know the effect his blatant admiration had on me, yet he made no effort to conceal his shameless regard. Darn him, anyway.

His body pivoted, following his eyes, to face me squarely and lavish his full attention. The fact that my own body responded so eagerly to that expression on that face was disturbing and I reminded myself again: My fabulous future did not include Jim Wills.

I had spent my first year out of the university as courthouse reporter for *The Bishop Clarion*. Before next October, Riley Wedge had promised to call me to intern with the wire service. Two months after that, Wedge would assign me to a bureau overseas, my dream job, my ultimate goal in life. I had trained for it, aspired to it, was on my way. But my grand plan had not anticipated Jim Wills.

He sustained his dark gaze and winsome smile as I gathered my wits and descended the stairs. "Good morning," he said. "You look very pretty." The man could do toothpaste commercials for a living.

My determined smile wavered with a passing thought and I whispered, "You, too."

Jim's grin broadened. I hadn't intended him to hear that.

As I reached ground level, he took my hand. Like an impartial observer, I allowed my hand to settle into his large, warm one before another thought prompted me and I scanned the room. Angela was gone. Jim didn't seem to have noticed her departure. That was good . . . and bad.

With a proprietary air, Jim put me in the car and I marveled again at such impeccable manners in such a manly man. Before he got into the driver's seat, he removed his blazer, folded it lengthwise and laid it on the back seat. It seemed like a stuffy old-man thing to do, yet the butterflies stampeded in my roiling stomach.

He smiled at me, almost *into* me. "Would you like some breakfast?"

"No, thanks. I'm too excited. Or nervous. Or something."

Jim's brows arched over his mischievous eyes. "Is it the homicide, or me?"

"What?"

"Giving you the jitters?"

He could yank me out of my dream world in a flash. The stampeding critters circled. "It's not you."

"No?" He caught my left hand and raised it to his lips. I tried to pull free, but only halfheartedly. He held fast.

"Why do you touch me so much?" My question sounded like an accusation.

His smile freshened. "I'm a hands-on kind of guy. I like physical contact. And I *really* like physical contact with you." He hesitated, as if waiting for me to comprehend some hidden meaning, to remember again how quickly I warmed when he kissed me and held me. My reliable blush must have signaled that I'd gotten the picture. He lowered his voice. "I also 'touch you so much' because you like me to. When I reach for you, you respond like shavings to a magnet."

His grin vexed me and I tried again to pull my hand away from his. Instead of releasing it, however, he turned it, pried my fingers open, lowered his mouth and nibbled my palm, sending chills pebbling my arms. Sheer force of will helped me snatch my captive hand from his grasp.

Chuckling, Jim started the car.

"Who's the victim?" I asked, thinking regular conversation might help defuse the fireworks going off inside me.

Jim grinned at the roadway. He knew perfectly well what he did to my insides. He did it on purpose. Glaring at him, I still felt queasy. Darn it, I liked him, especially liked him when he was ornery and teasing.

He watched the traffic as he answered, again reaching for and clasping my hand, but his tone became serious. "I don't know. I didn't recognize the name. Local law down there doesn't know him either."

I let my hand remain locked in his and tried to fill the air with words, mostly nervous chatter, random questions about the homicide. He answered in a businesslike tone. After that, I scrambled for other safe subjects. In the course of our forty-five-minute trip, I verbally waded in and out of a dozen innocuous topics: the university's football team, unbeaten through four games; fighting in the Middle East; Liz Pinello's new job; my other roommates—four in all—and their activities; the erratic stock market; football again, anything to keep my roller-coaster emotions on their rails.

I willed myself not to look at him, not to notice biceps straining beneath his shirtsleeves, not to admire his shoulders, his jaw line, his straight nose, his sun-bronzed skin, his one hand deftly steering the car, his dark, dark eyes that settled on me occasionally and held for long seconds at a time as if slaking a thirst.

I didn't dare stop talking and thought maybe he understood my dilemma when he made an occasional comment, helping maintain the conversational momentum.

Finally, as we pulled into a parking lot dockside, Jim released my hand. I swallowed a groan, immediately missing the warmth.

Police cruisers blocked dozens of other vehicles in the lot.

Stepping out of the car, I didn't say a word, struck dumb by my first glimpse of the *Choctaw Gambler*. It was glorious, a stately three-deck replica of the paddlewheel showboats once abundant on southern waterways, the white sheen of the vessel's skin a striking contrast to its mahogany decks and trim.

Oklahoma's late October sunshine baked my shoulders as Jim put his hand to my back to nudge me forward. We walked toward the boat and I was aware of heat—the unusual glow of that spectacular, freshly washed morning, and the warmth of Jim's guiding hand. River water gliding by sparkled and lapped against *Gambler*'s sides, muffling the murmur of voices that sounded far away.

I roused from that dreamlike state when Wills snaked his arm around my waist. Pushing me in front of him, he flashed his badge to several uniformed policemen near the gangplank. Security waved us through, up the ramp and onto the lower deck of the riverboat.

Stepping onto *Gambler*'s deck was like being transported back in time to simpler days when innocence and naiveté were virtues rather than liabilities. My breathing slowed and I swelled with a quiet reverence for the past, even as I inhaled present reality in the smell of fresh paint and new carpentry.

I had almost, but not quite, forgotten Jim's proximity until he again took my hand to lead me through a double-door glass entry. Wordlessly we followed the sounds of voices up a broad stairway to the boat's second level. Neither of us spoke.

At the top of the stairs another set of double doors opened into a ballroom.

Inside, the air hung heavy with the musk of stale cigarette smoke and booze. Releasing my hand, Jim stopped to talk with a uniformed patrolman at the door. I wandered further in and quickly counted at least six investigators—uniformed and in plain clothes—milling among fifty or sixty people in the ball-room.

Three detectives prowled, stooping occasionally, their heads bent as they searched for anything on the floor beneath the gaming tables that occupied the middle of the room.

Others interviewed civilians who were gathered at tables, which radiated like spokes from a small, half-circle, parquet dance floor fronting the stage to my right. To my left, banks of slot machines stood dark and silent.

I flipped open my reporter's notebook and eased closer to one of several clusters of people to eavesdrop. Movement on the stage, however, caught my attention. The curtains stood open, the stage itself empty, except for an officious-looking man with a badge on his lapel who waved, then began working his way

Sharon Ervin

down the stage stairs and strode briskly toward me. He stopped immediately in front of me just as a hand touched my back. Jim's voice crooned near my ear. "Jancy Dewhurst, newspaper reporter, meet Murray Serago, New Bedford Police Chief."

Of course, Serago had intended his wave for Jim, who apparently had walked up behind me.

I stuck out my hand and Serago shook it absently, his bloodshot eyes focused not on me, but on Wills.

Serago was probably five-foot-ten and paunchy. Broken blood vessels along his cheeks and in the bulb of his prominent nose gave him a perpetually flushed look, emphasized by the way he appeared to bustle, fidgeting even when he was standing still. Sprigs of chestnut-colored hair bristled from his balding head. The pockets on the chief's brown suit coat sagged. One bulged with a retractable measuring tape visible inside the gaping pocket. The pocket's opening was white with chalk dust.

Wills reached around me to shake Serago's hand before pulling a small notebook from his own pocket. "Brief us, Murray."

Serago dropped a piece of chalk into his protruding coat pocket and dusted his hands together. His movements seemed spasmodic.

"*Gambler* here is Jesse Chase's favorite toy." Serago's eyes darted around the room without pausing long at any place or on anyone. "The victim, Larry Potter, was a croupier. One point of note:" Serago suddenly stared hard at Wills. "Potter bore a striking resemblance to Chase."

"Oh, yeah?" Jim obviously got the point the chief was trying to make.

Serago extended his bottom lip as he nodded. "That's what I thought, too."

I stopped writing and looked from Wills to Serago to decipher the meaning of their words. As I did, a young man twenty feet away caught my eye. He smiled. I didn't recognize him and cut

16

my eyes from him without responding.

Serago continued. "Chase moved his office upstairs onto the upper deck, after he turned this tub into a secure little fortress. It's like a military installation. They brought Potter on board the same week Chase moved his office over.

Jim jotted in his notebook. "What's the M.O.?"

"Looks like a pro. One shot. Probably a hollow point from a twenty-two. Back of his head. Bullet's still in there. Clean. No litter. No one heard it. We think it happened between two and three this morning. We'll have more on the weapon later."

"Did the killer see the victim's face?"

Serago shook his head slowly. "Doesn't look like he did."

"Did Potter have enemies of his own?"

"None we've found. He was a transient. We think they spotted him as a ringer for Chase, cleaned him up and set him on here as a decoy for just what happened."

"Where was Chase?"

"He was supposed to be in his office." Serago took a notebook from his inside coat pocket, leaving telltale white chalk wherever his fingers brushed the brown suit, and thumbed through pages. "He had an appointment with an agent for a new band for the ballroom."

"At two o'clock in the morning?" My abrupt question drew surprised looks from both men.

"Yeah," Serago verified, again consulting his notebook. "Casino owners keep odd business hours."

Wills looked at me, but his face was expressionless. He didn't appear either to condemn or approve the interruption. Just when I really wished I knew what he was thinking, he winked. Okay, I knew. I lowered my gaze and tried not to smile.

"Anyway," Serago shuffled loose papers in his notebook, "Chase's daughter called him sometime Sunday night and he took off. He asked Potter to stick around until the agent got there, give the guy some complimentary chits and reset their meet."

"Where'd you get that information?" Wills' eyes seemed reluctant to leave my face. I knew he was looking at me by the way my neck warmed and the familiar blush crawled up from under my shirt collar.

Serago thumbed to a different page in his notebook. "Chase and Kyle Morgan, Chase's right hand, told the same story, separately."

"Were there a lot of people here on a Sunday night?"

"Maybe three hundred guests, total. Not a crowd for them. Something else. They had a full wait staff, thirty, in addition to their regular people, dealers and all. There's a big turnover in the wait staff from night to night. The bookkeeper told me they only paid twenty-nine. That's all they had social security numbers for. Kitchen manager insists he had a full thirty-person staff. Looks like the killer got inside posing as a waiter or waitress but didn't sign on for pay."

Wills glanced around. "What did Chase's daughter want to see him about?"

Serago shrugged and shook his head.

"I'll find out." Wills again wrote in his notebook.

Serago shuffled toward the stage. "Come on. We're interviewing employee witnesses, or you could say *non*-witnesses, backstage."

I lagged behind. When Jim looked back, I smiled and motioned for him to go without me. I knew I would concentrate better if we were separated, and figured it might be the same for him.

When he was out of sight, I wandered through the room listening and watching and jotting notes occasionally. Everyone, law enforcement and employees alike, looked tired, washed out. Some sat, elbows braced on the tables, hands supporting their heads. What I got was: The band had been loud and no one had seen or heard anything out of the ordinary.

"Do you like the boat?" The young man who had smiled at me earlier grinned as he approached.

This time I returned his smile. He seemed harmless enough, about my age, mid-twenties. "Yes."

He flushed slightly. "I saw you wandering around. You a reporter?"

"Yes. Jancy Dewhurst, with *The Bishop Clarion.*"

"Chuck Orb, public relations." We shook hands and I asked him a couple of questions. As it turned out, Orb was an information gold mine.

"*Gambler*'s privately owned," he said. I already knew that, but kept quiet hoping he would tell me things I didn't know. "It's permanent, built on a foundation like any other building, anchored right where it sits."

That tidbit definitely piqued my interest. "What do you mean? What about the paddle wheel?"

"They've got it rigged so water runs over it to make it look like it turns, but it doesn't." Orb seemed pleased to have my undivided attention. "It *can't* go anywhere," he reiterated. "It's built on piers."

"Why?"

He squared his shoulders, puffing up with something that looked like standard-issue male pride. "It's on tribal land. That makes it immune to state gaming laws."

I waited and watched as if I were fascinated, and actually I *was* pretty interested. He rambled on, providing details of security measures and staffing, along with other salient odds and ends.

"The guy who owns it, Jesse Chase, lives aboard sometimes," he added.

"Oh, yeah?"

19

Orb's chest seemed to expand a little more each time one of his revelations surprised me, so I kept being surprised.

"Yeah. A bunch of other people, too."

When Orb had run through his store of knowledge and had begun repeating himself, I tapped the notebook with my pen, decorating the page with a generous coating of dots. "Chuck, who do you work for?"

"Like I said, I'm public relations." He hesitated a minute. "With the police department. Truth is, this is my first day on the job."

"Oh, really? Hey, you seem very knowledgeable, like an old pro." He'd been helpful and I felt like I should reciprocate with a little praise. "Are you a journalism school grad?"

"Nah, history and government."

"And you're doing public relations?"

"Yep."

I laughed lightly, preparing to slip away. "Well, I'm sure you have other things to do. Thanks for your time and your help. You've given me some valuable background."

He cleared his throat, obviously self-conscious about something. "I'm afraid I can't let you just drift around alone."

"Why not?"

"Well, reporters . . . well, truth is, they pocket things. Evidence. I'm supposed to keep an eye on you." He looked a little sheepish. "It's part of the job."

My temper peaked, almost slipped its leash. "Look, Orb, I'm not interested in scarfing off evidence." I drew a breath ready to flay him, but froze as a familiar hand touched my back. Both Orb and I whirled to confront the intruder.

"Agent Wills," Orb said, obviously relieved. "I believe you know Ms. Dewhurst. I saw her interviewing you and Detective Serago earlier. I was just informing her about our policy. . . ."

"She's with me." Jim's proprietary hand circled my waist,

providing a visual aid. Orb cleared his throat. Jim's arrival at that precise moment annoyed me. I did not need a nursemaid. I could darn well look out for myself *and* my First Amendment rights.

The younger man's Adam's apple bounced. "I see. Well, then, if you'll excuse me." Orb pivoted, started to leave, then looked back. "Nice meeting you, Ms. Dewhurst."

I flashed him my best plastic smile and wheeled, ready to straighten out Wills' error.

If he saw it coming, my fury didn't seem to phase him. "Notching another conquest, Dewhurst?" I took one step forward and he retreated, throwing up both hands as if to defend himself. "Come on, Jance, it looked like you were about to disembowel the nice young man." He took advantage of my stunned silence to continue. "I butted in for his sake, not yours." His expression darkened as his thoughts apparently shifted gears. "I need to go see Chase's daughter. I've got all I need to get here."

He caught my elbow and turned me toward the exit. I sputtered objections as he deftly guided me out the double doors and down the stairway.

Crossing the parking lot, my vexation ebbed and I whirled to get a look at Jim's face. Although he seemed deep in thought, I interrupted. "Did you know *Gambler* isn't a boat? It's a permanent structure."

He gave me a solicitous grin. "Yes, I knew that. It's been written up several times in your own newspaper."

I ignored the jibe. "If this is tribal land, how can you and Serago investigate a murder here? Indian property's immune from local law, isn't it?" I repeated as my own, information Orb had provided only moments before.

"They called us. In Oklahoma, there is what is known as 'cross deputizing.' Like other law enforcement agencies, the

Indians can invite us in, if they want us. Today, apparently they did."

"Did you know people live aboard?"

His know-it-all grin faded. "No. Who?"

At last. I felt vindicated to be able to provide information he didn't have. "Jesse Chase and others. Also, he has a regular office staff and a substantial security force, full-time, on the dock and ashore."

"Serago told me about the security. He didn't say anyone lived on board." Apparently pondering, Jim took me to the passenger side of his car. He reached around me to grab the handle, but didn't open the door. "Do you want to go with me to see Chase's daughter?"

I turned and found myself looking directly into his broad, generous mouth. "Yes." I swallowed and tried not to stare. The scent of him wrapped itself around me and I felt the familiar flutter in my stomach as my gaze drifted up, totally without my permission, to engage his.

"You're playing me like a drum, aren't you?" he asked.

I was playing *him?* Give me a break. When I didn't answer, he leaned slightly and I raised my face, drawing him.

He nibbled on my lower lip and an involuntary little laugh escaped my control. He put one broad hand in the small of my back and tugged, sealing my body to his. He smelled heavenly and he was warm and so beautiful. I yielded to his mouth's gentle prodding. I loved the taste of him, the way his tongue toyed with me. I had never necked with anyone so early in the day. It might get to be one of my favorite pastimes.

But *it* was happening again, the thing that made me absolutely skitsy when I was with him; the thing that always happened when he kissed me. I stopped thinking. I hated when that happened; hated myself for the lack of self-discipline that allowed it to happen. Yet the yielding, wanting to yield, set my nerves singing, created sensations beyond any I'd experienced before. The disorientation was only one of my body's many subtle, independent responses to the man. He wielded some kind of power over my anatomy, power that short-circuited my mental dictates, and losing control that way scared the dickens out of me.

Alert to abusive, presumptive, arrogant, possessive males, with Jim I was befuddled by his gentle determination. This man held himself under strict control, yet relentlessly he came and just kept coming, luring me, drawing me to him, in spite of my own better judgment.

In order to dodge the threat that was him, I had to think. In order to think, I had to distance myself from him physically. When he was close—when I breathed the scent of him, felt his strength, heard his voice, looked into his eyes, particularly when I tasted him—I experienced this peculiar brain lock. And it happened again right then as he deepened the kiss.

As usual, he reacted immediately to my slightest effort to oppose him. When he gave way, I shuddered and turned, putting my back to him.

He drew a ragged breath before he wordlessly reached around and opened the car door.

CHAPTER TWO

Lisa Chase Toburn lived in a quiet, upper-middle-class residential neighborhood with street signs cautioning drivers to slow down for "Children Playing." Wills had called ahead and our hostess opened the front door before the bell finished chiming.

Lisa was tall, thirtyish, fair and casual in jeans, Keds and an oversized silk sweater. After introductions, she ushered us down an expansive hallway to a bright, spacious sunroom. An older, well-dressed man stood as we entered.

"Jim, good to see you."

Wills smiled and shook the man's offered hand before he introduced us. "This is Arthur Fry, Jancy, a senior attorney in Fry and Fritch, Inc."

Mr. Fry smiled. "Jim worked for us for far too short a time back when he was fresh out of law school."

The man appeared to be about seventy, and wore an expensive-looking black suit flecked with tiny white stripes. The stripes emphasized his white halo of hair. Gold links glimmered in French cuffs and he wore an Ivy League school tie. His pale blue eyes squinted, indicating he probably wore glasses, and I wondered how much detail he could see without them.

Fry glanced from me to Jim and back. "We couldn't hold Jim's interest. I'm afraid we were too stodgy for his energy. We sure tried to hang onto him."

Jim shifted uncomfortably as Fry recited plans he said the

partners had had for this young protégé's future.

Lisa Toburn stood quietly remote from us and gazed at a pot-ted ficus tree as if she were in a stupor.

As Fry's monologue continued, his attention on me, Jim produced a miniature tape recorder from an inside coat pocket, placed it on the coffee table and indicated Lisa should sit on the sofa in front of it. Although she seemed to be uncomfort-able at the prospect of his questioning, she asked him to call her Lisa, rather than the more stilted Mrs. Toburn. He smiled as he positioned himself beside her. When he began speaking in a businesslike tone, his words effectively silenced Fry's narrative.

"I understand you called your father at the casino last night," Jim said after Lisa had stated her name, address and the date for the recorder. She shot a look at Arthur Fry, then nodded.

Though uninvited, Fry and I sat in occasional chairs on either side of the sofa.

Jim drew the recorder closer. "Lisa, I need you to answer out loud for the machine, please."

"All right. Yes, I called him at the *Gambler.*"

"Why?"

"Dean was out of town." She spoke softly. "He called to say he wouldn't be back until today. I was nervous. I wanted someone with me overnight."

"Do you usually need company when your husband is away?"

Lisa ventured another glance at Arthur Fry, who said, "I think we can speak freely."

She clasped her hands so tightly that they became mottled. "Sometimes I do. Usually I call Mom or we go to their house. But Mom and the baby were both asleep in their own beds by the time Dean called. I knew Daddy would be on *Gambler,* which isn't too far from here, and he probably wouldn't mind coming."

"What time was that?"

"Ten-thirty or eleven." She scrubbed her palms back and forth. I noticed and thought it was odd that she seemed to be getting more nervous rather than less.

"I see." Jim must have noticed her unease, too, because he looked at me like he was inviting my help. "Dewhurst here is my nemesis these days, Lisa. She's a newspaper reporter. It's easier to let her tag along than to spend time later trying to bring her to speed. Do you mind if she asks a question or two?"

He was obviously trying to help her relax. Toburn looked relieved and rolled her eyes toward me. Naturally, I smiled.

"You're an only child, aren't you?" I thought changing the subject might help.

Lisa nodded.

"Does your husband work for your dad?"

"Yes." She brightened and stopped swinging her crossed leg, which had been gyrating ever since she sat down. "How did you know?"

"I figured he might have a place for a son-in-law who showed an interest in his businesses."

"Exactly." Lisa smiled at her hands. "Daddy's crazy about Dean. It goes both ways."

I lowered my voice, trying for a more confidential tone. "When Dean called you last night, had he heard something? A rumor, maybe? Did he think your dad might be in some kind of trouble?"

The leg began swinging again and Lisa shot a furtive look at Fry. The attorney's affable smile was gone. "Go ahead, Lisa. Tell them."

She swallowed as if she were on the verge of tears. Her long thin face suddenly looked drawn, fatigued, and the nervous leg froze. I waited. Sometimes patience earns an answer better than prodding.

Jim's eyes darted between Lisa and me before they settled on me. Taking the hint, I nudged her, gently. "What did your husband say?"

"He said G.C. Gideon was drunk in the bar at the Waverly Hotel and was telling people Daddy wouldn't be pushing people around much longer, that he had taken care of that." Lisa's crossed leg swung slowly, more deliberately, and she seemed to stall. When no one else spoke, she continued. "G.C. owed *Gambler* money. Last week, Daddy threw him out of the place and threatened to call his dad if G.C. didn't pay up. When Dean heard about G.C.'s big talk, he wanted me to get Daddy away from the casino before the crowd thinned out."

"Did he tell your dad about the threat?"

"Good heavens, no!" Lisa's eyes rounded as they shot to my face. "You couldn't run Daddy off his own property. He'd never have come if he'd known about G.C.'s threats."

Wills cleared his throat. "Lisa, I'm sure G.C. Gideon is not the only regular customer who owes *Gambler* money."

"That's true. But . . . I'm probably not supposed to talk about this, so you need to keep it confidential." She hesitated and looked at Jim, who nodded, then to me. I gave her another nod. "You can't let regular people run a tab in a gambling casino, of course, but guys like G.C., with a fortune behind them, well, you can be a little lax."

When she looked at me, I gave her what I intended as a kindly smile. I thought Jim wanted us to encourage her to talk about this. "You sound like you've worked in the business."

"Sort of. I waited tables at Pinks."

I could not imagine how that happened. "Over your dad's objections?"

"Practically over his dead body." Lisa shrugged, then allowed a grudging smile and uncrossed her legs. "The truth is, I hated it. A waitress takes a lot of abuse, even when her dad owns the place. Cleaning up after people is very demeaning work. I was still in college. Dean and I were going out. He applied for a job and Daddy hired him. Dean worked every night, went to classes early, then slept until it was time for him to go back to work. I thought Daddy was trying to break us up with that grind and I got the waitress job just for a chance to see Dean. When I had had enough, I confronted Daddy. He said he was trying to see what Dean was made of. He may have been testing me a little bit, too."

She stalled and I prompted her again. "Apparently, he was satisfied."

Lisa gave up a winsome smile. "Yes. Daddy likes Dean and Dean likes Daddy, so much that sometimes I get a little jealous. Anyway, last night I was scared. Dean didn't think we should try to warn Daddy off *Gambler,* that I should call and say I was afraid by myself and convince him to come spend the night. It worked.

"I feel terrible about that man who died. I don't understand why somebody killed him." She looked to Jim as if expecting him to come up with an explanation.

"We think it was a mistake," he offered, taking his cue. "The victim resembled your dad. *You* probably couldn't tell the difference from the back. He was in your dad's office at two a.m. It was a natural assumption."

Jim looked at me oddly before I realized I was scowling. Apparently it was my line. "What else, Lisa?"

She stared at the recorder as if she were trying to make a decision about how much to reveal. "G.C. and I grew up together."

Jim stiffened and Lisa's eyes locked on him. "Tyrone Gideon and Daddy owned things together. They were friends. Not everybody knows that."

"You've got that right. They are reputed to be almost mortal enemies." His peculiar enthusiasm piqued my curiosity as Lisa wilted under the intensity of his gaze. "What kind of things did they own?"

"A boat. A stable. A couple of race horses. They kidded each other about not being able to pick a winner at the track or in the barn either. I think they lost their shirts on the horse deal but they had a big time razzing each other about whose fault it was.

"They had other things. I was a kid. I don't know what all."

"Do they still own things together?"

"I don't know. Maybe."

"How about you and G.C.? Were you friends, too?"

She looked stricken. "No way. He was a sneak and a bully almost from the time we could walk. In high school I was desperate to avoid him.

"We started out at the university the same year but G.C. was in one scrape after another. His dad kept having to buy him out of ugly situations." She paused and digressed, as if thinking she needed to offer an example to verify her claim. "G.C. borrowed a guy's car, got drunk and ran it into a house into some people's bedroom. That cost his dad a bundle.

"G.C. paid some guy a thousand dollars to beat up another guy for pantsing G.C. in the dorm cafeteria. He got a couple of other girls pregnant.

"Mr. Gideon was over seventy years old then. He thought G.C.'s antics were just a normal boy sowing wild oats."

Jim leaned forward, elbows on his knees, and regarded Lisa intently. "But you didn't think so?"

"G.C. got his first rifle when he was four years old. He threatened to shoot me about a hundred times and probably would have except my dad caught him pointing the gun at me one day and paddled him. His dad never knew about the paddling, of course. As far as I know, it was the only spanking G.C. ever got.

"His dad bought him a classic Corvette—the real thing—when he was ten. He was only supposed to drive it on their property. The rule didn't last long and neither did the car. G.C. totaled it and killed a ranch hand who was with him. He walked away with scrapes and bruises.

"G.C. started taking booze to school in his lunch in junior high. He always had plenty of money to bribe kids to do things for him. He's been buying people and big-shotting—'sowing wild oats'—ever since he could walk. His dad was always there with his checkbook to set things right.

"I can tell you truthfully, G.C. has no regard for anyone or anything. The only person he cares about is Number One. That's G.C. Gideon in a nutshell."

Jim remained quiet for a minute, the only sound the whir of the recorder. "Did your dad spend the night here?" he asked finally.

"Yes. They called from *Gambler* at six-thirty this morning. Daddy heard the phone and knocked on my door to see if everything was all right. That's the first he knew of it."

"Is there anything else you think might be pertinent to this investigation?"

"No, I think that's about it."

"Lisa?" Wills' voice was smooth, conciliatory. "If you think of anything else, jot it down and call me, will you?" He handed her his business card after writing his home and cell numbers on the back, turned off the recorder and stood, his movements drawing the rest of us to our feet.

In the driveway, Fry and Wills paused to review Lisa's statement. I listened without commenting.

"I think she told you everything, don't you?" Fry asked finally as the two men shook hands.

"Everything she thought of." Jim looked at me, but I averted my eyes. I didn't want him to ask me any questions. Not in front of Mr. Fry. Fry shook my hand and left. Without saying anything, Jim opened my car door and watched as I got in, then he just stood there.

"Jance, you need to tell me, whatever it is." He knew I noticed things he didn't, which actually I thought was one of the main reasons he invited me to go along. I just sat there quietly, refusing to meet his gaze. I didn't know how to say it without sounding like some nosy old woman. He closed my door and walked around to the driver's side.

As he pulled into the flow of traffic, he said, "What?"

"You don't know me that well."

"Well enough. Now, what are you mulling over so hard in that busy little imagination?"

"I just wondered . . . well, Lisa said G.C. got 'a couple of *other girls* pregnant.' "

"And you are thinking what?"

"It may have been awkward wording, or it may have been a Freudian slip, but it sounded like maybe G.C. got Lisa pregnant."

"What?" Wills' yelp sounded like disbelief. "That's a pretty big leap, even for you."

"Did you or did you not invite me to share my thoughts?"

"I didn't see that one coming." Despite his skepticism, Jim was quiet for several heartbeats.

"It's after twelve," he said finally. "Are you ready for lunch?"

"Sure."

"Do you like fish?"

"Yes." How did he know?

"It figures. Me too."

We parked on the street, then passed a gift store as we walked the half block back to the restaurant. A huge, stuffed lavender lion on display in the window caught my eye and I slowed briefly to admire it. Jim stopped, put his arm around my shoulders and pulled me close beside him. "What now?"

"That lion. I love his smile. What do you suppose his name is?"

Jim grinned. "A handsome, manly fellow. Too distinguished to be a 'Teddy.' Probably 'Theodore.' Would you like to have him? Come on, I'll buy him for you." He reached to open the door.

"No, no." I pulled his coat sleeve. "I'm a grown woman, much too mature for stuffed animals. Good grief, did you see the price tag? The brute costs forty-two dollars."

CHAPTER THREE

"How did your parents come up with your name?" Jim asked, after we ordered and the waitress left. We sat facing each other in a booth in The Hungry Pelican beneath fishing nets strewn from rafters that resembled yardarms; the waiters and waitresses wore pirate attire. The ambiance was cool and quiet.

"Mom wanted to name me Nancy after her sister. Dad was partial to the name Janet. They compromised."

"I'd like to meet your family."

"They'd like to meet you." It slipped out before I thought and I groaned inwardly, hoping he hadn't noticed, but he arched an exquisite eyebrow, grinning.

"Ah, you've mentioned me, then?"

I rolled my eyes. "Just in passing. It was no big deal."

"When?"

"When did I mention you or when can you meet them?"

"Both."

"I really don't recall when or why I might have said anything about you, probably in the course of talking about the ribbon murders." The blush ignited under his playful scrutiny. I tried to look solemn and stay cool, but my words came in a rush. "They're coming Friday. They have season football tickets and come for all the university's home games. They stay at the house. I'm taking them to *Phantom of the Opera* at the fine arts theater Friday night. You're welcome to tag along if you're interested."

"I am. Very."

Looking into his dark, mischievous eyes, I saw the glint, knew he was teasing and tried to cover my embarrassment. "I thought you might have family or someone coming for the game."

Jim shook his head and grinned. "My folks were sports fans when my brothers and I played, but they've lost interest. I think it's a case of bleacher burnout."

I pursued the opening he provided. "Tell me about your family, all seven kids."

The taunting grin faded. "First there's my sister Veronica." He enumerated with his index finger. "She was named after a nun friend of my mother's. She's thirty-two, married to an insurance agent in Dominion, lives a mile from the folks and has two boys. She teaches junior high English."

He held up a second finger. "Paul is thirty, a playboy promotion man for a small company that makes fishing equipment." Jim interrupted the account to distribute our food when it arrived.

"Is Paul good looking?" I asked, when we had settled to eating. It was an innocuous question to get us back to the subject of his family.

Jim's eyes narrowed in mock concern. "Why do you want to know?"

"Just curious." I couldn't help laughing self-consciously. Maybe it had been kind of a leading question.

"People who know us sometimes call me Paul and him Jim. I don't know if it's the physical resemblance or they just don't know which name goes to which face."

"I'll probably be able to tell you apart."

"You may not be meeting Paul until it's too late." Again he arched his eyebrows suggestively and I didn't dare ask what he meant.

"I'm third, twenty-eight years old, or will be soon. I'm single, have a juris doctorate, am a member in good standing of the state and county bar associations *and* have considered myself eligible until quite recently."

"When's your birthday?"

"The twenty-eighth."

"I'll try to remember."

He smiled, his eyes staring intently into mine. "You don't have to." In the awkward silence that followed, I tried to concentrate on my lunch.

After long minutes of eating with no conversation, I wanted to break the tension, lighten the atmosphere. "It might be polite for you to ask when my birthday is."

"I'm already privy to that information. I checked on you the first time I saw you." His dark eyes danced.

"You ran my rap sheet?" My put-on surprise made him laugh. "What? You wanted to know if there were any wants or warrants on me? You are some piece of work, Wills."

He feigned innocence. "I checked known associates too. Saves getting soft on someone's moll."

"Oh, yeah? Have you had a gun moll girlfriend in the past?"

His dark eyes narrowed. "Spoken like someone who cares. Do you?"

I wasn't falling into any more of those verbal sinkholes. And why did he persist in answering a question with a question? "No, I'm just trying to make polite conversation."

His rich baritone rumbled good-naturedly. "Try a little harder."

"Who comes after you?" We needed to get back to talking about his family, definitely the safer topic.

"Next up, the one younger than I am is Mary Elizabeth. Bethy. She's twenty-six. She's also married, has one kid, currently my personal favorite, a little redhead, Amanda, and is expecting a boy. Beth and I are close. She's laid back, unabrasive. Very easy to take. Very pretty.

35

"Then there's Peter who's twenty-four, a draftsman who designs marinas." As if anticipating me, Jim added, "Yes, I suppose women consider him good looking, six-foot-four, taller and slimmer than Paul or I. He and Andrew, the next brother, both have blue eyes. The rest of us have brown. Pete thought he was adopted. He was in junior high before we convinced him Roman Catholic parents don't adopt a fifth kid. He had to be ours.

"Andrew's twenty-two, just got his B.S. and wants to go to med school. I told him I'd help him financially but he signed a contract with a little town in the panhandle. They pay for his school and they get him for his first five years of practice."

"I never heard of a deal like that. Aren't they taking a big chance?"

"Not with Andrew. He's very reliable. Very stodgy. Tall, slim, fair. Also handsome."

"Who is number seven?"

"Ah, you've been paying attention." Jim was obviously pleased. "Evie is the baby. She's twenty, is still in school over at Eastern in early childhood education. Talk about good looking. Evie is a raving beauty."

"I guess she has a busy social life?"

Jim's expression fell to thoughtful. "Maybe now, away from home. With both parents, two older sisters and four older brothers, Evie's opportunities for social activity have been, shall we say, closely monitored."

"And your parents?"

"Dad's a plumber. Mom's always stayed home, answered dad's business phone and scheduled him." Jim smiled, obviously enjoying the mental picture of his dad. "He still works longer, harder hours than any of us. He's in shape too, for an old duffer. Not many people intimidate me physically anymore, but I'd think twice about taking on the old man."

Watching Jim's face, his enthusiasm for his family, I felt left out. "I'd be interested in meeting your parents."

"They're great. He's a little shorter than I am, but close to six feet. She's short, heavy, feisty, Italian. They play a lot of gin rummy in the evenings. She howls when he wins a hand." Jim allowed a rolling chuckle at the memory.

"Not long ago Dad had a bout with kidney stones. They put him in the hospital. Mom couldn't sleep, paced around the house most of the night, then went downtown. The nurses found them both asleep together on that little hospital bed." Wills snorted and shook his head. "That's the way it ought to be." He hesitated again. "How about your family? Are you close?"

I shrugged. I'd never thought much about my relationship with my family. "I guess we are. I'm the oldest, twenty-three. Greg's nineteen. He's smart and handsome enough but he isn't really ready to grow up. He laid out of school last year after high school. He started college this fall at Southwestern. Thinks he wants to be a vet.

"Timothy is sixteen and a heartbreaker. Greg says Tim is spoiled. I suspect Tim's the reason Greg didn't go to school last year, afraid he'd lose his first son standing at home."

"Are you your dad's favorite?"

"Well," I hedged. "Greg's his namesake. Dad and I get along. Mom's the one, though. Being outnumbered made us girls close." I folded my napkin and put it next to my ravaged plate. "We've stalled long enough. Will you please tell me about Jesse Chase?"

Something caught my eye and I glanced down. My napkin was pristine clean; however, there was an orange spot—cocktail sauce from the shrimp—dribbled in the middle of my chest. The groan just slipped out. Wills grinned but pretended not to notice as he picked the check up off the table.

"Is it your turn?" He offered it to me.

I shook my head, dabbing at the spill, smearing it. "You invited me. Don't you have an expense account, a way to write me off?"

"I wish." His voice dropped. "In more ways than one." He laughed as I raised my eyes to his.

"Look." Suddenly I wanted to jettison the charming chitchat and get down to business. "I'm going to the ladies' room. Also, I need to call the office. Ron Melchoir will be worried. He always worries when I'm with you. You have a reputation, you know."

Wills' mouth dropped. "I thought Melchoir liked me."

"He doesn't like you." I stood up and scanned for signs marking the way to the restrooms before I completed the thought. "As managing editor, he considers you a valuable news source. I'm the one who likes you." A little startled by my own admission, I turned to see a slow, satisfied smile ease his broad mouth.

"I see." He stuck two fingers in his water glass, wiped them over his hands, then dried them on his napkin. Still grinning, his gaze knifed the distance between us. Embarrassed once again by my own overly candid comment, I hurried away.

"I'm glad we cleared that up," he said, loudly enough for me to hear. I didn't look back.

Returning from the ladies' room, I tugged the edges of my blazer closed to hide the wet circle dominating the middle of my blouse. I had done as the *Clarion*'s family editor suggested and scrubbed the dribbled dressing with soap, then did not rinse it off. The spill had expanded to a huge smudge, but it was basically colorless. I caught Jim at the cashier's desk.

Looking beyond me, his jaws clenched as he stared at a black uniformed cop on the other side of the exit. Noisily and with a lot of unnecessary motion, he grabbed the door handle and shoved. The policeman jammed his foot at the base of the door, holding it shut. Jim's eyes narrowed and he hissed, "Hey, nigger, let go of that door."

I gasped and spun to stare at Jim, astonished that he had used that politically forbidden word, particularly confronting a man that size who looked that belligerent. I detest racially biased people and would never have imagined Jim was one of them. I glanced back at the policeman and my horror mounted as his face twisted into a snarl. The man was menacing, well over six feet tall and easily two hundred-forty pounds. His voice snapped as he spoke.

"I warned you about that, white bread." He yanked the door open and, except for Jim's quick side step, the cop would have caught his mid-section with a massive fist. "And this time I'm still on my feet."

The door out of his way, the policeman caught the front of Jim's shirt with both hands, banged Jim's chest against his and enveloped him in two burly arms. I stood paralyzed, not even able to yell for help.

Suddenly, both of the men—black and white—exploded into hawking guffaws, hugging each other and grappling like two big bears. My mouth probably dropped to my knees as I gaped at the two of them exchanging boisterous insults. Stunned, I was caught in a heady mix of annoyance and relief. Greetings done, they both turned and grinned at me. I managed a shaky smile, which was the best I could do.

"Jancy, this is Kellan Dulany." Jim and the patrolman affectionately shoved each other to arms' length.

My knees quivered as I offered to shake hands, then watched in horror as mine disappeared into Dulany's massive mitt, but his hand was warm and his grin reassuring.

"Nice routine, guys. A real breath stopper."

Both Jim and his friend grinned like a pair of bad kids. Maybe sensing my residual anger, Jim stepped close beside me.

"Dulany and I played ball together most of our lives, starting with the boys' club Raiders when we were in the fourth grade and straight on through high school."

"Nearly won the state championship our senior year," Dulany added. "We was great."

Wills' laughter rumbled. "Spoken with customary Dulany humility."

"Then here come the college recruiters," the cop said, taking up the story. He watched me closely as his voice dropped into a singsong vernacular. "We signed up to go to college together.

"Wills stayed on my butt all summer, had me liftin' and runnin' ever' damned day. I was skinny back then, but cocky. Wills knew the buttons to push." Dulany flashed Jim a threatening look. "Then come fall practice, three-a-days in that terrible August heat. I got tired, maybe a little homesick, too, and the coaches was on me hard. They didn't have no business treating me bad. Hell, I'd been a star.

"One afternoon they run me until I flat couldn't run no more. I fell down on the ground and told 'em I quit.

"Well, here come the fat man." He arched his eyebrows, indicating Jim. "He come at me with that deep voice and he say, 'Get up, nigger.' "

Jim arched his brows and gave me a sheepish shrug.

"He knew better than to call me that." Kellan's voice and gaze appealed as if wanting me to see his side. And I did. "I was gassed out," he continued, "but I wasn't dead. I got up all right. I 'as going to kill me a big-mouthed white boy."

Jim's chuckle again was muffled, but he didn't interrupt.

"Wills was quick back then. Over ten yards he was fast enough, for a lard butt lineman." The cop gave Jim a conciliatory smile. "After ten, though, I could smoke him. That day he just had more left than I did, plus. . . ."

"Plus," Jim chimed, his suppressed laughter becoming a rolling, infectious chuckle, "I knew I was dead meat if he caught me. I ran like hell."

Dulany nodded. "The coaches was watching. They got all excited to see I still had some juice left after what they'd put me through. Man, they was all over me, pettin' me, congratulatin' me, all that. I couldn't 'a very well killed the man who'd made me look so good, could I?"

I smiled without answering the rhetorical question and Dulany continued.

"But I warned him not to ever call me the 'N' word again or I'd take him apart."

Dulany glowered at Wills, who grinned innocently and, playing the straight man, asked, "And how did that work out, Kellan?"

Dulany's eyes shot darts at Jim before they settled back on me. "He called me the 'N' word all the time after that, twice in the Missouri game."

"But I overdid it." Wills moaned, shaking his head with feigned sorrow. "It got so every time I called him that, he'd collapse into this helpless heap, laughing."

Dulany grinned at me. "You had to see his face. He looked like a naughty little kid baitin' you to fight. Man, that look was funny, especially when he was always ready to run as soon as he said it. Broke me up ever' damn time."

Wills smiled sheepishly. "A guy's gotta be careful not to overuse his best material."

Still chuckling, the policeman looked me up and down unabashedly, but he was addressing Jim. "Fine looking woman, Wills. What's a quality gal like this doin' hangin' out with a loser like you?"

I couldn't stifle a smile, but it withered when I remembered I had, as usual, forgotten my appearance. I appreciated Dulany's reminder.

"Did you see her face?" Addressing Dulany, Jim arched his eyebrows.

The cop brayed like a mule. "She looked like she'd taken a shot."

Looking at me, the two old teammates threw their arms around each other's shoulders and started whooping all over again.

I muttered some unkind, also inaudible, invectives as I slipped by them and out the door, actually flattered to be the audience for their little routine. "Very funny."

Jim caught up and clamped his hand on my shoulder. He gave it a squeeze as we walked to the car.

"What's that for?" I asked without bothering to look at him.

"I don't know. Irresistible impulse. How long do you suppose you're going to like me?"

"It's funny you should ask that." I stopped walking and turned to study him seriously. "I was just wondering about that myself."

"What?"

We began walking again, slowly, his hand on the back of my neck. "All my life, I've usually had one close friend at a time, male or female. We would be inseparable. After a while I realized, I never kept one of those close friends for a full calendar year. Before a year was up, I'd be cultivating someone else. When I began to anticipate what a friend would do or say, I'd be ready to move on.

"It's like wringing out a washcloth. Once I squeezed the water out, I was ready to toss that one and get a new, full one. Does that sound crass, tossing out friends like wrung out wash rags?"

"A little crass," he allowed as we stepped to the passenger side of the car. "But everyone gets rid of chewing gum after it loses its flavor. How'd all these friends take getting tossed?"

I'd never thought of that. Looking at Jim, I laughed at myself. "That never occurred to me. Actually, they didn't seem to mind. Maybe they'd gotten all the flavor they wanted out of me, too." Inwardly chiding myself, I mulled that over another minute before I continued. "Anyway, I thought it was odd that you should ask how long I thought I'd like you."

Stepping in front of me before he opened the passenger door, Jim caught an errant strand of my hair between his thumb and index finger. He tugged, pulling my face to his. "The best I can hope for is to try to hang on until next October fifth, or as long as I can still come up with something unexpected, a surprise from time to time, is that right?"

I shrugged. "I suppose so."

His voice fell to a coaxing tone. "I guess I'll have to keep creating new material." Gently, he tilted my chin with one finger and lowered his lips. The kiss was full of promises, but no demands. When he backed off, we were both smiling.

"About Jesse Chase?" I reminded him when we were in the car.

Crediting Serago, Jim gave me the printable version of the facts of the homicide, promising to fill me in as he got more.

"That's basically what I said in the story."

He shot me a startled look. "Story? Today?"

"Yeah, when I called Melchoir. When I went to the ladies' room. I told you I was going to."

Jim looked perplexed. "I guess I need to remember to tell you if information has to be off the record."

"I guess so." I felt less than honest by not saying something more, but I didn't want to ruin the mood. I just hoped I'd be able to honor his wishes when push came to shove.

On Wednesday I received six tickets for *Phantom of the Opera*. They came by courier from the university ticket office, a gift from Jim Wills. When my brother Greg begged off, I took one back to the box office and asked them to mail the refund to Jim.

Jim was supposed to meet us at my house by five-thirty Friday for drinks, hors d'oeuvres and dinner with my parents and my brother Timothy. It took some maneuvering, but I finally prevailed upon my housemates to make themselves tactfully scarce. Angela complained the most, but finally, grudgingly, agreed.

When Jim did not show up by six-thirty, an hour late, I called his office. Although it was long past closing time, Mrs. Teeman answered. "They've been gone all afternoon, Jancy. I'll beep him."

He still didn't call.

By seven o'clock, getting frazzled, I suggested we eat without him. The casserole was a tad overdone but it wasn't ruined.

As Mother took the Italian bread out of the oven, she said, "Jancy, I'm sure he got busy and probably couldn't get to a phone."

By then, of course, I was mad at the world and focused that fury on my mother for making excuses for a guy she'd never even met. "He carries a cell and has another phone in his car. How tough could it be?"

Dad took his lead from Mom. "I've been in the doghouse for the same thing."

Timothy only snorted. "He'll pay. I know you, Jance."

Our parents glared at him.

CHAPTER FOUR

We loaded up and left for the theater at seven-forty. By then, my mood was vacillating from angry to concerned, both extremes accompanied by muttered declarations of indifference I really didn't intend anyone else to hear.

"This is important to me," I seethed to myself. "And he darn well ought to know that." This was not the kind of surprise that was going to maintain our friendship for another day, much less a calendar year.

The performance was unusually good, except that, sitting five seats deep in the center row on the far side of Dad, I got more and more morose as it progressed. My mom, Lucy, sat between Dad and Timothy. Without mentioning it, we had left the aisle seat next to Timothy available.

Just before intermission, Jim slid into that vacant seat. He wore what I figured were the jeans and blazer he'd probably worn all day, which made me madder. He was normally such a terrific dresser and now, when I wanted to show him off, he turned up looking like a good old boy.

He leaned forward, looking around my entire family, and caught my eye. Both livid and relieved, I could scarcely force myself to look at him.

His whisper carried. "Sorry, babe." I ignored him, but could feel some of the tension ease between my shoulders. Maybe he had a good reason for his behavior and appearance. All I knew was, it had better be a darn good one.

Jim smiled and introduced himself to Timothy in a stage whisper, and I heard him say, "I'm in deep poop, right?"

Tim obviously liked Jim right from the start. "I've been there," he said. "With Jancy, it can get a little dicey, but it ain't fatal."

"I can tell we're going to be real good friends." Wills sat back just as I leaned around my parents to shush them.

Mom and Dad both smiled and nodded to him, acknowledging his arrival and unspoken introductions.

At the intermission, Jim stepped into the aisle to let Timothy and my parents out, but he stepped in front of me.

"Where were you?" I hissed, not wanting to sound shrewish in front of the entire theater full of people.

"A sniper took a potshot at Jesse Chase in his limo about four this afternoon."

One thing about Jim, he knew how to get a news hound's undivided attention.

"We got there fast enough to recover a couple of shell casings."

"Was Chase injured?"

"No."

"That's a good thing, right? Finding casings?"

"Yes."

I didn't resist as Jim slid an arm around my waist, tugged me close to his side and kissed my cheek. I kept my head turned away, not allowing any additional public display of affection. He grinned and nudged me up the aisle where we joined my family in the lobby.

"Mom, Dad, Tim, this is Jim Wills." Everyone smiled, exchanged all the usual niceties and shook hands.

"Did you get caught in traffic?" my dad asked, then gave an embarrassed laugh as if it were a dumb question. Traffic around campus on Friday nights was light as cars loaded with students abandoned Bishop for Dominion, cruising twenty miles up the interstate to the city to party.

Jim covered Dad's embarrassment smoothly, which I appreciated. "No, sir. Jancy's got me hooked on murder mysteries these days."

It was Mom's turn to embarrass me. "Reading them?"

I rolled my eyes but Jim just gave her a kindly smile. "No, ma'am, solving them."

"Oh, of course." Mom flushed. "Jancy told us you worked for the SBI. But she said you were a lawyer and could practice, if you wanted."

"Yes ma'am." He flashed me a know-it-all glance, like he got some satisfaction out of hearing I had talked about him in some detail. "I could be a regular lawyer. Maybe I will be, when I grow up."

Everyone twittered good-naturedly and Dad took the conversation in a new direction. "You missed a good supper."

Jim gave us all a comical look as if he were mystified. "Oh, yeah? Who cooked?"

"I did, Smart A," I said. Not that I was pleased to be the brunt of anyone's joking around, especially about my cooking, but everyone had begun to relax.

Jim, the picture of innocence, looked at me. "I didn't know you knew how."

"I have cookbooks. I can read. Anyone who can read, can cook." Apparently no one else wanted to touch that and Jim let us off the hook.

"Maybe I can sample leftovers."

"We'll see." I sounded brusque, but I was feeling a lot better about things. I mean, a sniper shooting at Jesse Chase probably was more important than getting to dinner or a stage play on time.

During the second half of the performance, Jim sat next to

Sharon Ervin

me and held my hand. As the music swelled with the lyrics, ". . . say you'll stay with me, one love, one lifetime . . . ," he pulled my hand to his mouth to brush his lips over my fingers. It was a very romantic gesture and I gave him a half-smile, but his dark eyes on my face were serious. Butterflies danced in my stomach and I was happy the dark theater hid my blush. Did his probing gaze delving into the depths of me mean what I thought it did?

No, no, no. I was responding again, letting him think we could become more than friends. I must not let that happen. I shook my head and lowered my eyes. There was no room in my future for Jim Wills. Why wouldn't he understand? I told him often enough. And why did I keep toying with this completely untenable relationship, like some demented adolescent? Why didn't I just stop seeing him?

Because I didn't want to, my other self explained. Not yet. Not until. . . .

Until what? Until I was so entangled in this thing between us that I couldn't get away without breaking something? My throat constricted. I needed to escape his tentacles while I still could.

Then I had the most frightening thought of all. Was it already too late?

Liz Pinello and Ben Deuces were heating leftovers when Jim and my family and I returned to the house. Liz studied me cautiously, as if she were trying to determine my mood. "Do you mind?"

My volatile attitude had taken a turn for the better after Jim's arrival at the theater. "Not a bit. Is there enough for Jim?"

Ben chuffed, a half laugh, half cough. "Him and a dozen more. Who did you plan on feeding tonight, the Armenian army?"

I smiled, graciously ignoring the dig, and fixed cold drinks for my guests, whom I urged to get comfortable in the living room. As I carried Jim a plate of steaming leftover casserole, I felt pleased that my dad had served a conversational ball and had a volley going.

While Jim ate casserole as if he liked it, I served my family cherry cobbler. Jim regarded the dessert with obvious interest but continued downing casserole as he responded to some question my dad had asked. "That's right. Are you familiar with guns?"

"I bird hunt." Dad took a bite of cobbler and smiled, looking what could only be termed "amazed." Ready to ease onto the sofa with a plate of cobbler, I nearly resented Dad's obvious surprise. Surely the man knew I could cook . . . at least some things. Jim shoveled casserole into his mouth while he continued holding up his end of the conversation.

"Well, you have an idea, then. After a shooting, we try to collect any evidence lying around before it's lost or contaminated." He glanced up and I supposed it was to make sure I was paying attention. "This shooter was in a stand of trees near a busy street." He flashed me a private smile. "There weren't any news people around and we didn't call anyone."

I returned the smile, an indication of my appreciation, but didn't let my eyes linger, which is what I think prompted Jim to snort a half-laugh and launch into the casserole again.

"Jancy went with me last week after what we decided was an attempt on this guy's life. His name is Jesse Chase. You may have heard of him. He's on the financial fast track in this part of the state."

Dad shook his head. Apparently, the name wasn't familiar to him.

"Well, anyway, we think the killer shot an employee of Chase's by mistake the first time. After that, Chase beefed up his personal security and we've been keeping an eye on him. This time the shooter couldn't get as close as he needed to. He got away, but if we come up with the weapon eventually, the rifling on the recovered casings will be as good identifying the gun as fingerprints are identifying a person."

Tim was listening wide-eyed. "Won't he toss the gun?"

Sipping iced tea, Jim nodded. "He might. This guy's a pro. But even a pro'll find a weapon he likes and won't want to part with it. That's particularly true of a rifle because of the weight and balance and sight and all.

"If this is the same guy, he used a twenty-two-caliber automatic last time, close up. The tighter security is backing him off. If not for that, he probably would have come with a shotgun this time, which really fouls up our weapon identification. But he has to get real close for a shotgun to be fatal. The longer range weapon leaves evidence. He should have picked up the casings, but a bodyguard and a cop tailing Chase were all over the shooter in a heartbeat. He didn't have time to tidy up."

Wills took another bite. "Yes, Tim, you're right, if he's smart, he'll toss the gun. But if he was smart, he'd probably be in another line of work."

Mom, who had been listening quietly, cleared her throat. "I would think a hired assassin would make a lot of money."

Wills regarded her face, which friends have described as an older, softer version of mine, and smiled. "For this one he might get paid a little more—maybe ten thousand. If he's caught and convicted, ten grand breaks down to a pretty low hourly wage over twenty years of incarceration."

My mom and dad and even Tim all nodded thoughtfully.

I couldn't help taking a little dig at Tim. "Maybe you'd better stay in school." He didn't have a chance to answer before a cherry escaped my spoon and dropped right into the big middle of my chest.

Tim whooped and his voice broke. "Sister, you really should use a bib."

I leaped to my feet, ran through the kitchen and up the back stairs. I could hear the others laughing loudly, their hilarity enhanced by my hasty departure.

Locked in the bathroom, I giggled, too, as I looked at myself in the mirror. I was a total klutz, standing there all flustered and blushing and embarrassed. At the same time, I felt incredibly happy. There was just something magical about Jim Wills. I couldn't put my finger on it, but I found something about him intriguing and altogether too stimulating.

Jim joined my family and me when they came for the football game the next week on Saturday and church on Sunday.

The week after that, I couldn't decide how to acknowledge his birthday. A gift seemed to overstate our relationship. My thought was, our friendship didn't really qualify as a *relationship.* It was not exactly a *friendship,* either. And we weren't dating in the usual sense of the word. An impartial observer might consider us business associates, except for the occasional kissing, which no one would define as businesslike.

What would be appropriate for his birthday?

After a lot of soul-searching, I decided a card and a balloon bouquet delivered to his office on the big day would express my sentiments fairly well without overstating anything.

On Saturday, two days before Halloween, Jim called and invited me to seven-thirty church the next morning, then out for breakfast.

I had not seen him since the previous weekend when we were with my family, and I hesitated. I had my career to think about. I couldn't afford to get entangled. But just going to church together didn't seem like much of a threat. It certainly couldn't be considered a date, exactly.

While I mulled it over, he filled the awkward silence on the open telephone line. "I like your Episcopal service. We'll go there. What do you say?"

"Okay." Taking a visitor to church was not like dating, I assured myself as I hung up.

After church and breakfast at Cheeries, Jim stopped at a roadside vendor where he purchased an extra large pumpkin. "We can carve it at my place."

Warning bells sounded and I guess I must have looked suspicious. He was too handsome, too much fun, too witty, too sexy, too. . . . But carving a Halloween pumpkin? There certainly was nothing seductive about that.

Alone at Jim's condo? I remembered too well how I responded to him the only time I had been there before. I couldn't trust myself to think clearly when we were alone. And he knew it. I continued looking at him.

His expression was a little too innocent. He grinned and there was a definite twinkle in those dark eyes.

I drew a deep breath, knowing what was best. "No, thanks. We'd better go to my house. I want to change clothes."

Jim's smile faltered. "Okay, we'll swing by there on the way and let you change."

"I'd rather stay there—mess up my kitchen instead of yours."

Wills studied my face, evaluating, then his voice dropped. "You don't need to be afraid to be alone with me."

Mine was a silly laugh that revealed my doubts. Could he possibly not know the effect he had on me? Oh, yeah, he knew.

His expression darkened. "You aren't fooling me, you know."

"What do you mean?"

"I realize you're using me. Cultivating me as a sometimes-valuable news source."

I was genuinely startled by his conclusion. "That's not true."

"Sure it is. I'm a good one, certainly as good as the assistant D.A.s, as the judges, Sheriff Roundtree, the police chiefs, the other guys you flatter and flirt with."

"No. You're . . ."

He wouldn't let me finish. "Why do you think I didn't call you that Friday about the sniper attempt?"

I opened my mouth but couldn't think of an explanation in the face of his obvious disappointment.

"I didn't want you getting in my head any worse than you already are, acting like you're interested in me when you're only after the information I can provide."

At a loss for words, I waggled my head and stammered. "That's not so."

"What's really pathetic is I want to be with you so bad that I let you play me and, damn it, I lay it all out there, turn myself wrong-side out to please you. But I'm not stupid, Jancy. I see the game you're playing. And I'm willing to go along, but I think I should get more than an occasional goodnight kiss or a free meal or ball game when your folks are in town."

About then, some righteous indignation came boiling up inside me as I thought about how hard I was working to squelch my feelings toward him. Suddenly I raised my flattened hand like a cop stopping traffic.

"Now hold it just one minute, hot shot. I don't pay for leads with favors, if that's what you're angling for. No, sir, no story, no matter how big it is, is going to get me into somebody's bed. I thought I made that clear right up front. What do you think, every time you sack up a bad guy, you should get to bag me, too? No way."

This time when I shook my head, there was no waggle about it, and I didn't intend to let him press his case, either. "If you think giving me news tips earns you a piece of me, you're out of your mind. I have a great career ahead of me, one I want; a future I've prepared for my whole life. And you, Jim Wills, as I believe I have mentioned before, have no place in that plan."

He stared at me a long moment, then laughter began, rumbling like a volcano deep in his chest before it erupted.

"I wish you could see your face," he said. He rocked his head back and howled, his convulsive laughter unnerving. And the eruption just kept flowing until all that hilarity oozed in, filling the crevices of my anger and spreading.

Okay, so it might have been a little pompous of me to think he couldn't get a whole slew of ladies by simply crooking his little finger. I gave in and chuckled a little at myself, which only fueled his fizzling laughter all over again.

Finally, when we'd both sputtered out, I said, "Does this mean I win?"

"Only this round, cupcake, on points. No knockout. This bout's not over yet, much less the fight. You're not walking away from this . . . not yet." Sobering, he gazed at me. "You've left me about a teaspoon of dignity, you know. I've still got a little bit left. Not much, but at least a starter, maybe enough to build on."

I didn't know what he was talking about and was darn well not going to ask.

Housemates Rosie Clemente and Liz Pinello, and Liz's boyfriend Ben, drifted in and out of the kitchen during the afternoon, making suggestions and offering advice on the art of pumpkin carving. Angela, on the other hand, after a couple of passes, hovered, sidling close to Jim, rubbing against him.

I couldn't pinpoint exactly when or why I began to feel restless, then resentful, then righteously annoyed by Angela's every word, not to mention all that phony giggling.

Jim removed his coat and cuffed his shirt sleeves, baring his muscular forearms, and Angela got sillier. Jim didn't seem to mind. I fumed as Angela flirted and Jim appeared to get more and more focused on that stupid jack-o-lantern.

The dumbest thing, when I realized it, was that I felt more jealous of the pumpkin than of Angela as Jim braced it firmly with one of his thick hands while the other hand caressed it, stealing inside, scraping, removing the seeds. When Jim noticed I was staring at his arms, he grinned. It had been a mistake to tell him he had great forearms.

His dark eyes danced and got more and more playful as Angela chatted along making constant, inane conversation, brushing against him as she moved from one side to the other pretending to be mesmerized by his work. I gritted my teeth, wondering how he could endure such a ridiculously flagrant display. I mean, she was all but drooling.

Perched on the kitchen stool, I was steaming by the time Jim stepped back to admire his work. Leaning close to my ear, he murmured. "It doesn't have to be this way." Was he talking to me? "This was your choice."

Sizzling, I walked to the sink, grabbed the sponge and began wiping slippery seeds from the countertop. Jim said something to Angela, who twittered as they both flashed sly smiles at me, like they had some big secret. I'd had about all I could take and still maintain any kind of civility. I stalked into the living room, slouched onto the sectional sofa and folded my arms over my chest.

What was the big deal, I asked myself. Jim and Angela made a swell-looking couple. I darn well didn't need him cluttering up my life, distracting me from my career plans; my goals. I wished Riley Wedge would call right that minute. Not that I needed reinforcement. Jim was only a diversion. My knuckles were white and my arms dappled from my fingers digging into my own flesh.

Kissing Jim the first time had been a mistake. Groping with him later at his place had warped my thinking.

From the kitchen, I heard a burst of goofy girlish laughter.

Angela was so full of crap. Jim wasn't as smart as he thought if he fell for all that fawning. Even if he didn't know much about the wiles of women, he was plenty old enough to watch out for himself.

I closed my eyes and took a deep breath, trying to shut out the sounds of Angela's artificial merriment. She was getting on my last nerve. When I opened my eyes, thinking I needed to go upstairs before I made a complete fool of myself, there he was, standing in the doorway watching me.

"What're you doing?" he asked, as phony in his own way as Angela was, pretending he didn't have a clue.

I certainly did not want to give him the satisfaction of letting my irritation—and maybe those little shards of jealousy—show. "Nothing. I just got tired of all the hypocrisy going on in there." His smirk made me mad all over again and I stood defiantly. "You and Angela can take it from here. I'm going upstairs."

Jim didn't offer to move from where he stood, which was blocking the door to the kitchen and the back stairs, so I turned on my heel and started for the front stairway, which was just inside the front door.

As lithe as a cat, Jim was suddenly there, blocking my alternate route. My temper snapped. "Leave me alone."

His voice was a whisper. "Believe me, I would, if I could."

I froze there, staring into his dark, unfathomable eyes and battling the lump that formed in my throat. My husky whisper matched his. "Please, let me go. You know how things are with me. I'm just about as sorry as I can be about it, but. . . ." The words wouldn't come for a minute. "I've told you my dream. There's just no . . . no place for you in my life. Go on back in the kitchen. Angela obviously wants to be the woman you need. What I need is for you to be my friend. Help me get out of . . . this. Please."

He pursed his mouth and blinked thoughtfully.

Angela's piping little-girl voice pealed, "Ji-im."

Casting his eyes at the floor, he did an about face and walked decisively back to the kitchen.

It was Angela who walked Jim to his car a half-hour later as I monitored their movements from my darkened bedroom above the driveway.

Jim sidestepped Angela after she planted herself squarely in front of him. Shrugging, my most glamorous housemate waved good-bye and called, "See you later, then."

I figured that meant they had a date. My throat ached and my eyes burned. For lack of anything else to do, I threw myself across the bed and lapsed into a deep funk.

A week passed, but no suspect surfaced in the execution-style death of Larry Potter. There were no further attempts on Jesse Chase's life. Police did not find the weapon that had fired the hollow point slug that had cut a wide swath through Potter's brain mass, then lodged peculiarly against the inside of his skull.

Neither were they able to track down the shooter who had taken the potshot at the limousine, although they had plaster casts of footprints and the shell casings to match if they could come up with a suspect or a gun.

I called to get daily reports from Mrs. Teeman, the lone secretary at the local office of the State Bureau of Investigation. When I phoned there, I purposely didn't ask for Jim. There was no need. Mrs. Teeman said he gave her regular updates to pass along to *the press*.

I spoke with Lisa. Chase's family was pressuring him to travel less and then only with a bodyguard. I passed that information along through Mrs. Teeman.

Interviewing acquaintances of the Gideons and the Chases, Wills learned that someone had hired a bodyguard for G.C.

Sharon Ervin

Gideon. Mrs. Teeman relayed that information to me, even mentioned that Jim speculated the bodyguards might indicate an escalation in enmity between the one-time partners.

I browsed through old press clippings and photos and found several with the elder Gideon and Chase sharing the winner's circle at a small race track, their wives co-chairing a country club style show and their children, dozing toddlers, sharing a stroller at the Dominion Zoo. I delivered copies to the SBI office along with salient points from my interviews.

No one I talked with could remember what cooled the Gideon/Chase liaison. Whatever it was had occurred about the time G.C. and Lisa were high school juniors.

After some red tape, Wills recovered medical records indicating Lisa had undergone a "minor, elective gynecological procedure" that winter. Mrs. Teeman conveyed his congratulations that my earlier, off-the-wall observation might have had some merit.

Because I customarily used the back stairs in our barn-like house on Cherry Street, I seldom saw Angela, who had one of the downstairs bedrooms in the front. After work one afternoon, I found her perched on the back stairs.

"Is Jim out of town?" she asked as she stood and dusted the back of her super low-cut jeans.

I felt a peculiar pin prick in the area of my heart. "I don't know."

"When'd you see him last?"

"The day we carved the pumpkin."

Angela studied me a minute, as if trying to determine if I were telling the truth. Finally, she flipped her fingers through her short, blonde hair and offered me a washed-out smile. "I've left messages on his machine and with that bitch who's supposed to be his secretary. He hasn't called me back. Not once."

I nodded, hoping the gesture indicated I understood but had

58

nothing to suggest. Angela's smile broadened. "He's probably being a gentleman, giving you time to get adjusted to your breakup before he asks me out."

"Hmmm," I hummed, another noncommittal response, waiting for Angela to clear the stairway, but my housemate didn't budge. She obviously had more to say.

"Jancy, we've never pretended to be best friends or anything. I seriously do not understand how you can let him go, but I want you to know, I will be forever grateful to you for bringing him into my life. It's really big of you to let him make his choice without any pressure."

With that, Angela stepped down, clearing the way. My feet felt leaden as I climbed the stairs, which seemed steeper than usual.

I was walking across campus with my family, joining the throngs headed for the football game on Saturday, when my parents yoo-hooed and waved to Jim. He grinned and trotted over to shake hands all around and to meet Greg. In an attempt to brazen it out, I pasted a smile on my face and willed it to stay there.

Jim seemed inordinately glad to see my parents and Tim. "I didn't realize you were such avid football fans."

The men all talked at once, loudly voicing their undying loyalty to the crimson and cream.

"How about letting me take all of us to dinner after the ball game?" Jim offered. "Bullards is walking distance and I know a guy. I can guarantee us standing room at the bar, maybe even food."

"Not all five of us, Jim," my dad said. "I'll let you pay for you and Jancy and I'll spring for the rest."

My blustered objections went unheard, swallowed up in the repeated instructions and arrangements and good-byes signaling Jim's abrupt departure. He had scarcely even glanced at me, certainly hadn't asked if I had other plans.

Dad immediately began replaying details of the Gideon case for Greg, who had missed the earlier trips but who had heard the story, probably several times. I dropped the plastic smile. I'd make the best of it and hope we didn't run into Angela. It would be hard to convince her Jim had made a dinner date with my entire family without consulting me.

I was polite and made a determined effort to be pleasant through drinks and dinner, but was relieved as the evening plodded to an end, that is, until Dad insisted Jim join us again the next weekend when the Dewhursts would provide the after-game refreshments and a meal. Without so much as a glance at me, Jim happily agreed. I could have dropped through a hole in the ground and been content to stay there.

When I called Mrs. Teeman on Monday morning to get any updates on the Chase matter, she said I needed to talk to Jim.

He opened our conversation briskly. "Your parents are crazy about me. And I like them. Guess you'd better get used to having me around."

I couldn't help a little laugh. So he was plotting these little get-togethers. "You'd resort to consorting with my family?"

"Whatever it takes, Dewhurst."

All together for the final home game, Jim asked my parents to excuse me Thanksgiving and let me accompany him to his parents' home in Dominion for the day.

For some unexplainable reason, I didn't argue. I had been curious about his family, of course. Turnabout's fair play and, after all, he had wormed his way into mine. I just wanted to have a peek at his, see what kind of parents reared seven kids and if any of the others had turned out like him.

When we were alone, Mother complained, and she was right. It would be my first Thanksgiving away from my family, but even Mom thought I should go.

I think what I secretly hoped was that, within his family circle, Jim Wills would reveal the clay feet I needed so badly to see.

CHAPTER FIVE

I washed, then rewashed my hair Thanksgiving morning after my first attempt with the small-barrelled curling iron frizzed. I changed my clothes twice. Were his brothers like him? It didn't really matter, of course. What would his sisters think of me? His mother?

"There's no competition," Jim said when I voiced those concerns on the phone the night before. "None of the Wills' sons has ever brought a date home for a holiday before."

"Jim, I'm not going as a date."

"Whatever," he said, then he laughed.

That prospect added to the pressure. I kept repeating, "I'm not his date. I'm his friend."

Angela burst into my bedroom as the butterflies had my stomach in a proper roil that morning, and she was mad. "What's the big idea, Jancy?"

Trying to talk around the butterflies, I replied slowly and calmly. "He asked me to his parents' house to eat turkey, Angela. It's no big deal."

"It is to me."

"Then maybe you should have this conversation with him."

"Just don't think I won't. I'm going to find out what you're up to, birddoggin' my man."

The confrontation didn't do much for my frazzled nerves. I

was relieved there was no sign of Angela when Jim pulled into the driveway.

I was nervous to the point I couldn't think of much to say on the twenty-mile ride to Dominion, which went quickly in spite of my anxiety. I was surprised and a little relieved when he pointed out the Wills' family home. It resembled the house I shared with my roommates on Cherry Street: a rambling, two-story frame structure that appeared to be fairly bulging with humanity. Cars filled the driveway, lined the curbing and two were even parked on the front lawn.

Jim smiled at what must have been my obvious relief as he pulled into the yard. I sat very still while he walked around to coax me into the brisk air and up the front walk.

A little girl with auburn hair and freckles sat on the front stoop carefully licking the cheese filling from a celery finger. "Hi, Uncle Jim!" Her smile dimmed as she cast suspicious eyes on me.

"Hey, Amanda. This is Jancy. I think she's hungry. Can we get her one of those?"

Amanda brightened and shot me a conspiratorial smile. "They might not want you to have one." She raised her eyebrows, obviously accepting me as her new partner in crime. "But I'll help you. Come on." She stood, bent a little at the waist and tiptoed through the front door. "Walk this way."

I crouched down and tiptoed, mimicking Amanda. Grinning, Jim bent and followed.

A short, round, bustling woman in an apron, a large metal spoon in her hand, stood in the front hallway as I trailed Amanda into the house. The woman had smooth, olive-colored skin and very curly, white hair. Her dark brown eyes shone as they shifted from Amanda to me, saw Jim, then popped back to me. She jabbed both arms into the air and cried, "You're Jancy, of course. Oh, honey, we're so glad you're here."

Olivia Wills had to reach up as she caught me around the neck in a warm embrace, the spoon waving over our heads. At her words, the hallway filled with an assortment of people of varying sizes, shapes and ages, all obviously eager to check out the newcomer.

"Jancy, I'm Veronica, Jim's older sister," a stately brunette announced, smiling. Veronica had her mother's dark eyes and curly hair but a fair complexion. She placed her hands on the heads of two boys, obviously her sons. "And my boys. . . ."

"Curly and Moe," Jim interrupted. The boys, whom he'd said were five and seven, whooped and flew at him. He scooped them up together in a bear hug.

"Hi, I'm Beth," a shorter, pregnant version of Veronica offered. Her voice was soft and melodious. "You probably met our Amanda on the porch."

I nodded, smiling all around, looking for Amanda, but our guide seemed to have vanished amid the flurry of her cousins' flying feet. Both of Jim's sisters introduced their husbands, who appeared in the hallway as if on cue. The husbands, Johnny Collett and George Peck, both were pale, blond, freckled and resembled one another.

I turned to find myself looking at the profile of a wistful smile on a lovely, dark face focused on Jim. It had to be Evie, petite, with dark, movie star quality beauty. Eve Wills slipped her arm around her brother's waist, looked up at his face like an adoring pet, then cut her mahogany eyes to me. There was a warning in her glance.

"I'm Jancy Dewhurst." I offered to shake her hand. "I sure hope you're Eve." The younger woman studied me a moment, then relinquished both a smile and a handshake as she nodded.

Suddenly all conversation ceased as a man loomed in the doorway.

"Dad," Jim said, putting Curly and Moe back on the floor and stepping free of Eve's arm, "this is Jancy."

I have to admit, I liked William Wills at first sight. He had jet black hair—no gray—and roughly hewn features. His eyes were the color of charcoal.

Jim appeared to be almost a clone of his dad. Although Jim was taller, his were duplicates of the older man's thick hands, his broad, muscular shoulders, his stance and demeanor.

Glancing at Mrs. Wills, I saw in her Jim's now-familiar flashing chocolate brown eyes, his even, white teeth and the curling, quick smile. For a fleeting moment I pictured Mr. and Mrs. Wills snuggled together in a narrow hospital bed. That image broadened my already established smile. Physically, Jim appeared to be a combination of the best of both parents.

Then the taller, fairer, slimmer brothers, Peter and Andrew, squeezed into the entry and were introduced by their mother. Both had her smooth, olive skin, although their hair was brown, not black like Jim's, and their eyes, both sets, a vivid blue.

Peter gave me an exaggerated look up and down. "I don't see any wings." He drew a warning look from Jim.

Andrew grinned broadly. "Or halo, either. Come on, Jim, she's just a regulation-type earth woman."

Jim turned his cautioning stare from the two younger brothers to scan the crowd. "Okay, where is he? She might as well meet him and get it over with."

Surprised, I looked around. "How can you tell anyone's missing?" My question, of course, prompted twitters and laughs.

Jim's mother slid a broad arm around my waist. "He'll be a little late. I need to get back to work. Come on, Jancy, help me."

Glad to escape the spotlight, I tossed Jim a smile and followed his mother into the hot chaos and delicious aromas of the Wills' kitchen.

Settling in to cut up hot giblets as directed, I asked again, "Who's missing?" as I dropped bits and pieces of gizzards and liver and heart into gravy bubbling on a front burner.

Mrs. Wills slid a rack out of the oven that gaped open beside me. "Paul." The rack teetered precariously under the weight of the iron stewer, which she opened to reveal steaming cornbread dressing.

"Oh." I wasn't sure but I thought I recalled that Paul was the brother older than Jim.

Almost immediately, new commotion in the hallway heralded another arrival as the front door opened and closed. Unable to leave her post, Mrs. Wills scraped the sides of the pan and stirred the dressing again as I continued chopping giblets.

"And who have we here?" An almost familiar voice bellowed from the doorway and Paul Wills swooped into the kitchen.

My first impression was that Jim's older brother was handsome enough, but louder, his clothing flashier, his features finer than Jim's, even though he had Jim's same dark coloring and eyes.

He crossed the room in three strides and curled around his mother, hugging her from the back.

"Pauly, stop that!" A giggle mitigated his mother's protest. He kissed her neck and brushed a strand of hair back from her face.

I shuddered when Paul turned his playful eyes on me. "And you are?"

"Jancy Dewhurst." I offered a token smile designed to dampen his enthusiasm.

He laughed boisterously. "That demure little grin isn't going to save you from me."

"You can look," Jim's voice boomed just as Paul started toward me, "but you can't touch."

Paul stopped in mid-step. "My little brother's favorite girl?"

Paul didn't take his eyes off me. "She's a tidy package, bro."

I could not prevent the blush and hoped anyone who noticed would attribute my heightened color to the heat of the kitchen.

"If you can't stand the heat of a little competition, Jim, you'd better stay out of the kitchen," Paul chided.

Jim had stepped up to block Paul's advance when Amanda, a new cheese-filled celery finger oozing in her small hand, suddenly appeared and got to me first. "You can come out on the porch with me," she said in a stage whisper.

I glanced at Mrs. Wills for direction.

"Amanda, on your way out with Jancy, ask your Aunt Veronica to come in here, will you?"

Amanda nodded, took my hand in her clean one and led me from the room, right out from under the noses of Jim and his bellicose brother.

Too full of absolutely scrumptious food, my energy sapped by my earlier nervousness, I trudged along on the family's traditional after-dinner walk, unashamedly eavesdropping on the myriad conversations and occasional quips without making any effort to contribute. I would have had to interrupt to get in a word anyway. Jim was watchful, always intervening when a brother came on with me.

I didn't see any signs of clay feet, which was less of a disappointment than I expected.

Comfortable on the drive back to Bishop that night, I studied Jim's profile in the reflected lights from oncoming traffic.

As I opened the front door of the house on Cherry Street, he caught my hand, then he reached inside to turn off the porch light, pulled the door closed and shut the screen. Then he put his hands on the wall on either side of me. I realized what was coming. Instead of resisting, I welcomed his mouth as it closed over mine. His tongue roved experimentally, coaxing, and I yielded.

My groan was involuntary but it made his biceps strain and he pressed his body into mine. He kissed me ravenously again and again and I kissed him back. I just wanted to. I had liked him before. Now, against my will and my better instincts, those kindly feelings were intensified. I nearly objected when he stopped kissing me. He shifted and pressed his warm mouth against my throat. "Come home with me."

Oh, Lord, I couldn't speak. It took every bit of willpower I had to rock my head from side to side, no. But he didn't take no for an answer easily.

"Jancy, you're all I think about. In my dreams my hands and my mouth touch every inch of your warm, sweet body. I've never felt this way. I'll be careful. We'll take it slow. Anything you want. Any way you want. I'll be good. I'll be the best you ever have. Please. Just this one night, let me hold you. Please, baby."

I pushed his shoulders. He groaned and, with a ragged sigh, released me.

CHAPTER SIX

The second Friday in December, I was at my computer doing a story on a theft ring of teens stealing to get Christmas money for gifts when Don Lockwood, managing editor of *The Dominion Morning News,* called.

After exchanging the usual holiday cheer, Lockwood's voice dropped to a serious tone. "Would you run some records down there for me?"

Suddenly he had my full attention. "For the competition?"

"The deal is, our publisher heard that Tyrone Gideon is bankrupt." He paused. The line was silent. "If it's true, he could take the Lincoln Bank here in Dominion down with him. We are talking a major financial crisis. I can't get away or I'd come do it myself. It's that important. I have some hotshot reporters around the office here who couldn't find their fannies with both hands in a county clerk's office. If they asked for help, it could tip people, cause complications, even if it turns out nothing's wrong."

"Do you want me to look for mortgages or what?"

"Yes, mortgages. And liens, on property, cattle, anything you can find. But you have to keep it quiet."

"I'll go right now."

"Call me as soon as you can."

"Don, if it's a story, I'll have to write it for us first."

"I know, honey. Right now I'm not after the story. I need the information. I'm sticking my neck way out giving you this. I trust you, Jance. Play it straight with me."

"I will." I saved the theft ring story in draft and closed down my machine.

Managing editor Ron Melchoir glanced up. "I thought you'd already been to the courthouse this morning. What's going on?"

"I just have a couple of things to check." I grabbed my jacket.

One of the deputy clerks looked up as I breezed through the clerk's office on my way to the vault. "Hey, Jancy," she chirped. "Need any help?"

"No, I can handle it, Joy. Thanks."

Permanent county property records were kept in the fireproof chamber at the back of the clerk's office, the entry to which was guarded by a massive iron door with a combination lock. The thirty-by-fifty-foot vault was well lighted and usually alive with lawyers and oil company land men running records. I got there shortly before noon to find the chamber deserted.

I hung my coat on the rack at the back of the vault, pulled the latest mortgage index and began to search for the Gideon name. It didn't take long.

In late November, G.C. Gideon signed a note and mortgage assigning part of the Two Bell Ranch, Tyrone Gideon's private empire, to the Lincoln Bank in Dominion for two-point-five million.

"The ranch is G.C.'s?" I muttered, thinking aloud. I closed that book and replaced it in its slot before going to the tract index. I traced ownership for sections included in the Gideons' sprawling Two Bell Ranch.

There it was.

Tyrone Gideon, in his dotage, had deeded a joint tenancy ownership in his entire kingdom to his son.

"What are you doing?" Jim's whisper close to my ear made me jump. I whirled to stare at him, startled. I hadn't been aware of anything except the astounding information in the books.

And, of course, I needed to keep this project confidential. But I also needed someone to interpret things for me, to explain the ramifications in the joint tenancy deed.

Wills' expression slowly changed from pleasant to concerned. "What is it? What's the matter?"

I closed the tract index.

"Come over here." He slipped his arm around me and guided me to the metal stairs that led to the loft where the county housed its historical records.

I glanced around, but no one else was in the vault.

We sat side by side and Jim rested his arm on the step behind me. "Now, what is it?"

I gave him a token smile. "I need a good lawyer."

He grinned. "He's here. Speak."

"I need to hire you for a minute for some privileged communication."

"Have you got any money?"

I grimaced, annoyed by his teasing.

He shrugged. "Okay. I'll take the case on contingency."

"What does that mean?"

"It means if we recover money, I get a percentage."

"What percentage?"

"How much are you expecting?"

"No money."

"Okay, I'll take seventy-five percent."

"Seventy-five!" I started to get up but Jim pulled me back, laughing. "Seventy-five percent of nothing, Jance, ain't all that much."

Realizing what he meant, I couldn't help smiling at my own reaction. "Okay, you're hired. Let's say I own some land."

He nodded.

"And let's say I deed this land to you and me as joint tenants. What does that mean?"

"Well, for one thing, my creditors can attach our joint holdings for payment of my debts."

That didn't sound good. "Could you sell my . . . our property?"

"I could if you signed the deed with me."

"Could you borrow money on the property without my knowing about it?"

He pursed his lips and nodded thoughtfully. "Theoretically, I could encumber it, but if I borrowed money on it at a bank, they'd require you to sign the note with me."

"What if you had clout? What if you were a very important customer?"

"In that case, I could probably borrow on it without your signature."

"How much could you borrow?"

He shrugged. "Pretty close to fair market value, probably."

"Oh." This was looking worse and worse for the Gideons.

Jim smiled. "My answers don't seem to be making you happy." He touched my chin and turned my face toward his. I smiled and he took a deep breath. "Would you like to buy me some lunch?"

I twisted to remove my chin from his hand. "I have to keep looking for something."

"Come back and do it this afternoon."

"I'd rather look now when no one else is around."

He winced. "Thanks a lot."

"I don't mean you."

Jim looked at me a long, sobering moment. "We really need a little time together."

"We're together enough."

"Not alone."

"I think that's probably smarter, don't you?"

"How about if we just sit here and neck. You'd be safe, a

public place, lots of lights. Let me just go pull that door closed."

I looked at the vault door and rewarded his little joke with a laugh. "Wills, what exactly is it you want from me?"

He shot me a disbelieving look and a derisive laugh.

"Okay, let me rephrase that. What'll you settle for?"

Formulating his answer took only a minute. "A evening alone at my condo. A fire in the fireplace. Soft music." He lifted my hand to his mouth, then turned it and kissed my palm. Whoa, that was exhilarating.

"Look," I indicated my arm, which was pebbled with goosebumps.

He raised his eyebrows and his voice was soft. "When?"

"Soon." I leaned against his arm, which was around my back, and kissed him full on the lips. I had longed to do that for days. I had thought about it and pretty well concluded Jim didn't like aggressive women. A change of tactics might discourage him.

He returned the kiss, gently at first, then more urgently. I set my hands at either side of his chin and leaned away. "I like your face."

He allowed an evil little laugh. "There's a lot more of me you might like if. . . ." Suggestively, he stopped the sentence there.

After a pause, he took another deep breath. "Let me help you." He stood and gave me a hand up, suddenly all business. "With both of us looking, we can finish in half the time. What's the name?"

I considered his offer, then shook my head. "No. I promised to keep it confidential."

"Your loss. How about if you come by my house after work?"

"It's Friday. You're playing handball with Dulany." He frowned. Then I remembered my new tack. "But I'll take a rain check."

He nodded without speaking, kissed my cheek and left.

Returning to the mortgage records, I began with the date of

the joint tenancy deed and tracked forward.

G.C. had started out small, borrowing only three hundred thousand dollars and obligating three hundred acres the first time. He doubled that the second trip and was up to one-point-two million by the third call.

Over six months' time, the heir apparent had drawn twelve-point-three million dollars and mortgaged every acre of his dad's ranch, seven separate herds of cattle, all the equipment—trucks, tractors, hay balers, personal vehicles, everything—including two dozen riding horses.

I made copious notes, carefully put away the books and got back to the office shortly before three. Melchoir glanced up as I returned to the newsroom but he didn't ask any questions. I called Don Lockwood.

"He's twelve-point-three million dollars in debt."

"What does that mean?" Lockwood's voice sounded hushed, almost reverent.

"Well, Don, if it were you or me, I'd say we were in bad trouble. With G.C., I don't know. I don't know what other assets they have. He's put the entire ranch on the block but they may have stocks, bonds, cash. We are out of my league here."

"What did he do with all that money?"

"That's not in the property records."

"Could you find out?"

I hesitated. I didn't know G.C. Gideon and, if Lisa's opinion were accurate, I wouldn't care to get acquainted with the man. But I had met his dad, Tyrone. I wasn't sure if he would remember me or, if he did, if he would talk to me. The elder Gideon had been a junior livestock judge at the county fair the year before. He had been patient with me, describing the criteria for evaluating sheep, hogs and year-old polled Herefords.

Thinking aloud, I said, "I guess it couldn't hurt to ask."

CHAPTER SEVEN

Tyrone Gideon did remember me and, when I asked about the new mortgages over the telephone, he insisted I come out to the Two Bell to talk with him in person.

The highway drive took only about twenty minutes, but the winding way through the rolling terrain to the main ranch house took nearly forty minutes more. The December days were short. Dark was coming by five-thirty.

The weather was raw, the wind snarling and snapping at the branches of nearby trees and I made a mental note to keep our visit brief.

Cattle stood bunched together in pastures lining the drive, all facing south, their backs to the north wind. Occasionally, the bunches moved en masse toward pickup trucks from which ranch hands unloaded feed.

I assumed it was Mrs. Gideon who answered the door, although she looked very little like the sophisticate in the newspaper photos. The woman neither smiled nor said hello, just mumbled, "Follow me." Without another word, she led me through the one-time screened front porch whose screens had been replaced with glass, and a huge living room to a panel-lined den. A fire blazing in the rock fireplace filled the room with the sweet smell of cedar.

Tyrone Gideon, sitting in a worn recliner beside the fireplace, wore tinted eyeglasses, even in the semidarkness of the room. He had lost so much weight in the last year that I scarcely recognized him as the robust fellow I had met.

"How are you?" He teetered as he stood and reached awkwardly, groping for my hand. Obviously, he could not see.

"I'm very well, thank you." I caught his flailing hand in both of mine. "And thank you for inviting me out. Your place is beautiful, even this dreary time of year."

"What'd you think of all the new activity?"

Caught off guard, I floundered trying to remember any activity. "I guess I was too preoccupied to notice." I had paid close attention as I negotiated the winding drive but had missed any "new activity." I glanced at Mrs. Gideon, who stared blankly at the wall and offered no enlightenment.

"G.C. has really taken the place over." Mr. Gideon motioned me toward the leather divan as he shuffled backward into his recliner. His wife withdrew. "He's had to hire a lot of new people to manage that quarter horse operation, and those bulldozers are running us a pretty penny, preparing the hog lots and new ponds. G.C.'s got some strong ideas about farming in the new millennium. I knew he'd take hold someday. I'm just glad I lived to see it."

"Well." I stalled, reserving a place in the conversation, then cleared my throat and pulled my steno pad out of my purse. "I guess reinvesting profits is the way to make money."

"Oh, no, we're not just reinvesting profits here, Miss Jancy. We are talking about a major, calculated risk, investing millions to make millions. And it's all come from G.C.'s vision for regenerating the place. His dream is to double my fortune for his son someday. I think he'll do it, too. He's really studied to get ready for this expansion. I can't remember when I've been so proud."

I stared hard at the man, trying to see through any pretense, but he convinced me he was sincere. "I guess he's made your bankers a little nervous. A man called us from Dominion. He said G.C. had mortgaged the ranch."

"Well, that's probably an exaggeration, but the boy's had to put up a considerable amount of collateral to get the funding he needs for the new programs."

I chose and delivered my next words quietly. "Mr. Gideon, he's borrowed twelve-point-three million dollars."

The room was silent except for the pop and crackle of the logs in the fireplace.

The expression on the old man's face remained unchanged, his smile frozen in place, but his prolonged silence gave him away. We sat without speaking for several moments.

"They've called from the bank when G.C. needed money." He spoke oddly, as if more to himself than to me. "I've okayed every transfer. I didn't ask how much he was getting. I was just glad he was interested."

He gazed toward the fire and I wondered if he actually could see the flames.

"All this'll be his someday anyway." The man seemed to wither before my eyes, suddenly looking terribly old and weary. "I'm eighty-seven years old. I don't even have the pleasure of being able to look at the place anymore. I can still feel it, though, feel that bristly cold air and smell the pine needles and leaves rotting in the winter sun. I'm afraid if I enjoy feeling and smelling it too much, God'll take that away from me too."

Studying the man, wondering if I should have spared him, I was only vaguely aware of a car approaching until the roar intruded into my conscious mind and brakes squealed in front of the house.

I heard the front door slam as someone entered the house. Heavy steps thudded on wooden floors as they stomped across the glassed-in porch and the carpeted living room until suddenly G.C. Gideon's silhouette appeared in the doorway. Hatless, his thick hair tousled, five-foot-ten or so in cowboy boots, jeans and a Carhart coat, G.C. stood stiff, hackled like an angry mastiff. He braced his hands on the doorjamb and his eyes burned through the darkness, his glare emphasized by thick-lensed eyeglasses.

"What the hell do you think you're doing here?"

I smiled civilly and, without standing, introduced myself. "I called your dad to ask about rumors that you had mortgaged the Two Bell. He invited me out to see the progress."

"What business is that of yours?" G.C.'s words seethed between clenched teeth. I smelled the distinct odor of bourbon.

"It's better to stop ugly, hurtful rumors before they get out of control, don't you think? I wanted to swap rumors for truth."

"Maybe you should have asked me."

"Okay, I'm asking you."

"It's none of your damn business."

I glanced coolly from G.C. to his dad. Slumped in his chair, the elder Gideon did not offer to defend me.

"Your dad has already explained about your putting in new quarter horse and hog operations. He's very proud of you."

Even in the half light of the room, I saw G.C.'s eyes grow bigger and the muscles in his neck constrict. He appeared to be about to explode, but by some force of will, he was able to control the detonation.

"You'd better get out of here. Now!" He stomped over close in front of me but stopped just short of making physical contact. The bourbon smell pervaded the room.

I cast another look at Mr. Gideon, trying to figure out the blank look on his face. When he neither moved nor spoke, I closed my notebook, picked up my purse and stood.

"Good-bye, Mr. Gideon," I said. "It was awfully nice getting reacquainted." I meant it and, at that moment, I wondered if I would ever see him again.

The old man nodded, but remained seated and mute, his

head bowed.

Squeezing by G.C., I shivered as the old man's heir fell into step behind me. I could hear him wheeze as he stalked, dogging my steps all the way to the front door and out.

Night enshrouded the landscape. It was nearly six o'clock. The north wind whipped my clothes in a most inhospitable way. Any natural night light was hidden behind dark restless clouds.

As I reached for the car door handle, I turned to look at G.C. Gideon. "Your dad asked if I noticed the new activity around the place."

He glowered at me.

"I guess I missed it."

"That isn't all you're going to be missing if you don't get off my property, smart ass." His jaw quivered and his eyes bugged even rounder behind the thick lenses of his eyeglasses. "I suppose someone knows you're out here."

Staring at him, I shivered again involuntarily. I had never seen anyone so menacing. In his enraged, drunken state, injuring, even killing me might not be difficult for him. At that moment I could see it in his face. I knew G.C. Gideon had done murder—at least had ordered it done—before.

"It's a long way back to the main road." His voice grated. "I'd be very careful driving it tonight, if I were you."

"Thank you." I got into my car, locked the doors, snapped my seat belt and pulled it tight.

There were only rare occasions on which I might have wished I had a cell or a telephone in my car. That night was one of those.

I took the winding drive much too fast, but I wanted to escape, get off of G.C. Gideon's property before he got any angrier or came up with a way to stop me. His property, I thought self-righteously, at least for the time being.

I'd just begun to calm down when a light-colored pickup truck materialized suddenly, barreling toward me from the opposite direction, taking the middle of the road. I slowed and moved as far to the right as I could without rolling into the bar ditch and stopped. The pickup fish-tailed out of control as the driver accelerated, fish-tailing more as he spun around me.

The dust cloud kicked up behind the truck blinded me to the road for a couple of minutes, which was all right as I needed the time to settle my nerves and calm my heart.

When Mrs. Gideon hurried G.C.'s bodyguard, bigger and stronger than G.C., inside the main house, he used his brawn to haul his enraged employer out. It took several minutes to calm him.

"What I done in there was that bitch's fault," G.C. wheezed. "I want you to kill her. I want her to feel it hard when you do it. Stick her with the big knife. Gut her. Yeah, that's what I want you to do, stick it low in her belly and rip it up and around. While she screams, I want you to slice that big mouth side to side, too, so her jaw drops on her chest. I want her to know she's dying and I want her to feel it deep before she does, understand."

"Sure, G.C., I'll do it just like you say, but we gotta get you calmed down, man, or you're going to stroke out or something."

"Tonight. I want to do it tonight. And I want to see it. Come on, let's go."

"Man, you've had a lot to drink. Are you sure you feel like . . . ?"

G.C.'s eyes bulged. "There was no reason for that poor old man in there ever to know about the place. He was happy thinking I was makin' improvements. He was proud of me. Tellin' him that way, like she did, she hurt him, man. Hurt him bad. Meddling bitch. She had no business comin' in here telling stuff that's got nothin' to do with her." His eyes narrowed. "Promise me, man! Swear on your mama's life you'll kill that meddlin' bitch for what she done here tonight to me and my family. Promise it!"

"I promise, G.C. I will kill her. I'll do it just like you said."

"Tonight. I want it done tonight."

"Okay, okay. Do you know her name?"

"I don't remember it. All I know is she works for the damn newspaper and goes around stickin' her nose in where it don't belong. Tonight she made me do something I never woulda ever done. Not in a hundred years. She's got to pay for what I done."

"She will, G.C."

"Do you promise?"

"I already promised, G.C. She's as good as dead. I promise on my mama's life."

"Where have you been?" Jim stepped from the front porch as I pulled in and parked at the house on Cherry Street. Suddenly feeling safe for the first time in nearly an hour, I tried to answer, but words caught in my throat and I couldn't speak. Instead I walked straight into his arms. There, finally, I was home, secure in the safest place I knew. Then, instead of savoring the moment, I burst into tears.

"Are you hurt?" He tilted my chin to examine my face in the beam of the porch light. I turned away from his scrutiny, buried my face in his shoulder and boohooed. Giving it up for the moment, Jim locked his arms around me and waited.

"I'm sorry." Sniffling, finally, I took the tissue he fished out of his overcoat pocket and blew my nose. "I had kind of a rag-gedy day." I mopped my eyes with what was left of the tissue. "Why aren't you playing handball? Where's Dulany?"

"You don't get off that easy. Kellan and I canceled. I wanted to know why you were acting so odd today. I came over here to find out. Rosie said you hadn't been home. I went by the office but your car was gone so I came back. I just drove up. Where've you been?"

"Can we talk about it later?"

I could feel my own resistance, my pride, revive and could tell from the look on Jim's face, he was aware of it too.

Eventually and with what looked like an effort, he shrugged and nodded and yielded again, which was totally unlike him. "I thought we'd go out to Roper's, two-step a couple of rounds."

That sounded good and normal. I drew a breath and swallowed any objection. I felt wiped out, too weak to be alone with him, but I had the distinct feeling he wouldn't leave as long as I was still upset.

"I don't mind, if you want to. I've gotta dust off a little first."

"Take your time. Kellan and Kit are meeting us out there later."

Roper's was crowded as we eased into the hall and staked out a corner table for four, but we didn't sit. Jim guided me onto the floor and into a smooth two-step. Darn it, I thought, half pleased, half chagrined, did he have to be a good dancer too?

He swung me behind him then into an easy spin and ducked me under his arm. Each maneuver brought our bodies closer. His warm, thick hands caressed and comforted me with every touch.

I began to relax, shuffling in perfect union with Jim's lead. Laughing eventually, I glanced up to see an angry G.C. Gideon and his bodyguard, Bubba Valentine, come through the door. Bubba and I had had freshman classes together at the university years before.

As soon as he saw me, G.C.'s face turned so red it was almost purple and he began shoving Bubba and pointing at me. Seeing them, my recovery nose-dived and I went stiff all over. I have never hidden my feelings well, and my angst must have shown. Jim's eyes followed mine. I shuddered. "Jim, I need to get out of here."

G.C. bent and began clawing at Bubba's blue jeans above his ankle. Bubba flapped at G.C.'s hands and talked hard and fast. I couldn't hear much, but Bubba seemed more concerned about Jim than me. I clearly heard G.C. say, "Damn it, Bubba, get your blade and do it."

Bubba answered, but all I caught was the one word: "alone."

Unperturbed, Jim looked at my face, then back at the newcomers before his docile expression tightened. This was a side of him I had not seen. He set his jaw and shook his head, no. His voice was quiet. "I'm not going to let a couple of cowboys ruin our evening. You don't have to tell me what's wrong, but we're not leaving until we're ready to go. I like dancing with you." The music started again and he gathered me tightly. "I like holding you. Now straighten up because I intend to keep right on enjoying you."

It was no time to be playful. "Please, Jim." I glanced at G.C. and Bubba and pushed against Jim's shoulder, but he wouldn't yield.

"No." He held me firmly.

Not wanting to attract undue attention, I relented, for the moment.

That set ended and the band took a break. Someone plugged in the juke box.

Jim led me back to our table where he ordered himself a beer and me a Bloody Mary. I felt numb and stared at my hands, trying to think how I could convince Jim to leave. I didn't say anything until Bubba Valentine stood in front of me.

"Jancy?"

"Hey, Bubba." I gave him the best smile I could manage, but my mouth quivered. Bubba was close to six feet tall and heavy, but he'd gotten soft. I figured he relied on his girth for the occasional intimidation necessary in his professional pursuits as a bodyguard.

"You and me's friends." Bubba glanced warily at Wills. "G.C.'s been drinking pretty heavy. He's a little bit out of control and talking pretty wild. He's awful mad at you tonight. It might be better if you and your friend left."

Jim gazed up into Bubba's puffy face. "We're not ready to go. I guess G.C. will have to coexist peacefully or *he'll* have to move along."

"Jancy," Bubba tried again, avoiding Jim's eyes, "I don't want no trouble."

"Oh, it won't be any trouble." Jim stood, obviously calling Bubba's attention to his advantage in height and brawn. "Why are you over here talking about what G.C. wants anyway? Let him come speak for himself, if he's got a problem."

Bubba shifted his attention from me to Jim. "He can't do that." He grimaced. "He's too drunk."

"Oh." Jim's look of concern ebbed. "Well, okay then." With that, he caught my hand and pulled me to my feet. "Come on, Jance, let's dance." Jim whirled me onto the floor for a schottishe.

Bubba returned to G.C., obviously confused.

Wide-eyed, watching Bubba's face, I couldn't help giggling. "Jim, you took a really big chance."

He laughed. "Nah. I got brave when I saw Kellan come through the door."

I scanned the room. "Kellan's not here."

"He's not?" His grin broadened and his eyebrows arched. "Whoa, that was risky."

Twenty minutes later, Bubba Valentine half carried G.C. out of Roper's.

Kellan and his lady Kit Wyands arrived late, just as Jim and I were ready to leave. We talked briefly without sitting back down, then separated.

"Let's go to my place for a little while," Wills suggested when we were out of the stiff north wind and alone in his car.

I wanted to. I really did. I wanted to snuggle with Jim on his sofa in front of a roaring fire. I wanted to kiss his handsome face and run my hands over his muscles and enjoy his features close up—his mouth, his chin, his thick warm hands. I tingled just imagining it. Mostly, I realized, I wanted to turn him on, make him lose a little of his usual cool. Oh, yeah, I would love to make that happen. If I were immune to the heat we generated during one of those sessions, I would go for it. If. Instead I settled for giving him a quiet, "No, thanks."

When we got to my house and it looked like no one else was home, however, I asked him to come sit on the couch and "talk" for a while.

He grinned at my stammered, rather ungracious invitation. "Is this going to be another privileged communication?" he teased. "Am I on the clock?"

I shook my head.

When he was on the sofa, I settled beside him and leaned across, putting us face to face. I wanted to be close to him, able to read his expressions when I told him about my unpleasant encounter that afternoon with G.C. Gideon.

Obviously pleased with the way I had positioned us, Jim propped one ankle on the other knee to give me a brace to lean against.

I kissed him, a glancing, indifferent little smooch. His eyes narrowed to a studious squint and he waited. Feeling safe, I smiled and kissed him full on the mouth. He continued to sit unmoving, watching my face. When he finally spoke, I realized my little subterfuge wasn't working.

"So what is it you're working up the nerve to tell me?" he

said. "I'm getting some really bad vibes. Let's get your confession out of the way before we get down to the fun stuff."

This was it. Choosing my words carefully, I told him about Don Lockwood's call, but he interrupted before I got to the nitty gritty.

"Is it all right for you to work for the *Dominion News* on *Clarion* time?"

I assured him it was, in this case, and gave him my rationale. Then I continued, speaking faster and faster as I provided a full account of my findings in the clerk's office, Tyrone Gideon's invitation and my pleasant visit with him at the ranch. Jim listened without commenting.

Finally, reluctantly, I told him about G.C.'s arrival, his appearance, his behavior and his thinly veiled threats.

Jim's expression and body language looked like a summer squall had hit. I was barely finished when he clasped my shoulders in a sobering grip and shoved me off his lap. With me out of his way, he stood. He paced, flexing his hands, and didn't say anything at first. Then he turned to face me. He put his fists on his hips and glowered at the floor as his jaw muscles clenched and unclenched. Eventually, he lowered his hands, still balled into fists, and set them firmly at his sides.

"What in hell were you thinking, woman?" His voice rasped with barely contained fury. "You heard Lisa Toburn. That jerk's never known any limits. He may have people cut up and buried all over that place out there." Jim took a breath. "What do you think would have happened to me, to your mom and dad, if you'd vanished?"

"Lockwood knew where I was."

"Great. Who would have thought to ask him? Oh, sure, sooner or later he probably would have heard about your disappearance and come forward. But by then, your beautiful bod would have been deteriorating somewhere on Gideon's thousands of acres beyond recovery."

Jim rubbed his palms together, snorted and hung his head, obviously exasperated. "Talk to me." He raised his eyes and they burned into my soul. "Tell me stuff." He shook his head. "If you'd told me about this today at the courthouse. . . ." He seethed, unable to finish the sentence, obviously struggling to control himself and his words. "I could have gone with you. I carry a phone everywhere I go. The office insists on being able to contact me. What happened to you today is why they keep close tabs on us."

He paused and shook his head again. "Jancy, I can keep secrets." He snorted with a sort of quiet desperation. "I'm good at it. I know a lot of secrets. When are you going to start trusting me?"

I repositioned myself to sit properly on the sofa. "I already do trust you, but I promised Lockwood I wouldn't tell anyone else about this."

"That was stupid. You tell me everything, from now on. I mean everything."

Watching him pace, a little bit frightened and a whole lot intimidated by his manner, I nodded. When he sat down again, I slid close beside him, wrapped my arms around his near arm and hugged it tightly between my breasts.

"Oh, that helps a lot." Regarding my intimate gesture with disdain, he shook his head and exhaled. He seemed to have lost all interest in necking. He left a short time later, beginning to thaw a little, but still angry.

I was not out of the woods yet.

On Monday morning, I had just called Lockwood to update him when Ron Melchoir motioned me to confer privately in the coffee room.

"We've been summoned to DeWitt's office," he said, always a

man of few words. "I think we're going on the carpet. Have you been investigating Tyrone Gideons' financial status?" He waved off my stammering attempt to come up with an acceptable answer. "DeWitt got several calls over the weekend from advertisers, big ones, folks who don't influence editorial policy officially, but some who have clout, unofficially. I didn't tell him I hadn't authorized it, Jancy, but he's got serious questions. I need answers."

I told Melchoir about the call from Lockwood and my thinking that the *Clarion* could have an exclusive if Lockwood only wanted information for his business office.

"Lockwood provided the lead," I said. "All I did was pursue it," which was true.

When Melchoir frowned, I decided to give him the whole thing, the twelve-point-three-million-dollar debt, my visit to the Two Bell, no evidence of either quarter horse or hog operations and, finally, reluctantly, I told him about G.C.'s noisy arrival and his threat. I could tell by the look on his face, I had struck a nerve. Melchoir looked like he now had answers to beard the lion or, in this case, Bryce DeWitt.

The *Clarion* publisher was brooding at his desk when Melchoir and I entered his office. It had been nearly forty minutes since we'd been summoned. DeWitt was not accustomed to being kept waiting. He stared at me as he motioned us into chairs on the visitors' side of his desk.

"Young woman, are you working for me or for the competition?"

"For you, sir." Those were the last words I was allowed to utter until "Good-bye."

Sufficiently incensed, Melchoir retold my account, succinctly and with an infectious passion that roused Bryce DeWitt to indignation of his own. It wasn't me he cared about, it was newspapering and First Amendment responsibilities.

"How dare he try to intimidate a member of the press!" De-Witt stood to stride in circles behind his desk. "Money and prominence are no substitute for integrity." His voice rose. "G.C Gideon's run roughshod too long. The boy's been an ill-mannered, stupid oaf all his life. If his money's gone, he's squandered his only redemptive quality."

As Melchoir and I left the office, my immediate boss winked at me and I smiled at him.

"Poured it on a little thick, didn't you?" I said.

"Only what was necessary to accomplish the task at hand." He looked terribly pleased.

CHAPTER EIGHT

"Man, I did it today!" The Friday night before Christmas, Kellan Dulany strutted into Jim's kitchen from the garage. Kit trailed him quietly, looking around for Jancy.

Jim, his shirttail out over his jeans, stood at the kitchen counter patting a mixture of Worcestershire sauce, salad dressing, seasoning salt and pepper onto two sizable sirloins. Outside the patio door, in downpouring sleet, a charcoal fire flamed high, too hot for cooking.

Jim smiled a greeting to both his guests without interrupting Kellan.

Wordlessly, Kit took the jacket Kellan handed her, slipped off her own heavy coat and carried them to the living room where she tossed them on the back of one of the two accent chairs.

She smiled, first at the lighted Christmas tree filling the far corner of the room and hovering over a dazzling array of gifts, then at the blaze in the fireplace. She eased onto the raised hearth to warm her backside and glanced at the second-floor loft overlooking the living room. She liked Jim's place.

Kellan appeared with two drinks and handed her one, still talking loudly to Jim in the other room.

"I was trying to cuff him, but he was putting up one hell of a fight. I remembered what Doc Prichard told us, drew my trusty slapper and, instead of thumping this character on his head, I popped his collarbone.

"You should have heard that bird chirp when that bone

snapped. His whole attitude changed in one heartbeat. Man, I'm here to tell you, pain makes a guy cooperative.

"Where's Jancy?" Kellan lowered his voice, looking around the room. Kit shook her head and shrugged. Kellan bellowed, "Hey, Jimbo, where's your woman?"

Jim appeared in the doorway with a drink of his own. "She was supposed to be. . . ." Interrupted by the doorbell, he hurried to let her in, but opened the front door to find his brother Paul, a box in his hand, shivering on the stoop.

"Hey, Pauly, what are you doing here?"

"Actually, I came to have another look at your lady, but Mom sent egg rolls to give me an excuse."

"Jancy'll be here pretty soon. Do you want to come in or wait out there?"

"It's twelve degrees and sleeting, man. Believe I'll come inside."

Jim motioned his brother in and introduced him to Kellan and Kit.

"You don't suppose she's lost, do you?" Paul asked, after he was armed with a wine cooler.

"No, she called from work. She was just finishing up."

Paul settled on the overstuffed love seat adjacent to the fireplace. "Is she coming home with you for Christmas?"

"Maybe Sunday, Christmas afternoon."

"Did you get her a ring?"

Kit shot Kellan a dark look.

Jim shook his head. "No."

"You mean you struck out?"

"She marches to the beat of a different drummer, Paul." There was a cautioning tone in Jim's voice. "She's not ready for that yet."

Kellan's face fell with horror. "But you are?"

Jim grinned. "I'm getting there."

"Afraid it's too late for you then, old buddy." Paul stood. "You've had your at-bat and didn't tag up. It's my turn. Time for a heavy hitter. You just take a bench, son, and watch a man at the plate."

Jim raised his eyebrows and winked at Kit before she could speak. "Be careful, Paul, you don't know her," Jim said. "You don't have any idea who you're dealing with."

Paul returned his drink to the kitchen. Jim and Kellan sat sipping quietly. Kit picked out some holiday music and started the CD player as they listened to Paul concocting. They could smell cinnamon. He appeared in the doorway.

"Jim, where's your rum?"

"Lower right, next to the sink." Jim chuckled. Kellan and Kit looked puzzled. "It's his best time-honored ploy, get a girl good and drunk, then insist on taking her home."

Kellan's eyes rounded. "It might work." He frowned at Kit. Obviously he didn't like the way things were shaping up, the brothers competing for a woman.

Jim laughed. "Listen, if it does, he's a better man than I am and I'll admit it. Paul's used to high-mileage bimbos. He's never played the game with anyone in Jancy's league."

As if on cue, Kit told me later, I blew through the front door smiling broadly, nose and cheeks rosy from the cold. I carried a laundry basket loaded with gifts.

"Ho, Ho, Ho! Guess who?" I shoved the door closed with my foot, put the basket on the floor, shed my mittens, which I stuffed in my pockets, and unbuttoned my coat as Jim got there to take it.

"Ooh." Shivering, I gave him a quick hug, relinquished the coat and hurried to the fireplace. I had on the clothes I'd worn to work, dark slacks and a blue chambray shirt under an open vest that I pulled closed to hide dark smudges on the shirt's placket. "What smells so good?"

Paul made his entrance from the kitchen carrying two steaming cups. "A toddy to warm your bones, my pet."

I was surprised and, to tell the truth, not particularly happy to see him. Thanksgiving, Paul had kept trying to put moves on me, which made Jim a little testy with us both. I smiled and tried to mask my disappointment. "Hi, Paul. Terrific. Thanks." He crossed the room, handed me one of the cups, then sat on the hearth right beside me. I looked at Jim. "Is this supper?"

"I promised you a charcoaled steak. You get it."

"You're not cooking outside. Jim, it's snowing."

"A promise is a promise. Neither sleet nor snow nor dark of night. I deliver."

Paul looked from Jim to me. "He's steady but he's basically a dumb schmuck."

Kellan and Kit frowned but Jim smiled tolerantly. I pretended not to have heard and sipped the hot buttered rum, shivering again, this time at the warmth.

I followed Jim when he went back to the kitchen and leaned against the counter to discuss events of the day.

Deputy Gary Spence had gotten a speeding ticket in Rogers County, earning him a noisy reprimand from Sheriff Dudley Roundtree—a report that made Jim laugh, just as I had planned.

"And Ron Melchoir gave me Monday and Tuesday off," I added, "and I didn't even ask."

Jim put water on the stove to boil corn, wrapped the garlic bread in foil and put a bowl brimming with salad into the refrigerator. "How did he happen to give you time off?"

"I told him you were off between Christmas and New Year's. I guess it was a Christmas present. I'm tickled pink."

Suddenly Paul burst into the kitchen. "You kids been in here by yourselves ten minutes already and you're not naked yet? Jimbo, you're losing your touch."

I tried to smile, but his being there and saying crude things made me feel awkward. Jim ignored him, but Paul wasn't in a mood to be disregarded.

"Jancy, you need to loosen up. Here, let me freshen your rum." Paul eased the cup from my fingers in a move calculated so that his hands caressed mine. He looked deeply into my eyes, with a squirrelly Rudolph Valentino stare.

When I looked at Jim for some explanation, he only smiled and went back to rubbing goo into the steaks. Kellan, carrying his coat and Jim's, joined us in the kitchen.

"Where do you think you're going?" Jim asked.

"With you, man. Can't be any colder outside than the treatment I'm getting in there from that one." He tipped his head, indicating the living room. "She just told me to drop dead."

Even without an invitation, Paul assumed he was staying for supper. I nursed the fresher and stronger buttered rum and endured Paul's escalating, sometimes embarrassing attention. He switched from buttered rum to rum and Coke after his third. I kept sipping my second and trying to make it clear I had no interest in him.

Kellan and Kit obviously were in the throes of an ongoing spat.

The more Paul drank, the more he belittled Jim, which elevated me from uncomfortable to angry. The atmosphere at the dinner table was strained in spite of the wonderful meal. The only one who seemed to be enjoying himself was Jim, who was oddly lighthearted, as if he delighted in the awkward exchanges among his guests. Paul ate sparingly and drank a lot.

"Jancy?" Paul said my name too loudly. "I can tell you are too much woman for old Jimbo, here. Hell, he's never joined the fraternity of real men. Of course, trying to find a real man around here is like trying to find a virgin on campus, isn't that right, Calvin?"

Kellan grimaced. "My name is Kellan."

Tempers seemed to be getting a little raw, so I tried to defuse the tension with a potshot at Paul. "What would you do if you found a virgin on campus?"

He laughed boisterously and addressed Kellan, who, looking back at him, emitted a wicked chuckle. "I'm a charitable guy," Paul said. "I'd offer her the benefit of my services." He winked. "Jancy doesn't know me very well, does she, Kevin, old man."

Kellan's smile wilted. "The name is Kellan."

"Right. Kellan, old man. You see, people, Jim's always been a goddamn altar boy, embarrassing me every time I tried to take him out in public. To this day, some of my friends still refer to my little brother here as 'the old sheep herder.' "

Jim flashed him a warning look. "You've got the wrong audience, Paul. You don't know her."

I was surprised that the peculiar strain in the air seemed to have something to do with me.

Paul lowered his voice, drawing all of our undivided attention. "When we were in college, we formed this elite little club. The initiation was special, required concentration, certain skill."

Jim tried again. "Paul, you're going to regret this."

"Shhh. Quiet. She needs to know about you. Now, for initiation into this very exclusive little group, members got the new guy soused and drove him to Fagan's sheep ranch late, after the Fagans and the sheep were all asleep. Did you know sheep sleep? Try to say that three times when you've had a drink."

Kellan snickered behind his hand. Paul gave Kellan an appreciative nod.

Jim said, "Don't encourage him."

"Anyway, the new guy had to *do it* with a sheep. The new guy went first and then any other horny guy was welcome to take a shot. The sheep . . . well, weren't any of 'em pretty, of course, but mostly they cooperated, especially when a couple of guys held one's head while someone else had his way with her."

Kit and I looked at each other and cringed. I'd heard wild stories like that when I was in high school, but I thought they were just boy noise. Kellan covered his mouth with his hand and spewed laughter. Jim scanned each of our faces.

Paul continued, goaded by our responses. "When the boy scout/altar boy here saw what was required, he wouldn't do it. He was plenty drunk enough, but he refused to copulate.

"I, myself an upperclassman, had recommended him for membership in this group. Goody Two-Shoes here almost ruined the Wills' family name in that pasture that night except, of course, everyone was so drunk that no one knew if he did it or not. I told 'em he'd done the men in our family proud.

"The trouble was, the next time we got a guy ready for initiation and out to Fagan's, guess what? No sheep." Paul hesitated, but no one else spoke. "We were all disappointed as hell. I mean, who could come up with another initiation ritual to equal it? It was tradition. We went back to the bar and drank ourselves blottoed.

"It turned out when Jim heard we were having an initiation, he talked old man Fagan into moving the sheep up by his house. And the old man got a dog."

When Paul finished his story, an awkward pall of silence settled over the room. He stood and swaggered to the kitchen to pour another drink while the rest of us sat in strained silence. I didn't want to look at anyone else and couldn't think of anything to say.

Kit finally said, "You know he can't drive, don't you?"

Kellan nodded. "We'll take him with us. Do we take him to your folks' house?"

Jim shook his head. "No, he's got an apartment in Cleary Village. I'll take him. I don't want you to have to haul him all the way up there."

"No trouble. Let's let him finish this drink."

"Good idea. When he's this far gone, he gets belligerent."

"Not with you or me on him." Kellan arched his eyebrows significantly. "I told you how easy it is to snap a guy's collarbone."

"We can wait a while," Jim said. "It's early."

"Kit and I need to go. We've got to talk over our little problem. Early is better."

Paul reappeared with his new drink, dropped onto the love seat in the living room and propped his feet on the glass coffee table. "Come here, Jancy." He patted the cushion next to him. "Sit down here beside me."

I could feel Jim watching my face as I got up from the dining table and walked to the love seat. Instead of sitting beside Paul, however, I perched on the opposite arm and peered down my nose at him. "You don't know it, Paul, but I'm a goody two-shoes myself."

He squinted against the glare from the floor lamp behind me. I didn't offer to turn it off. "I made a deal with the Lord a long time ago that whenever anyone used His name in vain, I would absent myself from that person."

"You don't mean me? I didn't do that, did I?" He looked at the others. Kit nodded. Kellan and Jim, too. Paul groaned. "Oh, God, a good Catholic girl. Jim, you S.O.B., why didn't you tell me?"

"Episcopalian," I corrected, regarding him with what I intended to be a tolerant smile.

"Does this mean you won't be tucking me in tonight?"

"Right."

"Maybe some other time?"

"I doubt it."

"But you won't be sleeping with Jimbo either, right?"

"He hasn't asked me."

"Damn!" Paul's eyes got round and he looked at me as if he

were startled. "*Damn*'s not against your code, is it?"

I shook my head slowly, struggling to squelch the smile.

Paul heaved a sigh, obviously for effect.

CHAPTER NINE

"What little problem?" I handed Jim plates rinsed and ready for the dishwasher. Earlier, all of us patronized Paul to get him into his coat and out the door. Eventually, he and Kellan and Kit left in a flurry.

"Kit's pregnant." Jim said it softly without looking up.

"They've gone together a long time. Can't they get married?"

"Yes, they could, except there's something else."

"What else?"

"Kellan's dating several girls."

"Sounds to me like he's narrowed the field."

Jim scowled at the dishwater. "Two of those several are pregnant."

"Oh." I didn't want to appear judgmental, but what in the world was the man thinking? "I thought Kellan had some street smarts. What's he doing having all this unprotected sex? Hasn't he heard of STDs? HIV? AIDS?"

"He says there's no problem. None of the girls is dating anyone but him."

I gave a little snort to demonstrate my contempt for that thinking. I was naive but I wasn't stupid. "Yeah, right. Why does he think that?"

"He's sure none of his women would cheat on him."

"While he's running around cheating on all of them." Mulling over Kellan's typical male logic, I dried my hands on a paper towel on my way to the counter across from the sink

99

where I lifted myself to sit and contemplate. No wonder awful diseases kept spreading, with help from people like Kellan and Kit—college graduates, for heaven's sake—educated people who should know better.

Jim closed the dishwasher and turned it on before he looked at me. His face relaxed as our eyes met, just as he snapped off the overhead light, leaving us only the reflected glow from the living room. In the semidarkness, he strolled over in front of me and casually rested his hands on my knees. Still mired in thought, I didn't object.

He stood half smiling, studying my face, specifically my knitted brow as I considered Kit and Kellan's situation. When I realized he was watching me, I sat up straighter. Puzzled by his concentration, I smiled. When I did, Jim leaned forward. I swayed toward him, aware, as usual, of his marvelous, compelling scent. He caught my shirt collar with both hands and pulled my face close enough to kiss. He kissed me gently at first, then deepened it as heat ignited along with our mutual desire. Definitely interested, I draped my forearms over his shoulders.

Slowly, keeping my mouth occupied with his, he unbuttoned my shirt. I didn't object—didn't want to—nor did I when he grabbed handfuls of fabric and pulled my shirttail free of my slacks. I felt totally comfortable, relaxed, fingering the back of his head, then watching as I followed the line of his ear with a fingernail. Something about us together seemed totally natural, as if we were intended to share a little intimacy.

When he saw my new bra with the front closure, he smiled. Naturally enough he probably assumed I had changed styles to facilitate his occasional survey, and I supposed he was right, although I had not selected the new item with that conscious thought.

His hands had grown hot by the time he flattened them against my midriff, then walked them around, following the line of my waist, to my back.

I put my hands on each side of his face and playfully dropped kisses around his mouth, slowly at first, then more urgently. My breathing quickened.

Jim fumbled with the closure on my bra before he freed my breasts and I wondered about the fumbling. He had a reputation as a smooth operator; certainly he had been with me.

Tossing the bra aside, he froze and just stared at me. His concentration made me squirm. I had never before been that exposed for a man's study. Self-conscious, I sat straighter and kept my eyes steadily on his face, becoming more and more curious at his reaction.

He licked his lips, raised his eyes to mine and smiled before his gaze dropped to drift hungrily from one breast to the other. Then his fingertips took up the study, tracing from my throat, skimming the tops of both breasts and back. I sat there like a zombie, not moving or making a sound. He didn't look up but gradually his eyes narrowed to slits and his breathing became labored.

A moment passed before he carefully touched his tongue to one nipple. I gasped. The incoming air felt hot in my lungs.

When I didn't move back or resist, Jim put his mouth around the tip, closed his eyes, sucked that breast into his mouth and titillated the captive nipple with his tongue.

I swallowed hard. Struggling to breathe, I didn't try to speak and, honestly, couldn't think of any words appropriate to the moment.

When his mouth released that breast, I pushed the other one forward, offering it for his attention.

He smiled without looking up and whispered, "Right. We won't be playing favorites."

Cupping one breast in each hand, he kissed first one, then the other, back and forth, again and again, crooning softly, voicing his admiration for their symmetry, their size and firmness.

Still cradling my breasts in his hands, Jim nibbled a path to my throat, over my chin and again settled upon my mouth. I ran my fingers over his ears and to the back of his head before I locked my arms around his neck and opened to welcome his tongue.

It wasn't enough. Wanting more, I pushed him back a little. My heart pounded so loud I didn't think he could hear me if I tried to speak and I didn't see any reason to ask for what I wanted when we seemed to be so perfectly in sync. I unbuttoned his shirt, pushed the fabric to either side and tried to breathe. He was magnificent, the hair on his chest abundant, mesmerizing the way it narrowed and trailed the middle of his stomach, down, down. I brushed my open hands over his torso, marveling at the heat of his bare flesh and the way his muscles flexed beneath my touch.

When the hard plates of his pectoral muscles tightened, I smiled and combed his dark body hair with my fingers, raking it to a natural trough in the middle. Then, surprising us both, I clamped my hands firmly to his ribs. Watching me as if he were an impartial observer, Jim moaned, a compelling sound that issued from somewhere deep within him. I glanced at his face and smiled again only to be a little disconcerted by his intensity.

Surprisingly, he planted random kisses over my face, confusing and distracting me while he slid a hot hand between my knees. He pressed forward, nudging my legs apart while his mouth continued nuzzling my face and neck and his hands again fondled my breasts. I couldn't think.

Deftly his fingers drifted up the outside of my thighs, which cradled his torso. Slowly, carefully, those fingers crawled toward my hips, fondling and exploring as they came.

His face was flushed as he pulled me forward on the counter and pressed himself more firmly into the valley between my legs. I was vaguely aware that he was careful to keep the lower part of his torso in the recess beneath the counter top.

Jim's naked chest scrubbing mine sent chill bumps up and down my arms and over my legs. At the same time, driven by curiosity and the heat we generated, I massaged the muscles in his upper arms and shoulders. My breath came in desperate gasps, yet I drew him nearer, pushing against him, movements that developed a jungle rhythm. I couldn't seem to get close enough. My thoughts wavered between reality and fantasy. Our intimacy produced peculiar aches inside, particularly in my nether regions, a longing I had never imagined igniting in my own body. In those moments I knew that what had been my dormant sex drive was awake and becoming fully functional.

An annoying groan roused me and I was startled to discover the sound was coming from me.

"Wait." I wheezed, at the same time pushing against the burgeoning muscles in his shoulders.

Jim froze.

I planted my hands firmly against his bare, heaving chest and shoved him to arm's length. I hated separating myself from his warmth, but warning sirens wailed inside me. When I could see him clearly, I stared, gasping, startled and confused. "We're getting close, aren't we?"

"A hitch and a zipper away." The hoarseness in his voice surprised me. He had always been such a disciplined, self-controlled person. The lower part of my body throbbed with unanswered need.

Jim looked down, drawing my eyes. My legs were spread, the most intimate part of me—though clothed—appeared vulnerable and totally open. If he stood up straight. . . . If we were naked. . . . He fingered the closure on my slacks. I wriggled back on the counter, struggling to put some space between us.

"I need to go home." I stopped and held perfectly still. "Don't I?"

Jim frowned and nodded, but his hands remained at my waist, steadying and coaxing. Gradually he pulled me forward and again pressed himself to that highly sensitized area between my legs. He lifted my hips and rocked me, swaying, scrubbing my naked breasts against his bare chest, making me feverish.

"Please," I rasped breathlessly, my lips against his ear, my arms again locked around his neck. "Help me. Help me get out of here. Please." I was begging, nearly defeated by my own heart-pounding desire. "Please."

He put his forehead to mine, ground his teeth and squeezed his eyes closed. Then, slowly, tantalizingly, he relaxed his hold. Finally, he dropped his arms to either side and I was free.

I shivered and swallowed the lump burning my throat. Oh, Lord, how I wanted him. I knew he could sense the desire in me. Like the man of sterling character he was, he made a valiant effort to overlook it.

"Are you cold? Let's go in by the fire." He splayed his hands on my thighs and studied his thumbs, so close to that magical spot.

Totally conflicted, I became aware of perspiration beaded on my forehead and upper lip. My whole body felt clammy. I was immediately self-conscious until I looked at him.

Jim's hairline was wet, his face flushed but set with grim determination. I trembled and he smiled into my face. "We're a mess," I said, stating the obvious.

His hands, which somehow were back on my hips, retreated again, tracing my thighs to my knees.

"Please quit feeling me up." I was too embarrassed to look at him more than seconds at a time.

He gave me a self-conscious grin. "That's hard to do. The thing I want most in this world is to touch all those places you want me to touch you. The problem here, you see, is. . . ." He hesitated, then lowered his voice. "Jancy, I don't want to scare you, but I've gotta tell you, sweetheart. I love you."

My mouth dropped open, but I didn't even attempt to respond.

"All I can think of these days—and nights—is getting you into bed. I have this nearly overwhelming desire to carry you upstairs right now." He looked wistfully toward the reflected light from the living room, the path to the bedrooms above. "I want to hold you and do all kinds of exotic, wonderful things to and with you. Then, when the storm of making love with you is over, I want you to sleep in my arms. But one night of you, Jancy, isn't going to be enough for me. My feelings are so intense I'm afraid of scaring you. I want you for more than just one night. I want you again and again, night after night, from now on, as long as I live."

I stared at him. "You love me?"

A startled laugh escaped him. "Damn straight! Why else would I torment myself like this? I love you, Jancy Dewhurst. I have from the first time you turned those insolent chocolate brown eyes on me. You had me from that annoyed, 'Damn.' I love you in my dreams when I'm sound asleep. I love you so much, I feel sorry for myself. This is the damnedest thing I've ever gotten into."

"That's good." Not able to look at him, I gazed at the blank wall behind him. Surprisingly, the two words emerging from the emotional turmoil inside me sounded matter-of-fact.

He remained very still, his eyes locked on my face.

I reached for my bra, put it on and fastened it with no interference. Aware that he was watching me closely, waiting, I didn't look at him as I buttoned up my blouse in the ensuing silence. Then I did a peculiar thing. I smoothed his shirt, pulled it closed and buttoned it for him. He got kind of a quirky smile, but he didn't say anything or move.

By then, I had sorted my thoughts and was ready to share. "I liked you that first afternoon too, Jim, but it's like I stumbled into a Brer Rabbit/Tar Baby scene. All I ever meant to do was say 'Howdy.' Before I knew what had happened, my fists and my feets were so stuck up with you, I didn't know if I could get myself loose, or not."

Jim began laughing, a rolling, infectious sound rumbling up from inside him to erupt in a sound that fairly filled the room. He threw his arms around me, swept me off the counter top and whirled me around the kitchen, laughing like a crazy man, and I laughed right along with him. For that moment, things seemed fine, no problem insoluble.

When he put me down, he kept his arms around me as his momentum carried us into the living room. There we collapsed side by side on the sofa facing the fire.

"There may only be one way out of this." He laughed lightly. "We may have to get married."

I sobered quickly, as if he had slapped me. I could tell the minute he saw the pain on my face. He tried to recant, sort of. "That's what people usually do."

By then I was staring at him, stunned that he would even suggest such a thing. My words came fast and my voice sounded frantic. "No. Jim, I told you, Riley Wedge is going to call me to work for the wire service in October. I have a huge future, a wonderful career planned. I'm going to interview and write about exotic people all over the world."

He looked deflated and sounded that way too. "I'll take you anywhere you want to go."

"But I want to meet royalty and prime ministers and mercenaries and villains. I want to be where things happen. I want to contribute; to be valuable and important."

"You're already valuable and important to me." His sorrow

got worse with every word. I had to make him understand, even if it ripped us both up inside.

"That isn't enough."

"I see." He was quiet for a long minute and I had nothing more to say right then. "What does that mean?" he asked finally. "If I push things, knock you up, we can get married, otherwise, it's tough shit. You'll go pandering after the rich and famous and I'll mope around here hoping if I hold on long enough, you'll come to your senses?"

There was another long silence, which he interrupted again, speaking quietly.

"Marriage obviously is a brand new idea for you. Think about it, about your options, including this new one. Decide what you want. But first, ask yourself: what's the most important thing you'll ever do in your life?" He waited, but I didn't attempt an answer. I'd never thought about that before. But he didn't seem to require my input.

"You're a good reporter, sweetheart. Really good reporters win Pulitzers, cash awards, fame. People know them and turn out at auditoriums to hear them recall highlights of their rich careers."

I regarded him quietly.

He took a deep breath and dropped his head. "Hell, I'd probably come hear you talk."

We were both silent a long time, listening to the fire crackle and gazing into the flames.

Thinking about what he'd said, I wanted to ask him the same question. "What's the most important thing you think you'll ever do?"

He didn't look at me as he spoke. "I've had some minor successes already." His quiet words soothed me. "I've gotten through college and law school. I'm a solid law enforcement officer and an adequate lawyer. But, Jancy," he lifted his eyes to challenge mine, "even if I eventually got to be a justice on the United States Supreme Court, I think the most important thing I could do in life would be to father and rear productive, God-fearing children.

"That may not sound ambitious enough for you right now, but I have given that question some serious thought and that's the bottom line for me." He bowed his head. "It may not be for you.

"I told Paul tonight, you march to the beat of a different drum. I believe you and I belong together. Mom could tell we were a match in the short time you were at their house Thanksgiving. But Mom and I can't make that decision for you. You have to consider your choices and reach your own conclusions."

Moving slowly, I got up and crossed the room to retrieve my coat from the closet. I glanced at the laundry basket of gifts still on the floor.

"Those are for you and your family. They aren't Christmas presents. They're thank-yous for Thanksgiving, so no one has to feel guilty or anything."

Painstakingly, I pulled on each mitten, then fumbled trying to button my coat. Watching, Jim shook his head and came to help.

I spoke without looking at his face. "I think this is the first time you've ever helped me button anything up."

He gave me a grudging smile. "You know I love you, don't you?" He snugged my coat collar around my neck as I bobbed my head in the affirmative.

Finally I stammered, "I was afraid maybe you did. But that was before. . . ." I blinked back tears welling in my eyes and kept swallowing to soothe the lump in my throat. I had to get out of there before I dissolved, so I just turned on my heel and marched straight out into the freezing night.

CHAPTER TEN

I slept in snatches, too upset to settle down. Finally, at three-thirty Saturday, I gave up, tossed some things in a bag and left the house on Cherry Street in the chill predawn darkness.

Snow plows had cleared the main streets and truck traffic had beaten down the slow lane on the interstate highway. I drove slowly, in absolutely no hurry. If I took it easy, I would get home about the time Mother had the coffee made. They didn't expect me early, but then I hadn't expected to be traveling so early either.

Sometimes I cannot recall faces or feelings, no matter how hard I try. In the early morning solitude of that Christmas Eve, I could not forget the myriad emotions that had played over Jim's face, the inflections in his voice, his laughter, his warm hands and mouth touching me places no hands or mouth had touched before.

I tried having a serious, insightful talk with myself. "It's called 'groping,' stupid. How could you be twenty-three years old and still be this naive?"

I decided Jim was an evil, insidious serpent, charming his way into my clothing and into my heart, taking everything I was willing to give and wanting—no, demanding—more.

A few miles further, I decided, instead, that he was an innocent, a boy scout herding sheep out of harm's way. I began to cry. He said he loved me. Was that the serpent or the boy scout?

The problem was my insatiable curiosity. I had always been

curious to the point of being nosy, but I simply had never been stimulated enough to pursue my occasional passing interest in sex. Not until Jim.

That thinking carried me deeper. I liked touching Jim's bare chest and stomach. And I really liked his touching me. But what was it about me that aroused him when my sexy housemate Angela apparently did not? Angie and other smart, attractive ladies chased him blatantly, and he seemed to understand and maybe even respond physically to their overtures.

"A man should stay with his own kind," I muttered. "He should be with someone who knows what she's doing."

That's when I quit making the heroic effort to stanch the tears. Creeping along the snow-packed highway, I started blubbering. It got worse until I was sobbing uncontrollably.

The one hundred-thirty-five-mile trip to Carson's Summit took nearly four hours on the snowy highways. When I opened the front door at home at seven-thirty, my eyes were completely dry. The house smelled of coffee and sausage cooking.

"Honey!" My mother hurried from the kitchen in her robe and scuffs to see who was coming in so early. I took one look at her unsuspecting face and I suddenly burst into tears all over again.

She took a hard look at my face, then she, too, began to cry. We fell into each other's arms bawling to beat anything.

Then, suddenly, realizing she was crying, too, I became alarmed. "Mom, what's the matter?"

"I don't know." She shook her head, blinking at me, puzzled.

"Why are you crying?"

She pulled a tissue from her pocket and blew her nose, looking confused. "Because you are."

We just stood there a minute, gazing intently into each other's faces before we began to laugh. The laughter grew into noisy guffaws and we hugged each other, fairly convulsing with giggles.

Greg came from the kitchen wearing the bottoms to his pajamas and a T-shirt. "What's up?" He smiled, then frowned.

Mom dabbed at her streaming eyes. "We don't know." She shrugged at him and looked at me and we again collapsed into each others' arms in peals of helpless laughter.

"It's too ridiculous to explain," Mom told Dad when he came down the stairs wearing his robe, house shoes and a puzzled expression.

As we sat down to breakfast later, I told them—Mom and Dad and both little brothers—that I had Monday and Tuesday off.

Mom looked overjoyed, though no one else seemed impressed. "Great," she said. "By the way, Stephanie Stone is having a little get-together Monday night for your high school bunch. She called to ask if you would be here. I told her I didn't think so. You need to call her."

Timothy's mouth was crammed with food when he choked out another message. "Max Binder has a Hummer, the big one." He swallowed. "He wants to show it to you, expects you to swoon or something. I think he's going to ask you out."

Now there was someone more my speed. Max Binder. Big, soft-spoken, dull Max, whose goal in life since the ninth grade was to be a mortician. Max oozed compassion and sensitivity. But most of all, Max was determined to be rich. Someone like Max would be easy to leave when Riley Wedge called, easy to forget when I was in the company of presidents and kings.

Dad passed Timothy the sports section of the morning paper, gave me a quick glance, then did a double-take. "Why so pensive, pet?"

Suddenly overwhelmed by volatile emotions mustering all over again, I hopped up from the table. I was no longer their little girl and Tim and Greg's big sister. I was maturing into . . . what? A wanton woman? "Excuse me." I tossed my napkin and ran for the stairs.

"Are you sick, baby?" Mom asked, when she opened my bedroom door a while later. She peered at me as if looking for clues to my erratic behavior.

Lying on my stomach across my bed, I gave her the best tremulous smile I could manage. "I'll be okay. I was up late."

"How's Jim?"

"Fine."

"Are you getting along okay with the girls at the house? At work?"

"Un-huh," I answered affirmatively.

"Did you buy gifts for everyone?"

"Yes." I had been more selective choosing gifts for the Wills clan than for anyone else, but Mom didn't need to know that. She began folding a quilt across the foot of the bed and I knew she was stalling, wanting me to talk about what was troubling me. I would have if I had been able to narrow it down and, honestly, I didn't know where to begin.

"A couple of presents came for you early in the week," she said.

"From Grandma?"

"No. They have a Bishop postmark."

The telephone rang. Saved by the bell, I scrambled to my feet and raced to answer. It was Max.

"Oh, hi, Max." I didn't feel nearly as pleased to hear from him as I sounded.

After we exchanged some pleasantries, he said, "How would you like to go riding around town in my new, top-of-the-line, four-wheel-drive, off-road vehicle?"

I gritted my teeth and wondered idly if a sport like Max ever actually ventured off paved roads anytime, but what I said was, "That would be great."

He sounded excited. "Right. I'll be there in half an hour."

Cruising town with Max, I saw several old friends and classmates home for the holidays, which lifted my spirits. Pretty soon I was whistling and yoo-hooing to people out the open car window and waving. When we stopped for a red light, two girls galloped up from the car behind us, skidding through the slush, squealing and bubbling. Catching their enthusiasm, I jumped out of the Hummer to exchange hugs right there in the middle of the street. In the Dairy Queen parking lot, we were besieged and I laughed out loud at all the hugging and chatter.

Taking me home, Max looked smug. "Stephanie's having a bash Monday night. Do you want to go?"

I looked at Max's soft belly that hung over so a person couldn't tell if he wore a belt or not, and gave him a smile. Good old Max. Harmless Max who was no threat to a woman's future. "Thanks," I said. "I'm not sure if I'll be here or not. Can I let you know?"

The smug grin broadened. "Sure."

Back at my house, my mother's parents had arrived with enough packages to fill one end of our very large den.

When noisy greetings calmed down, I casually asked the room at large, "Did anyone call?"

Dad looked embarrassed. "Yes."

I caught a quick breath.

It took him a minute to recall the message. "Stephanie Stone wanted you to call the minute you got back."

I exhaled my disappointment. "No one else?"

"No. Who are you . . . ?"

His question was cut short by Mom's sudden cough. When he tried again, she cleared her throat. Sometimes my mother is not even a little bit subtle.

I gave him a smile. "Thanks anyway, Dad."

On the telephone, Stephanie gave me an excited run-down of who was home for Christmas. She rattled off twenty names, reciting news of marriages and births and divorces as she went.

Our traditional Christmas Eve north wind was howling by nine as my whole family dressed for church—caroling at ten-thirty, Mass at eleven. I settled down, actually got serene, content or maybe just numbed, I supposed, back in Carson's Summit where I had reverted to being Lucy and Gregory Dewhurst's little girl again, trooping off to Christmas Mass without being asked for my preference. And it was fine with me. Really.

People at the church where I grew up seemed genuinely glad to see me. Ada Nelson, the organist and my old piano teacher, caught us in the hallway. "Jancy, no boyfriend yet?" she chirped, her voice carrying.

I forced a smile. "No, ma'am, not yet. Maybe next year. Merry Christmas, Ms. Nelson."

"Don't worry, dear, some nice young man will come along someday."

I waited until she had trundled off down the aisle before I mumbled, "I appreciate your confidence."

Standing right behind me, my brother Greg said, "What?"

I shook my head, motioned him to come around, then followed him into the pew.

Feeling buoyed by the service and the music, my mood darkened again when I saw there were no messages for me—or anyone else, for that matter—on the answering machine at home.

Traditionally, on Christmas Eve we put milk and cookies on the hearth beneath the stockings lining the mantle, then all slip off to bed. Later, each of us takes a turn sneaking down to stuff the others' stockings.

Christmas morning there was another four inches of snow on the ground and the stockings looked ready to explode.

I never cease to be amazed that wrapping paper, which looks so thin and well behaved around packages, can swell to such massive, unruly proportions when wadded and tossed around a room.

Granddaddy seemed pleased with the small pocket knife I gave him and he immediately put it to good use, cutting tape, ribbons and seals on request.

I had given Greg the game *Outburst* and Timothy *Jenga*. Mother was delighted with *The Phantom of the Opera* CD. I had gotten Dad a jigsaw for his Saturday carpentry and Grandmother a wristwatch with enormous numbers on the face so she could see it without squinting.

"Open your gifts," Mom said, nudging me. "You'll be here the rest of the day."

Timothy piped, "Open that big one."

Thinking it was from Tim, I pulled the big box over in front of me and squared myself on my knees. Granddad cut the tape with his pocket knife before I ripped into the tissue, burrowing down to something fuzzy and lavender.

"What is it?" Timothy asked, tearing into another of his gifts.

My heart skipped a beat. It felt like something caught in my throat, which caused me to whisper the response. "It's Theodore."

I buried my face in the thick, downy mane of the stuffed lavender lion I had admired the day we went aboard the *Choctaw Gambler*. Jim had paid attention when I pointed out the silly stuffed animal. It wasn't the gift itself, or even what I considered the exorbitant price. It was his remembering.

I glanced up to find Mom watching me curiously. "Who gave you that? Honey, who does the card say it's from?"

I tossed the tissue paper around inside the box. "There isn't a card."

"Oh, dear, how will you know who it's from?"

"I know who it's from." I wrapped my arms all the way around the lion and squeezed, Christmas joy revived.

When, at Mom's prodding, I finally set Theodore down beside me, I hurried to catch up with my brothers, who probably could compete in gift opening as an Olympic event.

Several packages later, there was another with my name written in Jim's same familiar scrawl.

Mom whooped when I peeled the paper away from the box. "A cellular telephone? Oh, sweetheart, you need that so badly. I never would have thought of it. Gregory, honey, what a wonderful idea."

Dad looked up, obviously perplexed by the compliment. "I didn't give it to her. You know I'm not into all that electronic gadgetry."

Greg winced. "Dad, you should have had one of those years ago. An insurance man should be accessible. We're going to have to drag you kicking and screaming into the twenty-first century."

Mom did not follow that red herring as she continued studying my face. "Is that from Jim, too, honey?" She asked the question softly, as if she were not quite sure she would like the answer.

Grinning from ear to ear, I nodded and her concerned expression gave way to a smile. He shouldn't have done it, of course. It was too much, considering our fizzling friendship.

I really perked up after that and helped out cheerfully, getting meals prepared and on the table, rifling through boxes before stacking them in the garage to put out for the trash on Tuesday.

Theodore sat grinning on my bed as I read the instructions, agreements and guarantees packed with the cell phone. One paper said the three-hundred-dollar deposit would be refunded at the end of one calendar year if all monthly statements were kept current.

I groaned, thinking he had spent so much. But that was before our little session the night before Christmas Eve. I probably should offer to return the phone. Would that injure his pride, or would he be pleased to recover such a big investment? I wasn't sure, but I decided not to activate it.

I thought long and hard about that and many other things. I did not, however, think about reconsidering my career choice. After all, it was a holiday. I was off duty.

When Jim did not call on Christmas Day, I assumed I knew why. He must have forgotten inviting me to his parents' house. That was, of course, before I got the two extra days off work and before the fiasco at his condo.

Embracing the no-thought-required freedom of the return to my childhood home, I decided to stay an extra day in Carson's Summit.

Monday I drove Mom and Grandmother downtown to exchange gifts that didn't fit for ones that did, I had lunch with two close high school friends, and I went to Stephanie's party with Max that evening.

Max was . . . well, he was Max. He spoke in the hushed tones he perceived to be a necessary affectation for any decent mortician and kept his hands folded together and propped on his prominent stomach all evening.

"Image in my business is everything, Jancy," he assured me, for about the dozenth time. Circulating, I tried to ignore the derisive remarks other people made about Max, but all the time I kept thinking his behavior was more than a little over the top.

At the front door when he brought me home, he licked his fat cherry red lips and leaned close. Yuck! I dodged, as if we were sparring, which was my not-so-subtle way of avoiding contact. I would have thought he was clowning around, coming at me with the exaggerated pucker, except Max had reminded me several times that humor was taboo at the mortuary.

He looked pained. "Thanks for the honor of letting me haul you around all weekend in my top-of-the-line wheels. Hope you enjoyed yourself at Stephanie's. It's nice one of us got what they wanted." With that, he whirled and stomped back to his car. The whirl and the stomp didn't play well on a guy as broad as Max. On video, even he might have seen the humor in his moves.

Inside, I laughed and snapped off the lights before I climbed the stairs. I shivered at the memory of Max's ridiculous mannerisms and his lurid lips. Giggling, I realized I was recovered, back to my usually happy, well-adjusted self. Being at home with family and friends had healed my uncertainties. I was ready and able to return to the emotional roller coaster that was my life in Bishop. I was even ready to face Jim.

Mom opened my bedroom door and peeked in. "Honey, there was an urgent call for you."

"Urgent?"

"Yes, Mr. Melchoir at the paper. I told him you'd be back in Bishop sometime tomorrow. He said to tell you he needs you there early, that your second day off is canceled."

"Did he say why?"

Mom shook her head.

CHAPTER ELEVEN

I was up and dressed and pulled out of Carson's Summit by
five-thirty a.m., thinking that would put me in the office before
eight. The roads were sloppy, the traffic heavy and I didn't get
to the newsroom until eight-fifty.

"What's urgent?" I asked Melchoir, who was obviously
relieved to see me.

"Late yesterday afternoon someone shot and killed G.C. Gideon."

"Oh." I felt taken aback by the news and, at the same time,
relieved. "Where?"

"At the ranch. You should have heard DeWitt. He wanted
you on it. No one else would do. There was no appeasing him.
When no one answered at your house here, I called Wills to see
if he knew where you were. He said you were at your parents'
and that he'd called there several times but hadn't talked to
you. I called there, too, but you were out. I told your mother it
was urgent. I hope I didn't alarm her. I'll make it up to you—
the day off, I mean."

I shelved some of those juicy tidbits of information in the
back of my mind to take out and mull over later. "Did you run
a story yesterday?"

"It broke after four o'clock, too late for us."

"Where was Bubba Valentine?"

"Who's that?"

"G.C.'s bodyguard."

"I don't know names, Jancy. You're our man on the scene. Ask your questions there, not here. I don't even know the players."

"Is it Roundtree's case?"

He bristled. "I said ask questions of someone who knows."

I made a beeline for my desk and made several quick phone calls.

G.C. Gideon had been murdered in Bishop County. Sheriff Dudley Roundtree and Deputy Gary Spence were investigating in close cooperation with the State Bureau of Investigation. Neither one could be reached until after noon. That information came from the holiday dispatcher.

Was there an incident report on file in the sheriff's office yet?

"No. They're sending all paperwork to Wills, the SBI agent in charge. He's holding all reports."

I smiled as I hung up, visualizing Jim. "You sly dog. Think you'll cut off my pipelines, do you? We'll just see about that."

But several more calls—to Robert Beams at the morgue; Dr. Crane, the pathologist; and even Don Lockwood at the *Dominion News,* who said he was "counting on" me—turned up nothing.

Investigators were gone, would return my call "as soon as possible."

Dispatchers were "not authorized to give out any information."

Even I was not crass enough to call the Gideons. I had seen the old man's pride wounded once. I didn't want to think about confronting him after the loss of the son he practically worshiped.

Then I got an idea and I called Roundtree's home.

"Mrs. Roundtree, you may not remember me. This is Jancy Dewhurst." Mrs. Roundtree did remember me. I explained my dilemma.

"The way I understand it," Mrs. Roundtree confided, assuring me she would not say anything Dudley would not tell me himself, "G.C. and his friend—Bobby, I think his name was— went to a cottage to wash up. They were due at the main ranch house for supper later.

"Bobby had gone upstairs to run G.C. a bath when a killer or maybe two or three killers burst through the front door and fired their guns, point blank. By the time Bobby what's-his-name grabbed his weapon and got downstairs, they had driven off at a high rate of speed. They were in a big black car. He didn't get the license number."

"Did they find the weapons?"

"No. The killers took their weapons with them. The highway patrol found a car in a roadside park about forty-five minutes later, but the slush and all the traffic in the gravel parking area had wiped out any tire tracks or footprints."

"How are they approaching the investigation, then?"

"Well, it seems G.C. had indebted the ranch for several million dollars. That's just a rumor, of course."

I hummed agreement.

"About six weeks ago, G.C. purchased a big life insurance policy. He named Chloe Conklin the beneficiary. The Conklin woman lives in the Gideons' manager's house with her two kids. People say the kids are G.C.'s. I've heard that the old man is awfully good to them. I don't know if it makes up for G.C. They say he's brutalized everyone out there, mentally, verbally and physically, the hired help, Chloe, the kids, everyone. Dudley's not surprised someone had him murdered."

Alarms sounded in my head. "The sheriff thinks it was hired?"

"Definitely. He said the biggest problem is they have too many suspects. G.C. ran up huge debts on the *Choctaw Gambler*, apparently reneged on bets on horse races and borrowed a lot of money from the wrong people. Also, of course, there's Chloe Conklin."

When we got to details Mrs. Roundtree couldn't provide, I thanked her. I had enough to get a foot in the door. If I framed it right, I had enough information to prime the pump to get Wills talking.

I called Mrs. Teeman. After we exchanged greetings and pleasantries about our holidays, I asked her where I might find Agent Wills.

"He's . . . oh, he and the sheriff are just pulling into the parking lot now. Shall I ask him to call you?"

"No." I tried to quell the butterflies scrambling off the runway in my stomach. "I'll just run over and see if he has time to talk to me."

"I imagine he will, dear." Mrs. Teeman's suggestive words were followed by a twittery little laugh.

I grabbed a new steno pad and tucked it into my coat pocket as I started toward the door.

"You on it?" Melchoir called.

I gave him a thumbs-up. He leaned back in his chair, patted his stomach with both hands, laced his fingers together and grinned.

Despite my snow boots, I slipped and slithered as I hurried by the courthouse and across the green way—a misnomer in winter—to the annex parking lot. Deputy Gary Spence came out the side door of the courthouse just as I trotted by, but I didn't have time for the B-team right then. I was aimed straight for the top. There was the personal thing, too. I wanted to see Jim's face when he first saw me. Out of the corner of my eye, I saw Spence bend and gather a handful of slushy snow and pack it as he trailed me.

Engrossed in their conversation, Jim and Roundtree leaned on the front fender of Wills' vehicle, their backs to me as I approached. My breath caught at the sight of Jim, one of the few men who looked good even in a trench coat. Of course, I knew which of the bulges were muscle.

Oblivious to everything and everyone else around me, I felt lightheaded when I got close enough to see the line of his jaw, his strong chin, the shape of his perfect ears, reddened by the cold. My heart pounded and I wished I hadn't put on the gloves that would keep my flesh from contact with his.

Looking at him, I marveled at how a person like me could be self-assured and have it all together in Carson's Summit and come completely unraveled at the mere sight of him.

I was nearly there and neither Roundtree nor Wills had seen me when Spence yelled, "Hey, playmate!"

I wheeled in time to see Spence finish his windup.

Wills and Roundtree turned around too, just as the deputy hurled the heavy snowball squarely at my head. Naturally, I ducked. The missile whistled over my head . . . and caught Wills mid-chest. Fragments splattered his face and dropped inside the front of his overcoat.

Standing upright again, looking at the total disbelief in his expression, I couldn't help the gurgling laugh that sputtered. I kept it under control for a heartbeat, trying to ignore the look of incredulity on Jim's face, but I couldn't hold on. I totally lost it.

Spence sputtered, laughing and apologizing, barely able to contain himself, spewing words every direction, as if trying to explain his behavior to an invisible audience.

Roundtree, probably burdened by the strain of the grim holiday murder, saw the direct hit and the surprise all around. He looked happy to see me, and my breathless, galloping giggles spread like a grass fire. The sheriff's laughter began with a low rumble that grew thunderous as both Spence and Wills turned dark looks on me. I guess they were mad at me for ducking.

As Wills' eyes narrowed, I whooped all the harder as he swiped snow from his face with exaggerated movements.

"Thought that was funny, did you?" He took two steps and scooped a handful of snow off the hood of a car.

Spence yelled, "Jancy, run for your life," but his warning came too late.

Still laughing uncontrollably, I didn't actually realize Jim was coming until he got there. He wrapped one arm around my neck, pushed my chin back with the other forearm and held the handful of snow poised just above my face. It was his turn to laugh, only his cackle sounded villainous.

"Don't do it, Wills." I tried to sound serious, but I couldn't pull it off. My own choking laugh undermined the threat. I squirmed and tried to push him away, shoving with both hands, but he held me fast with the single arm, leering down at me. His nose very close to mine, he whispered, "God, I missed your face."

He looked strong, handsome and completely unpredictable. His teeth seemed whiter, his eyes darker, his body larger, but I wasn't the least bit afraid. This Adonis, this marvelous man was crazy about me. It showed in his face and in his body language. And he didn't seem to care that his admiring me was on display in front of anyone who happened to be watching. How had I ever resisted him?

"It's only been a couple of days," I said, trying to calm the intensity surging between us.

He stretched the arm locked around my head out of his coat sleeve and peered at his watch. "Eighty-two hours and thirteen minutes. I hardly noticed."

"You are such a wuss." I didn't want him going all soft on me. I thought challenging him might snap him out of it.

He arched an eyebrow. "Ah-ha, now I see how you are."

I recognized the pseudo-danger and I began struggling, uncertain about what he might do. I realized too late, I'd pushed him a tad too far. His diabolical laughter and my squeals drew onlookers as he slowly smushed the snow into my face, then scrubbed it round and round.

A lot of people heard me shrieking, but those near enough to do anything about it were too astonished or too weakened with laughter to help.

Blinking, I thought I saw Mrs. Teeman—watching from the second floor offices of the State Bureau of Investigation—smile and nod her approval.

CHAPTER TWELVE

"So what do you know that's fit to print?" I asked breezily when Jim and I were settled in his office facing each other across his desk. If I were going to concentrate on business, I couldn't afford to look at him, at least not until I had all those renegade emotions in check.

Mrs. Teeman quietly produced a cup of steaming cocoa for me and brought Jim his usual black coffee. We both thanked her and remained silent until she left, closing the door behind her.

Jim continued the silent treatment. I could feel him looking at me and did not intend to look at him. I sensed a change and risked a quick look. Sure enough, he was grinning. Then he began speaking.

"A person or persons unknown shot and killed G.C. Gideon in his home about two o'clock yesterday afternoon."

"And they called you?" I regarded him solemnly and he returned my look as if we were strangers—polite ones.

"I got into it the way we always do. The sheriff called central office and asked for help. You know we have no jurisdictional authority. We have to be invited. Our people in Dominion called me."

"Why did the bureau get *invited?*"

"The sheriff didn't have the manpower to tackle this particular homicide, one with such high visibility."

I focused on scribbling in my notebook. "G.C. was killed at the ranch?"

"Yes."

"At the main house?"

When he didn't answer immediately, I looked up. His eyes narrowed suspiciously. "No. Most of the time G.C. actually lived with Chloe Conklin and her two children in what they call the manager's house. It's just beyond the swimming pool, which is at the back door of the main house, Tyrone Gideon's home. G.C., however, also had a two-level cottage away from the others. The killing occurred at the cottage."

I wrote frantically, things I had already gotten from Mrs. Roundtree. I risked only an occasional peek at Jim's face, trying to read behind his words, looking for any tidbit that needed pursuing.

"Where was Bubba Valentine at the time of the killing?"

"A very perceptive question. As luck would have it, he said he was upstairs running G.C. a bath. Valentine's story is he thought he heard a noise and turned off the water to listen. An M-16 fired indoors probably shook the rafters."

"One M-16?" Again concentrating on my notebook, I was forced to look up when he hesitated.

Capturing my eyes and my rapt attention, Jim nodded. "Yes." But he looked suspicious.

I wanted to keep this interview one professional to another. "Is that a rifle?"

"Yes." He smiled slightly, a look that appeared to have little to do with our questions and answers. "The civilian version is an AR-15, modified to make it semiautomatic. But this weapon actually was an M-16, fully automatic, supposedly available only to military and law enforcement types."

Although I stopped writing, I kept my eyes glued to the notebook page. "Have you found the weapon?"

"Not yet."

"How much does a gun like that cost?"

"Depends. Ballpark, around fifteen hundred."

"So the shooter probably wouldn't toss it in a dumpster?"

Jim shook his head. When I didn't hear a verbal response, I looked at him. Did the man's eyes never leave my face? I set my jaw, determined to keep my mind on the business at hand. "What about the casings? Does the M-16 drop casings when it shoots?"

"You are a quick study, Dewhurst." His answer was crisp. "Yes, the M-16 spits and no, we did not find any casings."

"What does that mean?"

He shrugged as if the detail were not important. "It means someone picked them up before we got there."

"Bubba?" I honestly wanted—needed—his answers, but even more importantly, I was desperate to keep us on the subject, not allow myself to drift, to get mesmerized by this man or his dark Machiavellian eyes, or think of how demanding his mouth felt on mine or about the incredible warmth of his hands beneath my clothing. No, no, Jancy, don't go there, my angelic self pleaded, battling that other influence.

It was as if Jim sensed my problem. His words became clipped. "According to Bubba, he was the only one there. He insists he doesn't know what happened to the casings."

I felt breathless. "Go on. Please."

"Valentine said he ran to his bedroom for his gun, then downstairs. He had to leap over G.C.'s body on his way down. Blood on his socks verified that, as far as we can tell.

"According to his statement, the front door was standing open. He said a big black car was speeding down the road. He said it was too far away to read the plate. Couldn't even tell what state it was from. He swore there was more than one oc-cupant. He fired a couple of rounds from his .45, but the car was out of range. He went back to see about G.C.

"Gideon had seven bullet holes in his body. He was dead

before he hit the stairs."

Wills hesitated, watching me closely, but I remained silent, waiting.

"Apparently the incident happened about noon. Then Bubba waited almost two hours before he called the sheriff's office to report it."

I stared at Jim intently. "Why the delay?"

He gave me an approving smile. "Bubba was a little confused about that himself. He first said he couldn't find his boots. Then he said he hid, thinking the killers might come back to finish him. Then he couldn't decide whether to go to the main house to tell old Mr. Gideon, afraid the killers might have been there too, and/or he didn't want to give the old man that kind of news. He had a lot of reasons."

"What else?"

Wills glanced at the single sheet of paper on his desk. "That about sums it up."

I knew he had more. "Jim, did G.C. have any life insurance?"

Wills mulled over the question a long moment before the dark eyes glinted directly into mine. "Who've you been talking to?"

"It was a guess."

"I know you didn't get it from Roundtree. He was with me. Everyone is under orders not to discuss the case. The sheriff's the only one who might cross the line, but only for you."

I concentrated on holding myself steady. I didn't want to do any telltale twitching. "You said I was good. It's instinct. Did he or did he not have life insurance?"

Jim's face became a mask, veiling any emotion. "He did."

"A substantial amount?"

"Yes."

"Twelve million dollars worth of substantial?"

He stiffened, balling his hands on the desk into fists.

"Jim, that's how much he borrowed against the ranch. I figure he wanted to cover it. Was it twelve mill?"

"Twelve-point-three. The exact amount he owed."

"Who's the beneficiary?"

His eyes narrowed to a squint and he glared at me.

"It's only a natural progression." I prodded gently. "I assume it's his dad, but I don't want to speculate."

Jim shook his head. "Chloe Conklin."

"His live-in? Not his dad?"

"Right."

That gave me new food for thought. "Jim, Conklin's kids are G.C.'s, aren't they?"

"I don't know that it matters."

I watched his face carefully. He was getting defensive, approaching saturation. I didn't want to push him over that edge. I needed to get back to something less threatening. "Where exactly is this cottage?"

He relaxed his fists and spread his hands, palms down on the desk. "It's a two-story studio. The Gideons own a trailer park off Highway Thirty-one, the back way. They rent trailers to their ranch hands. The park's probably three miles from the main house. The cottage is midway between the house and the trailer park."

His guard lowered, I felt safe prying into the sensitive stuff again. "How did G.C. treat his family?"

Jim's eyes narrowed and he straightened. The question obviously struck a nerve. "Why?"

"He was threatening with me and I was a stranger. I figure he was probably hard to live with."

"He beat Chloe and the kids. Yelling worked on his mother. I guess his dad just gave in."

"How did he treat his employees?"

Jim stared at me several heartbeats before he answered. "He

had a temper. He hit a man with a shovel last week, broke the guy's nose. From all accounts, he hit and kicked his employees—even threw things at them—when he had his tantrums. Apparently he'd had a lot of them lately."

"Could someone at the ranch have killed him?"

"It looks more like a professional job. G.C. had welshed with gamblers and bookies. He'd borrowed a lot of money, not all of it from banks."

Now we were rolling, the easy give and take carrying us onto safe ground. I slid my chair closer to his desk. "What did Bubba Valentine do before he worked for the Gideons? After he bombed out of professional wrestling?"

Jim's mouth set in a hard line and his eyes again became slits. I'd inadvertently struck another nerve. He stood. "I want to know who you've been talking to."

I slumped back in my chair, surprised and puzzled by his sudden agitation. "I just wondered."

He walked to my side of his desk. "We've plowed this ground before. I want you to come clean. Trust me. Tell me who?"

"I do trust you." My nerves jangled as he stepped closer. "It was just a passing thought. Why are you so uptight?"

He eased into the client's chair beside me. "We're off the record now."

"Okay."

He hesitated a minute, studying my face, before he began. "Valentine was a suspect before."

"You mean earlier today?"

"No. Two years ago we had an unsolved murder in Dominion. His name was mentioned. A year later his name popped out of our computer, a possible suspect in an execution-style slaying in Kansas City. Bubba was charged, then released. He never stood trial, but people up there quit looking for the killer."

"Bubba Valentine is a hit man?" All I could think of was how

Jim had baited Bubba at Roper's the night after my visit to the ranch.

Recalling that little sojourn to the Gideons', I felt a jab of delayed terror. I had thought it strange that Mr. Gideon did not defend me that night, in light of G.C.'s behavior. Maybe he had been afraid of his son or his son's bodyguard.

I realized Jim had not answered. He sat looking at me quietly, perhaps recalling the same afternoon.

"Jim, did G.C. hire Bubba?"

"No." Wills' voice was soft. "Off the record, right?"

I nodded.

"His dad hired Bubba indirectly, through a friend."

"What friend?"

"Are you sure you're just cutting your way through this on instinct?"

"You know how nosy I am. I want to help you untangle this mess. Who hired Bubba Valentine as a favor to Tyrone Gideon?"

"Still off the record?"

"I've already said yes three times."

"Jesse Chase."

"What?"

Jim coughed a laugh. "We've done some digging. Bubba is on the Chase payroll. Not only is he now, he has been for the last five years."

I looked at him hard as if the answers to all my new questions might be found in his expression. "So, now is Bubba going to be a target? Is he in big trouble?"

Jim shook his head almost imperceptibly. "Not exactly."

Light began to dawn. "Oh. This is turning into one weird can of worms. What now?"

"You're into theory. Think. Draw me a picture."

I pursed my lips, giving the scenario some serious thought. "Bubba went from professional wrestling to being a professional in another line of work." Without waiting for Jim's verification, I plunged ahead. "He killed people for a living. Is that right?"

Wills nodded. "Along with other duties."

"He worked for Jesse Chase, a prominent citizen with legitimate business enterprises that sometimes attracted a less than legitimate clientele?" Jim continued nodding, encouraging me. "Chase's old friend Tyrone Gideon had this jerk kid who somehow fouled up the old guys' friendship."

Wills smiled. "Chase put up with G.C. for years because of his regard for Tyrone."

"Then Lisa Chase, her daddy's pride and joy, got pregnant." I waited for his nod. Confirmation. "With G.C.'s kid?"

Stoically, he nodded again.

"So, she had an abortion, right?"

Another nod.

"But it caused bad feelings between the dads." My mind raced, my brain in high gear. I laid the spiral notebook on the desk, stood and walked around to the back of my chair.

"Using his dad's influence and money, G.C. was spitting in Chase's face when he ran up that big tab aboard *Gambler*. Then he made a lot of noise and refused to pay."

Jim bowed his head but I could tell he was smiling. On a roll, I didn't want to get distracted. "There was no love lost between Jesse and G.C. to begin with and G.C. kept making things worse." Then my racing brain hit a dead end. I stopped talking and sat back down in my chair. I could not understand this part.

"What triggered the killing? If Jesse didn't ice G.C. for Lisa, what in the world could have provoked him so much that he'd have his best friend's kid murdered?"

Wills smirked like a proud parent. "Very good, Dewhurst. It's my guess—total conjecture, you understand—that G.C. assaulted the old man."

"Beat up on Jesse Chase? No way. Chase is an old time tough guy and G.C. was mostly mouth. I can't see that happening."

"No, I don't think he touched Jesse Chase. I'm thinking G.C. beat up Tyrone Gideon, his own dad."

"Oh." I exhaled the word as if someone had knocked the wind out of me. It seemed unconscionable that even a man like G.C. Gideon would beat up an old blind man, especially his own father. "You're saying Mr. Chase held back on pounding G.C. for years out of respect for his friend, until that *friend* became G.C.'s victim." I made no attempt to hide my admiration for Jim's theory. "Is that what you think?"

"Yes."

"Wow." Suddenly I had new regard for the man in front of me. "It's great. Can you prove it?"

Jim relinquished a modest smile. "We're not ready for court yet, but at least we have a theory. That's a step in the right direction. Some murders are like a big jigsaw puzzle. You have a jillion pieces. If you put them together in the right order, you produce a picture. When you build a puzzle, it helps if you have a picture to use as a guide, to help you put the pieces in the right spots. Having a theory to go by is like having a picture of what the puzzle is supposed to look like. See?"

"Yes. Do you have the jillion pieces?"

"We're collecting them."

"But you don't think Bubba was involved?"

"Oh, yeah, up to his neck. We think maybe he stood back and let someone whack G.C. without putting up a fight."

I scanned my notes, looking for loopholes. "Jim, do law enforcement people go after bad guys who kill other bad guys as hard as they go after bad guys who kill good guys?" Again, my question provoked a smile.

"Yes, we do. Absolutely."

"Does that seem right?"

"Yes. There are no mitigating circumstances for murder. No matter how mad you are or how you've been victimized, one person cannot kill another one. Write that down in your little notebook, news person. Don't do it."

I flashed what I hoped was a comical grin. "*Don't do it?* Agent Wills, you've certainly changed your tune."

He grimaced, pretending to have been squelched. "Some phrases fit some situations better than others. Now, I hope you have all the information you need because you've picked me clean. I didn't hold back even one little tidbit. If you want more, you'll have to find someone else to grill."

Beginning to feel more comfortable with him again, I leaned back in my chair and gazed at him unabashedly. "Good."

Smiling, he returned the look. "Thanks for the Christmas presents." He flipped back his blazer to reveal the wild holiday galluses that were one of my packages to him. "I'm saving the shirt and tie for New Year's, if I can get a date. Do you think you might go out with me New Year's Eve?"

"Sure." The question had me a little confused. "Except I thought we were kind of . . . well . . . over."

Ignoring my comment, he reached over and linked his fingers with mine. "Did you get anything special for Christmas?"

I nodded, looking at our hands but not making any effort to withdraw mine.

"Why didn't you charge it up and use it?"

"It was too extravagant for you to give me a cell phone, something that expensive, especially when we seemed to be so . . . out of sync."

"I want you to keep that phone with you at all times." He had become deadly serious. "You have a talent for painting yourself into corners. When you do, dial up the cavalry."

"How did you know I wasn't using it?"

"I tried to call when I couldn't get you at your house."

"I didn't get any messages."

"No? Well, you were gone a lot. The last time I called, you were out on a hot date."

My surprise seemed to please him.

"Your brothers, Yin and Yang, answered on two phones the other night. One said you had a date, the other said, 'Yeah, with an undertaker, can you dig it?' They both howled. From my end, it was not a very satisfactory conversation. How was Max?"

"Dull."

"You didn't let him corner you in the kitchen, did you?"

I shot him a warning look.

Jim smiled and arched his brows, brushing his thumb over the inside of my wrist. "My kitchen has a whole new aura. It'll never be the same."

"Neither will I, I'm afraid."

"That's the kind of talk I want to hear." He smiled warmly. As an afterthought, he added, "Did you remember the purple thing?"

"Theodore? Remember him? Of course. And he's lavender, not purple. His smirk reminds me of you."

"Where are you going to put him?"

"On my bed."

Wincing, Jim nodded. "Glad to know one of us made it."

We regarded each other quietly.

"You knew you had me Friday night, didn't you?" I whispered the admission.

"I'm glad you remember it that way. You are a brand new experience for me, Dewhurst. I want us to have some real time, not just a couple of hours of heat, but long leisurely days and nights together."

"That's the kind of talk that scares me." It wasn't fair for me to encourage him. "I don't have that kind of time, Wills. I have plans for my future and I'm determined to achieve those goals.

It may wind up breaking my heart, but those plans do not include you."

I withdrew my hand from his and clasped mine together to quell my nervousness. "My goals were set a long time ago, Jim. I told you. Everything I do, the choices I make, all are designed to further my career plan. You're asking me to rethink things that are already decided. That makes me . . . squeamish."

"You can't alter your big plan a little? Squeeze out a tiny bit of space and time for me?"

"No."

"A couple of weeks?"

"I'm already hooked, like on some drug. What do you think two weeks of using would do to an addict? Don't say I'd be able to walk away. You're turning out to be my best friend. I've been totally honest about this all along. As my friend, it's your duty to help me stick."

Jim shook his head. "What, you honestly expect me to help you run from me? Honey, I'm the best thing that ever happened to you."

I couldn't help smiling.

He again captured my hand and raised it to his mouth. "This is one fine mess you've gotten us into, Dewhurst." He nibbled the back of my hand before he turned it over and put his warm mouth into my palm. Chills pebbled up my arm. Watching him, I felt tender and very receptive.

"I cried a lot in Carson's Summit," I said, which I thought was rather an odd thing to say.

He spoke to my hand. "I grieved a little myself, here and in Dominion, too."

"With your huge family and all the activity?"

He raised his eyes to my face. "I was relieved when my week off got canceled. Here in Bishop I have vivid mental pictures of you. Also, there was G.C.'s murder to think about, tracking

137

evidence and lining out suspects."

Our faces were so close I could feel his breath and I wanted more. I wanted to kiss him soundly and forget homicides and cherry-lipped morticians and, generally, everything and everyone beyond that room. But how could I surrender so easily? Staring into the hypnotic pull of his gaze, I knew how. I had to try to cover all these fomenting emotions with talk, say something. Anything. "Personally," I said, "I think you should have suffered longer."

"You're the one who said we had only been apart 'a couple of days.' I'm the one who knew it was eighty-two hours . . ."

"And thirteen minutes," I finished. "I heard. Now, how much time are you asking for? I mean cutting it to a bare minimum?"

Wills smirked. "Negotiations have begun, huh? How strong is my position?"

I shrugged, pretending to be indifferent and hoped with all my heart he couldn't guess how important he was becoming. I tried to sound blasé. "Make me an offer and we'll run it by management. I'm not making any promises."

Wills nodded solemnly, but he bit down ever so slightly on my fingertips, which trembled between his lips.

CHAPTER THIRTEEN

From the newspaper office that afternoon, I activated my new cell phone. A short time later, I called the Floyd Valentine residence in a rural area between Bishop and Dominion. Bubba's mother answered on the fourth ring and called him to the phone. He sounded calm when I identified myself.

"Bubba, I'm sorry about what happened to G.C. I know you were friends, more than just employer and employee."

"Yeah." His voice sounded husky. "It's awful hard."

"Will you tell me about it?"

"About what?"

"About the last few days of his life, right up to the minute he died. What you did. If you had trouble any place. Who might have been mad enough to kill him. The way I hear it, G.C. was not an easy guy to like."

Bubba cleared his throat. "You just think that because of him bein' mad at you. You didn't know him. He was a really good guy, deep down."

I snorted my disdain. "Bubba, of all the people who've described G.C. Gideon lately, you are the only one who's said anything nice, do you know that?"

"We was friends. Now he's dead. What do you say about dead friends? That they was rats?"

"Was G.C. a rat?"

"No, I just told you. He was okay."

"Bubba, out of regard for his memory, I think we should talk.

139

I'll do an article, let our readers see the G.C. you saw. A story like that might make his parents feel better. It'll be something they can keep for his kids to read when they're grown, a word picture of their dad from someone who liked him."

"Yeah." Valentine obviously was thinking it over.

"Chloe Conklin's kids are G.C.'s, aren't they?"

"Sure. Whose did you think?"

"I guess they'll be staying there on the ranch then, if Mr. and Mrs. Gideon will let them."

"Or maybe the Gideons can stay if Chloe'll let *them.*"

"What do you mean?" It was hard to keep the eagerness out of my voice, but here was a new wrinkle.

"Nothin'. I didn't mean nothin'."

"You know we ought to do this story, don't you?"

"Yeah, I guess you're right."

"Do you want to come by the office?"

"Nah, there's too many people watching me. Some of 'em think I done it. Some of 'em hated G.C. and wished I had. Nah, you better come out here to my mom and dad's."

"I can do that. When?"

"Now's okay, I guess."

He gave me directions to the house. On my way, I grabbed a new notebook and my purse. I was almost out the newsroom door when I thought of something and hesitated. I ran back to my desk and picked up the telephone.

"Mrs. Teeman, is Agent Wills available?"

"Jancy, he's gone to the morgue to talk to Robert and pick up the autopsy on G.C. Gideon. Can I give him a message?"

"Yes. Tell him I have an interview with Bubba Valentine this afternoon at his parents' house. Be sure and tell him Bubba's mother is home. Tell him I called to let him know where I would be. He likes to know." I gave her my new cell phone number.

140

Mrs. Teeman laughed lightly. "Right. I'll give him the message."

The sky was gunmetal gray with dark clouds roiling and the temperature dropping rapidly from the forties to the thirties. I was nearly twelve miles from the Bishop city limits when my cell phone buzzed.

"What do you think you're doing?" Jim sounded tense.

"The news. I figured you were through interviewing Bubba, or debriefing him, as you say. I called to ask him some questions. He invited me out to talk about the last days of G.C.'s life. It'll make a good follow-up. I might even turn up a puzzle piece or two for you."

Jim was silent on the other end.

"Agent Wills," I said frostily, "I didn't call to ask your permission. I called to tell you where I would be. It was a courtesy."

"Jancy, I'd rather you didn't do this."

"I like what I do and I'm good at it. I know you want to protect me, but I'm not some porcelain doll. I have to have space."

"Jancy, I wish. . . ."

"Jim, you like me like I am. If I were like you say you want me to be, you probably wouldn't." It was convoluted, but I thought the theory sound.

There was another long silence.

"Okay." He sounded disappointed. I tried not to care.

There were two dirty pickup trucks, a grimy older sedan and a shiny new black town car in the gravel driveway behind the Valentines' modest frame farmhouse. I had seen Bubba driving one of the pickups but didn't recognize the other vehicles. The back door looked like the one they used.

Standing on the top step, I knocked on the screen door

several times before the inside door swung wide, opened by a woman I assumed was Bubba's mother.

The woman's face had red splotches and there were dark circles under her eyes. She stood mutely in the doorway, one hand kneading something in an apron pocket. She made no move to open the screen.

"He can't talk to you." The woman choked and cleared her throat.

I put on my most pleasant smile. "It's okay, Mrs. Valentine." I backed down a step and pulled the screen toward me to get a better look at the woman and to encourage an invitation inside. "Bubba asked me to come out to talk to him about G.C."

The woman's pale blue eyes widened, but she shook her head resolutely. "No. He can't talk to you. His lawyer's here. He said Bubba can't talk to anyone."

Peering around the woman, I could see the shapes of two men in chairs at a kitchen table two rooms back inside the house. One of the men, in a suit, was facing me, his face concealed behind the other one's head. I recognized the shape of that back and one shoulder as Bubba's soft bulk. I tried a different tack.

"This killing has been hard on your whole family, hasn't it, Mrs. Valentine? I guess all of you were pretty close to G.C., weren't you?"

The woman dabbed at her eyes and her nose with a shredded tissue she pulled from the apron pocket and nodded. "We all loved G.C. Him and Bubba has been friends since they was little, bitty boys. My husband used to work over to the Gideons'. Bubba would have did anything in this world for G.C." Her chin quivered and she began weeping. "I have to go now." She started to close the door.

"What could Bubba do for G.C.?" I craned my neck to see around the door closing in my face. "G.C. had money to spend, cars to drive, family, girlfriends, everything."

The woman pulled the door wider for a moment, coughing a little, and folded the shredded tissue over and over with both hands to mop her tears. "Bubba was G.C.'s friend. G.C. didn't have too many of them. Bubba would have did anything G.C. asked him to do. Anything."

I searched Mrs. Valentine's face. The woman obviously was trying to tell me something but didn't feel free to reduce it to straight talk.

I spoke very quietly, watching her face. "What did G.C. need Bubba to do for him?"

Mrs. Valentine's voice was almost inaudible. "All I can say is no one ever had a better friend in this world than to do what Bubba done for G.C." She was interrupted again by her own sob and her effort to catch a full breath. "There wasn't nothin' G.C. asked him to do that Bubba didn't do. Can't you understand?"

"I don't think so." My thoughts went off like popcorn popping as I speculated wildly. My voice dropped to a confidential whisper. "What did G.C. ask Bubba to do?"

The sobs overcame Mrs. Valentine. Leaning, peering into the house again, I could see the one visible shoulder of the man with his back to me, the one I thought was Bubba, quake. The man in the suit appeared to lean forward and speak quietly to his companion.

"I can't tell you." Mrs. Valentine coughed. "I can't say it out loud. It's too awful."

I waited for the woman to regain control, then remained silent several seconds longer, hoping if Mrs. Valentine had some time, she might fill the quiet with words she obviously wanted to say and I really wanted to hear, by that time for confirmation.

"All I can say is G.C. never had a better friend in this world than to do what Bubba done for him."

In one motion, Mrs. Valentine stepped back and pulled the door around, shutting it in my face.

I eased down the steps, let the screen swing closed, and walked slowly down the dirt path to my car. Could she have been trying to tell me something else? I couldn't imagine what it could have been. No, there was only one way to interpret her words, surprising as it seemed.

Inside the car, I made notes. I wanted to get our entire conversation down while it was fresh in my mind. As an afterthought, I also jotted down the license tag number off the town car. It probably belonged to Bubba's lawyer.

It was nearly sundown, five-thirty. As I drove toward Bishop, I used my new cell phone to call Jim in his office. "How about if I buy you a burger at Cheeries?" I asked.

"When?"

"I'm twenty minutes away."

"I'll meet you there."

He slid out of a booth when I got to the diner, took my coat and waited for me to sit, then he slid in beside me.

"How'd it go?"

The waitress came to take our order.

"Well?" he prodded when the waitress had gone.

"I didn't even get inside the house." I checked my notes to keep the report accurate. I described my reception and repeated my conversation with Mrs. Valentine as nearly word-for-word as I had written it, teary interruptions and all.

Jim stared at me. "G.C. asked Bubba to kill him? Is that what you think she was trying to say?"

"That's what I got out of it and I can't think of any other scenario that would fit the way she acted and looked and what she said."

"These guys were no brain trusts," his eyes roved to the

window behind me, "but this would be out there, even for them. G.C. insured himself to bail out the ranch, then got Bubba to murder him?" He gave me a deep, questioning look.

"I never heard of any life insurance that paid on suicide," I said, then proceeded to tell him about Bubba's remark on the phone about whether Chloe Conklin would allow the Gideons to remain on the ranch and my conclusion. "It looks like she'll be calling the shots."

Jim shook his head. "This is unbelievable." He gazed at me with puzzled, wide-eyed admiration. "You did good."

"Mrs. Valentine's veiled comments do give your puzzle picture a different look, don't they?"

"Yeah. And it really does make a difference in the direction our investigation takes. Instead of combing the country for a nondescript black automobile or hired killers, we can look closer to home. This time your meddling paid off."

"As it has in the past, if you'll remember."

"You're right, it did then, too. What can I say? Thank you."

"Your turn. Was there anything new in the autopsy?"

"How did you know . . . ?" He grimaced. "Sure. Mrs. Teeman told you that's where I'd gone earlier, right?"

"Well?"

"Yes, there was something. G.C. was shot seven times with two twenty-three millimeter shells from one M-16. Oddly, two of the hits left powder burns. The two—Robert's pretty sure it was the last two—were fired from very close range."

"What does that mean? That the killer was especially thorough?"

"When a hired gun squeezes a round, he can pretty well tell if it's fatal. The powder burns may indicate this particular killer didn't want this particular victim suffering if he had to wait a couple of minutes to die."

"Oh." I drew and exhaled a breath, staring at the milk

machine behind the counter. I remained that way for several ticks of the clock, lost in dark thoughts, mental images of Bubba shooting G.C., being careful to make sure his friend died as painlessly as possible.

The burgers arrived and both of us ate quietly. As we shared a piece of Cheeries cherry pie, Jim regarded me seriously.

"What?"

"I was just wondering when you think Riley Wedge will call about your wire service job."

"He did call. Called the office the Monday after Thanksgiving."

"It didn't just slip your mind, did it?"

I didn't answer.

"What'd he say?"

"Not much, just wanted to know how I was. He talked to DeWitt and Melchoir first. They gave him glowing reports. He asked if I was thinking in French yet. I told him I was. I got to that level once before, in school, my second semester of French as a freshman."

"So, is there a date?"

"No. He won't call until fall, for sure."

"Were you glad to hear from him?"

"Sure. He's a wheel. When he calls and talks to the bosses about me, my stock goes up around the office."

"When he calls in the fall, what happens? Do you go overseas right away?"

"No. Wedge said I'll train in a bureau office with an experienced correspondent for a couple of months to learn the drill."

"Where?"

"Wherever the experienced person is, I guess. It could even be around here, in the Dominion office or someplace close. Why? Do you want me out of your hair so you can go out with someone else?"

He smiled wryly and swirled his coffee cup. "The director asked if I'd be interested in some special training. He wanted to sign me up for a school next fall. I figure if you're gone, I'll be pretty low. The change of pace and scenery might be good therapy."

For some reason, I felt deflated.

Apparently seeing the change in my expression prompted a puzzled look. "Why do you care, Jance? You'll be gone anyway."

"I don't know. I guess I just didn't expect you to be making plans for after I leave."

His eyes narrowed as he tried to read my face. "You know how I feel. If you were going to be here, I wouldn't consider going anywhere. You're the one in hot pursuit of fame and fortune. I'm the one in hot pursuit of you. I'm content to sit right here with you from now on, in front of the fireplace, necking, or whatever.

"I talked to my dad about us, Jance. I laid it all out for him. He said I should encourage you to go. He said if you can be happy any other way, with any other people, in any other place, I shouldn't try to hold you. He used that old saw about the captive animal. If you set it free and it leaves, it wasn't yours.

"He said if we separate and we're both miserable, we'll work out a way to be together, regardless of our career goals. He suggested I plan ways to occupy myself until we find out if you can be happy without me.

"When the director asked if I'd be interested in this school next fall, I remembered Dad's advice and said yes. That's assuming you'll be gone. If you stay, I'll cancel."

I shifted, unsure about why I felt so disappointed that he would be filling any void I left in his life. "What kind of training?"

"There are several phases, using and identifying various

weapons, evidence, physical conditioning, negotiating, handling hostage situations, liaison between state and federal agencies. It runs three or four weeks. It also involves some Homeland Security."

"Do you think you might want to work for the FBI or Homeland Security later on sometime?"

"Maybe. If I did, having gone to this school would be a plus."

"You don't sound very enthusiastic."

His mouth puckered and he shrugged. "I like what I do. I like the quality of life here. I don't envy people who commute. Dominion's too big for me and it's not real big, for a city.

"I like jogging in the mornings, reading the newspaper on the patio, catching a leisurely shower, dressing and driving seven minutes to work. I like the people I work with and for.

"My folks have this fishing cabin up by Skelter, a couple of hours' drive. We lived there summers when I was growing up. Life there makes sense."

Watching him, I was envious of his contentment, of his high regard for what he termed "the quality of life." I thought of my parents and my brothers. I'd struggled to break free of my parents and my childhood. I wondered if the anticipated prospect of being a wire service correspondent was more of my imagined independence from their influence.

Jim smiled. "What are you stewing about?"

"Oh, nothing much. I'd like to see your cabin."

"Okay."

I felt as if I had just taken the bait on a hook. Then he continued. "Are we on for Saturday night, New Year's Eve?"

"Sure."

He grinned. "Good."

"Don't get excited. You're the only one who's asked me."

"Do you want to wait to commit to see if Max calls?"

A rolling chuckle escaped my throat. "No, I'll settle for

you." I made a face and we both laughed.

Walking to my car, Jim asked if I would like to stop by his house for a little while.

"No, I have to unload my car and get ready to get back to the grind first thing tomorrow morning."

"You're not afraid to come back into my parlor, are you, little fly?"

"No." I arched my eyebrows. "But I'll wait until I'm well rested and alert."

"Thanks for the information on Valentine." Jim kissed me lightly and closed my car door.

No arrests were made that week in the death of G.C. Gideon.

CHAPTER FOURTEEN

Jim and I began party hopping on New Year's Eve at nine o'clock at the home of Sandy Bennett, the *Clarion* society editor who invited the newspaper staff along with her husband's coworkers from a nearby office machines business. The crowd was sedate as we began getting acquainted.

I wore long, jade and royal harem pants with a matching low-cut, long-sleeved blouse, which floated above my waist and showed my belly button.

Jim had surrendered his ever-present galluses and necktie and showed up unusually casual in slacks, a dark blue shirt unbuttoned at the collar and a gray blazer. He said he was saving the new shirt and tie for another occasion.

Thanking the Bennetts, making excuses, we grabbed our coats and moved on to his office party at ten.

The SBI director visiting from the head office greeted Jim warmly. "Is this the lady we've heard so much about?"

Jim smiled, nodded, and nudged me along. I had the distinct impression he didn't want me interviewing people or gathering information there.

With the director and all three division chiefs present, conversations were stilted, the local agents and their guests inhibited.

Jim whispered. "They're here to keep the lid on any uncontrolled merriment. The bureau's got a reputation for hiring serious, law abiding, non-imbibing personnel. Like I told you, one drink, one dance, some helloes and we are out of here." He propelled me through attendees as if we were on a mission.

Jim whooped as we turned the corner onto Cherry Street at eleven-fifteen and found ourselves in the traffic congestion and commotion of party time at my house. The barn-like structure fairly rocked with raucous music and the thunder of many dancing feet pounding wooden floors.

We parked in the first available spot, half a block away, then hurried through the nighttime chill to the warmth and excited welcomes of the revelers.

"They've got a good lead on us," Jim shouted loudly enough to be heard over the din of music and voices as he guided me through hugs and handshakes to the bar set up in the kitchen. "Now *this* is a New Year's Eve party!" He poured himself a double bourbon to sip as he fixed me a whiskey sour.

Yielding our positions at the bar, Jim handed me our drinks and he picked up two kitchen chairs, carrying them high, each by one leg, to maneuver through the crowd and into the living room. He put the chairs down against the wall just as the music changed.

Rosie Clemente, holding hands with a freckled-faced, red-haired man I had not seen before, introduced him. The music started just as Rosie spoke and I missed his name. He held out his arms, indicating we should dance. I put our drinks on the window sill, smiled at Jim and followed freckle-face into the mob already gyrating to the music.

When that music changed, Ben Deuces, unable to locate Liz, grabbed me for the next selection. I scanned the room looking for Jim and found him, deftly guiding Angela through the crowd, obviously bound for the kitchen/bar. Angela had her arm linked through his and gazed up into his face chatting happily. Jim nodded from time to time.

After a fast dance with another fellow I didn't know, I worked my way into the kitchen looking for Jim. It was getting close to midnight.

I found him standing with his back to the sink, a glass in one hand, his other hand on the counter top. Angela was pressed against him, her face tilted, inviting, enticing. Jim looked up in time to see me turn back toward the living room.

Jim pushed through people who filled the doorway behind me and caught my eye as I started up the front stairs. He didn't try to pursue me, but doubled back toward the kitchen. He probably didn't want to lose his place with Angie. I flounced into my bedroom and slammed the door. The sound was loud enough to be satisfactory upstairs, but I doubted anyone below heard my statement. In a minute, however, someone rapped lightly on that same door.

"Who is it?" I called, trying to keep the venom out of my voice.

There was a second knock and reliable feminine intuition told me exactly who it was.

Striding to the door, I flung it wide. "What do you want?"

All innocence, Jim peeked inside. "I've never seen your bedroom." He was obviously trying to stifle a smile.

"Go away."

"Not very cordial to your guests, are you?"

"Probably not nearly as sweet as Angela."

"What's this? Why, Jancy Dewhurst, I believe you're jealous. I didn't think you were the type."

I shot him a pained look, then considered his statement. What I said next surprised me as much as it seemed to please him. "Honestly, I didn't either."

He stepped closer and I backed up, letting him into the room.

He inhaled deeply. "It smells like you." He looked around the room. "Do you always make your bed or is this a special occasion?"

I looked at the bed, returned Theodore's smirk and thought a minute. "I always make it." When I turned back, Jim was easing toward me, watching my face closely. "Oh, no you don't." I planted my hands against his stomach and pushed.

Without yielding, Jim put his drink on the bedside table, sat on the edge of the bed, caught my wrist and pulled me down beside him. "This sure is a little bed."

"It's big enough." I looked around. "The room would have been too crowded with a double."

He smiled, nuzzling my neck, and repeated, "Big enough."

"How much booze have you had?"

"Not enough."

We heard the horns and shouts as "Auld Lang Syne" played loudly below. Jim pushed Theodore off the bed and pulled me across his lap. "Happy New Year."

As his mouth devoured mine, he put a hand across my knees and rolled me over, still in his arms, fitting me lengthwise on the bed, then he shifted to stretch beside me.

When I tried halfheartedly to push him away, he caught my hand, pushed it behind my back and caught it in his other hand which had snaked beneath me. I moaned as he slid his warm hand up my bare midriff to fondle my breast over my bra.

Lifting the filmy fabric of my blouse out of his way, he popped the front closure on my bra one-handed, pushed that garment out of the way and put his mouth to my bare breast. I lay still until his marauding fingers slipped beneath the elastic waist of my harem pants.

Still holding me tightly, in spite of my halfhearted squirming, Jim eased the harem pants down, kissing my midriff and nibbling his way around my belly button and down.

Unable to free my hands, I struggled, but it was not a genuine effort.

Holding me firmly, Jim leaned away to study my face. His

voice rasped. "You *do* want to, don't you?"

Tears stung my eyes and I blinked, trying to clear them. Droplets seeped out, one slithering across the bridge of my nose to join the other in a race. Oh, Lord, he was so beautiful—his body big and hard and perfect, his smile teasing, his hands warm and ever so gentle. I squeezed my eyes closed and nodded.

He didn't speak for a moment, then he wheezed, "Swell." Suddenly angry, he released me, stood, picked up his drink, opened the bedroom door and walked out, closing the door firmly behind him. Now what had I done? I heard him make a stop in the upstairs bathroom, then heard him take the back stairs to the kitchen. I supposed he was going to fix another drink.

The crowd at the house had thinned out by twelve-forty. I found Jim on the sofa alone in the dark listening to music and brooding. Uncertain about his mood, I eased onto the couch beside him. He put his arm across my legs and pulled me closer to him. Wordlessly, I wrapped both arms around his biceps and pressed my face into his shoulder. We sat like that for a long time, neither of us speaking, just listening to the music.

Jim drank a lot of bourbon. Sometime before dawn, I insisted on driving him home. He agreed only after I promised to pick him up later for breakfast.

We spent all of New Year's Day together but an awkward pall hung over and between us. We helped my housemates wash glasses and mop at the house early, took a brisk walk in the winter afternoon sunlight, ordered pizza and watched football games on TV at my house that evening. He suggested we go to his condo. I politely declined.

He looked and sounded contrite. "Have I scared you off for good?"

"You're not that lucky."

Still, we stayed at the house on Cherry Street, in spite of his repeated invitation and the many interruptions by my often flirtatious housemates.

CHAPTER FIFTEEN

Relentless snow made traffic sluggish at seven-forty Friday morning, January sixth, when a burly man approached my car at a stoplight, his face partially hidden by a ski mask, appropriate in the icy weather. He tapped on the passenger side window, which I lowered halfway. When I did so, he reached through and unlocked the door.

Too close to the car ahead of me to drive forward, I sat dumbfounded as Bubba Valentine swiped off the hat covering his face and head and clambered into the passenger seat of my Beretta.

Although I was startled, I attempted a smile. "Does this mean I finally get that interview?"

There were circles under his eyes. His eyelids were puffy and the whites of his eyes bloodshot. "Drive to the highway." It was a command, not a request.

My mind raced. "Let's go to my office, Bubba."

"I don't want people to see us." Anxiously, he peered out at cars and pedestrians nearby. "Drive out to the highway."

The light changed and the traffic in front of us moved forward. I sat, my foot planted firmly on the brake as I tried to decide what to do. Bubba glowered. "If they find me, we're both dead. Now drive."

"If who finds you?"

"People who want to keep me quiet."

"What are they afraid you'll say?" The driver behind us honked.

"Drive," Valentine repeated and his voice was urgent.

I stepped on the accelerator and lurched into the flow of traffic. "Where will you be safe?" I turned right and drove out Johnston Boulevard toward the highway.

Bubba ducked his head, staring at the floorboard, his shoulders slumped. "I hadn't thought that far yet."

"Bubba, let me help. I know people who make things happen. Let me ask them to help you."

When he looked at me, his face was mottled behind several days' growth of whiskers. Obviously either he hadn't been sleeping or he had been crying or a combination of the two.

"I have a friend," I said softly, allowing the tenderness I genuinely felt to express itself in my words and to shape my facial expression. "He'll tell us what to do. I can call him." I reached back to grapple in my purse, which was in the back floorboard, as I continued driving.

I produced the cell phone and held it up for Bubba to see.

"You won't have to stop any place? I mean you'll call him from here in the car?"

"Yes."

He seemed to be considering the idea, so I prodded him a little.

"It can't hurt."

Bubba scowled but finally his head bobbed up and down in agreement.

I turned onto Country Club Drive and checked the rearview mirror. No one followed. I drove slowly along the quiet, snow-covered residential street that wound up the hill to the country club. I pulled through the open gate and turned the car into swimming pool parking. I left the motor running as I punched Jim's pre-programmed number.

"Mrs. Teeman, is Agent Wills available?" I waited only a moment. "Agent Wills, this is Jancy Dewhurst," I said, wanting to alert him to the fact this was a business call. "Can you meet *us* at the country club swimming pool right now?"

"What? Why?"

"I can't discuss it on the phone. Could you come?"

"Is someone with you?"

"Yes. We'll wait."

As I punched the button to close the line, Bubba wiped the palms of his hands up and down his Wranglers. "I don't know if this is the right thing to do or not."

I wanted to call the office to explain my tardiness but thought better of it as Bubba grew more agitated. I tried to make small talk, the weather, basketball standings, the weather again.

"You probably need to think what to tell this man," I suggested finally. "Can you simply tell him the truth?"

Valentine looked as if I had slapped him.

"Bubba?" I prodded when he didn't answer, "what about your lawyer? Should you be talking to anyone without him?"

"He's the one didn't want me talking to you at the house the other day. They hired him. He tells 'em what I do, everything I say, everything I'm thinkin'."

"Does he know you're afraid of *them*?"

I saw Jim's car grinding up the long country club drive. Bubba twisted in the passenger seat to stare at the nondescript brown vehicle with the antennas as it approached. As the car got close, Bubba slid his massive frame into the floorboard, locked his hands around his legs and touched his forehead to his knees, his chin against his chest, almost in a fetal position, which was extremely weird for a guy his size.

Jim studied my car closely and waved as he cruised by and parked twenty or thirty feet beyond.

I rolled down a window as the dapper, overcoat-clad agent

approached on foot through the snow. "What's up?" His jaunty smile faded and his step slowed when he got close enough to see Bubba cowering on the floorboard.

"He's terrified." I indicated Bubba, who risked a glance. "He thinks someone's trying to kill him."

Jim's face hardened. "Valentine, I can't talk to you without your lawyer present." His voice was as brittle as his glare.

"Jim, the bad guys provided the lawyer. Bubba thinks his lawyer is relaying information to them. He's running from the lawyer too."

Jim fixed a hard stare on me. "Jancy, anything Mr. Valentine tells me, I will use against him at his trial. He's going down for killing G.C. Gideon. You need to remember I told him that and that I advised him to have his lawyer present during this conversation. Will you remember those two things?"

I nodded, as much to appease his obvious anger as assurance he was allowing Bubba his constitutional rights.

Wills leaned both forearms on the open window and focused his full attention on Bubba. "Having made that clear, I can say we might be able to help him work a deal with the prosecutor, if Mr. Valentine is willing to implicate whoever hired him. Probably the same person he's afraid is after him. Is that right, Valentine?"

Bubba didn't respond, only struggled back into the passenger seat, studying the armrest as if he were unsure of where to direct his eyes.

Jim appeared to be making a heroic effort to be patient. "How did you happen to turn up here with Ms. Dewhurst?"

The armrest held Bubba's attention. "I gotta trust someone. None of my people is smart enough or connected enough to help."

"And you think Ms. Dewhurst is?"

Valentine shot Wills a harsh look from under his thick

eyebrows. "She got you here, didn't she?"

Wills nodded grudgingly, then gave me a sheepish shrug. "Yeah, I guess she did. The question is, what'd she get me here for? Why didn't you run?"

"I loaded my truck this morning to do exactly that." Bubba turned coldly accusing eyes on Wills. "I got in and almost turned the key. Then I remembered something. I got back out and raised up the hood. There was this package back of the carburetor. I know a guy who works like that. I used him a couple of times. I introduced him to people. I guess he's working for them now."

It took a minute for me to notice my mouth had dropped open. "What about honor among thieves?" I asked, looking from Valentine to Wills.

"There is none," Wills said. Valentine nodded mute agreement. Jim's voice sounded noticeably kinder. "Bubba, who hired you to kill G.C. Gideon?"

"You mean who paid me?"

"Yes."

"You just want to know the ones who paid me cash money?"

"Bubba," Wills was getting testy again, "what part of the question don't you understand? Who gave you money, or anything else, to kill G.C. Gideon?"

"They was more than one." Bubba paused, sucked his lips into his mouth and bit down, then released them. "A bunch of people was in this, one way or the other."

"Okay." Jim shifted to balance his weight on both feet. "Who was the first person who asked you to kill G.C.? Can you tell me that?"

Moving my head to follow the conversation between Jim leaning in the window on my side of the car and Bubba in the passenger seat, I felt like I was watching a tennis match. "Jim, why don't you get in the car?"

The morning air was crisp and, like me, he probably realized this was not going to be a short conversation. He nodded. I climbed out, pushed the seat forward and dived into the back, leaving the driver's seat for him. Jim smiled his appreciation, then slipped in behind the wheel. Settled, he looked again to Valentine. "Okay, go."

"I work regular for Jesse Chase." Bubba focused on the glove box. "I do collection work and odd jobs. Sometimes he needs me to talk to someone who owes him. I don't mind doing that work, as long as I've got my health. It pays good. I enjoy it. It's like what you do. I'm out for justice, you might say."

Jim nodded and looked as if he were conceding the point. "Okay. Go on."

"Mr. Chase has had a hard on for G.C. for years but I told him a long time ago, G.C. and me was friends and I would not do nothing to him, even for Mr. Chase, who I love like I love my own daddy.

"I also admire Mr. Tyrone Gideon. Mr. Gideon sat me down when I got hired to be G.C.'s bodyguard and he told me what G.C. meant to him, his only son and all. He said if I ever heard of anyone wantin' to hurt G.C., I should tell him and he would make it worth my while. Also he would need my advice on how to handle it." He shot a quick look at Jim. "Not too many people ask me for my expert advice on things."

Jim said a muted, "Un-huh," and glanced at me. I was lined up squarely with his eyes in the rearview mirror. Ignoring the look, I sat unmoving, keeping even my facial expression set.

Bubba glanced at me, then back at Jim. "I was real proud he talked to me like that and I gave him my solemn word I would protect G.C."

Valentine hesitated, but when neither Jim nor I spoke, he continued. "Last fall things got complicated.

"G.C. beat on the ranch hands pretty regular, but they all

161

knew it before they come to work there so you figured if they took a job at the Two Bell, they knew he'd be knocking heads some. It was part of the job. Of course, the Gideons always paid good and ever' week. They didn't never miss a payday, like some.

"I don't know how to tell you this next part except just to say it like it was." Bubba looked hard into Jim's face. Solemnly Jim met the look and nodded for Bubba to continue.

"G.C. was a mean drunk. It wasn't bad if you was bigger than him since he never got so drunk as to pick on any body big, but he could be mean with people littler than him.

"One night I brought him home and Chloe had locked the door. Hell, he only stayed there part time and he had a key, but her locking him out made him crazy. He pounded on the door. Made so much racket, he roused his folks at their house. She finally opened up.

"Man, Chloe looked beautiful that night, standing there in that door in that long nighty. With the light behind her, you could see her whole figure real clear. I tried not to look but it was more than I could do.

"She usually kept her hair tied up, but it was hanging down that night, all the way to her waist. She's full blood. Probably the prettiest Indian I ever seen. But she was scared when she opened that door. She shouldn'ta let it show. Her showing her fear got him boiling and he started slapping her around.

"I didn't butt in. It was like between a man and a wife. It wasn't my place to interfere. But he knocked her across this chair and I could tell it hurt her bad. She couldn't even get up off the floor.

"He was screaming and throwing furniture around, almost hit her in the head with the same chair. She just laid her head down there on the floor and started crying, real soft and quiet. I figured I'd let him go long enough, maybe too long, even.

"I saw his kids peepin' around the door from the hall. I knew that big one, the boy, was going to be grown up enough soon to try to defend his mama. Seeing their faces, I knew I had to do something.

"I just picked G.C. up. He kicked and screamed like a woman. I got him outside, but he would not quiet down. I tried talking to him, but he just kept cussing and screaming and fighting me.

"Finally, I tossed him in the swimming pool, in the deep end. It was right there handy. He had on them boots, which filled up with water. He had a time getting out of there. He struggled and slapped the water around and wound up kind of walking on the bottom all the way up to the shallow end. By the time he come out of there, he was pretty well spent.

"I went back inside to see about Chloe.

"She was still laying there on the floor crying.

"I don't think she knew who I was because she put her arms around my neck and cozied up to me. I picked her up real gentle and took her back to her bed but she kept hanging onto me and crying real soft.

"I never will forget how wonderful she smelled. That brown skin of hers was smooth as a baby's butt. She kept hugging me and begging me not to leave her. I stroked that silky black hair of hers and I promised her I wouldn't leave. I didn't see how I could.

"G.C. come in to get some clothes but I didn't move from off that bed. He said he was going to the cottage. I just stayed there in that room watching Chloe. She pretended she'd gone to sleep, but I knew better.

"After that, I told G.C. I wasn't going to let him hit Chloe or the kids no more. I told him I was starting to see hate on his boy's face. I asked him how he would have felt if his daddy had beat up on his mama. He said it wasn't the same. Chloe wasn't his wife.

"That started me thinking.

"A man could do worse than a woman like Chloe and those two kids. That's why, when Chloe come to me, I was more or less softened up for it."

My legs were getting stiff. I stirred in the back seat and Bubba jerked as if he had forgotten where he was. Wills kept his eyes on Valentine and said, "What did Chloe ask you to do?"

"Nothing, exactly, but from that night on, Chloe liked me better."

"How did you know?" I asked, then I worried that I shouldn't have interrupted his flow, but it didn't seem to throw him off track.

"She did all that stuff women do when they like a man. When I come over to her place, she'd go comb her hair and put on perfume. She'd fix me a sandwich or a glass of tea or sew a button on my shirt. She fussed over me. And she'd stand and sit close to me so we was touching one another all the time.

"One evening when I stopped by, her arms was bruised and she had a shiner. She wouldn't tell me G.C. done it, but I knew. I was ready to kill him that night on my own, no matter what I'd promised his old man. She begged me not to. I was going to anyway. She started crying. Man, I couldn't take that. I put my arms around her, just to comfort her, you understand, but pretty soon I was kissing on her. Next thing, we was on her bed and . . . well, you can pretty well figure out the rest of it.

"After that, I thought of Chloe as my woman, not G.C.'s. He didn't love her. I did. And she loved me." His eyes darted to Wills' face. "She told me she did.

"She knew G.C. was gambling and drinking away the Two Bell. She talked him into getting insurance in case anything happened to him and she had to raise them kids by herself. He was drunk, thought he was signing insurance for the kids. It was for better'n twelve million dollars, which would be paid to her if anything was to happen to him. She told me it was to save the ranch in case G.C. should wind up dead. She wanted the place for her kids. Said it was theirs by right.

"Chloe thought a lot of Mr. and Mrs. Gideon. It hurt her they took G.C.'s side when he beat on her. She believed his folks would let him throw her and the kids out, if he wanted to. She worried about that. But not Chloe or me thought G.C. would ever raise a hand to the old man.

"That night you two was at Roper's and we come in? Well, that was right after G.C. pounded his poor old blind daddy. I pulled him off quick as I knew it was happening. The old man wasn't hurt much, except the damage showed pretty good. I hauled G.C. out of there.

"He'd been drinkin'. He blamed you, Jancy. Said it was your fault for buttin' in and tellin' his daddy about him borrowin' against the place. Said his daddy would never have known, wouldn't have started in on him. G.C. swore it was you who caused him to beat up on his daddy."

My heart dropped to my knees. Surely I had not brought more suffering into that kindly old man's life. "Jim," I began, but he flapped a hand signaling me to be quiet. Seeing Jim's gesture, Bubba looked pleased and continued.

"The old man didn't call the sheriff or nothin', but Mrs. G. called Jesse Chase. She'd had enough. She wanted her boy taught a lesson. The way I heard, she didn't have to say it twice. Like I said, Mr. Chase had had a burr under his saddle about G.C. for a long old time.

"I was living in the cottage then. Sometimes G.C. stayed there, sometimes he went down to a woman he knew at the trailers. That night, after Roper's, I dropped him at the trailers. When I got to Chloe's she was waiting up for me. She didn't come right out and say nothing, just told me how beat up Mr. Gideon was. We was sitting on the sofa, her loving on me, and I asked her straight out what she wanted me to do."

Bubba paused and took a deep breath. Neither Jim nor I spoke. Bubba exhaled. "Chloe said she wanted to be with me but that G.C. would kick her off the place, and me along with her, if he found out. She said Mr. and Mrs. Gideon loved me like another son. I asked her if she wanted me to get rid of G.C. She didn't say nothin,' just nodded her head like she was real sorry to do it."

Jim spoke quietly. "So did you kill G.C. for Chloe?"

"No, not then." Bubba stared at his hands clenched in his lap. "I told her I'd study on it.

"Every way I could think of, it seemed like G.C. passing would be best. Still, we'd been friends a long time and I kind of understood him better than any of them. Anyway, I was thinking about it.

"During the time I was doing my thinking, Mr. Chase called. Wanted me out to the *Choctaw Gambler* to talk to him.

"Mr. Chase told me he'd pay me ten thousand dollars to kill G.C. and asked me was I interested? I said I was." Bubba looked at Jim. "I mean, ten thousand dollars is a lot of money to a guy like me, what with thinking about marryin' Chloe and all. And I'd been thinking hard about killing G.C. anyway. But I told Mr. Chase I had to think on it."

"When did you decide?" Wills seemed to be encouraging Bubba to move the story along.

"I rocked along there several days studying it. G.C. was drinking hard every night, getting some serious phone calls that was scarin' him plenty. He was afraid to go off the place, afraid someone would catch him out and beat him up or worse. He kept getting scareder and scareder. They was threatenin' him with some pretty raw stuff.

"I kept telling him I wouldn't let nothin' happen. He wasn't a scrapper. He didn't like fighting. He liked whipping up on people, but he didn't never get himself involved in no fair fights and sure not no one-sided ones goin' against him.

"Anyway, one night he was drinking real heavy there at the cottage, just him and me, and he asked me was I still his friend. I said sure. He said he needed someone he could trust to do something important for him. We already had this one little project sort of still hanging." Bubba glanced at me, but I didn't know what I might have to do with any project Bubba and G.C. had going. Bubba frowned and nodded and looked back at Jim. "I said I would do whatever I could to help him.

"He asked would I kill him."

Chapter Sixteen

It was a wild theory we'd tossed around, but I couldn't believe it actually had been what happened. I looked at Jim in the rearview mirror, but he didn't take his eyes off of Bubba. His expression remained set, revealing nothing of the shock and horror I knew had to be written all over my own face. He didn't even exhibit mild surprise. Was Jim that immune to the idea of one man making such an outrageous request of another?

I knew, of course, that Jim had seen death close up. He had worked more than eighty murder cases his first year with the bureau. Had his experience hardened him, made him jaded and indifferent? Or did he consciously maintain that look for Bubba's sake? Certainly, by then Bubba was talking to Jim, not to me. The fact of the matter was, both men seemed to be intent on ignoring me.

Bubba slouched in the seat. "G.C. said some goons was after him, wanted to squeeze him, set an example for other guys thinking about stiffing them. They was going to kill him, but they wanted him to hurt real bad first. In them phone calls, they was telling him all about it.

"I said I'd try not to let that happen. He said he knew it was going to happen all right. He told me he had some cash put away and that he'd give it to me, if I'd kill him fast and painless."

Bubba seemed to want Jim to understand, maybe even approve his actions. Looking at Jim's face in the mirror, I was afraid maybe he did. There was a long silence.

Bubba's eyes scanned Wills' bleak face before he turned them toward the patches of green grass barely visible where the snow had blown into drifts on the eighteenth hole adjacent to the swimming pool. I followed his gaze and thought how peculiar golf greens look in the dead of winter, mostly hidden but maintaining their color, like the cedars and pines nearby. I wanted to say something, to stop the silence, but I couldn't come up with any words equal to the moment so I just kept quiet.

"I don't know if I ever would've done it for Chloe or for Mr. Chase or even for the ten thousand dollars," Bubba mumbled, staring at the eighteenth green, "but when G.C. himself asked me. . . ."

He turned pleading eyes to Jim. "I got to thinking if that Dr. Kevorkian could help people who were dying or just in pain, I mean, I couldn't see no difference. I'm no doctor to know about diseases, but I do know something about killing. You do a man a favor if you take him out quick. I've seen guys crying and begging and wishing they was dead quite a while before they got that way.

"Of course, Kevorkian 'fessed up and took his chances in court, beat the system plenty of times before he got put away. I wasn't plannin' on doin' it exactly that way.

"I just told G.C. okay I'd do it.

"Well, after I agreed, he got real quiet. I thought he was thinking what business he needed to take care of first. The next thing I knew, he was cryin' and huggin' on me. Man, I couldn't hardly take it. I hugged him back and I started blubberin' too. Hell, we'd been friends since we was little kids and I just thought I'd probably miss him, even if it meant I could marry Chloe and have his kids and live on his ranch and everything.

"He said I was the best friend he had in this world to do

something this good for him. It felt funny, him talking like that about what he'd asked me to do."

Jim cleared his throat. "How much cash did he offer to pay you?"

"I didn't ask. He said we both had some business to take care of first. He reminded me about a job I'd promised him I'd do." Again, he glanced at me and I wondered why. "After we got those loose ends tied up, then we could kind of set a time, but that didn't exactly work out.

"The day after Christmas, in the evening, this big black sedan come rolling up the road and G.C., he pitched a fit. He thought it 'as them, coming for him.

"He come running down the stairs in his socks, pulling on his pants, one arm in his shirt. He had the gun slung under that arm.

"The car cruised right on by, but he thought it was because they didn't know exactly where he was and they'd be back. He jammed the gun in my hands, then he buckled up his belt and pulled the shirt closed and he told me to be sure to put his shoes on him and to make everything look right before I called the law. And he reminded me about the promise I'd made to finish up a favor I was supposed to do for him.

"He told me to describe the black car and say it had four people in it, because it probably did and one of the hands or someone might back up my story.

"Then he handed me this wad of cash that'd choke a horse. I stuck it in my pocket.

"He got up on the steps, like he was coming down, and closed his eyes real tight and told me to shoot.

"I did just what he said, but hell, he hadn't put no ammo in the gun. When I told him, he sat down there on them steps and started bawlin'.

"I run upstairs and got the shells and loaded that sucker on my way back down.

"He made me stand at the front door so the angle'd be right. He said the most important thing was that I just be sure I killed him.

"He had to hold onto the banister to keep himself standing there. He'd messed his pants. I felt real embarrassed for him.

"I went to the door and aimed and fired off five rounds, following his body down when he fell. His nerves was still flinching. I was sure he was dead, but I stepped up close and fired off two more, just to be sure he wasn't in no pain."

Bubba stopped talking and a pall of silence descended. The three of us just sat there as if we had been frozen in time, not speaking or even looking at each other.

"Seein' him crumpled that way made me kinda' sick." Bubba choked on the words as they tumbled out of his mouth. "I had to sit down there on the step to think. Sitting wasn't too comfortable because of that wad of money in my pants pocket."

Jim's expression didn't change. "Where's the gun now?"

Valentine had tears in his eyes and he was quiet for a long moment. When he regained his composure, he looked at Jim and sniffed.

"It's disposed of. So, what do I do now?"

Crossing his arms over his chest, Wills shook his bowed head. There was another long silence. Valentine squirmed in his seat, looking out the side window.

"Did you ask Chloe to marry you?" Jim's voice broke the ominous silence.

Bubba nodded mutely.

"Did she turn you down?"

Valentine swung his head quickly to frown at Wills. "How'd you know that?"

There was another long pause before Jim spoke. "The first

thing I need to do, Bubba, is arrest you for the murder of G.C. Gideon."

Valentine started to object but Wills held up his hand to halt the words.

"That gets you off the street and into protective custody. That's what it'll be, too. I'll jail you here in Bishop County. Sheriff Roundtree will see to it that you live to see trial.

"We'll need a full formal statement, everything you've told us and anything else that comes to mind. Will you do that?"

Valentine nodded haplessly.

"And you'll need a lawyer, a good one, one working for you this time. Did Jesse Chase pay you?"

Valentine's brow furrowed. "Do you mean for G.C.?"

"Who else?" Jim's voice dripped sarcasm.

"I done jobs for Mr. Chase before . . . well, back before. . . ." Bubba hesitated.

"Recently?"

"I ain't talking about other stuff. That's one of the reasons I ain't givin' up the gun."

Jim looked at me and rolled his eyes. "This is one can of worms." He sighed, then turned his attention back to Valentine. "For now, let's just talk about jobs you've done this past year."

"For Mr. Chase, you mean?"

"Yes." Wills was again obviously struggling to maintain his composure.

Bubba cringed. "Well, remember the guy who looked like Chase who got killed aboard *Gambler*?" Wills nodded. "It turned out the shooter was a pro out of Miami. G.C. hired him. G.C. thought if Mr. Chase was gone, no one would be around to collect what he owed. He didn't know *Gambler* was a regular business with stockholders and everything."

"So?"

"I took care of that for Mr. Chase."

"You mean you iced the assassin?"

"I mean you don't need to be looking for him. That's all I'm saying. You can see, me and Mr. Chase has what you might call a silent partnership. I keep quiet. So does he. I don't think he's worried I'm going to start discussing our business."

"So you don't think Mr. Chase hired someone to kill you?"

Bubba winced. "I don't think he would."

"Did Chase pay you for killing G.C.?"

Valentine nodded uncertainly. Wills turned his hand palms up and wiggled his fingers, motioning Bubba to give him more.

"He dropped it."

"What do you mean?"

"We have this bank box. It's got both our names on it. We share. He puts cash in, kind of like installments. I take cash out, but I'm not suppose to ever take out the whole price of any job at one time."

I cleared my throat, drawing the attention of both men. "Does Chase ever take money out of the box?"

Valentine regarded me as if I were crazy. "No, woman."

"How much money was in the wad G.C. handed you?" Wills asked.

"I don't know."

"You didn't count it?"

"No. I just put it in the box with the rest."

Too curious to let it pass, I chimed in again. "Why didn't you count it?"

"It was however much it was." Valentine looked annoyed. "If it was too much, I couldn't very well give any back, could I? If it wasn't enough, I sure wasn't going to be gettin' any more."

I raised my eyebrows, marveling that despite what I thought of as the man's astonishing stupidity, he occasionally made remarkably good sense.

Jim prodded again. "Who do you think is after you?"

"I don't know." Pensively, Valentine turned his gaze to the covered swimming pool. Jim and I glanced outside as well. Our vantage point on Country Club Hill gave us a full panoramic view of the area. There were no vehicles parked on the streets and only an occasional car parked in the visible driveways. No one had followed us up there.

Bubba sulked. "I want to call Chloe."

"You'll have to be careful what you tell her," Wills said.

"She'd never rat on me."

"You're in the business, Bubba. With her kids for leverage, even a nice guy like me could break her. Some of the guys in your line of work ain't this nice."

Bubba smiled warily and nodded his agreement.

They talked a while longer until Jim asked Bubba if he was ready to go to the courthouse.

Valentine hesitated. "I might not tell them the story I told you. I might leave out about Mr. Chase and Chloe asking me, just tell about G.C. wanting me to kill him."

Wills nodded. "Make it easy on yourself."

They dropped me at the *Clarion,* then pulled into the courthouse parking across the street, where Jim escorted Bubba to Sheriff Roundtree's office.

They were still behind closed doors when I made my courthouse rounds about two.

Jim called me in the newsroom at three-thirty. "Buy your lunch?"

"I'll take you out to pick up your car first," I suggested. "Meet me in the parking lot?"

"Okay."

"What did you think?" I asked when we met at my car in the courthouse lot.

"You knew what I was thinking."

"Another fine mess you've gotten us into," we said, almost in unison, and smiled at each other.

I took the driver's seat and he handed me the keys, but I didn't start the engine. "Do you have any idea who's after him?"

Wills snorted. "Looks to me like half the civilized world. There's Chloe, who propositioned him to kill G.C., and Mr. Gideon, doting father of the victim, and probably half-a-dozen past and present employers who all know he's no genius. The D.A. is filing the information this afternoon. He'll be arraigned before the judge on Monday."

"I'm off Monday."

"So, they gave you your birthday off, did they?"

"I didn't know you remembered."

"Yeah. I've already got you a present."

"Is it something shiny and sentimental?"

"Yes, it is."

I felt a momentary surge of panic and my voice quailed. "Not jewelry."

He shook his head, regarding me solemnly. "No, not jewelry."

"Tell me." I felt a flood of relief.

"It's more what you'd call a gift that symbolizes our relation-ship."

Puzzled, I smiled as I leaned over spontaneously and pressed my lips to his cheek.

CHAPTER SEVENTEEN

Following Jim's recommendation, Bubba Valentine hired Jackson Denson to plead him not guilty at the arraignment on Monday. In the courtroom Denson, a stocky, no-necked man with a mane of white hair that flowed to his collar, was smooth and caustic.

Since I was off, I had left Melchoir a story to run on Monday, confident Bubba would plead not guilty and the judge would set a preliminary hearing for February tenth, which was the date the judge mentioned when I phoned him.

Snow the week before had thawed into muddy slush. I was really happy to wake up on my birthday, Monday, January ninth, to a new snowfall camouflaging the muck and muffling sounds.

I stretched luxuriously and took a deep breath. I could smell coffee. Usually I didn't care much for coffee, but it smelled good that morning. And bacon, too? I sat bolt upright.

Schools might be dismissed because of the snow, but my housemates all had jobs that required attendance, no matter how bad the weather.

The smell of food lured me out of bed. In my nightshirt, I bobbed gingerly down the back stairs, which were cold on my bare feet.

Fully clothed, Rosie Clemente sat at the breakfast table sipping coffee. Jim stood, spatula poised, over a hot griddle.

"What's all this?" I smiled, squinting through eyes still puffy with sleep.

Rosie and Jim both looked up.

"Now, I see who you are." Jim grinned, looking me up and down. "Good thing I'm securely hooked."

"Am I real scary?" I giggled, expecting a negative response.

Jim and Rosie looked at each other, raised their eyebrows and nodded in unison.

"Never mind apologizing. I am not offended. Not on my birthday. Jim, where's my present?"

Rosie scowled. "Isn't a home-cooked breakfast enough?"

"It isn't shiny or symbolic is it?" I looked at Jim.

"Get some clothes on," he said. "Lots of clothes. We're going outside."

I darted up the stairs on tiptoe and returned in record time clad in faded corduroys, a shirt and sweater and socks and carrying an extra sweater, a second pair of socks and my boots.

Rosie ate with us. Because of the weather, the bank allowed its employees to come in an hour late. After "one more cup of coffee," Rosie left.

When we were alone, Jim went to the living room and returned with a box nearly five feet long and thick. Taking it from his hands, I staggered under its weight and bulk. Setting one end on the floor, I shook it. The contents thudded, but I could not imagine what it might be. I left it standing and walked around it, grinning, excited, and in no hurry to discover its contents. I liked being tantalized by the unknown.

"Is this a joke box full of bricks that has a little bitty present inside someplace or have you given me a steamer trunk for my birthday, you sentimental rascal, you?"

Jim laughed, but didn't hurry me.

I giggled. "This is just like you—methodical, thorough, allowing plenty of time for things. I love you most for your patience . . . your stodgy, dependable patience."

The smile on his face wavered slightly, then resumed as more

177

of a practiced expression. I knew why. I avoided those three little words in conversations with him, although he often said he loved me. Obviously he had heard the words and wondered at my careless use. He looked uncertain, as if he thought it was a slip of the tongue, a mistake, not to be taken literally.

"I don't care what it is." I laughed lightly. "I do love you, you know?" And I did.

His mouth spread to a broad smile and for a fleeting moment he looked vulnerable. Then, with new determination, he said, "Open it."

I returned the smile, hesitating just long enough to assure him my words were true, then I tore into the wrappings.

"A sled?"

I yelped and yanked the marvelous vehicle out of the box. "A brand new Flexible Flyer of my very own. Yes. Yes!"

I leaped up and, hugging the sled, I spun pirouettes around the center of the room. Carefully, wordlessly, I placed my new vehicle on the floor and, without taking my eyes off of it, I sat down and began pulling on my second pair of socks. "Maybe you can borrow one from a kid on the hill." I hurried to the closet for my heavy coat.

"Or maybe you can share," he said, feigning annoyance.

"Me? Why me?"

"Because you're the one with the new two-man sled."

I had already put on my mittens before I began fumbling with the buttons on my coat.

Jim grabbed my shoulders and turned me around to give him access to the buttons. "Maybe you should consider buttoning your coat before you put on your gloves sometime."

I pretended to be offended. "Surely you're not criticizing me? Not on my birthday? Today is my birthday, you know."

Jim laughed, finishing the last button. "Yeah, I heard."

I jammed a knit cap over my head, folded it up above my

eyebrows, then threw my arms around his neck. "This is the best present I ever had."

He grimaced. "How old are you, anyway?"

I flashed him a warning look. "Twenty-four today. Why do you ask?"

He chuckled at my pretended pique and raised his eyebrows. "And maturing nicely, I'd say."

Extremely pleased with his satisfactory answer, I scooped up the sled and trotted out the door to wait beside the trunk of his car.

Though the sun was shining, Jim carried several pieces of firewood in his trunk, which he unloaded when we parked near the top of Harold's Hill. The hill, actually part of Juniper Street, covered six blocks. When it snowed, city street crews traditionally blocked off the side streets intersecting Juniper to provide a protected course for sledders.

Schools might be inaccessible on such a day, but the same students who could not get to classes showed up undaunted at the crest of Harold's Hill.

When Jim and I arrived, dozens of people were already sledding down the hill or trudging back up it, dutifully packing fresh snow with their feet.

Someone had already cleared a spot for the bonfire, part of snowy Bishop tradition, and the site awaited the arrival of the first fuel, which Jim provided.

He suggested I soap the sled's runners and handed me a bar of soap from his coat pocket. He had thought of everything. I felt flushed, a mixed result of bright sunlight, north wind and excitement. Still, I wanted to be gracious. "You can go first."

Jim laughed at my thinly veiled attempt. "Get on. I'll give you a push." When I sat and put my feet on the steering guide, he said, "You'll go faster lying down."

"Maybe next time." I was tired of preparation and delays. "Push, please." His hands clamped firmly on my shoulders, he trotted behind me to the drop-off, then gave me a mighty shove.

"Wah hoo," I whooped.

I ducked to dodge snowballs hurled by returning sledders, and guided the projectile in a serpentine pattern, from one side of the street to the other, hoping to make the ride last. I sped past Seminole, the last blocked-off side street, still sailing.

I breezed through the parking lot and closed on the curb bordering the city park where Juniper Street dead ended. Realizing this was the end of the run, I braced for impact, but suddenly there was a snow-packed ramp. Leaning and steering, I hurdled the curb but lost momentum as my chariot crept into the park.

The climb back up the hill took much longer than my grand, sweeping descent. When I finally got back to the first drop-off, I looked up at Jim, breathless but grinning. "I've never gotten all the way to the park before." I wheezed. "Man, what a ride."

Jim shook his head and laughed. "Are you cold?" He took the sled's rope from my hand. "The fire's going pretty good."

"Are you nuts? I'm burning up. I've got on too many clothes. I want to go one more time, then it can be your turn. Really. But I want to sit up, so I can see it all again, just like last time."

Although the snow was packed even more firmly under the tread of more feet, I barely got beyond Seminole Street on the second run. That was disappointing.

"I should have used more soap."

Jim was such a good sport. He didn't claim his turn. Instead, he said, "Try it again."

"One more time, then you can go." I wanted to sound definite, but I wasn't really paying attention to what I said. I had to concentrate on digging the scrap of soap out of my pocket.

I rode two more times, short of the park on both runs, and the bonfire blazed brightly as other sledders provided more fuel, before I again offered Jim a turn.

He took the sled. Holding it in front of his body, he took three quick strides, tossed the sled on the ground and lunged.

I had enjoyed brisk runs, but Jim flew down that hill, running at the returning youngsters who hurled snowballs at sledders, to send them scurrying all directions. I could hear his diabolical laugh and noisy insults as he enjoyed the routs.

"Are you here with your children?" a voice asked. I spun and was surprised to see Jackson Denson holding his gloved hands over the bonfire.

"Why aren't you in court with Bubba?" I asked.

He gave me a wry smile. "I was, but it was brief, just the arraignment. My kids were out of school. Their mother's working so I brought them up here. How about yourself? What kid dragged you up here?"

I arched my eyebrows, fair warning. "It's my sled. It wasn't coming without me."

"Oh." He looked puzzled. "Where is it, then? Your sled."

I glanced down the hill. Jim was just stepping off the curb, returning from the park. "Darn, I missed it."

Denson looked even more confused.

Jim didn't trudge back up the hill, as most of the other sledders did, but returned double time.

"Wills," Denson called as Jim got closer. "What the hell are you doing? They said you'd taken a sick day. You don't look sick to me."

"My first day out for illness in four years. You?"

"I had to bring my kids. I'd rather be almost anywhere else."

"Oh." Both men removed a glove as Wills stepped forward to shake hands. "I'm surprised anyone noticed I wasn't there."

Denson's smile waned. "Probably wouldn't have, but Chloe

Conklin, G.C.'s live-in, wanted to meet you, so I stepped into your office to arrange it. That's how I knew you were out."

"Really?"

"Where are your kids?" Denson looked around for likely prospects as he slid his hand back into his glove.

Jim gave me a phony quizzical look, as if I'd forgotten something, before he looked back at Denson. "We didn't bring any. Aren't you allowed to come sledding without kids?"

The serious look on Denson's face prompted laughter from both Jim and me. "I never heard of it," he said, sounding very sober. Our humor obviously was lost on him.

Jim turned the sled to line it up on the run. "It sounds like Mr. Denson is not interested in a ride, Jancy, which makes it your turn."

"I want to lie down this time. You flew."

"I weigh more. It gave me more thrust."

"But I want to zip down like that."

"Okay." His one word sounded like a threat. He motioned me on board. I lay on my stomach, my hands on the guide. "Bend your knees and I'll push your feet to get you started."

He ran, pushing until the snow, spitting in my face, blinded me. Then he lunged.

"Ooof!" I wheezed as Jim's full weight landed in the big middle of me.

Laughing, he put his hands over mine, guiding the missile as we flew, the passing trees and returning sledders a blur. I looked up just as he aimed us at the snow-packed ramp over the curb into the park. I don't think either of us saw the slush pit until it was too late.

I braced myself, expecting a plunge into the watery mire, but at the very last second, Jim rolled, yanking me off the sled with him.

His body cushioned my impact as we toppled, rolling a full

turn. I wound up on my back, on top of him, staring at the sky, spewing snow.

The riderless sled cleared the slushy trap and stopped just beyond it.

"Thank you. Thank you. Thank you." I shouted into the air, not bothering to get off of Jim first. "That was an all-time best. Incredible."

I rolled sideways onto my knees in the snow. Jim got up, shaking snow off his clothes and laughing before he offered me a hand up. "Did anyone ever tell you, you're very easy to entertain."

I pretended a frown. "Do you feel dumb? Did you realize we were the only adults up here sledding with no kids for an excuse."

"No. Are you worried about your reputation or mine?"

I retrieved the sled without answering. "The awful thing is, I want to go again."

"As many times as you want." He flicked a clump of snow from the side of my cap. "Do you want to ride up?"

"And let you pull me?"

"Sure."

"And have you get all worn out and ready to quit before I'm through? Not a chance."

After another run together, dark clouds billowed in the north. Jim pointed out the snow flurries in the sky above our heads, flakes falling but not yet reaching the ground.

Denson gathered his three children and left.

After another two-person flight down the hill, the overcast blotted out the sunshine and more sledders left. The fire, which had dwindled to red coals, sizzled as the snow began falling in earnest.

I didn't want to be a bad sport, but I felt like crying, disappointed that we had to quit, or maybe it was just fatigue. "I guess we'd better go."

Jim caught my arm and turned me back toward the run. "We can stoke the fire and keep sledding for as long as you want to, even if it pours."

"What time is it, anyway?" The glowering darkness made it seem late.

"Why do you want to know?"

"I'm hungry."

"Then it must be time to eat."

"Jim, you didn't even look at your watch."

"A real day off is a day without time, don't you know that?"

I wasn't exactly sure what he meant. Jim wound the sled's rope around his hand and I fell into step as he started toward the car.

"We only have one clock at the cabin and Mom keeps it behind a door so you don't have to know what time it is unless you go to the trouble to look. Being free from time is real freedom."

That seemed rather primitive. "How does she know when to feed people?"

"When we're hungry, we eat. When we're sleepy, we sleep. We fish and swim and play as the spirit moves."

"That would be nice." I trudged more and more slowly, imagining.

"You're going to like it there, Jance."

"I hope I get to see it before. . . ."

"Before what?"

I recovered quickly and smiled. "Before you forget you invited me."

"We'll go in the spring and summer, as many times as you want." He patted my shoulder. "You won't be leaving before fall. That's still the plan, isn't it?"

I stared at the ground. "Probably October." The odd thing

was, I glanced up just in time to see him turn his head away. What was he grinning about?

CHAPTER EIGHTEEN

Because the charge was first-degree murder, Judge Cecil Smith did not set bond for Bubba, who remained confined to the Bishop County jail under Dudley Roundtree's protection.

The preliminary hearing was set for nine a.m., February tenth. Assistant D.A. Reese Mabry provided a short witness list for the hearing, only enough to show that: One, a murder had been committed and, two, it was reasonable to assume Valentine had committed it.

Bubba's family visited him regularly. The incarceration was not a psychological shock, since he had been locked up before.

Chloe Conklin's appearance at the jail the Sunday after Bubba's arrest prompted the jailer on duty to call Sheriff Roundtree at home for permission to allow her inside. After giving the query only a moment's consideration, the sheriff authorized the meeting.

Denson feared that Chloe's visit might weaken his client's resolve to fight the charges and said he was surprised to find that, although Bubba would not confide the gist of their conversation, seeing Chloe seemed to boost his client's morale.

Denson and Bubba studied the prosecutor's list of witnesses together and reviewed the probable testimony of each. They would listen, then demur to the evidence when the prosecution rested, declaring it inadequate—no matter what it was. They would not mount a defense at that time. Denson did not want to tip the prosecution to his strategy.

Denson made a motion that Bubba be allowed to wear civilian clothing rather than prison garb at his court appearances, argued and won.

At the hearing, Mabry called a steady stream of law enforcement personnel to establish the fact of G.C. Gideon's death and Valentine's presence at the scene.

Cross-examining an evidence officer, Denson was able to confirm that Bubba had been a boyhood friend of, confidant to and was employed as bodyguard for the decedent.

There was testimony that the accused refused to submit voluntarily to a lie detector test. Denson asked the witness if lie detector results were admissible in court, to which the answer was, of course, that they were not.

"But they can prove . . ." the officer attempted. Denson cut him off, asking the judge to instruct the witness to answer only the questions asked and not to elaborate.

The judge looked bored. "The court is aware of the standing of lie detector tests."

At the end, Judge Smith ordered Valentine bound over to stand trial.

The only unusual aspect of the hearing was Chloe Conklin's behavior. She gazed almost steadily at Jim through the whole thing. Occasionally, he glanced at her. When he did, she flashed a stunning smile as if they shared a secret.

As we left the courtroom, the woman squeezed close against Jim. I didn't know what to think. If Jim noticed, he didn't mention it, but I really doubt he noticed. He could be so obtuse.

CHAPTER NINETEEN

Jim bought a kite for us on Valentine's Day and the sun came out, an unlikely occurrence in February. Watching him run in jeans and a T-shirt, positioning the kite to catch the updrafts, I marveled at his coordination and admired the bunching muscles in his arms, his shoulders, his back and hips and thighs. God sure knew what He was doing when He made Wills. Really good workmanship there.

Glancing away from the soaring kite, Jim did a double take and stared into my face. "What?"

I pretended to be captivated by the kite and tried to remember that members of royal families and prime ministers and presidents of foreign nations might call me by name someday, if I could stick to my career plan. Faced with Jim Wills and his pumped biceps, my dream was losing its luster.

Jackson Denson scheduled both Jim and me for depositions as he prepared for Bubba's trial. He asked peculiar questions, raising our curiosity about what was looking like an odd defense strategy.

Jim complained when Denson asked me out to dinner—alone—an invitation I genuinely mistook for more trial preparation. I thought he was trying to curry sympathy from the hometown press.

"My wife and I have been separated for two years, Jancy, even though we still occupy the same house." Denson spoke just as I popped a raw oyster into my mouth and I almost spewed it right back out.

"We don't share a bed," he continued.

Now there was more information than I needed. I chewed quickly and swallowed hard.

"But I am there for my children. That's the kind of man I am, the kind who honors his obligations regardless of the personal sacrifice."

What was that, a public service announcement?

"The arrangement is terribly hard on me." He reached across the table and took my hand. "I'm a passionate man, Jancy."

The oyster might not be conquered yet. I just sat there and stared at him without comment. Denson must have taken my silence as encouragement because he lowered his voice. "Honey, I feel a strong attraction between us. I have a small, private place, an efficiency really, near the courthouse in Dominion. A convenience. I'd like to show it to you." He smiled seductively. "I have a spare key I'll let you have so you can use the apartment anytime you like."

I still sat dumbfounded. I might have a hard time withstanding Jim Wills' charm, but Jackson Denson was totally resistible. When I didn't say anything, Denson began caressing my hand with both of his. I thought I might barf. Instead I gave him a wan look, slipped my hand free and excused myself.

In the ladies room, I scrubbed the fondled hand with soap and dried it thoroughly, then repeated the procedure.

I didn't bother to sit down when I went back by the table. "Jackson, thank you for a lovely evening. I need to be going now." I had met him at the restaurant. Denson stood, started to say something, but I held up a hand, my open palm signaling a half-wave. "See you. Thanks again."

My first instinct was to call Jim from my cell to report Denson's peculiar behavior and conversation, but I waited until I got home.

"Did he get romantic?" Jim asked before I could even begin my report.

"How did you know?"

"That was obviously what he had in mind."

"Why didn't you tell me it wasn't a business dinner about Bubba?"

"Everyone within rock-throwing distance knew what he was after, Jancy. He's not subtle."

"Thanks a lot. Next time give a girl a hint, will you?"

"Maybe it'd be better if you wised up."

In light of Valentine's confession to Jim and me that he had killed G.C., Jackson was compelled to come up with an unusual defense, and he did, taking his lead from Bubba.

His colorful approach was particularly welcomed after two days of jury selection and drab technical testimony from prosecution witnesses regarding the location and position of the victim's body and the numbers and kinds of slugs recovered. The prosecution had the jury nearly catatonic with details of the chain of custody of each and every tiniest bit of evidence.

Assistant D.A. Reese Mabry had Sheriff Dudley Roundtree read Bubba's second confession, the one taken at the jail, all about how he had murdered G.C. Gideon at the victim's request.

Chloe Conklin testified G.C. was sole provider for their two small children and his elderly parents, something of a reality reach. She said her lines well and was careful not to exchange glances with Bubba, but she seemed unable to keep her eyes off of Jim. I was beginning to get annoyed about what she might be thinking.

Under Denson's probing cross-examination, Chloe reluctantly told of G.C.'s tirades and the physical abuse. G.C.'s mother and father, sitting on hard wooden pews in the courtroom, stared fixedly as Chloe drew a graphic, ugly picture of their son.

Cross-examining ranch employees who were prosecution witnesses, Denson established G.C. as a man who abused his employees, as well as his common-law wife.

Also in cross-examination, Denson steered the prosecution's precise, unsmiling bankers into tales of G.C.'s squandering of the Gideon fortune.

Neither Jim nor I were called as witnesses, which was good as someone would have asked for "the rule" and banned both of us from the courtroom if we had been listed. Reese considered our testimony redundant in light of Bubba's admissions.

When the state rested its case, Jackson Denson stood and with a flourish of feigned humility said, "Your honor, the defense rests." He had not called a single witness.

Jim said Jackson Denson was too shrewd to put Bubba on the witness stand. "If he got up there," Jim said, "Bubba would have to answer questions about his past, his police record, and his prior activities as a contract killer."

In closing argument, I grudgingly thought Denson was masterful, hammering one point taken from the defendant's confession replayed over and over again by the prosecution.

"G.C. Gideon wanted to die." Denson's voice dripped with regret. "He wanted to die as he had lived, comfortably. G.C. appealed to Bubba Valentine, his boyhood friend, to provide him a relatively painless escape from the financial and family dilemmas elaborately detailed for you by the many prosecution witnesses.

"Bubba was a good friend." Denson drew a tissue from his pocket, walked to the defense table and handed it to Bubba, who swabbed it over his eyes and blew his nose. The jurors looked spellbound, as if they were moved by what I considered cornball theatrics. Then Denson continued. "Certain that he was going to die, G.C.'s only request was that he die at the hands of his boyhood friend, quickly, humanely and with dignity."

I caught a glimpse of Jim standing just beyond the doorway into the judge's office. He stared at the floor.

Denson's voice quavered. "And Bubba," he hesitated, "provided his friend the same service Dr. Jack Kevorkian has made available so often . . . to . . . to virtual strangers."

Wondering if Denson practiced that warble in his voice, I looked at the jury. They appeared totally enthralled by his performance. Three nodded understanding or agreement.

"And," Denson's voice became stronger, "if jury after jury refused to convict a man like Dr. Jack Kevorkian for his compassion, how can you possibly condemn this man for helping his closest boyhood chum?"

In his closing shot, Mabry actually gave credence to the defense by saying Kevorkian had merely implemented the desires of his patients, provided means and opportunities for ending their lives. "To my knowledge, Dr. Kevorkian never actually pulled the trigger," Reese said. "The only testimony we have of Bubba Valentine's victim's alleged request is from the defendant himself, in his confession."

All the time he was speaking, I knew Reese was chalking up points for the defense and his own defeat. The assistant had insisted Roundtree read Bubba's confession in court, which served to give the words added credibility. Also, that made it unnecessary for Bubba to give testimony himself. Oh, yeah, Jackson Denson was slick.

During a recess, Mabry asked Jim what he thought of asking the judge to let him call Jesse Chase as a rebuttal witness.

Jim shook his head. "Chase's attorney will have him claim his Fifth Amendment rights. But you probably should produce any other tricks you've got left in your bag. Jackson did a good job."

Investigators had found no evidence that anyone paid Bubba for the killing. Mabry had no ace left to play.

The jury of eight men and four women deliberated four days, the last twelve hours after they told the judge they were hopelessly deadlocked and he sent them back to deliberate some more. Judge Smith finally relented and declared them a hung jury.

Their vote was evenly split, six for acquittal, six for conviction.

Not to be thwarted, Mabry, the D.A.'s top gun, geared up for a second trial and another run at Valentine.

Out of jail on bond, Bubba went into seclusion, working out his keep aboard the *Choctaw Gambler*.

On March second, Beth Wills Colette had a baby boy. With daughter Amanda's enthusiastic approval, they christened him James Paul after Beth's two older brothers.

Jim and I spent most of our leisure time together. Occasionally we necked in the car or in the living room of the big house on Cherry Street, always subject to my housemates' interruptions. I didn't have enough confidence in my own self-discipline to be alone with him anywhere else.

A warm early spring whetted our competitive juices and we engaged in frequent, hard-fought tennis matches. It seemed a safe way to enjoy each other's company, although I seldom won a set. When I did, I accused Jim of holding back.

Wrapping me in his arms, he insisted he was giving me his best effort. But when we were goaded into playing doubles, he came up with tougher serves and more vicious returns.

Just before Easter, Jim stood up with Kellan as he and Kit married in a small church ceremony. Six months pregnant, Kit was a glowing bride. As far as I was concerned, Jim stole the show, the blue-black of his hair emphasized by the black tuxedo, his thick, capable hands dark beneath white, white shirt cuffs. I chastised myself royally for admiring him so much. It was harder and harder to maintain my aloofness when our conversations turned to sex, which they did more and more often.

Annoyed by his constant touching and coaxing, I finally made a hard decision, summoned all my courage and braced him. "You think we should be sleeping together, don't you?"

He eyed me suspiciously. "It'd be okay with me."

That wasn't the answer I wanted. I thought he understood. "I can't, Jim. What if I got hooked and couldn't walk away? I'm a commitment kind of person. I don't want to sacrifice my future, my freedom. Can't you understand that?"

He nodded solemnly.

I bit my lips, hating the words I had rehearsed, but felt duty-bound to deliver. "I think you should find someone else."

His expression turned grim. His response nearly broke my heart. "You're probably right."

My only consolation was that I was being true to myself and to my own promising future.

After that exchange, however, our routine didn't change one iota.

May brought Bubba's second trial. The attorney general brought in a special prosecutor, Anissa Featherston, a statuesque beauty with a sultry voice, who fawned over Jim and insisted he participate in every leg of preparation.

I tried hard not to be jealous. After all, I myself had suggested he find someone else. The lurking jealousy was bad enough before Jim noticed.

"You don't seem to like Ms. Featherston," he said casually one day. When I turned away, he leaned to keep my face in sight. When I whirled and put some distance between us, he chuckled. "I believe you're jealous."

I shrugged, which was answer enough.

"You don't need to be. Not yet, anyway."

Jim told the assistant D.A. he was annoyed by Ms. Featherston's persistent sexual overtures. Finally, after several late-night sessions, he declared he would be available to work on the case only during regular, daytime office hours.

I tried to ignore my relief.

"What is your problem?" I asked myself. "If you don't want him, let someone else have him." From then on, I refused to think about it.

In the second trial, Denson had to initiate the sheriff's reading of Bubba's confession during cross-examination. Again, he went with the Kevorkian defense and the new jury, this time eight women and four men, also deadlocked.

The attorney general directed the district attorney to schedule yet a third trial. Bubba remained free on bond.

All spring I looked forward to our visit to the Wills' fishing cabin. My enthusiasm waned when Paul casually recalled past occasional late-night, in-house visits from snakes, scorpions, ticks and mosquitoes.

"Paul hasn't been swimming in the lake since he saw 'Jaws,'" Jim countered, eying his brother in that ornery way. "He won't spend nights at the cabin any more, even when the whole family's there, including the babies."

As it worked out, Jim and I both could get away from work by two o'clock, Thursday, June eighth. By being back in the office on Wednesday, June fourteenth, I would use only three days of my vacation.

On the way through Skelter, a settlement with a grocery store/bankette and small post office, the last chance at fast food and civilization before the cabin, we stopped to buy minnows. I couldn't tell if I was nervous or excited.

No one else was at the cabin when we arrived.

I stepped out of the car feeling isolated and glanced at Jim nervously. "Where is everyone?"

"In town doing laundry or something." He grinned and I blushed. "You're safe, sweetheart. I won't rip your clothes off . . . unless you ask me to." Hesitating, he flashed a suggestive smile.

"No, thanks," I said and turned our attention to the cabin.

A screened porch wrapped three sides of the structure, which was shaded by lush, graceful oaks, giving the place a feeling of cool, sprawling spaciousness, not at all the cramped, bug-infested place I had expected.

We entered what Jim called the back porch, which faced the road and where there stood an ancient refrigerator and four enamel-topped tables, lined up along the wall, all of which appeared to be of nineteen-fifties vintage.

The cabin's furnishings and appliances were a happy blend of history and new technology. On the tables were two ice chests and two water tanks, also a coffee maker and a microwave. Underneath one table, a battery charger hummed, recharging one marine battery while a second appeared to await its turn. Under another table, a mute electric ice cream freezer held definite promise.

Jim was silent. I looked at him to find him gauging my reactions.

To our left a bunk bed marked the beginning of the sleeping porch, which occupied the long east side, with its line of beds.

Instead of guiding me to the sleeping porch, Jim took us straight ahead through a small kitchen. Ground beef simmered in tomato sauce in a skillet on the stove.

Jim paused to breathe in the aroma. "Sloppy Joes. Ready when you're hungry. Do you want one now?"

I shook my head, no.

A large bathroom was actually a glorified breezeway with

doors at opposite ends.

The only other interior room was occupied by a dining table and ten chairs. Twelve-foot, beamed ceilings invited hot air upward. The walls were knotty pine. A fireplace occupied most of the outside west wall.

Shelves on both sides of the fireplace contained dusty books, leftover fireworks apparently from years past, and a variety of tackle boxes and fishing equipment. Dozens of fishing poles dangled from cork hangers on wall boards above the shelves that partially concealed a row of very dirty windows.

Opposite the fireplace, yawning French doors opened to the sleeping porch on the east. Behind one of the French doors was a well-stocked gun cabinet; behind the other, a small table on which the cabin's lone clock provided the time of day. Notably, there was no telephone, nor was there a television. Boxes containing board games—*Scrabble, Monopoly, Trivial Pursuit*—teetered precariously on a small desk. An open door and windows allowed the south breeze access to the interior across a broad, screened sitting porch that spanned the southern exposure of the front of the cabin, which overlooked the lake some fifty yards beyond a sweep of grass.

Absorbed by the rustic atmosphere, I was distracted by the breeze coming off the water, whispering an invitation. It enveloped me as we stepped onto the sitting porch, which was laden with a variety of comfortable-looking, dated furnishings. There were a dozen chairs and an aged glider. Some of the seating was canvas/duck padded, some wicker. All of it rocked or glided or bounced.

A chrome and glass dining table and six chairs anchored the west end of the sitting porch. A game table between two rocking chairs was covered by pieces of a jigsaw puzzle in progress. Small occasional tables hosted containers of candy, peanuts and fat red grapes. Also, there were several small footstools about. A screen door in the screen wall opened onto a broad deck on which a hammock swayed lazily with the breeze.

Walking east on the sitting porch, I looked down the sleeping porch at the beds. Four doubles, two of which had single bunks above, and two twin beds, separated only by night tables.

I couldn't help smiling. "This looks like the attic where the seven dwarfs lived."

"It's pretty clubby. The first bed, on this side of the French doors, is the folks'. I'm next, then Veronica or Beth and spouses, then you, then a kid, then Peter and Andrew in the bunk on the end.

"There was quite a bit of discussion about your placement. I volunteered to share my double. It caused some conversation. Anyway, Mom thinks you'll be safe down there. We'll see." He raised his eyebrows and grinned.

"This is great." I turned to gaze at the lake. A volleyball net rocked easily in the breeze on a flat grassy area between the cabin and the lake. "Can we walk down to the water?"

"Yes. We need to take the minnows anyway."

I stepped out onto the deck as Jim went back to the car for the plastic bag of water and minnows. He grabbed two pieces of stale toast from the top of the stove as he returned through the kitchen.

We had started down the grass-covered knoll to the fishing dock when I heard a thump. I turned, saw an enormous black reptile and slapped both hands over my mouth to muffle the scream.

The huge snake lay on the ground beside the birdbath near the cabin steps.

Jim wrapped an arm around my shoulders. "That's Blue."

I buried my face in Jim's shoulder.

"Blue's a fixture," Jim said, patting me comfortably. "Been here for years. He eats mice and bugs and other snakes." I risked a peek. "Dad won't let us kill him. Mom hates mice. Since Blue's been around, we haven't had one rodent. He's so old and slow no one knows how he catches anything.

"He won't hurt you. When it's hot, you'll see him dangling out of the birdbath or out of that cedar beside the hammock. Ignore him. Come on."

Jim nudged me toward the water. I glanced back several times to make sure Blue wasn't following, but he was winding his way up the birdbath pedestal.

The dock was a twelve- by thirty-foot, over-the-water, wooden structure bordered by a low railing and furnished with plastic-coated chairs and benches. An aged wooden plank secured to the dock served as a diving board. About fifty feet out from the fishing dock, a twelve- by twelve-foot wooden float rocked against its anchor with the subtle movement of the water.

Jim pulled a mossy minnow bucket out of the water with a rope tied to one of the dock railings, opened the cover and dumped in the new bait, closed the lid and dropped the bucket back into the lake. Wadding the plastic bag, he stuffed it into one of the hollow steel posts anchoring the dock.

"Here," he said, offering me a pinch of the toast, "toss this in the water."

The morsel attracted an assortment of vivid sun perch. I turned to Jim for more toast. He handed me both pieces. Soon small red-eared turtles swam up only to be comically outmaneuvered by the much quicker perch. I laughed at their antics.

The sun was warm, the breeze cool, and I eased onto one of the benches as I continued tossing tiny nibbles of toast. When it was gone, I took a deep breath and closed my eyes, tilting my face toward the sun. "Can we go swimming?" I didn't open my eyes.

"Now?" Jim asked.

"Ummm."

"Go get your suit on." I stood slowly and dusted the last of the toast crumbs into the water. The country silence was broken only by the clattering of locusts. It didn't seem like a place or a time for hurrying.

"I see why your mother doesn't want clocks around." I smiled and took Jim's hand as we strolled up the hill. I had forgotten Blue, didn't even notice him. On the deck, I remembered and looked back to see the snake, literally, hanging out . . . of the birdbath.

Jim set my bag on one of three straight-backed chairs in the oversized bathroom. "Be sure to latch both bathroom doors," he said. "The cabin's old and the wind's tricky. The doors can be snug when you shut them, then pop open unexpectedly and catch people in all kinds of awkward activities."

The switch that turned on the light also started an overhead fan. Terry cloth curtains with rods at both top and bottom billowed at the open window as the fan moved the air. Tapping the latch as a reminder, Jim stepped out.

Dutifully, I locked doors at opposite ends of the bathroom and quickly changed to one of the three bathing suits I'd brought—a modest one-piece. I slipped a white cotton cover-up over it and was surprised when I emerged to find Jim already in his trunks and a sleeveless T-shirt. He had also put on worn tennis shoes with no laces and a water-stained baseball cap. I'd never seen him so inelegantly attired, yet even in grungy clothes, he looked delicious. We had gone swimming in Bishop, always in public places, but I had not quite gotten over the inevitable tingle at the sight of his amazing physique.

"Did you have your bathing suit on under your clothes?" I asked.

He laughed. "With you in there, I could change anywhere. Modesty is a luxury we couldn't afford around here with two adults, seven kids and one bathroom. Do you want to take an air mattress?"

"No." Sliding my feet into my scuffs, I trailed him out the door.

Remembering again as we went down the path to the lake, I glanced back and smiled to see the motionless snake still dangling from the birdbath.

CHAPTER TWENTY

I kicked off my shoes on the dock, dropped my towel and cover-up on a bench without looking at Jim, tiptoed quickly over the hot wooden planking, ran to the end of the diving board and leaped.

The water was tepid to four or five feet. Below that, the cool darkness startled me. I surfaced to find Jim in the water beside me. Without a word, we raced the fifty feet to the wooden float. He caught me around the waist as I started up the ladder and hauled me back. Playfully, I struggled, trying for my own sake to avoid touching his bare chest, but he was too strong. When I finally gave up my death grip on the ladder, Jim unceremoniously dunked me.

Surprised and giggling bubbles, I yanked on his arm, pulling him under. His downward momentum propelled me back to the surface.

"Oh, ho!" He sputtered when he came up behind me. "So you want to play rough, do you?"

"Uncle Jim." Amanda squealed, jigging barefooted on the hot dock. She wore a swimsuit and had a ski belt buckled around her waist. "Uncle Jim, I'm here."

Turning away from me to swim toward her, he yelled, "Jump to me," and held out his arms.

I gasped, "Jim, no!" before I thought. Then I did think about it and grew even more concerned. "What if she can't swim?"

His answer was a rolling, infectious laugh. "Jancy thinks

maybe you can't swim. A four-year-old who can't swim. Not in this family."

Amanda ran out the wooden plank full speed and dived. She surfaced, blinked to find Jim, then kicked and paddled, closing on him quickly. He gathered her up as she wrapped her little arms around his neck.

"You do me proud, imp."

The little girl giggled and wiggled her way to his back. "Grampa's Aunt Leta got here."

"Yea! Now we'll show Jancy some serious fishing. Where is everyone?"

"Uncle Paul and Uncle Peter and Uncle Andrew took the pickup truck to town for ice and minnows. Aunt Leta brought minnows too." Her expression melted into a frown. "I can't remember about Aunt Veronica and Curtis and Maurice." She brightened again. "Evie can't come because she has to work tomorrow. Momma and Daddy and my new baby brother can come Sunday. Grandma made them let me come with her and Grandpa."

Jim regarded her small face suspiciously. "Did you have to cry to make your mama let you come?"

Amanda looked earnest. "Only a little."

I couldn't help laughing at the candor between them.

"I'm glad you're swimming so I could come down. Grandma was going to read me a book . . ." she arched her eyebrows, "on the bed."

Jim clenched his teeth in a horrible grimace. "We all know what that means."

Amanda's face twisted as if she had eaten something sour. Without meaning to, I gave Jim a puzzled look.

"A nap, sure as anything." He spoke with authority. "Boy, I'm glad we got you out of that. Come on, girls, I'll race you to the dock. We may need to help put all those minnows in the water."

There was a lot of unnecessary splashing and kicking as we covered the distance to the dock together. Amanda won the race and went up the ladder first. Wrapping his arm around my waist, Jim pulled me back and turned me around to face him. My hands flattened on his marvelous chest before I could grab the ladder rung. As if he enjoyed my being so flustered, Jim kissed me and it was not a calming kind of kiss.

"Just a reminder about whose girl you are, for when the wolves come sniffing." He grinned and cocked an eyebrow. "The two-legged kind."

On the dock, I watched Jim pull on his T-shirt, settle the baseball cap low over his dark, dark eyes and slide his feet into the laceless tennis shoes. Struggling to tend to my own business, I slipped into the cover-up and scuffs. For some reason, I was terribly aware that Jim didn't hold my hand as we started toward the cabin. I walked stiffly at his side as we trailed Amanda, who negotiated the path barefooted, stepping gingerly.

Olivia Wills, putting groceries on the open shelves of the cupboard, greeted us both with hugs as she announced she was scalding milk to make ice cream and Aunt Leta was in the bathroom changing clothes.

"Jim, would you mind taking Leta fishing until Andrew or Peter get back?" Olivia shot a doleful look at me in way of apology.

Jim grinned. "We can all go. Amanda, get your pole. Come on, Jance, let's find one for you. Mom?"

Olivia declined and looked pleased to have some preparation time to herself.

When Aunt Leta emerged from the bathroom, she introduced herself to me with a firm handshake. Jim's dad's maiden aunt was a brash woman in her seventies who wore a floppy bonnet over her short bluish curls, a long-sleeved plaid shirt, baggy denims and Grasshopper tennis shoes, an ensemble she declared to be an unbeatable sun block.

Jim and Amanda and I had made one trip down the trail to load the john boat, which skulked in the eerie cool of a teetering boathouse. The boathouse was only a short distance east of the fishing dock but was barely visible, hidden in a clump of cypress trees.

The john boat had two substantial oarlocks that held two long wooden oars, devices that looked like they would be terribly cumbersome to operate.

A speedboat was also parked in the boathouse, but it was reserved "for water skiing and fast rides, not for fishing," Amanda explained patiently when I asked.

A canoe leaned bottom-side-up against an upright anchoring the most substantial part of the boathouse. The paddle peeked out from beneath it. When I reached for the paddle, Jim cleared his throat loudly, drawing my attention and halting my movement.

"What?" I asked.

"We are very careful around the boathouse." He looked to Amanda for the explanation.

She peered up at me, her face solemn. "Snakes live down here. We have to watch out for them. If we startle them, they might bite. They like hiding under boats where it's shady."

I clamped my hands together and backed up a couple of steps.

Jim's voice was a soothing balm. "We don't panic or let the snakes spoil our fun. We just keep an eye out for them."

I glanced around nervously. "And what do we do if we see one?"

"Except Old Blue." Amanda's blue eyes were orbs.

"Of course. Goes without saying. Except Old Blue."

"Aunt Veronica screams bloody murder." Amanda's tone was matter-of-fact.

Jim laughed. "And what does your mama do?"

"She just plain screams, but not bloody murder." Amanda schooled patiently.

"And what do you do?" I asked. "Maybe I'll do that."

"I yell for someone to bring the gun. That's the best thing." Amanda hesitated and thought a long moment, her small mouth twisted sideways on her face, then shrugged. "It really doesn't make any difference. No matter which one you do, scream or yell, someone brings the gun."

I looked at Jim, who winked.

"I see," I said. "What gun?"

Amanda turned to Jim, who lifted an aged four-ten shotgun from among the handful of fishing poles, landing net and other paraphernalia he carried.

"That one, the four-ten," she said, the schoolmarm tone again in her small voice.

Surprised that she should have noticed when I had not, I looked at Jim. "She knew it was there."

He beamed. "Certainly. She sees and hears everything. Very observant. Reminds me a lot of you."

We three women—Amanda and I and the indefatigable Aunt Leta—fished while Jim rowed, changing locations at Aunt Leta's frequent commands, baited lines, removed fish from hooks, weighed each catch regardless of size, and maintained morale by responding happily to all requests.

I discovered the pure pleasure of watching the muscles in his arms and chest ripple beneath his damp T-shirt as he rowed. I let myself survey his powerful thighs, perfect knees and prominent calves, happy that he seemed oblivious to all that shameless admiration until he caught Leta and Amanda both distracted. Looking directly into my face and exaggerating the movements, he flexed his pecs, working one oar at a time, grinned and then said, "Poor baby," when I looked away embarrassed. "She can have what she wants, but she has to ask."

Aunt Leta and Amanda both cast him puzzled looks but didn't demand an explanation. I couldn't help laughing . . . at myself.

The sun set and the breeze died. Twilight brought a still coolness. Aunt Leta waited until almost full dark and the onslaught of the mosquitoes to command our little party back to port.

"You really are good." I held the flashlight and waited to help Jim carry equipment back to the cabin after Aunt Leta and Amanda trooped on ahead.

"I hoped you'd notice." His arms loaded with gear, he stepped close, tipped his head to regard me from under the bill of his baseball cap and puckered.

He was sweaty, smelled fishy and had a definite five-o'clock shadow, but looking into his laughing eyes, I melted. He was absolutely irresistible. Giggling, I met his pucker.

We trudged up the hill slowly, enjoying the cool breeze that was just reviving after allowing its usual period of mourning for the passing of the daylight.

We greeted Jim's dad on the path, in his swimsuit and carrying a soap dish and towel, obviously a nightly excursion. I wasn't sure if I was expected to hug him or shake his hand, but he solved the dilemma by waving me off. "I smell like a goat. You've been downwind up to now. Unless you're fond of filthy animals, you'd best get stepping, gal."

At the cabin, Peter, Andrew, Paul and Olivia all sat on the porch listening to the newly arrived Amanda and Aunt Leta's embellished accounts of our afternoon's expedition.

The men stood and crooned appreciative hellos as we walked in, making me terribly self-conscious to be the object of such a thorough study.

Jim's brothers wore shirts and shorts: Peter fetching in cutoffs, a muscle shirt and flip-flops; Andrew in nicer cargo shorts with a T-shirt and tennis shoes; and Paul clean and handsome in walking shorts, a shirt with a button-down collar and deck shoes. They all had great legs and builds, but not one of the others was as spectacularly endowed as Jim.

"Sit," Paul invited, indicating the glider beside him.

Dropping off the fishing equipment and taking what I carried, Jim interceded. "Come on, Jancy, let's go get a bath before it gets any later." He grabbed two towels and my hand, pulling me out of reach of any of his three brothers, who—no longer captivated by the fishing stories—had drifted close, casually encircling me.

"We barely said hello to everyone," I said, trotting to keep up with Jim.

" 'Hello' with those guys is more than they deserve." He paused to let me catch up. "They've all got the hots for you, sweetheart. Better stay close so I can protect you from the riffraff." He licked his lips and moved his eyebrows up and down.

I laughed out loud. "Ah, yes, the fox guarding the hen. How dumb do you think I am?"

"Thought maybe you'd feel safe enough to let your guard down with all these people around. That's when I'd make my move."

He reached for my hand. I was not only willing, but flattered. Then Amanda, clamoring to catch up, joined our march down the path to join Jim's dad in the communal bath. As we approached, a security light on the dock blinked and came on automatically, washing the area with an orange glow.

William Wills had finished his swim and had settled in one of the dock chairs to dry.

"I'll wash your hair if you'll do mine," Amanda said when we had soaped and rinsed, working skillfully around our bathing suits.

"How?" I asked.

"Get on the floating dock. I'll show you."

We girls lathered each other's hair and then both scrubbed Jim's cropped top, before we dived in together for the rinse. Jim caught me submerged, pulled my face to his and breathed me an underwater kiss. I surfaced burbling.

Amanda was first to the dock. "I'm starving."

Jim winked. "See there? It must be time to eat. But if I get there first, Amanda, there won't be anything left for you." He stepped into his laceless shoes and ran toward the cabin, Amanda squealing along behind like a siren in hot pursuit.

I hung back to wait with Jim's dad, who watched Jim and Amanda's antics from his chair, smiling. After a while, as he and I walked up the hill together, he spoke quietly. "You seem comfortable, Jancy, here in our little Garden of Eden." William Wills breathed easily despite the trek uphill.

I looked at the sky clear all the way to a three-quarter moon and beyond to a thousand stars. I turned my face to catch the evening breeze, allowing it to cool the sunburn I had just begun to notice. "This is as good as it gets." I sighed. "It probably is like those early days of mankind."

The patriarch smiled and hummed agreement.

During my chance at the bathroom, I got out of my swimsuit, pulled on underwear, dry shorts and a T-shirt. Because of the sunburn heating my shoulders, I decided to keep to the shadows and not bother wearing a bra. As I pulled my hair up, my face glowed back at me from the mirror. I helped myself to a generous portion of a bottle of After-Tan lotion on the dresser.

There was no organization to supper. People ate as they pleased, including Amanda. Clad in shorty pajamas, she dished up half of a sloppy Joe sandwich, poured a huge orange juice, took a nectarine, a handful of grapes and a kitchen cup of the newly churned ice cream.

After we ate, Amanda enticed me onto her bed—a double beneath a bunk single—with a coloring book and a brand new box of crayons. We lay on our stomachs coloring under a small wall lamp, listening to the others conversing on the darkened front porch. Their voices carried back on the south breeze.

I didn't notice when Amanda quit talking and was surprised to find my little companion sleeping, her face on her arm, the red crayon dangling limply from her small fingers.

Jim was there a short time later to transfer Amanda to the next bed. He motioned me to get up while he turned her bed down.

A sleepy voice whined, "I didn't finish my picture yet," but she was only half awake. He tucked her in, assuring her she could work on her picture again tomorrow. Amanda wrapped her arms around his neck as they said her prayers together. He kissed her goodnight.

"Jancy," a man's voice called quietly from the darkened front porch, "how about a little Monopoly?" It was one of Jim's brothers, but I didn't know which one.

Scarcely able to keep my own eyes open, I shook my head in the direction of the voices. "No, thanks."

"Do you play Spades?" another voice asked.

"Or we can turn on the overhead light and work on the jigsaw puzzle."

"No thanks," I whispered, concerned that we might disturb Amanda.

"How about riding to town with me?" Paul's voice sounded the most like Jim's. "Sleep at home, in civilization."

"I like it here." I stood by my assigned twin bed waiting as Jim turned it down and checked between the sheets with his flashlight, as he had done with Amanda's.

He smiled and motioned me in. "Just making sure nothing crawled in that didn't belong there." He withdrew to his chair on the front porch. I could feel eyes watching me in the dark as I lay down. I pulled the sheet over me before I removed my shorts and slipped the rubber band off my ponytail. Feeling strangely safe under the scrutiny of all these people, I dozed off almost immediately.

I roused when Jim crept down the sleeping porch. I could feel him smile and I made a halfhearted effort to smile back.

Jim turned toward his dad, who was suddenly beside him, and the two smiled into each other's faces. It was nice, but didn't concern me and I drifted off again.

CHAPTER TWENTY-ONE

Birds chirping and commotion outside woke me early. I squinted at the brightening sky, with only the screen wall at the foot of my bed between me and all out-of-doors. I always liked Tarzan movies where Tarzan and Jane woke up in their home in the treetops and that's exactly what this felt like.

The lyrics to a hymn popped into my mind: "When morning fills the skies." I rubbed my eyes and leaned up on one elbow.

An armadillo scraped at the ground next to a tree root not fifteen feet from me. Beyond and ignoring him, a family of cottontails munched clover, pulling up long stems, then sucking the reeds comically like strands of spaghetti. I had to muffle a laugh and glanced down the sleeping porch.

Amanda slept soundly in the bed next to me, breathing long, steady draughts. On the other side of Amanda, Jim slept on his side facing us, the bed sheet covering him to the waist. The sight of his hairy, man's chest, his tanned, muscular body—quiet, vulnerable in slumber—made me tingle with unimaginable pleasure.

His mother in the next bed also faced us, her back nestled against William Wills' T-shirt clad stomach and chest. Seeing them, I felt like a voyeur peeking at something private, something not intended for my viewing.

Turning, I looked at Aunt Leta flat on her back in the bed on my other side, snoring softly, her breathing uneven compared to the others. Beyond Aunt Leta, Peter slept in the lower, double bed part of the end bunk. I could see only a lump that I assumed was Andrew in the upper, narrow bunk. Apparently Paul had gone back to town.

Soundlessly, I slipped out of bed, stepped into my shorts, picked up my scuffs and tiptoed across the porch. I unlatched the screen door, crept out and stepped into the scuffs before starting down the rocky path.

"Good morning, Blue," I whispered as the snake slithered under the deck. I was surprised and pleased with myself for feeling so comfortable. Even the snake seemed to be a lovely part of the early morning stillness. Vapor rose off the lake. I had no earthly idea what time it was and didn't really care. I supposed it didn't matter. All I knew was that the sun was not yet up.

I ambled slowly to the dock where I settled in one of the chairs and propped my feet on the railing. If people knew how gloriously a day began, we'd probably all be up to watch each dawn. Like a tease, gradually, down in the east end, the sky progressed from light to rosy to peach to a dazzling yellow. As the light spread, puffs of clouds chased each other across the changing hues. On the horizon I thought I saw occasional water spouts catching glints of sunshine.

It would be another scorcher, heat accumulating mercilessly on the cement streets in town. Out here, I doubted it would get nearly so hot.

I felt the dock vibrate and looked to see Jim in cutoffs, a T-shirt and baseball cap, walking toward me. He carried a Styrofoam cup, probably coffee, for himself and an orange juice in a clear plastic for me.

He spoke softly. "Good morning."

I smiled and self-consciously ran my fingers through my uncombed hair in a futile attempt to neaten it. He eased into a chair, handed me the orange juice and propped his feet next to mine on the railing. We didn't talk. It didn't seem necessary.

In a little while, Aunt Leta interrupted the early morning quiet by rattling down the path to the boat house juggling an armload of fishing gear. Jim grinned, shook his head and went to help before she dropped the whole load. Leta ignored me altogether. Obviously she intended to claim Jim's undivided attention. She could be a little jealous, I decided. Any woman any age probably envied me for having his interest. I could afford to be gracious. I only felt bad that being gracious took such a fierce, conscious effort on my part.

I watched them push off in the cumbersome old john boat and Leta begin dabbling lines in the water grass along the shoreline before I went back up to the cabin where other people were beginning to stir and I could get my mind off my generous gesture.

Stepping into the flow of things, I helped produce breakfast.

William Wills was on a second plate of eggs and fried potatoes when his beeper sounded. He got to his feet slowly and carried his coffee cup.

I stood, too. "What's going on?"

Olivia grimaced. "His helper probably needs a hand. It's awfully hard for William to get a real day off. He'll have to go to the store in Skelter to call, find out what it is."

"Why can't he use the phone in Jim's car?" William and Olivia both regarded me as if I'd grown a second head, but I led him out to Jim's car where his cell phone was charging. "I'll show you."

Two quick calls revealed the beep was not an emergency. The problem would wait until Monday. The older man's stride quickened as he returned to the cabin.

Aunt Leta and Jim had not returned when Veronica and George Peck arrived late in the morning with Curtis and Maurice (Curly and Moe).

Badgered by the kids and finally his wife, George agreed to take Curly, Moe and Amanda tubing off the speed boat, promising Olivia he would keep to the middle of the lake so as not to disturb the fisher persons in the east end.

The sun was high before its heat drove Peter and Andrew from their beds and into the kitchen to forage. After they located leftovers, they insisted their mother let them manage on their own.

William was reading the newspaper the Pecks had brought along and Olivia and I had settled to quietly piecing the puzzle when we finally heard muted voices coming up the path, one of which revved my heartbeat.

Jim carried the equipment and a stringer of crappie and bass, which he hung on the deck railing. Steadying herself on his arm, Aunt Leta began retelling a fish story of another time—another generation even.

When Jim's eyes found mine from under the bill of his cap, I swear I saw a twinkle and his white teeth flashed. I couldn't help smiling, marveling. He never flagged no matter how many requests were made of him.

I looked around. Olivia saw the exchange between us and smiled a little herself. "Peter, you and Andrew come help Aunt Leta clean her catch." There was no equivocation in her voice. To my surprise, both Peter and Andrew appeared immediately. I wasn't certain if they saw her as a threat of some kind, or if she had just gotten her bluff in early. Or maybe it was her backup who made the boys jump to that tone.

Jim skimmed by me as I held the screen door open for him, his arms loaded with gear. He whispered, "Let's go swimming."

I pulled up my shirt to show him my swimsuit—a fetching two-piece number I'd bought especially for this trip—was already in place.

Just as Andrew took the tackle box from Jim's hand, we heard a woman's loud shriek from the lake.

Andrew said, "Damn."

William slowly got to his feet.

Jim waved him back. "I'll get it, Dad."

Unceremoniously, Jim dropped the rest of the gear, reserving the shotgun, and grabbed a handful of shells from the tackle box Andrew had opened and offered.

Leaning close to my ear as he passed, Jim whispered, "Meet me at the dock. Bring towels."

Confused, I looked to Olivia, who had not even glanced up from our jigsaw puzzle. "Who's screaming?"

Olivia calmly tried another piece. It fit. "Veronica saw a snake. She likes to cut cattails at the edge of the water. She forgets to look where she's stepping."

"Now and then she flushes a moccasin," Peter finished as he carried the stringer of fish through, headed toward one of the tables on the back porch. "The scream will have scared the snake out of his skin and he'll be long gone by the time Jim gets there, but someone has to go or she won't stop hollering."

Quietly, hoping no one would notice, I got towels from the line on the back porch, picked up the rubber raft, watched Andrew and Peter scale and gut fish for a moment, then stepped outside, around the cabin and down the path to the dock.

I left the towels, my shoes, clothes and the raft on a chair and dived into the water. Again, the water was warm down to about four feet, then cool and dark and inviting. I surfaced in time to see Jim doff his cap, run out on the diving board and achieve a distance-gulping dive. I also saw the rubber raft blow off the dock into the water.

Jim grabbed my legs and followed the outline of my body up. He dunked me roughly, but when I threw my arms around his waist, my momentum pulled him under with me. We groped each other in the cool depths, our first private moments in the twenty-four hours we had been at the cabin. I felt daring and extremely sexy. We were holding each other, chest to chest, thighs to thighs, when we surfaced.

"Your raft's going to the weeds," Veronica yelled from the dock.

Jim and I exchanged looks, then took off, racing to see who could be first to recover the runaway raft. I got there first and slithered aboard, then flipped to lie stretched on my back. Close behind, Jim pulled himself up over my feet and legs. With a bawdy laugh, I pushed against his shoulders to fend him off.

"Jim Wills!" Veronica shouted indignantly, "that doesn't look very nice."

His pained expression turned into a lecherous leer and he groaned. "She's always been a tattletale." He flipped the raft, dumping me into the water squarely on top of him. Submerged, he caught my ankles. Two minds in sync, I paddled and he kicked as we swam in tandem, aimed again toward the rubber raft skimming over the water, wind driven.

Surfacing, I caught my breath and dived again, my feet lifting Jim to the surface for a breath before he followed, still holding my ankles.

We caught the raft and swam it to the wooden float, clambered aboard and stretched side by side, breathless and grinning. The noonday sun was warm, the breeze cool.

"I don't want to kiss you in front of my family." Jim stretched on his back and cushioned his head on one crooked arm. "They know me. They'll see it's important."

Lying beside him on my back, I had one arm across my face to shade my eyes. "Is that a secret?"

He turned his head to look at me. "It is if it's unrequited."

I didn't say anything.

"Is it, Jancy? Unrequited?"

I would have made a poor gunfighter because, in a showdown,

I flinch. "You know it isn't." Neither of us moved nor spoke. "And it's worse here with your family." I returned his look.

Jim's dark eyes held mine. "Show me."

I rolled toward him as he slipped his arm under me and pulled us close. Poised over his face, providing him some shade, I smiled and licked his chin. He tasted salty and felt bristly. He still hadn't shaved. My teasing grin faded. I kissed each corner of his mouth as he lay motionless. Then, abruptly, I rolled away from him, onto my knees and dived off the far side of the float. He followed.

We surfaced on the side of the float away from prying eyes at the fishing dock and in the cabin. We were even hidden, for the moment, from the group tubing in the west end.

I felt naughty. "Hold onto the float."

He complied.

Holding his face between my hands to keep myself from sinking, I kissed his forehead, his cheekbones, his nose and circled kisses around his mouth. Inch by inch, I worked my way to his neck, holding myself afloat with one hand, and allowing the other to survey his chest and those marvelous flexing arms. I kissed his collarbones and his shoulders.

Taking a deep breath and holding onto his waist, I pulled myself under water. I had kissed his chest and his stomach and was moving south before he caught my arm and pulled me up, bringing us again face to face.

"No, no," I objected, about half seriously. "You have to keep your hands on the float. This is my game. Turn around."

He did as directed, clinging to the beams of the float just above his head, his biceps pumped. I proceeded, kissing the back of his neck and his shoulder blades. Again gripping his waist, I submerged, kissing his back and circling to nibble down his ribs. I came up kissing the area under his arms.

He let go of the cross beams. "No tickling."

"Keep your hands on the float."

Doing chin-ups on his biceps, I kissed the outside of Jim's boulder-like arm muscles, then ducked under one to kiss the inside of his arm. He watched as I came up under his chin, then he caught me and pulled, aligning my body tightly with his. The physical intensity of his desire set me reeling. I pushed away from him and he allowed a little distance between us before he pulled me back. His open mouth covered mine and, I swear, he could have had me there, at that moment, in the water. My body drifted to seal against his. Instead of retreating when I felt his arousal, I sucked his tongue into my throat. Our bathing suits were in the way. I wanted them gone and Jim and me alone, there in that lake in the great out-of-doors.

"Jim. Jancy." Veronica was again on the dock. "We need you for volleyball."

Jim groaned. "There are some really good things about a big family. Right now I can't think of one."

He gave me a quick, dismissive kiss and took off, again swimming several yards to retrieve the escaping rubber raft. More disappointed and sexually frustrated than I'd ever been, I did a slow side stroke to the dock.

As if we were the objects of a conspiracy, Jim and I were not alone again as incoming family members, Evie and her boyfriend and Paul, continued to swell the human population of the area. And they stayed, at least most of them did, days and nights.

Around twilight those evenings, after the heat and the water had taken their toll, Jim and Peter chose up sides for volleyball. The competition got fierce as each night the teams hammered their claims to the family championship until darkness forced bilateral concession.

In his natural habitat, Jim was patient, comfortable in and around the water, particularly proficient with boats—pulling skiers, rowing the john boat or paddling the canoe.

Also, there was a small catamaran.

When I remarked about the variety of water vessels, Olivia said Jim had provided all except the sturdy, old sheet-metal john boat, which William had gotten when the children were small.

When I expressed interest in the catamaran, Jim took me out and had me maneuvering the sails alone after one lesson. Amanda chaperoned.

Twice he invited me to a makeshift target range to practice with a twenty-two-caliber pistol. Both times Curly and Moe insisted on coming along.

At first nervous handling a weapon, I responded to Jim's praise and encouragement. On our third outing, I also fired a rifle and both the twelve-gauge and the four-ten shotguns.

In that rustic setting, with no clock dictating, I lost all track of time. I neither knew nor cared what day it was, much less the hour. I forgot my family in Carson's Summit, my housemates, my job in Bishop and, most surprisingly, I forgot Riley Wedge.

My attention centered on people and activities at the Wills' fishing camp. I turned down invitations to ride into town, in spite of the lure of an air-conditioned vehicle. I was more content than I had ever been. Peace reigned, that is, it did until Jim's car honked early Sunday morning. He hurried outside and leaned in to answer the persistent beep of the car phone.

After several minutes of conversation, he settled onto the seat to talk some more. He hung up, walked slowly back to the cabin and came directly to me. I was in the kitchen pouring orange juice.

I said, "What's going on?"

"Remember the school I told you about?"

An ominous chill crawled up my back and set a dark cloud in my mind. "Yes."

"There's an opening." He spoke to me but I realized by the silence all around us that everyone else was listening, too.

I stopped pouring juice and looked into Jim's face. "I thought it didn't start until fall."

"That was the director on the phone. There's an opening for the session that starts this week. I told him I wasn't ready. He's insisting. No one in the state has had this training. If there were a disaster, no one coming in from outside would be familiar with our resources or know who's qualified to do what. The director's talked to both the A.G. and the governor. They're all pretty well set on my going."

"When?"

"It starts tomorrow. I'd need to fly to Virginia this afternoon."

Without realizing it, I set the juice pitcher on the table. Jim took my elbow. "Let's go for a walk."

Olivia blocked Andrew, shushing the question he started to ask.

Jim and I walked to the water's edge and followed it across the dam and along the channel of water that ran over the spillway into a creek.

"You can stay here, Jancy, and ride back to Bishop with someone Tuesday. Or you can go back with me today." There was a long silence. "Or," he added as an afterthought, "I'll tell the director I'm just not available and live with the repercussions."

I inhaled deeply and stopped to watch water cascading over the spillway into the creek. "How long does this school last?"

"Three weeks. I'll be back by the Fourth of July."

"What about Bubba's new trial?"

"Third time's a charm. They'll manage fine without me. What I want to know is, can you?"

My eyes stung, but I wanted to let him go, guilt free. "Got along without you before I met you," I sang the lyrics from an old song we'd heard on local radio, "gonna get along without you now." I managed what I hoped was a confident smile, trying to mask the emotional turmoil chewing me up inside.

Jim's expression didn't change, but he paused a long moment, studying my face. "All right," he said finally. "I need to pack." He took my hand and turned resolutely. "Do you want to ride back to Bishop with me or stay here?"

My bravado wilted. I trudged silently, staring at the path in front of us, trying to swallow the unwelcome grief. I loved that quaint little lake and that cabin and my creaky bed and that whole collection of people. Most of all, though, I loved being there with him. It wouldn't be the same with him gone. But it would still be almost paradise. I didn't know whether to grieve for him there or in Bishop.

Finally, in the face of my strength-sapping ambivalence, Aunt Leta made the decision. "You can drive me back Tuesday. I hate highway driving. I'm having duplicate bridge at my house Wednesday and, of course, you need to be back at work then, isn't that right? That way you do me a big favor."

I agreed but remained unusually quiet, trailing Jim, smiling with some effort as he gathered clothes and personal items. "You're taking a bathing suit?"

"Yep." He didn't look the least bit contrite. "Gonna party some while I'm there. Whoop it up." He studied my face a long minute before he gave me a wry smile. Darn, he was teasing me, as usual.

"Where will you be exactly?" I asked.

"A training facility near Quantico."

"I thought that was a Marine base."

"I guess they use some of the facilities and teaching staff for this school." He dug through a box in the bathroom closet and came up with two dusty rubber scuffs that had seen better days.

"Will you call me sometime?" My voice broke before I got it

under control.

Jim looked surprised, pleased, and a little incredulous. "Yes, I'll call you."

My chin trembled and a surprised frown rippled over his brow as he smiled gently.

"I'll call and give you my address as soon as I get there. You can write to me."

The words boosted my spirits. Maybe this was not the end of us. Maybe it was just a temporary interruption. "Good idea. I will."

With his thumbs, he blotted tear droplets beading in the corners of my eyes as he continued the tender smile. "This is nice. Really nice." He just stood there staring into my face for a long time. I could feel strands of hair that had escaped from my ponytail dance in the breeze produced by the ceiling fan throbbing overhead.

"Jancy, you and I both know this is real. We have not got an 'out of sight, out of mind' relationship. You've been a long time coming in my life. Time, miles, nothing will change how I feel. We may have to get by a few time and distance tests over the next few months, but we'll manage, if we both want it to work."

Curly burst into the bathroom at that moment, desperate to use the facilities. Jim and I joined the others. I would've liked to have heard more, but I supposed the most important words had been said.

The Wills family milled near his car as Jim tossed his bag into the back seat. He hugged and shook hands with everyone else before he turned to me. "If you want to tell me good-bye, you'd better come here."

I blushed, but closed the distance between us until he gathered me in his arms. He kissed me firmly, with the authority of an alpha male claiming his mate. I tilted my head until my face was flush against his shoulder, the depth of our kiss hidden from the onlookers by those biceps I admired so often. Finishing the kiss, he held me until I was steady, then he put a hand on the top of my head and smiled into my face.

"May the peace of the Lord be with you, Jancy Dewhurst."

I ducked and stepped away, then smiled back at him to answer the traditional Episcopal greeting. "And also with you."

CHAPTER TWENTY-TWO

Jim had been gone two hours when Amanda's parents, Beth and Johnny Colette, arrived, distracting everyone with Amanda's new baby brother, Little Jim. Paul mentioned repeatedly that the baby had two names, James Paul, but people persisted in calling him Little Jim.

Obviously pleased by Jim's departure, Paul sat with me as I worked on a new jigsaw puzzle. I tried to be pleasant, but I just didn't feel like making a lot of conversation.

Paul objected when I left the puzzle to go swimming with Amanda, Curly and Moe, and later when I went fishing with Aunt Leta and Andrew. I felt totally comfortable with Jim's younger brothers, who resembled my own siblings. On our return, Paul challenged me to play Scrabble with him, his mother and Peter, then grudgingly gave in when I asked if he wanted to participate in the afternoon's volleyball fray.

The Colettes loaded Little Jim and a reluctant Amanda and left that night after charcoaled hamburgers. I turned down Paul's invitation to ride with him to the store in Skelter to make a phone call. It did not even occur to me to offer him the use of my cell phone, which had spent the holiday in a side pocket of my suitcase. I overheard Olivia explain to an offended Paul, in a stage whisper, that I had not left the cabin with anyone since our arrival there on Thursday.

"She likes it here," Olivia Wills said, smiling at me with obvious pride.

When he got back, Paul said, "I'm going to stay a couple of days." Olivia and William exchanged looks, then each glanced at me, as if I were responsible for his change of plans. Indifferent, I turned back to the puzzle.

Peter and Andrew loaded their gear in the pickup they shared and left for town shortly after I turned in for the night. Paul slept in Jim's bed. Curly and Moe slept next to me in Amanda's double. Leta was in her usual place in the twin on the other side of mine, and Veronica and George took the lower double bunk vacated by Peter.

Aunt Leta and I were on the lake fishing with Curly and Moe before daylight on Monday.

William Wills went back to work in town Monday morning.

Veronica, her husband and the boys left after lunch and the cabin, which had vibrated with humanity during the extended weekend, suddenly seemed deserted, with only Olivia, Leta, Paul and me there to hold the fort.

I welcomed the activity of sweeping and mopping the porches with Olivia, although we wound up drenched with sweat and had to take a swim to cool off. Paul declined to get involved in the sweeping, mopping or swimming.

In lieu of volleyball Monday evening, Olivia produced a five-pound bag of cracked pecans for shelling. Paul objected, then joined the ladies as we rocked and shelled pecans on the front porch, visiting pleasantly as I coaxed Olivia into talking about how she and William met, the courtship, highlights of their married life, their children and the kids' myriad antics. Aunt Leta threw in a memory now and then.

When Olivia asked if I was ready for my nightly bath, I hedged. While I didn't want to go alone, I did not want Paul to accompany me and knew Leta would rather wrestle with the cantankerous cold shower in the bathroom than risk her body to the lake. Without another word, Olivia closed herself in the bathroom and returned immediately wearing her bathing suit. Following her lead, I changed quickly.

I had not realized before Jim left that while I was at the cabin, he could not contact me. Again I did not think of the cell phone safely tucked away in my bag. I missed him terribly after he left Sunday and all day Monday. I pretended he was rowing Leta around the lake or cleaning fish on the back porch, imagining him there but out of sight.

Getting my cover-up from the bathroom closet Monday night for our bath, I found the shirt Jim had worn on our trip down on Thursday. I brushed the fabric against my face. It smelled like him, the mingled fragrances of his aftershave, his deodorant, his body. I closed my eyes and imagined him there in the room, his dark eyes, his white teeth, his warm, searching hands. I opened my eyes almost expecting to see him. As I looked around, a familiar lump crowded my throat.

After breathing in the shirt once more, I hung it back in the closet.

Armed with shampoo, soap and towels, Olivia and I went to the lake. William drove up just in time to catch up with us. Paul and Leta walked with us to observe from the dock. Paul fell into step beside me on our way back up the hill.

He spoke quietly so no one else would overhear. "Ride home with me tomorrow."

"I'm driving Leta back."

"She lives in Cosgrove."

"I'll drive to Bishop. It's just a little out of her way. Then she'll only have to manage the fifteen miles from Bishop to Cosgrove."

"Seventeen miles," he corrected.

"Okay, seventeen miles."

"It would be a chance for us to talk and get acquainted."

"We know each other well enough."

"Can I call you?"

"Why?"

"Mom said Jim'll be gone a month. You might get lonesome. Having another Wills around might help."

I looked at him, searching his face for some ulterior meaning, but he looked sincere. "Sure, call me, if you want to, when you're in town. I've got some good-looking housemates. One of them will probably be between guys. I'll set you up."

Paul looked injured.

We finished the puzzle Monday night. Olivia placed the final piece, then we glued the back to a sheet of newspaper and thumb-tacked it on the wall. Olivia wrote the date and the names of everyone who had worked on it on a piece of paper and stuck it on a lower corner of the finished work. We all stood back and admired the result of our joint industry.

Early Tuesday Leta and I made a last run in the john boat but, as we had done since Jim's departure, we threw back our catch rather than clean the fish ourselves.

Shortly after noon, I loaded our bags in Leta's car. Also ready to go, Paul reminded me he would call me. I said that would be fine.

The oddest thing happened when we were ready to go. It was terribly hard for me to leave Olivia Wills. The little woman hugged me tightly, pounding my back with a tiny hand. I struggled hard to keep all my unexpected emotions at bay and managed a husky, "Thank you for inviting me."

"Oh, honey, you *made* the weekend." Olivia stepped back and I noticed she looked a little weepy too. "Come back next weekend or the next, if you want to. I'll get a new puzzle and do a batch of ice cream, just for us."

"I'll call William to warn you, if I can come."

"Don't bother to call, just get in your car and drive. I'll have fresh sheets on your bed."

As I drove, absently listening to Aunt Leta prattle, I thought about the Wills family and their wilderness haven.

I have a mom and dad and brothers of my own, I mused. *I don't need to come back here. I need to get back in the language lab, get back on track. I'm getting confused. I'm letting my career get sidetracked. That place and those people are not part of my plan.*

I thought of Paul. He seemed smarmy. I liked thinking of him and his smarminess. It was better than mooning over Jim.

Aunt Leta quit talking and turned on nostalgia radio. ". . . or would I leave you running merrily through the snow? Or on a wintry evening when you catch the fire's glow? If ever I would leave you. . . ."

I had always loved the music from *Camelot,* but I couldn't help remembering Jim at Christmas, and after, smushing the snowball in my face; my birthday present, "shiny and sentimental," and sledding at Harold's Hill. Suddenly, I wanted that particular musical selection to end.

It was closely followed by a called-in request for a number I had not heard in years. I knew the words and sang along blissfully until they got to the refrain.

"You don't pull on Superman's cape, you don't spit in the wind. You don't pull the mask off the old Lone Ranger and you don't mess around with . . . Jim."

Oh, yeah. Now there was a universal truth. "That was my first mistake," I said, mumbling to myself.

Leta shot me a look. "I thought maybe it was."

Startled, I glanced at my little companion, who smiled knowingly.

"It doesn't matter what anybody thinks, I'm not caught." I wasn't sure if I were speaking to her or reminding myself.

Leta smiled and raised her eyebrows, indicating her skepticism. "I know you're not, dear. You still have your independence. No one's going to steal it away from you. If it's given, you'll give it of your own accord."

That seemed like a curious thing for her to say and prompted my natural inquisitiveness. "Have you never been tempted to give up your independence, Aunt Leta?"

"Yes, I was. Once."

There followed a rich history of Leta Wills, the story of a brief, unsuccessful marriage, family obligations that sounded like more of an excuse to refrain from further romantic involvements than the actual reason for her prolonged single status.

CHAPTER TWENTY-THREE

Jim had left messages on my answering machine Sunday, Monday and again Tuesday morning, casual reports of his arrival, accommodations, the weather. He always ended with, "I love you. I promise not to interfere with your career."

Just hearing his voice thrilled me and I played each message more than once.

He wouldn't be near a telephone until the weekend after next and they weren't allowed to have cell phones, but he gave me an address. I sat down immediately, addressed an envelope and stuffed it with the hodgepodge of notes I had written him from the cabin after his departure.

Beginning Wednesday morning, I threw myself into work with renewed vigor. I spent an hour or more at the language lab each evening. After hours, I cleaned my closet, my room, my desk, expelling excess clothing, memorabilia, belongings, except for those with serious sentimental meaning. Those I put in boxes to store with my parents.

I asked Liz and Rosie to go shopping with me, reminded every time how much I liked those two particular housemates.

Angela Fires asked about Jim. I asked if Angela would like to go out with Paul.

"Does Paul look anything like Jim?" she asked. I said he did. "Does he act anything like Jim?" Angela asked with less enthusiasm.

Sadly, I shook my head. "Not really."

Angela brightened. "Then I'd love to meet him. Let me know when he's coming."

The next Thursday night, Andrew and Peter caused commotion when they showed up at the house on Cherry Street.

"Wills, you say," Teresa said loudly when she answered the doorbell. I raced to the stairs and down, stopping midway, trying to mask my disappointment when I saw it was only his brothers.

Andrew walked to the bottom of the stairs. "We thought we'd take you to the show or something. A sandwich date. We're the bread, you're the filling."

Laughing, I thanked them for being so thoughtful, then rounded up Teresa, Rosie and Angie to go along.

After the show, we went to Roper's, where the Wills brothers displayed remarkable skill at the two-step. They were a huge success.

Jim wrote to me and I to him every day the first week. The next Friday night, I drove to Carson's Summit to see my parents and brothers, but I went back to Bishop on Saturday feeling restless and depressed.

The next week, I found I was repeating myself writing to Jim every day so I cut back to every other day. It seemed like I couldn't get him out of my mind. I thought things would be better if I could only hear his voice.

Morosely I decided Jim was wrong. Distance and time did make a difference. Gradually, they would wean us from each another. That idea sent my spirits plummeting into an even deeper funk, which was followed by another particularly unpleasant surprise. I did not have a picture of him, not a billfold mug shot, not even a snapshot.

Delving in the *Clarion* library, I found some old university yearbooks and combed through them until I found a thumbnail picture the year he graduated from the university. I found his face in another, later book, among a group of law students. Although both pictures were small and of poor quality and clothes and hairstyles badly dated, the images comforted me.

After work on Saturday of another long, determinedly busy, miserable week, I tossed two bathing suits and a change of clothes into my car and drove to Skelter. I took the asphalt road to the turnoff and followed the dirt road that wound down to the cabin. The closer I got, the higher my spirits. That's where I had seen him last and, somehow, in my subconscious mind, I felt he might be there, although intellectually I knew he wasn't.

Yoo-hooing, Olivia Wills was out the cabin door and greeting me before I put the car in park. We laughed and hugged, both talking at once, like a couple of giggling high school girls who had been apart all summer.

Olivia finally got to say something without my chiming along. "No one else is coming. I'm so glad you're here."

I laughed at her excitement.

It was terribly hot and humid, so we went for a swim. During my turn to change clothes in the bathroom, I opened the closet and slipped Jim's shirt off its hanger. I hugged it close and drew a long, reviving breath. In a way, my subconscious had been right. He was here, at least part of him was.

After we'd cooled off, Olivia and I launched the catamaran. We toured the shoreline until we were dry, then we freed the sail and jumped in the water to cool off, holding onto a tie to keep the vessel close. We clambered back on board, holding the crossbeam and working our way onto a pontoon and up, then lay back to admire the sun just easing out of sight. I felt content for the first time since I'd left there.

When he arrived just before dark, William Wills acted genuinely pleased to find me there, but wouldn't hug me, of course, until he had bathed.

After a supper of pork chops and fresh corn and tomatoes, he read selected items aloud from the newspaper while Olivia and I laid out pieces of a new puzzle on the game table. It seemed very late as I tumbled into bed, but time at the cabin was deceptive.

The car horn linked to my cell phone startled me from a deep, early sleep. I grabbed a flashlight and dashed outside to quiet the noise shattering the country hush.

"Where are you?" Jim's voice sounded deep, as if he were annoyed, but I didn't care. I was too happy to hear it. "I've been calling your house all night."

"I'm here. You woke me out of a sound sleep."

"Where's here?" This time his question was less urgent.

"At the cabin. I'm looking in through the screen and down the row of beds as we speak."

"Oh." He sounded relieved. "What are you doing there?"

"Your mom told me to come back. I went home to see my family last weekend. I've been missing you and wondering if I'd ever see you again. I keep wondering if the magic will survive." That was more than I might have confessed had he been there, but I gulped down my pride and just forged ahead. "So after work, I decided to come down here. You left your shirt in the bathroom closet. Did you know?"

"No." He sounded puzzled.

"It smells like you. I came down because I like your folks and this place, but the biggest reason I came, I think, was to smell your shirt."

His laughter burbled on the other end of the phone. "Have you see any other Wills?"

"Peter and Andrew stopped by the house the other night and a bunch of us went to Roper's. They were a big hit with the housemates."

"How about Paul?"

"No, but he said he'd call and be by to take me to lunch

sometime while you're gone."

"Do you and mom have a puzzle going?"

I shivered as a cool breeze wafted by. "Yes. We started it tonight while your dad read us the newspaper. Before he got here, your mom and I went swimming and cruising on the catamaran. My hair's still wet. The three of us might go fishing in the morning, if your dad doesn't get any emergency calls."

"Who all's there?"

"Your mom, your dad and me. That's it."

"I'll bet they're glad you showed up. They're used to a crowd." He hesitated. "I got an emergency call here tonight. It was Kellan. He was jabbering. Kit had the baby. It's a boy, as expected. Kellan's higher than a kite. He'd lost my phone number. Said he'd been calling you all afternoon. Finally traced me through the office."

"Is Kit okay?"

"Fine."

"Did they name the baby Jim, after you?"

"Yes, well, sort of after me but not Jim. His name is Wills Dulany."

"How did I know? Did you remember Bubba's new trial starts Monday?"

"Yes. Will you be covering it?"

"I'll drop in and out to keep an eye on things." I lowered my voice. "Jim, your dad just turned on the kitchen light checking on me. We were all asleep. I'm turning this phone off for the night so don't call back. We won't answer."

"Jancy?"

"Yes."

"Can you still feel the magic?"

I shivered again. "Yes." I hesitated before I asked, but I really did need to know. "Can you?"

"Stronger than ever. Can you see that fingernail moon?"

235

I glanced up. A wisp of a cloud veiled the silver sliver in the nighttime sky, but I could see it. I scarcely breathed the word, "Yes."

"So can I. It's almost like holding hands."

I laughed. "Not if memory serves. Jim, our shenanigans at the float . . . that was a mistake."

"Oh, yeah? What makes you think so?"

"It makes me miss you more than maybe I would have."

"Remembering you there has carried me these two weeks. The damnedest thing is, I don't have a picture of you."

Funny how we'd both noticed that. "I don't have one of you either. When will you be back?"

"A week from tomorrow. Eight more days."

"Jim, I've got to go in. Your dad flipped the kitchen light on and off again."

"Say it and I'll hang up."

I thought it over. I had already said it, so this was only confirmation of what he already knew. I whispered, "I love you." He didn't say anything, so I elaborated. "As it turns out, I'm afraid I may love you wildly . . . madly . . . passionately."

He chuckled, a rippling, victorious sound. "Good. Sleep well. In my dreams, I'm one bed over, on the other side of Amanda." After a minute, it was his turn. "I love you, Jancy."

"Good night." Reluctantly, I hung up. I hurried back into the cabin, snapped off the kitchen light William had left on for me and used the flashlight to scurry back to bed.

Later, rousing up, I realized I hadn't turned off the cell phone. It was too late. Turning toward Jim's empty bed, I closed my eyes.

Chapter Twenty-Four

Bubba's third murder trial began with jury selection Monday June 26, one week before Jim's scheduled return. Assistant District Attorney Reese Mabry again represented the state and Denson Jackson the defense. Jim and Anissa Featherston were noticeably absent.

It took just three hours to pick a jury, six men and six women.

Bubba's parents were again in the gallery. Tyrone Gideon was housebound with a broken hip and Mrs. Gideon stayed home to care for him.

Chloe Conklin was unavailable, appearing in court in Dominion where she was attempting to force the insurance company to pay off on G.C.'s multi-million-dollar policy.

I heard that Chloe was a remarkable witness. Late in the week the parties settled out of court for an undisclosed amount which, I heard later, was the full amount of the policy plus a healthy attorney's fee. The attorneys for the insurance company were concerned about getting hit with bad-faith punitive damages if they continued to deny the claim.

I tried to get interested in Bubba's trial, but it was a rehash of the first two, although the witnesses testified more skillfully.

An elderly black male juror and a young white mother of toddlers nodded off during the prosecution's tedious testimony regarding the chain of custody of evidence.

Barely able to concentrate, I daydreamed of the moment I would see Jim again. Usually I imagined I would be able to tell at a glance if the flame still burned. Other times, I was less sure.

After a week of trial, during which Jim called me three times, the jury got the case for deliberations. Both sides voiced confidence.

It took jurors only ninety minutes to find Bubba innocent of the first-degree murder of G.C. Gideon.

In an interview after the verdict, Reese told me he expected federal charges regarding civil rights violations to be forthcoming, but I doubted that. I figured everyone else was as tired as I was of the whole matter.

I was still at the office when Jim called late Friday. Hearing his voice made me lightheaded. All I could think of was seeing his face, holding him. "What time do you get in?"

"There's a glitch."

"A change in your flight?"

"No. I did pretty well here. My scores qualify me for additional training. I have to go to Arlington for a little while for another school—part of Homeland Security stuff."

At that moment, I didn't give a flip about national security. "How little a little while?" I struggled for some elusive level of maturity.

"A couple of weeks."

I whimpered, straining to swallow my awful disappointment. "When will I see you?"

"August one." His voice was soft, caressing, as comforting as a voice could be absent a physical touch.

I sputtered. I wanted to lash out, to hurt him as much as he was hurting me. I was losing the fight against the ache in my throat, the burning sensation behind my eyes. He didn't say anything. "I'll have to find someone else." My voice warbled, adding to my angst, so I struck again. "You've got me spoiled to holding someone, to feeling warm hands and lips where hands and lips haven't ever been before. You gave me chills and fever.

I'm addicted to the gleam in your eyes when you look at me."

Still, he didn't speak.

My breath caught, strangling my words. "I don't know what's happened to me. I don't know what's going to happen to me now, with you gone. I have this awful feeling, a premonition . . . that it's . . . over . . . that I'll never . . . see you again."

Overcome, drowning in my own tears, I hung up.

Ron Melchoir pretended not to notice when I folded my arms on my desk and laid my forehead on them. Other employees scurried around, finishing up, eager to begin the weekend. I doubted anyone else even looked in my direction.

My extension rang. I didn't answer. Sandy stopped beside my desk, but she didn't say anything. I imagine she understood a reporter's reluctance to answer the telephone at quitting time on a Friday.

My cell phone rang as I drove home. I turned it off.

He had left messages with Liz, who had put sticky notes on my bedroom door, and on both answering machines, the one for the house and the other one in my room. I didn't bother to read the notes or listen to either machine, and I unplugged the phone in my room.

That night I hoped Roper's might provide medicinal relief and I tagged along with Angela. I had always liked men, generally speaking, but suddenly I did not want to dance or laugh or drink with or even speak to a man. I bought my own drinks and danced on the line until I thought I was tired enough to sleep, then I bummed a ride home with the first people I knew who looked like they were leaving.

Usually an early morning person, I didn't wake up until nine-thirty and was annoyed at having awakened at all. I tried to go back to sleep but finally got up to prowl around the house looking for something, but I didn't know what. I didn't want to eat or read or dress.

After roaming upstairs and down, I pulled on shorts, a bra, a T-shirt and my tennis shoes, stuffed some money in my pocket and went outside.

The air was humid, the heat punishing. It helped.

Because it was too hot to jog, I walked, first over to the Jessup Y, near his house, carefully avoiding his block, then doubling back downtown.

I drank a long time from a water fountain in the park, then strained my eyes to read the marquis on the Center Theater two blocks away.

It was cold in the dollar movie, *Seven Brides for Seven Brothers,* which gave my sagging morale a boost. I hadn't seen that movie on a full-sized screen with the big sound in years.

The second feature started, another dollar movie, *The Way We Were.* I watched the beginning, but art imitates life, and when Streisand and Redford began having problems, I left.

The late afternoon sun beat mercilessly and heat waves shimmered from the cement walk. I couldn't open my eyes. The glare brought on a headache that felt like shards of glass in my forehead. I made it back to the park to sit on a bench in the shade, strategically close to the water fountain.

It was nearly sundown when I began the long walk home.

At the house, there were no new messages from Jim, which made me feel worse. I had not believed that possible. Down the hall, I heard Rosie humming and moving around in her room. I rapped lightly on her door. "Rosie, are you doing anything tonight?" She smiled as if we shared a secret and I had to ask, "What?"

Rosie slanted me a suspicious look. "Didn't you tell him to ask me out?"

"Who?"

Rosie looked as if she were accusing me, in a pleasant way, and I shook my head.

"No, honestly, I didn't. Who?"

"Peter Wills. Oh, Jancy, he is darling. I've never been out with anyone who was so perfect. And he's asked me out three times. He's so tall and handsome and built, has a good job, never wants to borrow money. Honestly, I think I'm in love."

I tried to generate some enthusiasm and a congratulatory smile. "Good."

"Come go with us. I owe you for this one. Come on. Don't be gloomy. We're just going to Roper's. How about it?"

I thought it over. I could mope at Roper's just as well as I could at home alone on a Saturday night. "Yeah, maybe I'll meet someone nice."

The statement made her frown. She started to say something, apparently thought better of it, and waited as if she thought whatever was festering inside me would work its way to the surface by itself eventually.

The walls in Roper's were vibrating when I walked in with Rosie Clemente and Peter Wills. I wore boots, jeans and a T-shirt under an open vest.

Peter shouted. "Do you want something to drink?" I shook my head and walked straight to the line dance, elbowing my way through the already rollicking crowd. I wanted to be out from under Peter's watchful eyes.

As usual, I danced until my hair lay plastered in ringlets against my face and sweat trickled down my neck. I turned down every guy who asked me to dance or offered to buy me a drink. Eventually I went to the bar and ordered a large water with lemon.

"Hey, honey," a man's voice crooned, "you got the mean reds? I can help."

I turned a jaundiced look his way. He was middle-aged, wore two flashy diamond rings, a gold chain around his neck and his shirt open to the waist. His gray hair was long, slicked back into a ponytail and his jeans were tight. "What happened? Your boyfriend stand you up?"

I answered with a grimace.

"No, he didn't." The male voice which came from behind me was marvelously familiar. I spun.

The profile was almost the face I longed to see, but not quite. An arm snaked around my waist. The voice, the familiar touching were nearly right, but not. And the scent was all wrong. Hope shattered as I looked into the face of . . . Paul Wills. With no regard for his feelings at all, I groaned and said, "I don't want you either." With that, I whirled and darted out the door. I flagged down a couple I knew just as they drove up and asked them to run me home. They were gracious and didn't ask any questions or complain at such an imposition.

At home, I shot through the empty house, up the back stairs, opened my windows to the hot south wind, stripped down to my panties, tossed on a T-shirt and flung myself over the bed. Not knowing what else to do, I buried my face in my pillow and bawled, great crocodile tears. Later, almost against my will, I slept.

In the early morning hours I roused when the back stairs creaked, then was frightened by a large, dark figure silhouetted in the doorway to my room. I started to scream but something prevented it. Two steps closer and he knelt beside my bed. "Are you awake?" This time the voice was right. Exactly right.

"Jim?"

"Yes."

"Are you a dream?" I waited, but the voice and—this time—the fragrance both were totally accurate.

He laughed quietly in the darkness.

"Is it really you?" I asked again.

"Yes. Who were you expecting?"

I didn't care about the earlier injury or my hurt pride or anything but holding him. I opened my arms and he came up over me and into my clutches. He kissed me once, then again and over and over, sealing our bodies until there was no space between us. Finally, as if it took Herculean effort, he stretched out beside me, although we remained attached.

"What time is it?" I whispered.

He yawned and stretched an arm over his head. "Nearly three-thirty. I have to catch a flight out of Dominion at eight-forty-five."

"You're here for five hours?"

"That's right."

"I'm sorry. . . ." I began, but the words caught in my throat. I didn't know where to start or how to explain my emotional upheaval.

"I know." He brushed the hair away from my face. "I am too. I wish you'd try to hold onto this one concept. When we're apart, the separation is harder on me than it is on you. Always has been."

"Not possible."

"Oh, yeah, possible."

"It keeps getting worse."

"For me, too." His voice sounded tired. "Would you mind if we. . . ." he didn't finish.

"What?"

"Could we sleep? Just for a little while?"

I turned onto my side to face him, allowing him half the narrow bed. He propped his head on his arm on his half of my pillow. The breeze through my south window was brisk. By the time I pulled the sheet up over us, Jim was already asleep.

The only light in the room was the night light of the cloudless sky through the windows. I lay there a long time gazing at his face, trying to sort out and maybe label my feelings.

Although he appeared helpless enough at that moment, I felt both comforted and threatened by such a virile presence in my bed. He always claimed I was free to go my own way. Why, then, did I have the feeling I was caught in a vise?

At the same time I lay there feeling threatened. How could such inner turmoil create a glow of pure contentment?

We had no commitment. I was not bound to him, certainly not committed sexually, yet this was precisely where I wanted to be. At the moment, my only desire was to stay close enough to Jim to be able to touch him when I wanted.

Recently I had noticed a subtle, peculiar change in my thinking. Once, in my eager enthusiasm, I had thought Riley Wedge would never call. More often now, I felt an odd dread anticipating the same call.

A frown pinching my face, I dozed, but close to the surface of consciousness, aware of every sound, every movement, enjoying his nearness and the scent of him. Yet I knew I must be sleeping because the time on the digital clock at my bedside galloped forward.

Sunlight roused me fully awake at six. I opened my eyes to slits. I lay facing the sunshine peeking through the east window. I heard Jim breathing deeply, steadily behind me and I smiled. I didn't dare move.

Several minutes passed before I rolled carefully. I wanted to be able to see him in the light. But he roused with my movement as I propped on an elbow to look at him.

His appearance surprised me. He was tanned, his deeper color emphasized by the icy blue cotton V-neck sweater he wore, and he was noticeably thinner. The waist of his khaki trousers appeared to be gathered in tucks but his belt was hidden beneath the sweater. His eyes were only slits, but he smiled.

I smiled back, tentatively. "You don't even look like you."

Jim rolled onto his back and stretched. Mischievously pushing my shoulder, he slid me precariously close to the edge of the bed before I grabbed his hand to save myself. He patted his stomach and locked his dark eyes on my face. "I lost a little weight."

"Doing what?"

"Calisthenics. Running eight miles a day. Surviving on varmint a couple of times. Jumping out of airplanes. Rappelling down parking garages and mountains, then sitting in classes and toiling in a chemistry lab. It's been tough. But the worst part was worrying about holding onto you while I was going through hell for you."

"For me?" My voice definitely sounded accusatory. "What are you talking about? You're not doing this for me."

"Yes," he said emphatically, rolling onto his side and propping his face on his hand, "I am. The more I can do, the better they like me, and the more valuable I am."

"But you like things the way they are. You like your job. You make plenty of money. You like your life the way it is."

"Yes I do, but you don't. So I've got to work my way into a job where we can hobnob with the fat cats. That's what you want, isn't it?"

"But it isn't what you want." I was getting confused.

He looked annoyed. "We always come back to this same conversation, Jancy. You are what I want. You want to travel and meet important people. You don't have to work for a news service to do that. Besides, the way I understand it, hanging out with big wigs comes later for a news hound. First, you have to pay your dues.

"I see pictures of correspondents reporting from gutted buildings in the Middle East and disease-infested villages in Africa, ducking live rounds and getting thin and sickly because there's starvation and disease and death in places where important news happens. I don't want you in those places."

Flabbergasted, I didn't speak, so he continued.

"Sweetheart, you liked covering Bubba Valentine's first trial but by the third go-round, you were bored. I think it'll be the same shaking hands with presidents and kings. When you've seen one, you've seen 'em all. But if it's presidents and kings you want, I'll try to get you there.

"Personally, I think those people in the press shoving and elbowing each other to ask some insipid celebrity some inane question is demeaning, not to mention that some of the crap reporters come up with is more gossip than news."

I glowered at him for degrading my profession, but I didn't really feel like arguing.

"You've got a lot of talent, Jance." His tone was softer. "In many different areas. I don't want to see you wind up with rigor mortis behind some sand dune. I want you with me. That'll make me happy. You want fame and fortune. That's what you think will make you happy. I'll do whatever it takes to get you there.

"Bottom line is just like I said: I'm going through this hell for you."

Twisting, I sat up on the side of the bed, putting my back to him, and drew a deep breath, then I peered over my shoulder into his smoldering eyes. "So you're saying I'm supposed to sacrifice my dreams and you'll sacrifice your contentment to try to provide your version of my dreams for me, is that what you're thinking?"

"I'm thinking," there was an edge to his voice, "that you don't have any idea what you really want."

"But you do . . . know what I want?"

"I watched you at the lake, coloring with Amanda, fishing, tightening the sail on the catamaran, working puzzles with Mom, talking politics with Dad. You belong there, Jancy, in that life. You know it as well as I do. You're just too stubborn to admit it."

I looked away, not wanting him to see my face.

"Don't deny it." He hesitated then he sat up on the opposite side of the bed, putting us back to back. "If you can't see it now, maybe you will later." He paused a minute. "Anyway, until then, I'm going to try to get us where you think you want to be. I can do it too. All it takes is determination and a little sacrifice." He looked back over his shoulder at me just as I risked a look at him and our eyes met. "To me, you're worth it." He rolled his shoulders. "But no more bellyaching or cracks about finding somebody else. I can promise you one thing, Dewhurst, there isn't anyone anywhere who will ever love you more than I do, or who will try as hard as I will to make you happy, no matter who they are or what they say."

I turned full around to study his face more closely. "I can't tell if you are real smart, Jim, or real dumb."

He shot me a disdainful glance. "I have above-average intelligence. Drooling over you just makes me look stupid. And here I am, AWOL, flying all night, my only night off, in clothes I've worn for two days, to set things right with you."

Awash with new understanding, I got up and walked around the bed. I knelt beside him, smiled and patted his knee. "I've never tried to see things from your perspective before. I appreciate what you're doing, now that I have a better idea of why you're doing it."

He winced. "Sure you do."

What we needed was a definite change of mood. "Would you do me one little favor?"

He shrugged and shook his head. "Well, sure, honey. What's one more?"

"Will you let me watch you shave?"

A slow smile relaxed his face. Roughly, he lifted me by my

elbows and threw me onto the bed beside him. He scrubbed my nape with the three-day growth of beard on his chin before he grabbed my hand and pulled me up to stand beside him.

He'd left his bag just inside my bedroom door. Rummaging in it, he found his dop kit. "Come on."

I was suddenly intimidated and embarrassed. "I can let you have a little time in there by yourself. I'll make coffee."

"Good. And, sweetheart, don't feel like you have to put on clothes for me."

Looking down, I realized I was wearing only panties and a T-shirt that was barely long enough to cover them. I grabbed the hem of the shirt and yanked it down, bending my knees to make it feel longer.

Jim laughed and shook his head as he picked up his bag and strolled to the bathroom.

Closing the bedroom door, I dressed quickly, rolling on deodorant, fitting a bra, topping cargo shorts with an olive drab T-shirt and a khaki vest, then splashing on cologne.

A glance in the mirror and I was horrified. Mascara from the night before had bled under my eyes—a result of my crying jag—giving me a distinctively raccoon look. My hair, wet when I went to bed, was plastered stiffly against my head.

I flew to the bathroom downstairs, scrubbed my face—with special attention to removing the mascara—brushed my teeth, combed my hair back and secured it.

Remembering the promised coffee, I ran to the kitchen to start the pot, then located my purse and hurried back to the bathroom to dab on my usual minimal make-up.

Returning to the kitchen, I poured a cup of coffee and practically jogged back up the stairs. I had just finished pulling up the bed when Jim called softly.

It suddenly occurred to me I hadn't bothered to alert my housemates to Jim's presence. It was probably wise not to wake them at six-thirty on a Sunday morning to tell them I had a male house guest, a violation of one of our cardinal rules. Besides, Angela wore very sexy sleep wear.

I tiptoed back to the hallway and whispered, "Ready." I took the straight-backed chair from the desk in my room and the cup of coffee.

Jim was wearing only khaki slacks, which rode a little higher over his hips and lower in front. He looked thinner, but somehow his muscles were better defined than they had been before. I could not take my eyes off his gorgeous upper body and the muscles in his arms. I put the chair in the hall outside the bathroom so I could get a full view both of Jim and of his reflection in the mirror over the sink.

Gratefully, he took a sip of the coffee I handed him, then set the cup on the lavatory and began patting shaving foam onto his face.

His biceps flexed as he smoothed his skin with his left hand in front of the stroke of the safety razor in his right. I watched, mesmerized. When he caught me flagrantly admiring him, he froze until my eyes met his in the mirror, then he smiled. Self-conscious, I diverted my gaze.

He laughed lightly. "Look all you want. It's yours."

With what may have been pride of ownership, I sat riveted as he rinsed off the soapy residue. I swallowed hard before I spoke. "Will you let me do that sometime?"

"Give me a shave?" He grinned at me in the mirror. "I don't think so."

"Please."

"Maybe. Sometime. When you've earned the privilege."

I knew better than to ask the obvious question. "Now, what?" I followed him down the hall as he returned the chair to my room.

"We shower."

"Excuse me?"

"We slept together. Showering together's not that big a leap."

"We shared a bed. We didn't actually sleep together."

"I've never been all that good at semantics." His taunting grin continued. "It was worth a shot. Anyway, I shower and dress, then you drive me to the airport where I get a boarding pass. After that we go to Mass or out to eat."

"We can't talk in church."

"Breakfast it is."

As we drove, Jim said he wished I could go with him, spend the Fourth of July in D.C. He would be gone for four weeks, would call me once or twice a week and would try to write every day.

At the airport, he got a boarding pass and we had breakfast at the restaurant there, talking, laughing, occasionally arguing about the merits of jury trials or how the Democrats might best prevail in the upcoming elections. As the hands on the clock passed eight, I got pensive. I held my marauding emotions firmly in check, until they called his flight.

I didn't want him to see my face distorted, but he caught my chin and forced me to look at him. My mouth and chin quivered. Nearly blinded by unshed tears, I tried to jerk my head to the side, but Jim held firm. When I risked a look, he was smiling.

"These are genuine, aren't they?" He rubbed a thumb through the tears that had begun trickling down my cheeks.

I nodded.

"Because you're going to miss me?"

I nodded again.

"Only God knows how much I love you." He grinned broadly. "May He watch between me and thee while we are absent. . . ." He kissed me then, actually for the first time since he'd arrived. Gently, he pushed me away from him, picked up his bag and hurried down the tunnel to his flight. I just stood there blubbering like a leaky faucet.

CHAPTER TWENTY-FIVE

Bubba Valentine called on Tuesday night, July eleventh, to ask if I would meet him. He wanted to discuss something we couldn't talk about over the phone. I stalled him until Thursday, thinking I needed to give his request some serious thought.

For one thing, I didn't want to be seen with Bubba. His reputation had deteriorated with the hoopla of each new trial. Still, I couldn't help being curious about what he wanted to tell me. After two days of soul searching, I called him back.

"Name the place and time," he said.

I suggested Como's, a small restaurant near the campus. Seven-thirty. Business on campus was slow in the summer session and I figured the chances of running into any of my coworkers or housemates at Como's on a Thursday night were slim.

I didn't mention Bubba's call or our dinner plans when I talked to Jim on the telephone Wednesday night, deciding the report would be easier for him to take when I had other information to put with it.

During supper, Bubba and I made small talk. I told him about my adventures at the Wills' cabin up by Skelter. Bubba pretended to be interested and asked polite questions—how long a trip it was and how a person was able to find the place out in the boonies like that.

He in turn provided gossip from the *Gambler,* which I absorbed with delight. Bubba used colorful phrases and his view of events and the behavior of gamblers was very different from mine; sometimes, I had to admit, more insightful.

"Chloe's pregnant," Bubba said, after a brief period of silence over dessert. He watched me closely. I tried to hide my surprise behind a hurried sip of water, then decided some surprise was to be expected.

"She's saying it's G.C.'s," he continued. "It's not. It's mine. She won't say so, but it has to be."

I dabbed my mouth with my napkin. "She must be pretty far along if she can even say it's G.C.'s. He died at Christmas."

Bubba nodded, looking at his plate.

"What do the Gideons think about it?"

"Them?" His face looked relieved. "They're tickled to death. They never knew nothin' about Chloe and me. I've been trying everything I can think of to get Chloe to marry me."

"Why won't she?"

"Says she don't love me. Says she never did. I told her I knew better. I could have told if she hadn't. She says I never loved her or I would have done what she asked me to do about G.C. when she asked me to do it, that I would not have waited around until he asked me.

"I done a dumb thing then. I told her about Mr. Chase asking me also. She hit the ceiling." He paused. "There's something else, which is why I really wanted to talk to you."

"What is it?"

"See them two guys over talking to the busboy?" I checked out the two men. One, his brown hair neatly styled, wore a nicely fitted, expensive suit and alligator tassel loafers. He stood with one foot propped in the seat of a booth, counting change in his hand and talking to the kid busing tables. He wore a large, flashy gold nugget ring.

The second man was of medium height and had acne scars that were obvious even in the dim light. His less expensive suit hung loose on his tall, slender frame and he kept swiping at the shock of brown, unkempt hair that persisted in falling into his eyes as he studied his reflection in a smoked mirror and scratched at something on his chin. His eyes met mine in the mirror. He suddenly turned and said something to his companion, and they trailed the busboy into the kitchen.

"Yes," I said, answering Bubba's question. "Who are they?"

"From out of town. I think they might be here working a contract."

"You think they've been hired to kill someone?"

"Yeah."

The hair bristled on the back of my neck. "Who?"

Bubba looked around, suddenly nervous when the strangers were out of his sight. "Me." He said it without emotion.

"Why?"

"Someone wanting to get even for something I done before. Someone wanting to keep me quiet about something. I don't know. They've been on me since Sunday. I wanted you to see 'em, so you can identify them later, if it comes to that. Did you get a good look at 'em?"

I nodded, but the bristling hairs moved down my arms. "Are you scared?"

Bubba got up without answering and I followed him to the cashier. He made me put away my money, insisting he'd pay since he'd invited me.

When we got outside, the parking lot was as dark as ink. Clouds had obscured all light from the sky and the area was sparsely lit by two single-bulb yard lights. Bubba bent over like he wanted to tie his shoe. Instead, he pulled up his pant leg and I glimpsed what looked like a holster of some kind. I was just going to ask about it when a carload of kids wheeled into the deserted parking lot. Since we were the only other people around, they hooted and waved like we were friends.

Bubba grabbed my arm and we walked quickly to my car, which was parked near the front of the lot a long way from his pickup truck in the shadows at the back.

The kids got out of their SUV laughing and talking, obviously in no hurry. Playing the gentleman, Bubba stopped beside my car to wait until I was inside, then proceeded to his truck. He seemed a little annoyed about the kids but they didn't really bother me.

Saturday afternoon, July fifteenth, Bubba Valentine's mother called. They hadn't seen Bubba since he left Thursday night to meet me at Como's. Mrs. Valentine thought Bubba might be staying with me. I told her we had parted in the parking lot at Como's about ten-thirty. I asked if they had checked with his other friends.

"He's not on the *Gambler,* and Chloe has not seen him either." His mother sounded worried.

I assured her I would let her know if I heard anything.

"We got kind of a strange call," Mrs. Valentine said, just as I was about to hang up. "A man who said he was a friend of Bubba's from the *Gambler.* Said he wanted to know the name of the girl Bubba was dating now. I told him I didn't know Bub was dating anyone. The man got rude. I told him to give me his number and I'd have Bubba call him back. He hung up."

I thanked her for the information. Each of us promised to call the other as soon as we heard from Bubba.

I hung up the phone and called Sheriff Dudley Roundtree right then. I told him Bubba might be missing, about my having had dinner with him on Thursday night, about Bubba's suspicions and then I described the two men Bubba had pointed out at Como's.

Roundtree listened attentively as I told him about the call only moments before from Mrs. Valentine and about the unidentified man wanting to know the name of the girl Bubba was dating. I assumed the caller was referring to me, since Bubba had taken me to dinner.

The sheriff had me repeat the descriptions of the men twice, then asked me to see the police artist in the fine arts building at the university on Monday morning for sketches of the two. Meanwhile, Roundtree would find Bubba's tag number and put out a bulletin on his truck.

Bubba did not turn up until the next Sunday when honeymooners from out-of-state camping up by the big lake made a grisly discovery.

He'd been dead several days. His wallet and jewelry identified the remains. Birds and animals had gnawed away most of his exposed flesh. The coroner said he was severely beaten, had suffered several broken bones before his death.

Early Monday Sheriff Roundtree called to let me know about Bubba's death before his identity was made public. The Valentines were being notified.

In the ladies' restroom at the *Clarion*, I wept angry tears. Not having anyone really good to confide in, after work I went for a walk to clear my head of cobwebs and disconnected thoughts.

G.C. Gideon had died quickly at his own request at the hand of his friend. Had others broken bones and tortured Bubba, taking out their frustrations at missing G.C. on the unknowing bodyguard? Did that make sense in some criminal's mind?

Valentine thought the contract on him might have come from some disgruntled customer from his past, but he hadn't given me any specifics. Had they tortured him trying to force him to confess something?

They must have wanted him to implicate someone, to name an accomplice or maybe an employer. They might have been after the name of someone who hired him for a specific job.

Another nagging question: G.C.'d had Chloe for years, treating her badly. Bubba had her a short while, treating her well. Why hadn't she preferred the kinder man?

Of course, G.C. had been rich or, at least, the son of a rich man.

I walked toward home deep in thought, oblivious to people or vehicles around me until sheriff's deputy Gary Spence cruised up and stopped.

"Hey, beautiful, want a ride?"

"Hi, Gare. What are you doing here?"

"Just passing. What are you doing wandering around this time of night?"

"What time is it?"

"Nine-thirty. Little girls need to be in before dark or at least be out with someone big and strong like me."

"Don't leer like that, Spence. If I was carrying my pepper spray, a masher like you would be in a world of hurt."

The deputy laughed, then his face turned serious. "The sheriff has us keeping an eye on you, missy. What are you doing tonight?"

"I'm going home right now." I felt a twinge of orneriness. "How do you feel about jogging in the morning? Six-ish?"

"Nah, I'll be sawing logs about then. Why don't we all just sleep in."

It was my turn to smile. "Okay." I turned and trotted home, waving to him as I jogged through our front door.

I called Jim and was surprised when he answered his telephone before ten. He was seldom in his room that early. I expected the answering machine. I told him cheerily about the pleasant events of the week before the lull in the conversation.

The man had telepathy. "What's happened?"

It was show time. I took a deep breath and started at the beginning. I told him about my having dinner with Bubba on

Thursday. He didn't comment. And about the men Bubba had pointed out at Como's, adding the fact that I was keeping Roundtree posted on all developments. Jim remained ominously silent, which probably shouldn't have given me courage, but it did. I spieled the story more slowly as I told him about Mrs. Valentine's call on Saturday.

"Did you call Roundtree after you talked to her?"

"Yes, I did." My voice sounded brittle. It was a struggle to keep from crying. "Jim, Bubba's dead."

"Oh." He didn't exactly sound surprised. "I'm sorry to hear that." I remembered all over again that Jim had never particularly liked Bubba.

Sputtering, I provided all the details I knew, then I told him about Gary Spence trailing me.

"Good for Spence," Jim said, but he sounded suspiciously cheerful. "That's easy duty for him. He's always had an eye for you." He paused a minute. "Jancy, be smart. Don't depend on anyone else for your safety. Stay alert. Pay attention to where you are and who's around you. It'd probably be best not to go walking alone any more after dark."

"They don't know who I am."

"They will."

"There's no reason for them to come after me." I wasn't sure whether I was trying to assure him or me.

"You saw their faces." He paused again. "Let Roundtree and Spence keep an eye on you. Make it easy for them. I'll be back in less than a week. Stay out of trouble until then."

I promised to try, but his warnings made me jumpy and my nervousness increased when, on July twenty-fourth, Jesse Chase walked out to the *Choctaw Gambler* parking lot, got into his town car, turned the ignition key and got blown to kingdom come.

Chapter Twenty-Six

Alarmed by the violent deaths of Bubba Valentine and Jesse Chase, I got concerned about Chloe Conklin and called her. She sounded untroubled on the phone but agreed to let me drive out to the ranch to talk to her.

I was nervous as I turned into the long drive that traversed the Two Bell. Activity at the ranch looked much as it had on my first visit, with spotty herds of cattle, this time collected in tight clusters at the shade of trees dotting the pastures. The heat prohibited most activity, with the exception of the spring's new arrivals who romped and cavorted, butting one another. I laughed at their antics and the sound brightened my gloom.

Full-blown pregnant in a loose, knee-length turquoise caftan, and barefooted, Chloe's bronzed American Indian skin glowed with vitality.

She invited me inside and then led me along a path through toys strewn about the living room. The house smelled faintly of ammonia or soiled diapers or a litter box or a combination of all of those.

We sat at opposite ends of a long sofa. Its flowered cushions were stained, felt damp and smelled faintly of Lysol. The worn upholstery flowers on the arms had faded to shadows. I perched on the edge of my seat, but Chloe leaned back, relaxed, comfortable.

I pulled a steno pad out of my purse and looked around for children. As if anticipating my question, Chloe said, "They're down for rest time."

I took the plunge. "Have any law enforcement people talked to you about Bubba?"

"Why would they? He was G.C.'s friend. He didn't hang around here after G.C. died."

"Bubba said you loved each other. He wanted to marry you." I was careful to keep any accusation out of my voice.

Chloe glared at me a moment, then lowered her eyes to her hands folded demurely in her lap. "So?" she shrugged. "I loved him, too, in a way. He was nice to me when I needed someone. What does he have to do with anything?"

I looked intently into Chloe's face, trying to see the truth. "Chloe, Bubba worked for Jesse Chase and now both of them are dead. Doesn't it seem to you like there might be a connection?"

The other woman shrugged again as if moving her shoulders would absolve her. "Could be, but it doesn't have anything to do with me."

"The coroner thinks Bubba was tortured before he died. His killer wanted information. Do you have any idea what information Bubba might have had that someone wanted that badly?"

Chloe shook her head. Ripples in her long, black hair caught the sunlight filtering through the window behind her, turning the color almost blue. It reminded me of Jim's dark, dark hair.

"Have you had any unusual visitors or phone calls?" I asked.

Again Chloe answered with a shake of her silken head.

I took a deep breath and decided to try another subject. "It looks as if you and the Gideons have worked out any differences you had in the past." I sat back on the divan. "Will you and your children be staying here permanently?"

Chloe cast a suspicious glance. "Why do you want to know?"

"I wondered if the ranch would be safe from creditors now, after the insurance company paid you."

"Yes, it's safe. Plus, Mrs. Gideon has decided I'll need more room with another child. They need less. We're going to switch houses. They're moving down here. The kids and I will be moving to the big house. It was her idea. Really."

"That's very gracious of her."

"Yes. Of course, I am the mother of their grandchildren, their only living relatives. They want the children to be raised in the house where their beloved G.C. grew up. They want my children to turn out to be just like G.C."

"Are they like him?" It was easier to follow the conversational path Chloe chose than to try to steer her where she obviously did not want to go.

"No, they are not. They care about other people's feelings. G.C. never cared about anyone but him, not his parents, not me, not the kids, no one. The Gideons want to buy my kids all the stuff they bought G.C." Chloe glanced around, indicating the array of toys. "I make the kids do chores. They help fix meals and wash dishes and fold laundry. My big boy is six. When he shows his temper, I paddle him until he screams. I'm not going to raise another G.C. Gideon if I can help it."

I nodded. "And the new baby, do you think it will be like the others?"

Chloe looked startled, then her eyes narrowed. "He might be different. He might be nicer, being the third kid and all. We'll just have to wait and see."

I stood up and closed my notebook. This was a waste of time. It was obvious Chloe was not willing to confide any secrets in me.

"Can I ask you a question?" she said out of the blue.

"Yes."

"What's the story on that guy you hang out with?"

Jim. She had eyeballed him often in and outside the courtroom. "He's an agent with the State Bureau of Investigation.

His name's Jim Wills."

"Is he . . . ?" she stammered. "Is he yours?"

I blurted an embarrassed laugh. "No. No, I wouldn't call him mine."

"Then you're saying he's fair game."

That seemed like an odd thing for a woman in her condition to say. Looking for a new man when she was full-blown pregnant seemed strange. Besides that, she didn't have a very good track record with men. Both of her most recent interests were deceased.

I didn't say any of those thoughts out loud. Instead, I said, "I suppose." I picked up my purse, stuck the notebook inside and dug out the car keys. "Chloe, I appreciate your talking with me. If I can ever do anything to help, give me a call."

Chloe rose and walked me to the door wordlessly, looking a little puzzled. "Did you ask me everything you wanted to know?"

I looked directly into her face and smiled. "Did you tell me everything you wanted to tell me?" Chloe's smile mirrored mine, but she didn't answer, so I added, "Maybe we can get together again another time."

She nodded. Her mouth was still smiling, but her dark eyes grew shrouded in what I assumed was an effort to hide other thoughts.

That night on the phone, I told Jim about the interview, detailing the conversation and also giving him my read on the undercurrent of meaning that seemed to flow beneath our words, particularly listening for any comment he might have about Chloe's veiled personal interest in him. He didn't comment on any of what I said.

"Do I get to pick you up at the airport Sunday?" I asked, finally, after giving him time to talk.

"Yes." His voice sounded deeper, more serious than usual, as it had the last week or so.

"Jim, is something wrong? Tell me."

"Nothing's wrong. Why do you keep asking me that?"

"You sound different. Have you gotten close to the people in your classes?"

"Yeah, a couple."

"Men or women?"

"Wrong." He barked a mirthless laugh. "They make it bearable. They are not substitutes for you."

"You just sound different."

"I've been a little under the weather since Quantico. I don't have much zip. I figure being around you will get me well in a hurry. Four more days. I can stand on my head for four days. My flight gets in at two-thirty Sunday afternoon. Can you be there?"

"Wild horses couldn't keep me away."

"Your enthusiasm coming over the phone gives me a lift, but I can't wait to hold all that energy in my arms."

On my usual courthouse rounds Friday I stopped by the court clerk's office, exchanging noisy hellos with the girls, including Angela Fires. But I was dumbstruck when the lone customer turned around and I was standing face to face with one of the men Bubba Valentine had pointed out at Como's the Thursday night before his death—the slouchy dresser with the acne.

Trying not to let him see I recognized him, I pivoted on a heel and left the clerk's office.

"Who was that?" the stranger asked one of the clerks.

Having noticed Jancy's odd behavior, Angela tried to signal the other girl, but it was too late.

"Does she work around here?" His interest earned him an earful about Jancy Dewhurst. Angela, meanwhile, stepped into the court clerk's private office and made a phone call.

Obviously satisfied with the outcome of his non business in the clerk's office, the visitor got to the exit just in time to open the door for Sheriff Dudley Roundtree, swelled to his full six-foot-four and looking decidedly grim. The sheriff backed from the doorway. "I'd like to speak with you a minute, sir." Roundtree's official baritone boomed, echoing in the silent hallway.

The man frowned, looked Roundtree up and down, then yielded. He started to retreat into the clerk's office, but Roundtree tipped his head, indicating he wanted to talk outside.

The sheriff led the way to a secluded spot near the water fountain. "Do you mind telling me who you are."

The man hesitated.

"Friend, we can do this anyway you want." Roundtree's tone made his voice sound like more of a growl.

Wordlessly, the man produced a Florida driver's license. His name was Jose Torres, thirty-seven years old. The picture and description matched.

Roundtree returned the license. "I understand you've been asking questions about Jancy Dewhurst." Torres didn't speak. "I'd like to know why."

The man shrugged. "She's an attractive woman." Torres had a distinctly Spanish accent. "Perhaps I will ask her for a date."

Roundtree shook his head, obviously not liking the answer, but Torres was cool and remained silent. The sheriff glared at him. "Jancy's a personal friend of mine." Again Roundtree's baritone became an ominous rumble. "She doesn't want to go out with you. Now, how long do you plan to be in town?"

"Not long."

"That's probably best. While you're here, we'll be keeping an eye on you." Roundtree turned away, then looked back over his shoulder. "And don't be asking any more questions about Dewhurst. Do we understand each other?"

Torres nodded and flashed what appeared to be an intention-
ally phony smile. His lips turned up at the ends but his dark
eyes stared coldly.

Roundtree watched Torres leave the building, then hurried
back to his office.

Deputy Gary Spence and I talked while we waited. As soon as
the sheriff walked into his reception room, however, I turned
my full attention on him. "I saw you talking to that guy. He was
one of the men Bubba thought was following him. Who is he?"

The sheriff strode quickly into his private office. "Funny you
should ask. He was asking questions about you." Rudely, he
closed the door in my face. Later, Spence told me the sheriff
had faxed a query to the Florida State Police and the Dade
County Sheriff's Office regarding Jose Torres and included the
number he'd memorized off the man's driver's license.

Meanwhile, in the outer office, Spence gave me a chastening
look. "You got some other guy on the ropes over you, Dewhurst?" My face must have betrayed my concern. Spence said,
"Come on. Lighten up, you don't need to worry about him."

I wished I could be as sure as he was.

It took me three changes of clothes to dress Sunday before I
was satisfied with a sleeveless, scooped-neck chambray dress
with white buttons neckline to hem.

I left for the airport at straight-up noon, took my time and
arrived there at twelve-thirty-two p.m., two hours early.

I located Jim's flight on the schedule board, verified it was on
time, walked to the designated waiting area, put quarters in a
chair/TV, then wandered away while it played.

Most of the shops on the concourse were open. I browsed
some, bought a couple of morning papers and a soft drink, then
ambled back to the waiting area where several people had

gathered. My stomach churned with anticipation as I imagined Jim coming through the doorway.

After what seemed like eons, I watched his plane land and then negotiate the taxiway to settle against the accordion tunnel that would usher him into the terminal. I stepped back to allow others surging forward to meet their arrivals. My eyes locked on the doorway as passengers appeared and then cleared the darkened opening.

My breath caught when I saw him.

He looked tired—his dark eyes couched in sunken sockets— and thinner than he had looked on his surprise visit. His shirt collar hung loose around his neck.

Realizing my face would give me away, I consciously brightened just as Jim's hollow eyes found me.

He carried his AWOL bag and an armful of reading materials.

I waited for him to thread his way through the crowd, then I stepped up to wrap my arms around him and kiss the side of his face when he didn't bend to let me at his lips. I thought maybe he was self-conscious among so many other people but, oh, he smelled good. He shifted his AWOL bag from one hand to the other and draped an arm around my shoulders. I was surprised that my own arm looped nearly all the way around his slim waist. That's when I looked hard into his face and again noticed the dark circles under his eyes.

"You look terrible," I said.

He laughed and squeezed my shoulders. "You look good enough for both of us."

I led him to the claiming area to pick up his other baggage, then to daytime parking.

Waves of heat radiated from the concrete and there was virtually no breeze. Jim walked briskly in spite of the heat. I felt relieved that he exuded his usual energy, despite his appearance.

"Where to?" I sounded like a cabbie. Unlike a pro, I failed to notice the gray mid-size car following us.

Jim sighed. "Home."

He put his arm on the back of the seat and rested his chin against it, his half-closed eyes focused on me. "I'm going to sleep for a week. Will you join me?"

I laughed as I pulled to a traffic light and returned his gaze. He needed a shave and his eyes were bloodshot. Even with all that, he was the most gorgeous man I had ever seen. Of course, a big part of the attraction for me was knowing the man.

We chatted pleasantly, exchanging newsy tidbits of mundane events in our lives apart from one another.

At his house, I helped carry his bags inside and was vaguely aware of a gray car that pulled to the curb across the street and parked. Normally there weren't many cars on Jim's street in the middle of the day when most residents were at work.

Jim seemed listless but I might not have noticed except that he didn't come on with me, touching and teasing and trying to coax me into bed.

"What's the matter?" I asked finally, watching him pace to the swinging door to the kitchen.

"I guess it's the heat. And the house is stuffy." He flipped the thermostat and the air-conditioning unit outside roared to life.

I was all but levitating, happy just to be in the same room with him. "Do you want to cook here or eat out?"

He looked a little embarrassed. "I'm not hungry now, are you?"

That wasn't like him and my casual concern put out roots.

"Jance, I'm beat. Let's crash a while, till I can get caught up, okay?" He picked up the remote, turned on the television and slumped onto the couch.

I relieved him of the remote and turned the TV off. "No. Come on, let's take you upstairs and put you to bed where you can really rest. I'll go to the grocery store and fix supper here. Steaks on the grill to celebrate."

Again his reaction was suspiciously subdued.

"Is that okay?"

He stood and let me bully him up the stairs without much of a fight. I was still wary. This was not the Jim Wills I knew and loved. He sank onto the side of his bed, on top of the bedspread, and yawned.

"It's awfully hot," he said. "Why don't you lie down here with me for a little while. As tired as I am, I'm harmless. You don't have to worry. We can stretch out, take a little nap together with no one around to interrupt."

I thought about that while keeping an incredulous eye on him. "Speaking of interruptions, what about your folks?"

"I have the week off." His smile looked like it took extra effort. "I'll run up to Dominion and maybe even on to Skelter Monday or Tuesday while you're working. Mom's nose was out of joint about my not calling them when I dropped in on you that night. One of Veronica's friends saw us at the airport and mentioned it. I've got a whole week to set injured feelings right before I go back to work."

I walked closer, scrutinizing him carefully. "I didn't even think about your family that night you were here. But you were only in town a couple of hours."

"And," Jim propped a hand on my waist, "a man has his priorities." He pulled me toward him but I dropped to a knee to untie and remove his shoes and lift his feet onto the bed.

"And right now," I said in my practical tone, "sleep is this man's top priority."

He caught my hand just before it was beyond his reach. "Not so." He tugged, forcing me to sit beside him. That's when I finally realized his arm wasn't just its usual warm. It was hot. I put my hand to his forehead.

"Jim Wills, you've got a fever." I scurried to the bathroom, where I rummaged to turn up bottles of aspirin, non-aspirin and another pain reliever. "What do you usually take?"

"Nothing. I'll just sleep it off."

I got two non-aspirin and a bathroom cup of water.

He took the offering without arguing, which was more weird behavior.

"It's nearly four o'clock," I said. "I'll be back in a couple of hours. Until then, you sleep."

He leaned back and closed his eyes, obviously relieved by that command. "Yes, ma'am."

I went grocery shopping alone, again only subconsciously aware of the gray mid-size that hovered right there in my rear-view mirror as I drove to and from.

I cooked steaks on the charcoal grill outside the sliding glass door at Jim's and baked potatoes in his oven. I sliced tomatoes, cleaned a cantaloupe and fixed garlic bread. During preparations, I ran upstairs several times. Jim didn't stir. He had broken a sweat and was sticky. When I felt his forehead, his fever seemed to be down but not gone.

About seven, I coaxed him awake. "Hey, big boy, are you about ready for something to eat?"

He grinned with his mouth, but didn't open his eyes. "Absolutely." He was gracious but faltered going downstairs and ate only enough to appease me. I didn't press it.

I escorted him back to bed, gave him more non-aspirin, cleaned up the kitchen and locked the doors as I left. Our reunion had been less than auspicious.

Relieved to see the gray sedan was gone, I noticed a white mid-size vehicle, again with no distinctive markings, notable only because of the two men sitting inside reading newspapers.

Of course, they could be looking for a house for sale or meeting someone, but when I glanced their way, little hairs bristled on the back of my neck.

When I didn't hear from Jim all day on Monday, I was reluctant to call. I didn't want to disturb him if he were sleeping. I figured he would let me know when he felt better.

Late in the afternoon, I got his voice mail on both land and cell phones and wondered if maybe he'd gone to visit his parents. Still, it was strange that he didn't call before he left. Of course, I had been at the courthouse all afternoon covering hearings with my cell turned off.

I called both of Jim's phones again on Tuesday and left new messages. I didn't try to camouflage the irritation in my voice. How tough would it be for him to pick up a phone and call? Agitation mounting, I decided if I hadn't heard from him by Wednesday night, I would break a long-standing rule and call him at his parents' house.

Late Wednesday morning Beth Colette, the sister just younger than Jim, called the newsroom. She sounded irked. Had I seen Jim?

"I picked him up at the airport Sunday. He had a fever. He's probably in Dominion at your parents' house."

"No, he's not. I just came from there. Mother called from Skelter. They haven't heard a word from him." Beth took several breaths. "Jancy, it'll take us a couple of hours to get there." Her voice had taken on new urgency. "Will you go check on him? There's a key hidden in a flower pot on the east window ledge in front. Check his house, will you, then call and let me know. Meanwhile, Mom, who is a basket case worrying about him, is on her way."

"I'll go right now." I felt a nagging urgency of my own.

CHAPTER TWENTY-SEVEN

The heat inside was stifling as I slipped through the front door of Jim's condo. I checked the thermostat. Someone had turned the air-conditioning off. The phones were unplugged except for the wall phone in the kitchen by the answering machine.

I called his name softly, not wanting to startle him or awaken him if he were sleeping. Hairs bristled a warning along the back of my neck, prodding me to hurry, yet at the same time making me apprehensive.

Upstairs the air was even more acrid than it had been below, hot, stale, stuffy. And there was a peculiar odor.

I found Jim lying spread-eagled on his back on the bed, breathing heavily, his face dark with several days' growth of beard, clad only in jogging shorts. The heat and the odor in the room made me gag.

I touched his forehead, which burned with fever.

In the bathroom, the three bottles of pain relievers all lay empty on the vanity.

I set my purse on the counter and fished through it until I located a tin of aspirin and shook three into my hand. The cup dispenser was empty so I rinsed and filled a used one, then returned to the bedroom.

"Wake up, Jim." I touched his shoulder. That close, I realized he was the source of the pungent odor permeating the room. "You have to take some aspirin. Come on, Jim. Wake up."

He groaned.

I propped his head, put the tablets in his mouth and forced him to sip the water.

Moving quickly, I opened the windows, allowing hot, fresh air to displace the hot stale air in the room. I had adjusted the thermostat, but it was going to take the a/c a while to bring things right. At the window, I noticed massive, white thunderheads boiling up in the distance, filling the summer sky.

I got a washcloth from the linen closet, ran cool water over it and began wiping Jim's burning flesh. I wet the cloth repeatedly, bathing him until the aspirin kicked in and his body began to cool. Finally I placed the wrung-out cloth on his forehead.

The room was airing nicely, the temperature dropping, getting some cooperation as the sun disappeared completely behind the approaching rain clouds.

Under the bathroom sink I found cleanser and a sponge and quickly began scrubbing and disinfecting the lavatory, the vanity, floor, stool and even gave the shower a quick once-over.

I tossed used towels into a heap on the floor and had just started to wipe the mirror when Jim roused and halfheartedly told me to stop.

"You have to get up and take a shower," I ordered, ignoring his mumbled objections.

"Get out of here," he said, "I don't want you to get this."

"Why didn't you call me?"

"I don't want you to get this." His voice was stronger with the repetition.

Again I disregarded him entirely, went to his closet and rifled through the built-ins between the hanging bars until I turned up clean jogging shorts and a T-shirt.

I found sheets and towels in the linen closet in the bathroom, hung clean towels on the towel bars and laid fresh sheets and pillow cases on the occasional chair at his bedside. "Come on, tough guy."

He smelled sour and his skin had an odd, yellowish cast, residue from profuse sweating, I supposed.

Using a mix of gentle persuasion and strong-arm tactics, I coaxed him to a sitting position on the side of the bed. His shorts, his pillow case and sheets were all sweat-stained.

Frowning, squinting, Jim tried to wipe away crusts around his mouth and in the corners of his eyes.

"A shower will make you feel better," I announced, sounding more confident than I felt. "If it doesn't, we're going to a doctor."

"No."

"What we do is up to you." I had to concentrate to ignore the way he smelled and keep my gag reflex under control. I helped him to his feet and guided him into the bathroom. "I put out clean towels and there are shorts and a T-shirt to put on when you get out." I indicated the locations of each as I turned on the water and adjusted the spray to tepid.

Jim reached a shaky hand in to test it. "That's too cold."

"It's warm enough. We've got to get your fever down. Leave the temperature set like it is."

He glowered down at the floor and his shoulders slumped.

I was not giving any ground. "I'm going to leave the bathroom door ajar so I can hear if you call me."

He nodded. Slowly, bracing himself on the countertop with one hand, Jim began pulling at the waist to remove his jogging shorts. I stepped out of the bathroom. I wanted to see all of him sometime, but this definitely was not that time.

Wondering that he had needed blankets in this heat, I tossed the two from his bed to the gathering heap of soiled things by the door and held my breath as I stripped the sheets. They were damp and smelled vile. I tossed them toward the hallway, along with the mattress pad, also damp, and his pillows.

I found a clean mattress pad and two new pillows still in

plastic wrap on a shelf in his closet and remade the bed with the fresh linens I had put on the chair earlier. The clean sheets were stiff and smelled as if they had been dried on the clothesline, a big improvement.

The air-conditioning mingling with air coming through the windows continued to cool the room. The bank of dark, dark clouds had completely obliterated the torturous August sun. I cleared a *Bar Journal* and other magazines and books from Jim's bedside table. I could still hear the shower running.

Collecting the dirty sheets and towels, I raced downstairs. The rooms smelled musty below but I would remedy that later. I didn't want to be out of earshot for long. I tossed the collected linens in the floor of the utility room off the kitchen, then scrubbed my hands before I opened a can of chicken noodle soup, added water in a saucepan, and started it heating.

I opened a bottle of vegetable juice, then one of grape, poured them into separate glasses, and filled a large mug with ice and water. I stuck straws in all three beverages.

I found a package of crackers and put it and a jar of peanut butter on a cookie sheet when I couldn't turn up a regular serving tray.

Pouring part of the bubbling soup into a bowl, I loaded the cookie sheet with the drinks, food and utensils and hurried upstairs to set it on the cleared bedside table.

Jim was toweling his hair as he emerged from the bathroom in the clean jogging shorts, minus the T-shirt. He was clean and clean-shaven.

Beaming, I walked over and took the towel to mop beads of water still clinging to his back and shoulders, then I stepped in front to appraise him.

Except for being so gaunt, he looked almost like himself. Even his muscular legs, however, were noticeably thinner. I gave him a gentle pat. He returned my smile but his eyes still had a glassy, feverish look.

"I see you made your bed." He smirked. "Will you lie in it?"

I tried to ignore him, but couldn't conceal the joy I felt at his teasing. "Eat first." I smiled pleasantly, led him to the side of the bed and showed him the tray. The room had grown darker and thunder rumbled in the distance.

Jim sat on the side of the bed. "You don't have to baby me. I'll eat, but I'd rather have some of that steak I left last . . . ah . . . the other night?"

The fact that he didn't even know what day it was prodded my conscience. How could I have let him lie there in that heat suffering for days without checking on him? I stacked the pillows, then pushed him back against them. He groaned as I lifted his legs back onto the bed. He sighed and closed his eyes for a moment before looking at me again.

"This is Wednesday, big boy." I tried to hand him the bowl of soup and spoon, but his hands trembled, so I pulled the side chair closer to the bed and held the bowl as he began spooning down the warm liquid.

"You've been wallowing in the awful heat up here for three days. It's a good thing you're strong. What do you think you've got? Do you think it's a summer virus?" He nodded uncertainly, but didn't look at me, which made me suspicious. "Or what?"

He lifted the bowl of soup to his mouth and drank it down, then wiped his mouth with the paper towel I provided in lieu of a napkin. The breeze through the windows became cool gusts carrying the sweet smell of rain. He breathed deeply, definitely looking more and more like himself.

"We were out of country a couple of days. We'd had shots—immunizations. They said we might have symptoms. It didn't sound like the symptoms would be this bad. They gave us pills."

"Did you take the pills?"

"No. They're in one of my bags downstairs. I was chilling so I went down to turn off the air, but I forgot the pills. I thought I'd wait until I felt better, get them on the next trip down. I haven't been back yet."

I had other questions, but humongous raindrops began pelting the windows. I ran over to close the two on the south, but left the one on the east up. No rain was coming in that one and we both were enjoying the cleansing fragrance.

His eyes followed me. "Could I have the steak now?"

I didn't want to overload his system with too much rich food, but he sounded definite and his hands seemed steadier and his color looked more normal.

"I need to do a couple of things downstairs. I'll be right back with the steak. Meanwhile, see that mug of water?"

Jim glanced at the container and nodded.

"You have to drink a mug of that every thirty minutes. Do you understand?" Before he could object, I added, "And both glasses of juice." I didn't intend to argue. I figure we both knew he was too weak to resist because he nodded solemnly.

Downstairs, I turned off the air-conditioning, then dug through his bags to find the dop kit. Inside, I found quinine pills, which I shoved into my pocket for transport upstairs.

In the kitchen, I put the steak Jim had left Sunday—he'd taken only a few bites—into the microwave to heat and popped two slices of bread into the toaster while I jotted a grocery list, with aspirin, non-aspirin, juices and pop for starters. I poured a cola over ice for him to drink with his steak.

His bedroom smelled like summer rain by the time I got back with the food. Jim looked comfortable as he proudly held up the empty water mug. I handed him the bottle of pills from my pocket, the plate of steak and buttered toast, and took the mug down for a refill of both ice and water.

The driving rain that peppered the windows let up a little before it settled to steady. I opened downstairs windows on the east and the sliding glass door.

I tossed a batch of smelly linens in the washer with extra soap and started the load.

Smiling as I walked back to the stairs, I drew a deep breath of air that smelled sweetly of damp foliage. The breeze was cool. Thunder rumbled in the south, probably heralding the advance of yet more precipitation.

Jim's plate was empty by the time I returned, except for bits of bone and fat. As I picked up his makeshift tray, he caught my wrist and his grip was firm. I put the tray back on the bedside table, then allowed him to pull me down to sit on the bed beside him.

I pretended concern. "The meat was a mistake, wasn't it?"

He laughed and lounged back against the pillows. His eyes had regained their normal glitter. "Big mistake. You'd have been smarter to keep me on the gruel." He gazed at me a long minute, then wordlessly, he shifted to allow me more room. Rearranging pillows, he motioned me down beside him.

Rain again began tapping against the closed windows on the south. I looked at Jim, admiring his face, his arms, his bare chest and legs, all the while slipping my feet out of my sandals. I smoothed my dress as I twisted to face him.

"I like looking at you," I crooned and couldn't help smiling. "The hair on your chest is like a lion's mane. On your stomach," I gestured timidly, careful not to touch him, "it all runs to the middle, like little tributaries flowing into a great river. And the river runs down, down past your belly button and disappears."

He shook his head. "No, it doesn't."

"Doesn't what?"

"Doesn't disappear. Do you want to see?"

Laughing, I shook my head, suddenly very aware of where we were and that we were alone.

Jim caressed my arm. When his hand reached my shoulder,

he applied gentle pressure.

The rumbling thunder grew louder. Yielding, I put my head on his outstretched arm and eased down, lying on my side facing him, the length of me aligned perfectly with the length of him. I loved the feel of his warm hand on my neck. He kissed my face as that caressing hand slid down my arm.

His mouth very close to my ear, he whispered. "The river flows into the grasslands, where the king lives."

Deftly, he unbuttoned the top buttons of my dress as he nuzzled my throat and the nape of my neck. Without really intending to, I stretched to give him better access. He released the front closure on my bra and pushed it to either side, freeing my breasts, which seemed to celebrate their liberation. I felt vibrantly alive for the first time in weeks.

Jim's tongue followed the outline of my ear as he murmured. "The king is restless. He wants me to bring him my woman." Jim raised up to loom over me and his teasing smile faded as his mouth devoured mine.

I felt his power revive. His arms grew taut and his body swelled with desire. As a reward to myself, I allowed my curious hands the run of his bare chest. He grabbed my leg and rolled, pulling and pushing me until I was astride him.

"Let me help you with that." He grasped the front of my open dress and pulled the unbuttoned top half of it and the unfastened bra back and down off my shoulders, but he stopped when the clothing twisted in the middle of my upper arms. The waded fabric effectively held my arms pinned behind me. I started to object until his mouth hungrily attacked my bare breasts swinging free in front of his face.

At that moment, it seemed the heavens themselves offered thunderous applause as his body began to throb beneath me. I had never felt so powerful, igniting him the way I did at that moment.

Pulling my clothing clear, freeing my arms, Jim rolled again, putting me on my back. He held himself poised over me.

Not at all threatened, I lay there comfortable in my entrapment. My hands followed the line of the bunching muscles in his shoulders and chest. He was magnificent.

Working quickly, breathlessly, he unbuttoned the lower half of my dress. When I felt the fabric fall to either side, exposing all of me, except the part scantily concealed by my panties, I groaned and grabbed for his hands.

My small cry only accelerated the movement of his fingers, exploring where they pleased. I placed my hands on his as they traveled, touching, fondling, caressing me.

"The king wants to meet his prize." Jim's voice sounded husky. He got to his knees straddling me, caught my waist with both hands and lifted, bowing his head as he kissed my stomach. His tongue skewered my belly button, prompting a tiny whine.

I couldn't think. Not only that, I didn't want to think. Jim's hot breath held me in place. My most titillating imaginings had never produced the erotic yearning that seemed to snap all restraints inside me as if they were threads.

Skillfully, the alpha male continued mesmerizing, his hands and his hungry mouth exploring swells and hollows in turn.

Using one knee, he coaxed my thighs apart and I yielded. My hands splayed on his rib cage, I marveled at the heat, the writhing of his body as it swayed to and from me, titillating overly sensitized nerves first here, then there.

My breath caught as he put one hand firmly on the flat of my stomach and inched it down over the lacy panties, which remained in place. His fingers pulsed as they reached and explored that pristine realm between my legs, stimulating eager, involuntary responses. I arched, pressing against him, eager for more, encouraging the groping hand, which I wanted to defeat the panties barring its way.

Sharon Ervin

Slowly, he fitted his body to mine and retreated. Then again.

I raised my torso to meet him as he brought his weight hard against me again and again. I welcomed the hot probe between my legs, that part of him still confined within the jogging shorts. I thrilled as he dominated my aroused body with his own.

I was aware of lightning flashes and the resounding thunder coming in rapid succession, the elements cheering us on.

Jim's mouth consumed mine, his tongue, like his hands, exploring intimate places as if he belonged in those places and I embraced him the same way, writhing and grinding with need, until it burgeoned beyond control and I became still, trying not to hinder him with my beginner's clumsiness.

Suddenly there came what seemed to be a lull in the storm outside and Jim's body froze.

Seconds passed.

I bucked slightly and tightened my arms around his neck. When he didn't respond, I pulled myself closer to scrub my breasts against his chest, hoping to renew his energy. Still, he didn't react. I couldn't quell the tiny cry of disappointment which began in my chest, slipped up my throat and broke from my lips.

Jim clamped a hand over my mouth. That's when I finally looked at him and saw that he was listening.

Between the retreating booms of thunder, there came another sound. A door closing. Someone stirring downstairs.

My sorrow emerged as a moan. I did not want an interruption. My whole body yearned for him. This was our time, finally. At last.

Jim scarcely breathed for a heartbeat, then, moving swiftly, he rolled off of me and reached into the bookshelf beneath his bedside table. His hand came back with a gun. He shoved the loose clip into the handle, listening.

"Jimmy?" It was his mother's voice. Olivia Wills was in the

house, right downstairs.

Jim leaped from the bed, reached back to wrap my open dress over me and pull me to my feet, almost in one motion.

I wobbled, feeling lightheaded and confused, as if I had been roused out of a sound sleep. At the same time, I was consumed by an overwhelming sense of sorrow, followed a split second later by mind-blowing panic.

"It's okay," Jim whispered, steadying me as I groaned and looked around the room trying to decide what to do first. He straightened my clothing, which barely covered me, and handed me my bra. "Go in the bathroom. Everything's all right." He nudged me.

"Hey, Mom." He called a little too loudly, his voice hoarse. "Bring a Coke and a glass of ice on your way up, will you?" He removed the clip from the gun and replaced both clip and gun behind the books.

"Sure, sweetie."

I heard Olivia talking in muffled tones to someone else. Jim swigged the cola at his bedside, cleared his throat once, then again. "Who's with you?"

"It's me, Veronica, and Curtis, too. Mom was worried about you. Do you have a cold? You sound like you have a cold."

"No." He peered into the bathroom where I was fastening the last button on my dress. He stepped in, wrapped his arms around me and lowered his voice. "I love you." He held me tightly. I frowned but didn't speak. "Why don't you finish the mirror." He motioned toward the glass cleaner and paper towel I had abandoned earlier. I nodded, then wilted again when I caught sight of my reflection.

I was flushed and sweating, my clothing totally trashed and my hair seriously mangled. I looked frazzled and terribly well kissed.

Jim smiled. "You don't look that bad. Fact is, you look great.

And I love you." He turned his attention back to the bedroom, where he fluffed and restacked the pillows, smoothed the rumpled bed and lay down as if trying to resume his earlier ailing pose as the visitors' voices came up the stairs.

When they appeared in his room, both Olivia and Veronica glanced at me in the bathroom, wiping the mirror. Both women regarded me peculiarly. Olivia frowned. "You've gotten too hot working so hard in there, Jancy. You'd better come out here."

"I'm just finishing up."

Silent, Veronica cast what seemed like a knowing, accusatory look, one that carried more than idle suspicion. I could not meet Veronica's gaze.

Olivia had brought food and two suitcases. "I knew you had to be sick," she said to Jim. "You look like death warmed over." She bustled, assuming command of the room and the house.

"You don't need to stay, Mom. I'm on the mend now. Jancy'll check on me."

But Olivia Wills was not to be thwarted when it came to restoring one of her children to full health. She stayed until Saturday.

Curtis asked to stay the next week while Morris was at church camp. The following week, Moe asked equal time while Curly was at camp. Jim appeared indifferent to their requests, a response that Olivia, Veronica, Moe and Curly all accepted as affirmative.

I felt cheap, abandoned, guilty and confused. I was surprised and disappointed in myself, that I had responded so willingly—so enthusiastically—in Jim's bed. I was, in stages, angry, relieved, righteously indignant with myself and then with Jim.

We had no opportunity to discuss the incident privately until Wednesday evening, a week later.

While Curly made a second run on the go-cart track, I

broached the subject as Jim and I sat together, alone on a bench waiting.

"You just got out of there by the skin of your teeth." Jim leaned forward, his elbows on his knees, and looked back at me over his shoulder.

I clasped and unclasped my hands. "I've never behaved like that before. I've been trying to figure out what happened to my conscience. To my good, common sense. You know I'm not that kind of person."

"Yes you are." He said it almost angrily. "With me you are. It's the magic. Our kind of magic, Jance, defies analysis. Rolling around with you cured me of my mysterious illness and took us to the thin air. Most people have to get there with drugs. It's only fair for you to get a whiff. I've been going there off and on for months, every time we're together, every time I think of you. And someday, baby, when we don't get interrupted, it's going to get even better than that."

I frowned at the ground, unwilling to look at him. "Jim, I don't want to be out of control like that. I have. . . ." I hesitated.

"A plan? A big career? I heard. Well, sweetheart, you'd damn sure better stay out of my bedroom then, because you are the sweetest thing I've ever missed and next time, I won't. You belong to me, Jancy. You and I both know it. And I promise you, I'm primed to take possession."

I raised my eyes, intending to challenge him. "What happened to 'trust me?'"

"Don't!" He said the word emphatically. "Don't trust me not to take you if I have the chance. You weren't the only one experiencing the intensity, baby. I'm telling you, don't be alone with me any more unless you're ready, because if you and I are by ourselves, I won't be responsible for what happens."

There was a lengthy silence. When Jim spoke again, his voice was quiet. "Jance, I lie in bed aching for you every night. Do you have any idea what I'm talking about?"

I saw the ferocity on his face and my own heartbeat had quickened with his words.

"Another fine mess . . . ," I began. He nodded and his rueful smile met mine as we finished together, "you've gotten us into."

"What am I going to do?" I asked quietly.

"Say yes."

"But what about Riley Wedge? The wire service? My career?"

"Your plan will never get you anything close to the pleasure you'll have in our bed. I promise."

I frowned, studying his face as if I could find the answers to the universe revealed there. "Is that what life's really about, Jim? Physical gratification? Sexual pleasure?"

"Name anything better."

I felt the furrows in my forehead deepen. That and the roar of the go-carts together with the diesel smell combined to provide the beginning of a wicked headache while I sat puzzling, thinking of and dismissing possible answers to what seemed a simple question.

CHAPTER TWENTY-EIGHT

I exited the interstate between Dominion and Bishop in the rain on Sunday evening as a car roared up from behind and whipped by. I heard the shriek of metal on metal and my steering wheel didn't respond as I careened off the pavement, onto the shoulder and dangerously close to a plunge thirty feet into a rain-filled culvert. As I struggled to get my car under control, the other driver roared off down the road.

My heart pounding, I sat trying to catch a breath with the motor running, staring into that rain-swelled pit not two feet from my right wheel. Finally I felt calm enough to step out and check the damage. The left fender was crumpled, barely cleared the tire. Cautiously I drove the car back onto the pavement, thankful that it was still drivable.

The other driver obviously wasn't aware of what a near-disaster he had caused.

I bummed a ride with Rosie Monday morning after I took my car in to have the wheels realigned and to ask if my mechanic friend could "buff out" the scrapes on the left side and straighten the fender. Rosie mentioned the close call to Jim when he stopped by the house Monday night.

When we were alone, he asked what happened. My answer did not please him. "Why didn't you tell me about it on the phone last night?"

"It was just some jerk in a hurry."

Although Jim didn't pursue it, he insisted on going with me to pick up the car after work on Tuesday.

The mechanic was playful. "Jancy, honey, you can't 'buff out' that kind of damage. You'll have to take that to a body man. Here." He took a note pad and pencil from his uniform pocket and jotted down an address. "This guy'll do right by you. His name's Da Vinci. Save the cute cracks. He's an artist, all right, just in a different medium. Tell him Steve sent you."

The Beretta drove fine, despite its appearance, so I didn't mind that Mr. Da Vinci couldn't get to it until the following Monday. They'd make it a priority job and have it out by Thursday. Jim loaned me his Civic. He would drive his SBI unit.

"It looks terrific," I said when I stopped by to settle up with the artist for the car at noon on Thursday.

Da Vinci gave it a critical look. "I want to keep it until this afternoon, buff the old paint a little, get a better blend between the new skin and the old."

It looked good enough to me but I couldn't drive two cars and hadn't had the foresight to bring another driver along. "I'll pick it up after work. But I sometimes get caught. If I'm late and you close before I get here, leave the key over the visor." I handed him the insurance check. "Is that right?"

"On the money. Glad to have your business. Recommend me to your friends."

By the time I got away from the office and drove to Jim's so he could take me to the body shop, it was after six.

Emergency vehicles working a car accident blocked the street and Jim detoured through an alley. But when we got there, my car was not on Da Vinci's lot.

We walked over to peer in the shop window, but my candy apple red two-door was nowhere in sight.

Turning around, his hands on his hips, Jim scanned up and

down the street, then stiffened. I followed his gaze.

Just beyond the ambulance blocking the street, I caught sight of something bright red. My eyes met Jim's. Wordlessly, we made our way toward the scene of the accident.

A tangled mass of what appeared to have been my car lay twisted in the middle of the street. The hood was charred and pieces of the engine were scattered to opposite curbs. After explanations about what we were doing there, I walked behind the car to check the license plate. It was twisted but legible. It was my tag—my car.

One investigator picked up large pieces of debris while another wrote down measurements just in front of firemen who were attempting to wash away gasoline and broken glass to reopen traffic lanes.

Medics loaded a sheet-draped body into their vehicle. Another body was already inside. Both bodies were covered. It looked like there was no hurry.

I approached a fireman I recognized but whose name I either didn't know or could not recall at that moment. "What happened?"

He shrugged. "An explosion."

"The gas tank?"

He shook his head no.

"That's my car. Whose bodies are those?"

"A couple of kids. Probably not old enough to drive. It looks like they grabbed the car for a little joy ride."

"Did they run into something?"

He shook his head again. "No. It was a bomb. Looks like it was set to go when the engine warmed up, and it did. They hadn't gone two blocks."

I turned around, practically leveling Jim with an accusing stare.

The fireman, too, looked at Jim. "The bomb guys from

Dominion are on their way. We'll hang around until they get here. If you've got questions, they'll probably be the ones to ask."

Jim nodded, took a firm grip on my elbow and walked us back to Da Vinci's. He put me in his car without even attempting to answer the questions I was too stunned and confused to reduce to words.

I slept fitfully that night, awakened several times by nightmares and the sycamore slapping against my window in the barn-like house on Cherry Street.

Jim picked me up for work Friday morning. At the *Clarion* he accompanied me upstairs where he asked to speak with managing editor Ron Melchoir and publisher Bryce DeWitt in private.

Naturally, I objected, but Jim was not to be deterred.

"Jancy's had two close calls in a week," Jim said, coming right to the point when the four of us sat down together in DeWitt's office. "She can identify people who may have been involved in two—now, maybe four—murders. I want her someplace where I can guarantee her safety. She'll need to be away from the office for a while. Give the police a chance to nail the bad guys."

Melchoir and DeWitt agreed. DeWitt insisted I be paid during the time off.

Melchoir, who knew me pretty well, studied my face. "I expect some good copy out of this, Dewhurst."

His challenge put some starch back in my attitude. I had become a darn good newspaper reporter. I didn't usually help make the news, but I might make an exception in this case. I definitely had an inside advantage on this story.

I phoned my parents to explain I would be out of town on special assignment for a few days.

Jim insisted I pack my clothes in Wal-Mart sacks, which he

loaded in his car. We drove to the sprawling discount store and carried the sacks inside. With no delay, we walked briskly through and out the back door to the SBI unit Agent Foxworthy had parked there.

Jim handed the keys to his unit to Foxworthy, while I tossed my "shopping bags" into the borrowed car.

"Give us an hour before you drive my unit out of the parking lot," Jim said.

In Foxworthy's car, Jim took the access road opposite the entrance we had used. He drove directly to Skelter, to the cabin.

Olivia, reading on her bed in the afternoon heat, jumped up, obviously pleased. "Jancy, good. Andrew and Peter are coming. We'll have enough for games."

I had been nervous and had not slept well at home the night before. In that place where I felt completely safe, I breathed deeply and relaxed. I noticed that Jim, however, remained stiffly alert, even after he changed clothes.

He wore a button-up shirt open over his T-shirt, concealing the weapon that would require an explanation.

That evening Jim told his family about the sideswiping and the car bomb, the two incidents that had made him so tense.

Peter sat up straight, his eyes bright. "Andrew and I can take shifts during the night, Jim, give you a break."

Jim snapped light switches up and down. Security lights outside blinked on and off. "Thanks, guys, but I think the cabin's pretty secure."

Despite his words, Jim remained vigilant as I again adjusted to the leisurely pace of our placid surroundings.

Jim checked with Roundtree by telephone twice a day. Law enforcement had not turned up the missing Jose Torres. The sheriff's theory was Torres left Bishop after their confrontation in the courthouse hallway.

By Wednesday, the sheriff was jubilant when Bishop P.D.

picked up Daniel Johnson, alias Dan the Dude, the other man I had described. Roundtree bellowed triumphantly over the telephone. "We've got a fingerprint match on him with a random print we got off of the driver's window on Bubba Valentine's pickup."

Jim listened attentively. "Did Johnson tell you where to find Torres?"

"Nah. He said he didn't know anyone in Bishop or Dominion, had never worked with a partner." Roundtree was adamant. "Jimbo, we've got this guy on murder one. He's a transient. No bond. He's going to be staying at my place for a while. We figure the other one's flown the coop."

Finally, Jim relaxed a little. He took me swimming and fishing. I remained on guard when we were alone against what to me was an equal threat, my weakness for him.

He needed to be back in the office on Monday. "I want you to stay down here a few more days."

Noting his concern, I didn't argue until Sunday.

Restless, faced with the impending Monday morning departure of William Wills, Andrew, Peter, and even Jim, coupled with Roundtree's good news, I began my campaign pleading with Jim to take me back to Bishop with him.

"I want to contact the insurance company about another car." I was annoyed when my voice came out as a whine. "I'm sunburned, Jim. I'm tired of being hot. I want to get back to air-conditioning, take a real bath and wear something besides swimsuits and shorts."

He raised his eyebrows. "I don't know, it doesn't sound like you're suffering much to me."

I ignored the gibe. "Please let me go with you."

"Stay here with my mom, just two more days."

I sulked.

He frowned and shook his head as he exhaled. "Will you stay if I do?"

My shoulders sagged as I nodded, satisfied for the moment with his concession, but I didn't smile.

"I'm not your hostage, you know," I said, gearing up for round two on Tuesday afternoon as I began wheedling again. I sat on the glider. He slouched in a wicker rocker.

"You love it up here," he said, sounding tired of this frequent conversation.

"And I want to keep loving it, but I need a little time off for good behavior, don't you think?"

He gave me a halfhearted grin. "You haven't been that good."

I made a face.

He relented. "Okay, we'll go back in the morning. Maybe it's over. The guy in custody can do his buddy more damage than you can do either one of them."

I rolled my eyes and wondered out loud for the hundredth time. "I don't know why they came after me in the first place."

"They have to think you know something that'll hurt them."

"I've told you everything at least a dozen times. Did you hear anything that sounded like I knew anything that could do them any damage?"

"No, but I don't know what they think you know, you know?" He shot me a look and I smiled at his attempt to humor me. He yielded a crooked grin as he reached for a deck of cards. "How about some gin rummy?"

I slid into the chair opposite his and pouted. "I already owe you thirty-eight dollars and change."

"Double or nothing?"

I brightened. "You're on." By the time we quit, doubling the bet each game, I owed him more than my next paycheck.

We left early Wednesday and got back to Jim's house in Bishop before ten a.m., where he handed his keys over to me and he picked up his SBI unit. He followed me home. All four of my housemates were gone to their various places of employment.

Jim insisted on checking the empty house before he left me there to bathe and dress while he went home to clean up.

By the time I was crisp in a freshly ironed shirtwaist, he was back, again the efficient, dapper agent. He brought along a cell for the Civic as mine had been in the glove box of the Beretta.

"Thank you." I whispered the words. "You're very thorough."

"It's my public duty to protect and to serve. I'd do the same for any citizen." When I looked surprised, he grinned. "Not."

Melchoir was glad to see me back, as were other beat reporters who had been doing their own jobs and covering mine as well.

Tired after the trip and a day of catch-up at the office, I dragged into the house at five-twenty thankful for air-conditioning and the pitcher of sweetened ice tea that Liz brewed most afternoons.

"You had a call on the machine," Angela yelled as I trudged up the back stairs carrying a fresh glass of iced tea and the afternoon issue of *The Dominion Times*.

"Who was it?"

"Who do you think?" Angela sighed. "He said it was urgent. He'd meet you at the cabin, for you to be there by seven."

I glanced at my watch. It was a good two hours to Skelter. I needed to get moving. I heaved a heavy sigh, hiked my purse back onto my shoulder and made a u-turn on the stairs.

I refilled my tea glass and went out the back door. No need packing. I had shorts and bathing suits at the cabin. Besides, I wasn't staying.

I stopped once for gasoline but made good time and was turning onto the blacktop road at Skelter by seven-fifteen, congratulating myself.

The cabin was all locked up. Jim was his usual inevitably late. I breathed in the aroma of baking foliage. Olivia had no doubt decided to spend the torrid August days in town, in the air-conditioned comfort of her home. Who could blame her? I couldn't help smiling just thinking of Jim's bustling little mother. The air here was always ten degrees cooler than the temperatures in town and the lengthening evening shadows promised immediate relief. I didn't mind waiting, but I planned to give Jim some flak for ordering me to hurry and then not showing up himself.

I lifted the key from its hiding place—dangling on a nail on the side of the cabin, in plain sight—unlocked the padlock, opened the hasp on the back screen door and returned the key to its usual place.

I checked the refrigerator. There was plenty of ice in the freezer, drinking water in the tank carried from town and, of course, food.

I stood still absorbing the quiet. No white noise here. Was that a car coming? No. No car. No Jim. Not yet.

A little uneasy, I guess from being there alone for the first time, I walked through the cabin. I turned on the ceiling fan on the front porch to give the variable south breeze a little punch and for the comforting hum of company.

I was used to Jim's being late, but I might call him on my cell anyway. Nudge him along. There was no answer on his car phone. The unit, the computer voice said, was out of range or had been turned off.

I left terse messages on the voice mail and the answering machine at his house. My pique would serve him right. He'd get the messages later, after he got back from here. I left my cell phone in the car.

In priority order, I got a cup of ice, poured a canned pop over it, dug the Dominion paper out of my purse, kicked off my shoes and stretched out on the glider directly under the fan, propping my head on the end cushion turned sideways. Everything was hushed. My unease ebbed. The steady drone of the fan and stale news stories of the day made my eyelids heavy.

Twilight, the sun's last call, didn't rouse me but I awoke with a start to rude honking. I jumped up, sliding into my flats as I darted out to the car.

"Where are you?" I said, instead of "hello."

Jim's voice was garbled. ". . . Gun . . . shells . . . run . . . !" There were more words too faint to hear.

"Gun . . . out of there . . . hide . . ." again, then static followed by an eerie silence.

I hung up, frightened, confused, and feeling very alone. Why did I need to run? What kind of threat had him so worked up?

CHAPTER TWENTY-NINE

If the threat were imminent, I shouldn't risk driving the one-lane road back to Skelter. I looked around in a frenzy. Unable to think clearly and uncertain about what danger was coming, I decided the smart course would be to follow Jim's instructions, if you could call the hodgepodge of words instructions.

I darted back into the cabin, straight to the gun cabinet in the living room. There were two twenty-two-caliber rifles, the shiny new twelve-gauge and the old four-ten shotgun. I felt nervous about firing the rifles. They carried too far and I wasn't that accurate. I had not liked the brutal kick of the twelve-gauge. By elimination, I chose the aged four-ten.

I tugged open the ammunition drawer, trembling so hard I couldn't get hold of more than one or two shotgun shells at once. They kept rolling under my fingers.

Was I supposed to use the red shells or the green ones? Darn it, I couldn't remember. One went farther, the other scattered wider or was more effective at a short distance. But which was which? So rattled I couldn't think clearly, I grabbed an assortment, one or two at a time, both reds and greens, jammed them into my dress pocket, then filled my purse.

It was getting dark. I grabbed a little penlight flashlight.

What else should I take? What would I need and for how long? Jim was coming. He would be there. But when? I needed to hide until then. But where?

In the weeds and cattails? It was too rough down there, and

snaky. And I was even more afraid of the woods at night. Under a bed or in a closet was more my style, but weren't those the first places someone would look?

"Outside. Maybe not near the water. Maybe in the water," I whispered, hoping to clarify my thoughts by speaking them out loud. Taking a firm grip on the shotgun, I flung my purse strap over my shoulder and hurried out the front screen door onto the deck.

I might be safer in the water, maybe under the dock or the float. Should I put on a bathing suit? No, there might not be time.

Would the gun work if it got wet? When it came to guns, I still had more questions than answers. The shells felt like they were made of cardboard. They probably would dissolve. I skimmed down the steps, reluctant to leave the cabin but driven by the urgency I'd heard in Jim's voice.

Something moved on the ground in front of me. I froze, not even thinking of the gun clasped tightly in my hands. But this threat felt familiar. I fumbled with the tiny flashlight and aimed it toward the sound.

"Blue," I muttered, glowering at the huge old snake as it indignantly dropped from the birdbath and slithered under the deck as if annoyed at being disturbed.

Seeing the snake, however, eased my rising panic. I knew this place. This was my home turf. Being on familiar ground should give me an advantage, but I'd need to think to make it helpful. I snapped off the light.

The night seemed unusually black and I looked skyward as I picked my way carefully down the path to the dock. I had been back and forth to the dock dozens of times at night, but I had never before negotiated the rugged course in leather-soled dress shoes, treacherous little rascals that slipped and skidded over the rocky terrain. I should have brought a big flashlight, but hadn't thought of it before and probably shouldn't go back.

At the ramp, I looked for a hidey hole. Nothing likely. I trotted out on the open dock and stooped behind one of the plastic-coated chairs. Maybe I could blend with the tree shadows that stretched overhead. Precisely at that moment the security light blinked to life, giving birth to its nightly glow, illuminating everything in the area, including me.

"No." I clenched my teeth in disgust at my own stupidity.

Running from the dock as if I were being chased, my foot came free, leaving a shoe on the ramp. I had to backtrack to retrieve it, a waste of precious seconds. I seemed to be moving in slow motion, stopping and starting. I had to lay the gun and my purse down long enough to put my shoe back on, then I picked them up and fairly flew over the ramp and to the path leading back to the cabin. Then I saw them. Lights were on inside the cabin. It had been broad daylight when I arrived and I'd been asleep. I didn't remember having turned on any lights, even when I was grappling for the shells for the gun.

I stood there, perfectly still, straining to see. Maybe I hadn't turned any lights on in the cabin, but I had turned on the fan, and left it running, a dead giveaway. Otherwise. . . . "The fan's not the only evidence against you, Sherlock," I chided, disgusted that my common sense seemed to have abandoned me entirely. "Your car's there, too. Duh."

My car was not only there, it was unlocked. But if I hadn't left the fan on in the cabin, they might have thought I had met someone there and left with them. In my stupor, I actually toyed with the idea of going back to turn off the fan.

Maybe the lights meant Jim was here. I brightened. Should I go back to the cabin and check? No, Jim would call or whistle to let me know it was him, if it were.

"You can't go back." I wheezed. "They're here, in the cabin, looking for. . . ." My breathing became short, shallow gasps.

"Calm down." I slowed my words, whispering in an effort to soothe my own panic. "I need cover." I scanned the lakefront. The boat house! Perfect. Someone who'd never been here would not know about the boat house and they wouldn't be able to see it, as dark as it was. I couldn't even see it and I knew it was there.

I heard gravel crackling on the road as a car pulled up behind the cabin, moving without the benefit of headlights. Jim or family or friends certainly would have driven up with their lights on. Only someone trying to be sneaky would douse their headlights on a night as black as this. Obviously, someone had arrived ahead of the others, a scout maybe, someone who came in on foot, the same someone who, moments ago, had turned on the lights in the cabin. How many of them were there? How many does it take to catch . . . kill. . . . No, no, don't go there.

Moving slowly, stealthily, I went to the boat house.

Midway, a rock turned under my foot and sent me sprawling. The palms of my hands and knees skinned over the rocky ground. I bit my lips closed, bottling the involuntary shriek, checked in a gingerly way to make sure I was intact, then jumped up to find I was again missing a shoe.

Crawling on my hands and knees, aided only by the dim glow from the security light on the dock, I found the shoe, sat on one leg to cram it back on my foot, and then was up and running again full tilt toward the boat house.

Approaching it, I slowed to regard the dark, dank little enclosure with some dread.

The aged, shed-like edifice was ominous in the daylight. At night, it seemed eerily occupied. It smelled of gasoline and minnows. I stood there for several heartbeats, staring into the darkness, screwing up my courage. The boat house creaked and groaned as water lapped against its supports. Boats inside bumped their moorings and the sounds they made had never seemed so loud. I looked back longingly. More lights were on in the cabin. It was lit up like there was a party.

Peering from under the cypress limbs, I could clearly see the forms of three men moving along the screened porches, bending to look under beds. I heard the closet doors slam and the fact that I had not chosen those beds and closets as hiding places bolstered my confidence.

Two of the men stopped, regarded the fan, and seemed to have an animated discussion. I knew I should have turned it off.

The lights blazing in the cabin cast squares of brightness along the path to the dock and I saw, in one of the squares, a familiar bundle. My purse. I must have dropped it when I stumbled in my flight from the dock to the boathouse. I stared at it, willing it to come to me. I've never considered levitation a possibility until those moments and doubt I ever will again.

"Dumbbell." No, no. I was my only ally. I mustn't chastise myself. "No dissension in the ranks." Should . . . could I risk retrieving the purse? Definitely not. The area was too open, too exposed.

The screen door banged as the men advanced out of the cabin and onto the deck. They were talking but their words didn't carry upwind. Slowly they moved down the front steps, peering into shadows. They were coming.

Suddenly the world rocked. Loud, angry shouts were followed by at least a dozen gunshots. I stood there paralyzed. My limbs refused to budge.

"Hate snakes!" one man yelled, excitement raising the volume of his voice.

"Man, he's big. Look at the size of that monster."

My shoulders sagged with the obvious. "Blue." I whispered his name and my throat tightened.

Contending with the snake appeared to have diverted the men, at least momentarily. Maybe it would encourage them to scrap their mission. Or maybe the encounter had only motivated them to rethink it. They muttered together another couple of minutes, then went back inside the cabin. Were they going away or had they just retreated to re-plan their assault?

Determined not to let Blue have died in vain, I hurried into the boat house, thrashing arms above my head to clear the newly spun cobwebs.

Amanda had told me how hard the tiny insects worked to build their intricate little webs. I had laughed at Amanda's description of industrious little cobs marching off to work, carrying their tiny lunch pails, to repair and spin. The webs hadn't bothered me as much after Amanda's visual aid.

Besides, I reminded myself as the darkness made me quail, Blue had given his life to allow me these few additional, precious moments. That thought again prodded me to action.

I placed the shotgun on a ledge above my head in the boat house, then fished in my pocket to retrieve and count shotgun shells.

Six. The pocket had seemed heavy. How could I have only six shells? Of course, I'd probably lost some in my flight or when I fell. Too, I remembered, the bulk of my arsenal was in my purse, lying in the middle of the path that was bathed in the light from the cabin. Six would have to do.

Carefully I returned five shells to my pocket and fingered the one.

At the cabin, the men turned off the lights. I peered toward the gloomy framework, straining to see. Were they leaving?

I waited, scarcely breathing. I didn't hear them start their car, nor did I hear the slam of car doors, but the breeze was behind me, coming across the lake from the south, carrying sounds at the cabin away from me.

I didn't see any headlights either and, while the men might have arrived stealthily, if they had determined no one was there, surely they would not risk driving back along the winding dirt road without benefit of headlights.

I hunkered there in the dark boat house, my thoughts racing frantically, when the rocking and knocking of the boats called my attention to them.

The speed boat had been suspended on lines above the water, its motor and battery probably at the cabin, but the john boat rocked gently against its mooring. I had reliable transportation and a viable means of escape right there in front of me. I could simply untie the john boat and row myself out of harm's way. How easy was that? Such a simple solution and so obvious. Why hadn't I thought of it before?

"Stupid." I berated myself, angry not to have had such an obvious revelation earlier.

Moving quickly, decisively, I retrieved the shotgun and climbed into the boat, laying the weapon on the middle seat. The boat bumped the boat house floor loudly with my movements. I felt around for the oars and found both, stowed beneath the seats along each side. I left them and stepped back to the boat house floor.

It took several long minutes and a number of attempts before I was able to untie the boat in the dark, distracted as I was by every perceived sound or movement. My dress, crisp that morning before work, was wet, soaked with perspiration. My skinned hands and knees stung as beads of sweat trickled into the open abrasions.

If the men were gone, all this effort was for nothing. But if they were not gone. . . . I shivered to think what the consequences might be if they caught me.

The boat free, I shoved it and stepped in, pushing off as the bow cleared the concealment of the boat house.

Suddenly there was rustling in the brushy cattails between the dock and the boat house. I tried quietly to extract one of the oars from its storage, but sensed there was no more need for silence. The oar banged the metal floor of the boat with a loud "bam" as I pulled it free. I dug it into the silted bottom of the shallow water at the boat house and shoved with all my strength.

Sluggishly the boat came about just as a man lurched into the boat house. Apparently banging his head into the low-hanging crossbeams, he came through cussing, his arms stretched as if he thought he could catch me up from that distance. Frantically, I dug into the silt once more and the boat responded, pitching toward open water. The man in the boat house lunged, reaching as far as he could, but the boat and I were well beyond his grasp. He hit the water belly first.

Using the oar as a paddle, I stroked on one side of the bow and then the other, building momentum with each thrust. A good flow of adrenaline pumping through my veins probably made me stronger. The man in the water thrashed about, burning precious seconds before he realized the water was shallow there. He stood up in water not thigh high and took another moment to see if I was watching. He probably felt ridiculous. His next move was stupider still. Without bothering to remove his suit coat or blazer, he leaped toward deeper water and began thrashing, swimming, following me, in hot pursuit. By that time, I had twenty yards on him. When he hit deeper water, he splashed more, making a bigger commotion but little progress as the expanse of dark water between the boat and his flailing grew.

I didn't feel safe yet, however, mainly because I didn't know the whereabouts of the other two men. Not knowing made me hypersensitive to every sound or movement, most of them caused by the wind, which seemed to be increasing.

Then I heard a noise I recognized, the distinctive sounds of the paddles clattering as they slid down the corrugated metal siding on the west side of the boat house. They had found the canoe.

I groped the seat in front of me until my fingers found the shotgun. Fumbling, I broke it open. I could hear the man who had jumped into the water. It sounded as if he were splashing back to the bank.

One of the things I liked best about the shotgun was that it was single action. It would fire only one shell, then have to be manually reloaded before it would fire again. Tonight, I decided, that might be an important disadvantage. With only six shells, each shot must be carefully calculated and, no matter how frightened I was, I needed to stay cool enough to remember to reload it each time it was discharged.

I loaded the first shell.

Idly, I thought it strange that I seemed to have no compunction about shooting human beings. Shouldn't my moral beliefs or humanitarian instincts inhibit me? I felt no such inhibitions, only certainty. If they got close, I would shoot.

There was no safety device on the aged weapon. The shooter had to physically cock the hammer for each shell to load. I pulled the hammer back, then carefully returned the gun to the boat seat in front of me.

The man who had been in the water had returned to the bank and there was a lot of excited conversation as he and another man positioned the canoe. They both talked at once. Snatches of their words indicated neither knew much about canoes or lakes.

Good. Their unfamiliarity with the water and boating might work to my advantage, especially in the increasing breeze.

I strained my eyes, staring into the night trying to locate the third man, but could see no sign of him in the dark, no human movement in the shadows.

The two men with the canoe shouted expletives as they

shoved it into the water. They teetered precariously, attempting to sit on the bars across the top rather than kneeling in the floor. The craft rocked violently from side to side, shipping water. Both men shouted.

The man in front slid to the bottom of the canoe, which made it more stable. His partner followed his example and they both began paddling at once on the same side, driving the vessel in a hard circle. There was more yelling. I couldn't help smiling at their dilemmas coming one right after the other.

I thought about the gun again as I paddled on one side, then the other with the single oar. I had loaded a green shell. That meant I needed to let them get close. That's what Jim had told me. As I calmed down, his words came back clearly. "At twenty to thirty feet, the green shell is effective over a broader area."

Calmly, I slipped the oar I was using into its lock. When it was secure, I drew the second oar from beneath the seats and positioned it. Moving to the middle seat, my confidence growing, I began to pull, driving the vessel toward the west end where the water was rough and dead limbs and other debris collected at the dam. It made good habitat for fish. I hoped the wind might give my pursuers fits and old trees might reach out and snag the canoe if it followed with the two inexperienced boaters in command.

I had a good lead on them when the wind kicked up strong out of the south as it often did late in the evening. The breeze hampered me only a little—the aged old john boat steady in the turbulent water—but I looked back to see whitecaps wreaking havoc with the canoe and its novice crew.

While they were concentrating on staying afloat, I turned the rowboat and pulled hard toward the dam, thinking to hide in the cover of the stone tower that stuck out of the water fifty or sixty feet from the dam. The tower housed the key to the spillway. I rowed steadily, looking back from time to time to see glints of light reflecting off the aluminum hull of the canoe. I felt terribly grateful that the Wills' had allowed their young sons years before to paint the john boat forest green like the cabin, effectively camouflaging it on this dark, dark night.

Jim had called Jancy from his office at five-thirty. She had left the *Clarion*. He tried her cell phone, got her voice mail but didn't bother to leave a message. He took his time, cleared his mail log and dictated answers to several letters before he drove home. When he had changed into casual slacks and a sport shirt open over a T-shirt, again to conceal the shoulder holster and weapon, he called her house.

Angela sounded surprised to hear his voice. "I told her you said to meet you at the cabin."

"What are you talking about?"

"The message you left on the machine this afternoon. You said it was urgent, that she should meet you at the cabin and to try to be there by seven."

"What time did she leave?" He kept his voice steady, his tone deliberately calm.

"I'm not sure." The pitch of Angela's voice rose with what sounded like alarm. "It was five-thirty, I think, or right after that. What's wrong?"

Jim looked at his watch. Six-forty. He hung up without saying good-bye and called Roundtree.

"Is there someone you trust in Davis County?" Jim glowered at the sweep hand on his watch.

"I've worked two cases with the Davis County sheriff. The guy was sharp and that's his name. Sharp. Wayne Sharp."

Jim drew a deep breath to calm himself. "Jancy's at our cabin at Skelter. Someone left her an urgent message to meet me there. She's got a good hour's head start and so have they."

"How would anyone know about your cabin?"

"I don't know." Jim was wondering the same thing. He hadn't mentioned the family hideaway to anyone.

Roundtree's voice deepened. "I'll call, have Sharp meet you at Skelter. Do you want me to ride with you?"

"No, I'm leaving now."

"I'll rally the troops, then I'm right behind you."

Jim made record time, running code three, lights and sirens as he flew, calling Jancy's cell phone every few minutes, trying to get in range. It was nearly dark when finally, still thirty miles out, she answered. He didn't know if she could hear him or not.

"Get away from the cabin." He was frantic that she didn't seem able to understand him over the interference. "Get a gun. Don't forget shells. Run. Hide. Get a gun and shells and get out of there. Run." He had shouted, as if more volume would carry.

A sheriff's unit waited with its lights on at the Skelter store. Jim shot by them, honking and waving for them to follow as he careened onto the blacktop and turned off on the dirt road, dousing emergency lights and siren, and raced to the cabin.

He pulled in as close as he could to Jancy's car. There was a rental car angled beside and in front of hers, blocking it.

Sheriff Wayne Sharp and a deputy got out of the sheriff's cruiser. A second deputy arrived as Jim bounded out of his unit. Jim introduced himself and told the men quickly about the attempts on Jancy's life. He hurried to the cabin, stepped inside and snapped on two lights. The uniformed officers followed, scanning the premises.

"No sign of a struggle," one deputy offered.

Jim nodded. "I called her cell phone and told her to run. I was out of range. Maybe she got some of it. I didn't want to call back. I didn't want it to ring and alert anyone to her whereabouts."

Jim led them onto the deck, then shushed them when he thought he heard voices carried over the water on the wind.

Men's voices. He smelled gunpowder.

Quickly, he crossed the deck, leaped the front steps and trotted down the path, following the sounds of the voices.

The eerie orange glow of the security light over the dock revealed no one there. Jim looked to his right, toward the thicket of willow trees. Nothing moving. No sound. He looked left along the path to the boat house hidden in the cypress grove.

There, on the path, in a patch of lamplight from the cabin, Jancy's purse marked her trail.

Running, Jim scooped up the purse as he flew to the boat house. The purse seemed unusually heavy.

The canoe was gone. Jim doubted she would have taken the canoe in this wind. Warily, he ventured into the boat house. The john boat was missing.

He sighed some relief. "Good girl."

The deputy, who was close on his heels, grunted. "Huh?"

"I think she took the rowboat. The guys following her are in a canoe."

The deputy raised his eyebrows. "They'd better be good, with this wind."

Jim nodded, straining to see anything moving on the water in the inky darkness. Voices floated from the west end. The stone tower would be the only choice for cover in this wind. At its nearest point, it wasn't fifty feet from the dam.

Breathless from his run down the hill, Sheriff Sharp joined them just as Jim made a decision.

"One of you stay here in the boat house, be here in case she circles back. Have one man wait at the cabin for Roundtree, then direct him to the dam. I'm guessing Jancy's gone to the west end of the lake. I'm going down to the dam, try to intercept her, give her a hand."

The sheriff agreed.

"Nab anyone you see and hold onto them for me." Jim

handed Jancy's purse to Sharp. "Hang onto this for her."

Assignments made, Jim took off at a lope toward the dam. Without missing a step, he removed his outer shirt and dropped it at the turn as a guide for Roundtree. The rocks that formed the dam slowed him only a little.

As he got closer, Jim could see the shadow of the bow of a boat sticking out beyond the outline of the tower. Something moved on the rocks some forty feet in front of him. Jim froze.

A large form crept stealthily over the rubble.

As Jim watched, a man's shadowy figure, bent double, eased over the rocks and slid into the water.

Staying low, Jim followed.

CHAPTER THIRTY

The pursuers in the canoe allowed the wind to carry them back toward the floating dock. They obviously lacked the know-how to maneuver the small craft against it.

Realizing they had been blown off course, I tied the john boat loosely to a rung in the stone tower and relaxed a little. I felt safe enough for the moment and thought it wise to collect my wits before choosing a next course of action. My first choice was to sit tight and wait for the cavalry.

Suddenly two puffy white hands caught the back of the boat.

Scrambling, I grabbed for the four-ten, but looking at the hands at the back of the boat instead of at the gun, I only succeeded in sending it clattering to the hull. Luckily, it didn't fire. I tried to retrieve the fallen weapon, still without looking at what I was doing, too intent on trying to identify the person attached to the strangely familiar hands grasping the stern. Fumbling, I finally fought the penlight out of my pocket, snapped it on, aimed it at the back of the boat and gasped at the pasty wet face leering at me. It was Bubba Valentine.

"Bubba?" My mind spun crazily while I entertained and rejected a barrage of ghoulish thoughts. Gradually, I narrowed my imaginings to fact.

Grinning, Bubba pulled himself up enough to hang his belly on the boat, then struggled, kicked and wriggled his way into the sturdy vessel.

"Surprised?" He sounded breathless as he teetered, on his

feet but holding both sides as water rolled off him and into the boat. "I'd have been here sooner, but I turned right at the store, like you'd said."

"I said?"

"Yeah, that night at Como's. When you told me about this place, you said turn right at the Skelter store."

"I meant turn *immediately* at the store, but I meant left. Anyway, I didn't know I was giving you directions."

The astonished look on my face must have told him I was a little confused. Slowly, suspiciously, I managed an uncertain smile. "We all . . . everyone . . . thought you were dead." My voice had a telltale rasp. "Bubba. I'm really glad to see you . . . alive. But where have you been? They had a funeral. Why didn't you call someone? Do your mom and dad know you're okay? And what in the world are you doing here?"

He kept the grin but didn't answer. Instead, he balanced himself, clutched the sides of the boat, which rocked violently, still being buffeted some by the wind in spite of the protection of the stone tower. He stepped over the back bench seat and worked his way forward. I thought maybe he was getting closer so he could hear me better.

"Jancy." Jim's voice called from the direction of the dam. Against the wind, it sounded strange. I jerked around to stare into the dark, but couldn't see anyone.

"Jancy," Jim's voice came again, "get out of the boat. Get away from him. Do it. Now."

I strained, trying to see in the night. I was sure it was Jim's voice but I thought I should be able to see him, to verify what he was telling me to do.

"What?" I called, not believing I'd heard him right.

"Get out of the boat. Now. Get in the water. Dive. Swim for it."

I looked back at Bubba, seeking assurance that I had heard

correctly. A huge knife glinted in his hand. The silly grin was gone. He looked almost apologetic.

"I promised G.C. I'd do this; do it with this weapon this way. He made me promise. Besides, Chloe wants your guy."

"What?" I asked in disbelief. "Chloe? You're going to kill me so the woman you love can have a chance with Jim? Bubba, that isn't going to happen, whether I'm around or not."

"I'll dope him, choke him down, lock him up, whatever it takes. With you gone, he'll be easy to handle."

"What about you, Bubba? Don't your feelings count?"

"When she's through foolin' around with him, I'll kill him and she'll be back with me. The beauty of it is, I can kill anyone I want to now, and go scot-free. No one'll ever suspect a dead man."

"But those men . . . you pointed them out to me at Como's so I could identify them later."

He laughed. "I wasn't fingering them for you. I was fingering you for them. How'd you think they happened to run you off the road that day or knew to blow up your car? Who do you think got 'em here? You told me all about this place, the night at Como's. Remember?" He shook his head. "People think you're smart, Jancy, but you're not. You're dumb as a post. Dumber than me."

The boat rocked as he shuffled another step toward me. "Hold still and I'll do it quick. It'll be over in a minute. I gotta do it for G.C. I owe him. And after you're gone, your man'll go down easy. I don't want to have to kill him tonight, you know, for Chloe's sake. Funny thing is, sooner or later we'll both be ghosts—except I'll be the one still breathing."

Bubba planned to kill Jim, tonight or later on? That suggestion sent rage shivering to the tips of my fingers and toes. To get Jim, he needed me dead first. Jim told me to get out of the boat. Good enough. I whirled and stepped up on the bow just

Sharon Ervin

as Bubba cleared the last bench seat between us. Things happened in a blink after that. First, Bubba stepped on the four-ten laying in the darkened bottom of the boat. He flailed his arms and staggered. Stumbling, doing a crazy dance, he grabbed for my arm. The boat yawed and Bubba fell forward, scrambling, trying to right himself. In that same heartbeat, I dived. I went deep, knifing through the water I loved.

Bubba's weapon clattered against the boat's hull as he toppled headlong into the water behind me. He grappled for me in the water, but I cut left and was well out of his reach as the dark water covered my escape.

As if I had superhuman strength, I pulled hard and fast through the water. Choppy above in the wind, it was calm and silent below. When I surfaced, several yards away, a tumultuous battle raged in the water on the near side of the boat.

Bubba was spewing, strangling, both hands clawing behind him at a huge forearm locked around his throat. The arm pulled him under. The water boiled where he disappeared and churned for what seemed an interminable length of time.

Finally, Jim's dark head surfaced ten or twelve feet from the tower. Obviously burdened, he pulled something unwieldy as he side-stroked back to the rowboat.

Straining, he hoisted his cargo. With massive effort, he wrapped the back of Bubba Valentine's shirt collar over a hook on the stern where a motor could be secured, if anyone ever used a motor on that boat. Suspended as it was, Bubba's body floated. His head bobbed forward and bounced on his double chins against his chest.

Once he had Bubba's body secured, Jim turned around looking for me. Treading water nearby, stunned by the wild events of the night that had culminated in watching one gentle, reasonable man take another man's life with his bare hands, I wasn't in any hurry to get too close.

Dog paddling toward me, Jim glanced back. I suppose he was checking to make sure Bubba stayed dead this time. When Jim got close to me, he began treading water, apparently warned off by my facial expression.

"Everything's okay." His croon reassured me that the reasonable man I knew had control of himself. In his rage, he had saved my life. Of course, he had taken someone else's while he was doing it. It was hard to reconcile all the things that had happened in the last hour. Then I looked into Jim's face, saw his uncertain smile and the truth written there.

Hovering, treading water, he said, "I'm sorry. I hope you'll be able to forget this . . . to forgive me for. . . ." He tipped his head toward the boat without taking his eyes from mine.

"For?" I asked.

"For losing it back there. It's just that . . . well, Skelter's always been a haven for me; a place for family and laughter and games and things like that. It's a place where a man brings people he loves to keep them safe. None of those guys—not Bubba or his cronies—belong here. When I saw he was . . . after . . . trying to hurt . . . well, you . . . I sort of . . . lost it." He shot a look back toward the boat without actually engaging his eyes. "I'd like to think I wouldn't have killed him if he'd surrendered. But I couldn't let him go on like he was. I couldn't take that chance, don't you see? I couldn't let him go after you again." His eyes glistened. "I had to stop him, Jancy. My main thought was I couldn't let him go. Not this time. If I'd been a lion, I guess I'd have gnawed his head off." He paused, but I didn't have anything to say.

"He shouldn't have fought me, Jancy. If he'd given up, I like to think I could have gotten myself back under control. That was his mistake. I think he knew it, too. His fighting gave me all the excuse I needed. I think he's gone for good this time."

We just hovered there, treading water, facing each other.

"I didn't only want him out of your world, I wanted him out of this world." He shivered. "I cannot tell you how bad I feel right now that I did that . . . or that you saw me . . . or how relieved I am that he's gone . . . even if you had to see . . . to see what a sick person I can be."

I swam two strokes, threw my arms around his neck and pulled him close. When I started kissing the side of his face, we sank. With one arm around me, the other treading water to get us back to the surface, he said, "Honey? Honey, we're not through."

"What do you want me to do?" I asked. At that moment, I was willing to do anything he said.

"First, let's get you into the boat. Then I have to go back for my gun."

He swam me through the choppy, wind-whipped water to the side of the boat and gave me a leg up. Groping my way to a seat, I sat stiffly upright, my eyes following Jim as he swam. I didn't allow myself to look at the corpse floating behind. I shivered occasionally and didn't know if the shaking was fear or relief or shock or the wind whipping my wet clothes and hair.

Barely audible above the rush of the wind through the trees and the slapping of the whitecaps against the stone tower, I could hear men's voices, faint cries for help and a steady "Thump, thump."

At the dam, Jim stepped out on the rocks and retrieved his weapon. He wrapped the leather strap around the holstered gun, then waded back into the water.

Holding the gun high, he side-stroked to the boat and reached over to place his gun on the boat seat next to me.

"Shift your weight over there, to the other side," he said before he hoisted himself up and in with one fluid motion. The boat rocked only a little. He bent and held both sides as he stepped briskly over the seats. I picked up the four-ten that had upended Bubba, then crept back to the middle seat.

"I didn't know Bubba hated me."

"He didn't hate you, honey. G.C. made him promise to kill you and he wanted to keep his word."

It was hard to follow that logic. I guessed it was a man thing.

"You brought the old shotgun. Good girl." He sat and positioned me close beside him. His slacks and shoes squished. He took the cocked shotgun from my hands and gently released the hammer. "I thought you'd take this one."

His small talk and matter-of-fact actions couldn't deter the tears as I locked his arm tightly with both of mine and buried my face in his shoulder. "Who did we bury before, instead of Bubba?"

"We may never know." He slipped his arm free and wrapped it around me. "Don't get too cozy. I told you, we're not through yet." He looked at the shoreline. "But it's about to get easier. Here comes the cavalry."

I rotated my face without lifting my head from his shoulder and I, too, saw the beams of the powerful searchlights coming toward the dam.

"Move up front," Jim ordered.

I hesitated. It was warmer beside him.

He nudged me with his elbow.

Wordlessly, holding onto the sides of the boat, I returned to the bench at the bow, turned and sat so I was facing Jim. I had to bite my lips to stop my chin's quivering.

Jim slipped the rope free from the tower and manned the oars. Deftly turning the boat, he yelled at the uniformed officers to meet us at the dock.

It was difficult for Jim to row the boat with Bubba's body dragging behind, but the wind pushed, lending aid.

The voices and the thumping sounds grew louder as we neared the dock. I began trembling all over. The cold came from inside as well as seeping in from the outside.

Having lost their paddles, the men who had terrorized me sat comically in the canoe as the wind slapped it again and again against the wooden swimming dock. The wind-whipped water lifted the vessel, bouncing it up and almost onto the anchored float. With each bounce the men cowering in the floor shrieked for help. Their voices were so high, they sounded like women.

Two sheriffs and several deputies on the fishing dock yards away trained their searchlights on the wooden float and discussed whether to swim out to rescue the men or to wait.

Jim brought the john boat up so that Bubba's body was not visible either to the men in the water or those on the dock. Of course, no one flashed a light on the boat's stern.

Relieved and struck by the absurdity of the men's predicament and our reversed roles, I suddenly forgot how cold I was and began giggling. Once begun, I couldn't get my ridiculous laughter under control. It seemed too preposterous that the men who had seemed such a threat earlier, now sat mewling for help. The more desperate they sounded, the harder I laughed.

Jim ignored my goofiness and sounded grim as he spoke to the men in the canoe. "Show me your weapons."

The anger in Jim's voice quieted me.

Both men produced forty-fives, which they held by the barrels as the canoe bounced and banged against the float and the south wind continued to pummel them.

"Toss them." Both threw their weapons into the water.

"Torres, who's your friend?" Jim yelled.

The second man answered. "I'm Lido. Peter Lido."

"Get us out of here." Torres' command was cut short by another abrupt bounce.

Jim didn't move. "What are you doing here?"

"Came down to do a little fishing." Lido sounded surly, his confidence obviously returning. A gust picked the canoe up and slammed it again, nearly dumping the men onto the float.

Jim allowed a wry smile. "Then I won't disturb you."

"Get us out of here, you dumb son-of-a-bitch." It was Torres.

Casually, Jim freed his thirty-eight from its holster. Our rowboat, too, was rising and falling with the swells. Jim steadied one hand with the other as he took aim.

Torres glowered back at him. "You've got too many witnesses, smart ass. You ain't gonna shoot nobody out here."

"Oklahoma's got capital punishment." Looking down its sight, Jim kept trying to steady the weapon. "I'll bet you didn't know that." The wind again buffeted the boats, making us all lurch unpredictably. Jim scowled and tried again to line up his shot. "The courts take longer, but it's the same finish. I might be doing you a favor. You're trespassing on private property, Torres. We're still not as civilized as people in other parts of the country. Didn't you see that sign down the road? 'Trespassers will be shot. Survivors will be prosecuted.' "

Torres turned and addressed himself to the law enforcement contingent on the dock. "You're not gonna let him shoot us."

Jim laughed triumphantly, as if he thought Torres was convinced. "I shoot snakes out here all the time. Vermin are not allowed in the swimming area. Club rules."

Torres started to respond but didn't get the words out before Jim's gun discharged. The scarred man cried out and grabbed his shoulder.

Jim spat an angry, "Damn."

I didn't know if Jim was angry that he fired or that he'd missed Torres' head. Either way, he again took aim.

"Jimbo," Sheriff Roundtree called from the dock, his voice placating, "better bring those peckerwoods on in here before someone gets hurt."

"Don't bleed over the water." Jim's concern sounded genuine. "Blood attracts the scavengers. If you have to swim, they'll be all over you. You don't want that."

"I can't swim," Lido shrieked.

Jim turned the gun toward him. "That's real bad. Now, let's try again. What're you doing here?"

I had never before heard that depth of malice in his voice.

There was silence. Then Lido spoke and there was new regard in his tone. "We're here for her."

Torres backhanded his partner, then winced and again grabbed his bleeding shoulder.

"Did you hear that, Roundtree?"

"Yes, Jimbo. I heard."

"Who sent you?" Jim peered down the barrel, still trying to train his gun on the second man.

"No one." Lido cringed away from his partner, obviously anticipating another blow. "Jose here and another guy come down to do a job for an old lady, but that stupid Valentine—he made sure the girl there got a look at 'em. No one's paying for her. She's Jose's deal because he said she could finger him."

Jim nodded. "How'd you know she was here?"

Neither of the men answered. Suddenly I understood. They didn't want to implicate Bubba, didn't want to reveal that he was alive . . . or had been last they knew.

Another gust lifted the canoe, shoving it rudely around the end of the float and into the swimming area bound for the fishing dock. It slid sideways, pitched violently with another punishing gust, took on water and began to sink.

"Help! Help!" Both men screamed, frantically appealing to the officers gathered on the fishing dock.

"Wait," Jim ordered, staying the officers, then added reluctantly, "I'm already wet. I'll get 'em."

He tripped the safety and laid his gun down, stepped up on the seat and dove into the water.

He fished Torres out first, grabbing the man's long, matted hair and pulling him to the ladder as the second man kicked and thrashed, beating the water but staying afloat. Hands reached down to haul Torres onto the dock while Jim returned for Lido.

He caught the back of Lido's shirt collar and held his head above the water. "Did Jose Torres and Dan Johnson murder Jesse Chase?"

"Yes. Yes, Jose and The Dude did Chase."

"On whose order?"

"Some old lady."

"How do you know?"

"They got her on tape, man. Jose's got a copy of it in his suitcase, in a pair of folded-up socks."

"And the car bomb? Who's the genius who set that little gem?"

"Torres. Now, get me out of here. Jose's blood's in the water. It's gonna draw sharks."

Jim yanked his subject toward the outstretched hands of the waiting Sheriff Roundtree.

"We've got the other one, too." Jim's gaze met Roundtree's. Jim swam to the back of the rowboat and lifted Bubba's body, struggling to work his shirt collar free of the hook, then he floated the corpse to the dock. Roundtree and a deputy lifted the body. All of the remaining law enforcement people watched in awed silence, holding their questions for later.

Then Jim swam back to the rowboat, lifted himself over the stern, picked up the oars and wordlessly began pulling toward the boathouse.

I watched him closely as we bounced along on the whitecaps. "I told you, you aren't afraid of anything," I said, finally.

He gave me an incredulous look. "What?"

"You're not even afraid of the sharks."

Looking startled, he peered into my face. When I grinned, he slumped forward. Slowly, ponderously, he began laughing. Lifting both oars out of the water, he threw back his head and laughed with what sounded like pure relief.

Everyone was gone.

The county medical examiner had sent an ambulance for Bubba's water-bloated body. After some discussion, Sheriff Sharp took custody of both Torres and Lido, saying he would get the injured man medical treatment for the flesh wound to his shoulder and then lock them both up and file a report with the local D.A.

Rummaging in the bathroom closet and chest at the cabin, Jim and I turned up a hodgepodge of dry clothes. Roundtree appeared reluctant to leave the willow rocker, the company, the evening breeze, the quiet or all of the above.

After Roundtree drove away, the last one to leave, I lagged behind.

Sadly, I told Jim about Blue and asked if we could bury the reptilian friend who probably had saved my life. Working in the light from the porch, Jim dug a deep circular hole beside the birdbath, beneath the cedar tree. He said a quiet, grateful prayer as we coiled bits and pieces of Blue's body into the earth and covered it over.

After we straightened the cabin, wiping away all signs of this nightmarish visit, Jim doused the lights and turned around waiting for me. Reluctant to make any other demands, I eased onto the glider.

Jim chose a chair opposite that would allow him to look at my silhouette in the darkness.

"Could we stay tonight?" My words sounded innocent, but I knew exactly what I was asking.

"No."

His terse reply brought me up short. "Why not?"

"Because I'm overstimulated. I may look normal on the

outside, but inside I'm still wired. We can't stay here alone tonight." He gave a caustic little laugh. "Neither one of us can depend on me tonight. It takes all the willpower I've got to keep my hands off you under normal circumstances."

"Jim, I. . . ."

"No, Jance. This is a guy thing. I've got this animal urge to beat my chest and ravage my woman. That's not how I want things to be for us but it's primitive and very hard to control, especially when we're alone, here, in the dark, when I can hear you and smell you and when I've wanted you so bad for so long."

I started to argue, but his voice dropped.

"Don't press it. Not tonight."

He stood and strode to the back door. I followed. He held the door but was careful not to touch me. We went to our separate vehicles, started them and turned toward home.

Jim was suspended with pay until a disinterested committee could investigate the death of Bubba Valentine. Law enforcement people at the scene said Bubba's second death was a matter of self-defense, the shooting of Jose Torres necessary to subdue the partners.

Within forty-eight hours, Torres and Lido were arraigned on charges of assault with intent to kill for their attack on me. Torres faced an additional count of first-degree murder in the death of Jesse Chase.

SBI agents with a warrant searched Torres' luggage and turned up an audio tape of a conversation in which Torres and Dan "The Dude" Johnson, contract killers from Kansas City, agreed to kill Bubba Valentine and Jesse Chase for a woman who, they later testified, had advertised in the personals of a soldier-of-fortune magazine. She was an elderly lady who insisted on paying their fee in installments. She still owed them half.

Jim and I, speculating that her name would come out in the trial, were convinced the client was G.C. Gideon's grief-stricken, elderly mother, determined to avenge the death of her only son.

Law enforcement teams also put together a substantial first-degree murder case against Lido and Torres for the bombing deaths of the two kids who unwittingly had taken the fatal joy ride in my car.

CHAPTER THIRTY-ONE

The last day of August was oppressively hot, sapping energy from everything that lived, plant or animal. Shortly after ten-thirty a.m., I walked from the air-conditioned *Clarion* building to the equally cool courthouse on the opposite corner.

Once inside, I took my time, trudging slowly through the corridors from office to office. There was little activity, only two incident reports on the sheriff's log, both domestic disturbances, probably results of the awful heat.

Reluctant to make the return trip to my office, I parked myself in the district attorney's reception area where I lounged in a chair shooting the breeze with Assistant District Attorney Reese Mabry.

A spare, bespectacled man of forty or so, Mabry propped himself sideways in a chair across the room. He swung one leg that was draped over the arm of the chair next to him.

Behind the word processor, Flora, the receptionist, sat on one leg, the other crossed over it. The toes of her empty shoes comically peeped out from beneath the desk.

After a while, Jim sauntered into the room and took the chair two down from Mabry, he too wilted by the triple-digit temperatures outside.

"People keep asking if it's hot enough for me," Flora complained, "like I ordered this weather." Everyone smiled. "I don't have any energy after nine a.m. My hair won't stay curled and my clothes sag by the time I get here in the mornings. I like

323

cold weather better, don't you?" She glanced at me.

I gave the question an inordinate amount of thought, hesitating so long Flora apparently thought I hadn't heard and prodded. "Huh?"

I drew a deep breath and smiled at Jim. "I like being around water when the air's this hot. I like swimming and boats. I even like walking through lawn sprinklers. I like summer best. It's lazy. No one expects you to rush in weather like this. Time doesn't rule your life as much."

Jim smiled at me and winked, back to his old self. We were going back to the cabin on Saturday for the Labor Day weekend, near and in the water, free of the constraints of time.

Sheriff Dudley Roundtree opened the office door.

"Here she is." Roundtree's voice had a triumphant note of merriment. "Jancy, who do you think waltzed into my office looking for you?"

Roundtree stepped aside and allowed the man with him into the room. "Who does this look like to you?"

I peered at the form behind him and laughed. "Looks like opportunity to me." I leaped to my feet, suddenly energized, and beamed. Jim frowned at the stranger.

The newcomer greeted me robustly. "Dewhurst, I've been looking all over for you."

The visitor was in his mid-fifties, stood probably five-foot-nine, was slender and walked with a slight limp. His hair obviously once had been carrot-colored, but white now dominated the fringe and the few strands combed over his freckled alabaster dome. He favored his right leg as he stepped into the room.

I imagine the stranger seemed unremarkable to everyone else, particularly Jim, except for the effect he had on me. I lit up like a Christmas tree.

"How are you," the man fairly shouted. He opened his arms, then seemed content to grab the hand I offered instead.

"Tres bien." I arched my eyebrows as I pumped his hand. "Et vous?"

Jim stood and crossed the room to stand beside Roundtree. He kept his voice low, but I heard him. "Who is this guy?"

"This, Agent Wills," Roundtree said loudly and with a flourish, "is your worst nightmare."

The stranger turned, as if on cue, and looked at Jim curiously.

"Jim Wills," Roundtree boomed, "meet Riley Wedge."

Automatically Jim smiled and reached to shake hands, but his eyes narrowed as he evaluated the average appearance of this man who, I realized, he knew was his arch-rival for my future. Jim looked as if he were struggling to quell his anxiety. He showed determination in keeping any concern from his face. It was still August, of course. Wedge was not supposed to claim me until fall. It was Wedge himself who had required me to have the two years' experience on the *Clarion*. The two years did not run out until the end of September. Policy was policy. What was he doing here?

Jim didn't ask any of the questions leapfrogging through my mind and maybe through his as well. Instead, he spoke only the usual amenities. "I've heard a lot about you and about Jancy's plan. She's been dedicated in the language lab." He hesitated. "I'm accidentally picking up a little French myself."

As Wedge looked at Jim, his face became more and more puzzled until his confusion was replaced with a pesky smile. "Agent Wills, you're not the S-O-B who's trying to beat my time with Ms. Dewhurst here, are you?"

Jim grimaced. "Without much success, I'm afraid." He raised an eyebrow and glanced toward me, but I saw it coming and kept my eyes purposefully set on the older man as Jim said, "Have I run out of time?"

Wedge shook his head. "Not yet, but the fellow who's training her for us gets back to the States in two weeks."

Wedge then turned to address himself to me. "Duke Mallory. He's got thirty days' leave coming, then he'll set up shop in San Diego. When he gets on board, we'll want you in California. I'm thinking probably fifteen October."

I nodded and smiled and ventured a look at Jim, whose gaze was locked ponderously on the floor.

Wedge addressed his next words to Wills. "You'd better take your best shot, my friend."

Jim nodded solemnly without raising his gaze. "I guess I'd better."

I forced a smile and simply pretended not to notice the tension in their exchange.

Roundtree looked at me. Lines formed at his eyebrows and pinched the corners of his mouth, as if this were the first time he realized I might actually be leaving.

Jim and I were pensive as we drove to Skelter after I got off work at noon on Saturday. I turned off the radio, which left us in total silence.

"I know you don't want me to go," I said.

Stoic, Jim kept his eyes trained on the highway.

"When I'm with you, Jim, I don't want to go." I gazed purposefully at his profile, but his expression was resolute, his attention on the road. "The truth is, I'm afraid to go. Afraid to be on my own, to rely solely on my judgment, my skills, on myself. Sometimes I'm wrong about situations and circumstances, even occasionally wrong about people."

When he didn't say anything, I plodded on. "You're not always right either. It's just that you have the confidence and the courage to get yourself out of the awkward spots you might get yourself into. I don't have either one because I've always had my folks or you or someone else bailing me out when I got in a bind.

"Jim, being somebody's wife always seemed like a trap, like something a woman did when she found out she couldn't make as much money or have as much power as a man. Wives were second bananas, married by default. That darn sure wasn't going to happen to me. I had talent. I was too smart to settle for less than all I could be."

Jim turned his head and started to object, but I held up my hand. "Let me finish." He exhaled and turned his attention back to the road.

"Newspaper journalists don't make much money, but men and women are pretty much paid equally.

"Men like Sheriff Roundtree and Ron Melchoir have always treated me like I was as good at my job as a man, even better than some. They respect me, but they expect a lot out of me. They haven't given me special treatment, at least they haven't very often. And I haven't asked for it.

"I thought I was too big a coward to be a really good reporter. You've helped me overcome some of my cowardice. You've praised me and chewed on me, just like Melchoir and Roundtree have, and helped me improve.

"I've been in the cocoon long enough. I've metamorphosed. My wings are wet, but I want to try to fly. Jim, even your dad told you to set me free."

Again I signaled, not allowing his interruption.

"You say you love me, then you ask me not to be me. Did you ever think that maybe it's not me you love? Maybe you're just ready to get married to somebody and I happen to be in your immediate line of sight."

I paused then, giving him an opportunity, but Jim did not attempt to speak.

"Maybe you need some ditsy girl who'll be content to roll

around in your bed and cook your meals and iron your clothes and have your babies. . . ." My voice broke and made a sound that could have been anguish. ". . . and have your babies," I repeated in a half whisper, "and go sledding and kite flying and. . . ." Tears stung my eyes and I shifted in the seat to look out the passenger window. Still, Jim didn't speak. We were silent for several minutes.

"My mom predicts you'll be married before Christmas." My voice was oddly off-key as I spoke toward the passenger window. "She said when a man is ready to get married, he takes the most likely available candidate. She's afraid I'll regret this decision for the rest of my life."

Jim cleared his throat. "Your mother doesn't seem to have a very high opinion of me."

"She just understands that a man's sexual needs have to be met." I shrugged and finally looked at him. My face was probably splotchy, like it usually gets when I'm upset.

His eyes remained on the road. "What about a woman's needs?"

"Darn it, I didn't even know I had sexual needs until I met you. I'd never cultivated an interest in sex. I thought a woman should adjust her sexual appetite to the man who chose her someday. I figured I'd get around to it sooner or later, but just not yet."

Jim smiled tolerantly. "Jancy, several men have chosen you already."

"So?"

"You didn't make any adjustments to fit any of those guys' plans, did you?"

"No, but I had a plan of my own. I couldn't afford to get interested in any of their plans."

"What about now? What about me?"

"I've let myself get way too interested in you, but I didn't plan to. I didn't want to." The explanation sounded as if it were as much for my benefit as for his. "And I told you right up front about my dream and how determined I was to achieve it."

"But you don't want some ditsy female having my babies?"

"I don't want her sailing the catamaran either." I smiled ruefully, shaking my head. "I know I'm not making sense."

"Yes you are. The road you're on is coming to a fork. You've made your choice, at least about going as far as San Diego. I don't like it. It leaves me out. But, Jance, there's no pressure here. I don't want to get married, generally speaking. I am ready to marry you, now.

"But I don't want some whipped pup, stuck with me because she was afraid to try to make it in the big leagues. I've got a sizable ego myself, in case you haven't noticed. In the final analysis, I want you to choose me against the best the competition's got to offer.

"Just between you and me, I expect you to knock Mr. Duke Mallory right on his keister. You'll probably be the best apprentice news correspondent anyone's ever seen. I expect you to pry and meddle and get under people's skin and be generally as obnoxious digging up information as you've been around here.

"What I'm hoping is that when you get to San Diego and conquer that lofty peak, you'll realize it's not enough. And I hope that when you start looking around for a bigger thrill, a greater conquest, you'll remember me." He flashed me a quick grin. "Meanwhile, my babies and I will wait.

"Now, I want you to relax and have a good time this weekend. It'll be hot. We'll have to stay wet to make the heat bearable. The heat can make people short-tempered if they're uptight about something else. We're here to rest and enjoy each other's company and the company of everyone else.

"You and I have cleared the air. We understand each other now, right?"

I really did appreciate his saying what he had and that made me smile. We drove in a companionable silence for a while until I had another thought. "Could I ask you one more thing?"

"Sure."

"What do you think of the old adage, 'If you can have the milk free, why buy the cow?' "

Jim laughed, shot me a sidewise glance and was obviously surprised to see I was dead serious. "Well, I guess it depends on how accessible the cow is and how much you like milk."

"How about, 'You don't buy a pair of shoes without trying them on first?' "

His grin broadened but he stared straight ahead at the road. "I'd say that was sage advice, if we were talking about shoes." He looked at me. "We are talking about shoes, aren't we?"

Annoyed by his teasing, I looked back to the scenery out the passenger window and remained quiet the rest of the way to the Skelter Grocery/Bankette and Post Office where we stopped to buy cold pop, minnows and ice.

"Want to go swimming?" Jim stood in front of me in his swim trunks. I stared at his bare stomach and chest and my breath turned hot in my throat. I forced my eyes back to the puzzle scattered on the table in front of me and shook my head. Jim hesitated. When I glanced back up at his face, he looked curious.

"I can't." My voice sounded thick, even to me, and I averted my gaze again, trying to avoid his scrutiny.

"Why not?"

I bit my lip. He grimaced.

"I know you aren't having a period."

"Jim!"

"Jancy, I've got three sisters. I did family trash detail for a dozen years. A guy learns to monitor these things. Now why

330

can't you go swimming?"

I looked around to see who else might be in listening range, then lowered my voice. "I can't even look at you anymore without wanting. . . ."

"Wanting what?" He'd lowered his voice, too, and looked sincere.

I lowered my voice again and he stepped forward, tilting his head, obviously trying to hear better.

"You, I guess." I thought about it a minute, then plunged ahead. "I want to rub against your fur." His face softened. "I want you to hold me and kiss me and touch me in intimate places, which takes us right back to what I said. The bottom line is: I can't go swimming with you."

A grim smile made his lips thin as he nodded. He walked around behind me, leaned down close to my ear and whispered. "I understand. You've just covered all the reasons I invited you. I love you. Let's get in the water and compare pelts."

He walked out of the cabin and down the path to the dock. I watched him go, trying to memorize the sway of his body. I didn't turn back to the puzzle until tears completely obliterated my view of him.

Sunday morning I was in the bathroom putting on a dry bathing suit to go swimming with Olivia. I heard Amanda singing as she came up the path with a stringer of small bass. Suddenly the singing stopped and Amanda's small voice called, "Uncle Jim."

The two words cut the air like a shriek. I yanked back the bathroom curtains and peered out. "Amanda, what's wrong?"

But Jim, hearing the tone in Amanda's voice, was already out the back door and rounding the corner of the cabin. He stopped abruptly.

"Jancy," he called calmly, "there's a hoe in the closet on the back porch. Hand it to me."

I darted out the back door of the bathroom, jerked open the closet door, grabbed the hoe and raced outside to place it in Jim's outstretched hand. He stood very still, looking at the ground right in front of him.

I had to look twice to see the copperhead, the textbook hourglass markings down the snake's back making him blend perfectly with the dirt and rocks under the outside water faucet. The snake lay about midway between Amanda and Jim, who were no more than ten feet apart. I looked at Amanda's face.

There was no panic, just concern as Amanda's eyes rolled from Jim to the snake and back.

Jim lifted the hoe slowly, then THWACK!

The snake's headless body slithered and knotted around itself as Amanda dropped her stringer of fish and leaped into Jim's arms, wrapping her legs around his waist as he swept her high off the ground with one arm, the other hand still holding onto the hoe.

The snake's mouth opened and closed several times as its eyes roved, searching for its attacker, but the bodiless head had no mobility except for the opening and closing.

"Don't get close to the head," Jim said. "He's still poisonous and he will be even after he quits moving. Don't try to handle him."

Amanda nodded solemnly.

I thought he must be kidding.

The snake's body slithered over close to a rock step used to rinse minnow buckets at the outside faucet. Still holding Amanda, Jim used the hoe to pull the body back into open view.

"Good job, Uncle Jim," I congratulated him, but my stomach churned.

He turned, apparently puzzled by my tone. "Thanks." He

regarded me uncertainly.

Late that afternoon, standing side-by-side in our bathing suits, tight-lining for crappie off the floating dock, I studied Jim carefully as he pulled his line up, hand over hand, landing a wriggling fish. Getting a minnow to bait my empty hook, I dipped a second one for him. "You actually aren't afraid of anything, are you?"

His attention remained on the minnow. "Sure, I'm afraid of a lot of things."

"Not snakes?"

"Yes, I'm afraid of snakes. That's why I kill the bad ones when they come into the area where we swim or when they get close to the cabin."

"But you don't ever run. Like today. My first reaction was to grab Amanda and run. It didn't even occur to me to attack. I was willing to vacate. But you didn't flinch. You were deadly calm when you told me to get the hoe. You became the aggressor. You weren't willing to give him any ground at all."

"It was my ground, not his. He was threatening Amanda, also not his."

"You were the same way with Bubba and those men. How do you see it so clearly, yours, theirs?"

Jim laughed, then glanced at me and his laughter evaporated. "If you get confused, you can ask me."

Neither of us spoke as I finished baiting my hook and let it down, hand-over-hand, ten or twelve feet into the crappie hole. Jim took a new catch off his line and dropped it in the basket with the dozen others we had already caught.

"If you're around." I muttered the words without looking at Jim.

"If I'm around," he confirmed quietly, not looking at me either.

CHAPTER THIRTY-TWO

After Labor Day, I couldn't concentrate. I fretted and worried about everything, including what to take to California and what to store in the attic of my parents' home in Carson's Summit.

Late in September, I tried to help Liz and Rosie decide on a new roommate to take over my room in the house on Cherry Street, but the thought of giving up my place there was entirely too depressing. Rather a little too brusquely, I suggested they make the decision without my input.

The *Clarion* advertised for a news reporter and accepted resumés, including two from promising new graduates of the university journalism school. That's where they'd found me. Ron Melchoir asked me to screen applicants with him, but I made excuses to avoid being available at the appointed times. My life seemed to be like a pool of water, like the hole caused by my leaving would be filled immediately and it would be as if I had never existed there at all.

I knew eventually I would have to take my replacement around to introduce him or her to the county officials and the university people I had grown to respect or disregard, and I dreaded doing that, turning over my well-cultivated sources to some stranger.

Adding to the pressure were the frequent calls from my parents. Was I sure this was wise? They were apprehensive about my living in California, much less in a foreign country. They cited all the political unrest worldwide. They even pointed to news accounts of correspondents taken hostage, terrorized, tortured and even killed.

When I reminded them they'd had two years to adjust to my well-advertised plan, each of them in turn admitted they had thought it was just a phase, one I would mature out of.

Riley Wedge faxed me a reminder to get a passport, which cranked my anxiety and excitement up another notch.

Then there was Jim.

I actually tried to avoid Jim, thinking to wean myself from him, but I longed to hear his voice, to smell him, to look at him, tried to etch the memory of him so deep that I would be able to conjure the reality of him at will when we were again separated by the inevitable time and distance.

Most of all, I wanted to hold hands, to wrap my arms around him, to experience the ever-present heat of his desire for me.

At the same time I was careful to limit our time alone to places where our privacy was provisional. I politely refused to go to his condo and I think we both knew why.

So I rocked along, sidestepping emotional pitfalls, unable to concentrate on routine efforts until Chloe Conklin called and asked to see me.

When I suggested Agent Wills accompany me to the ranch, Chloe hesitated until I denounced my own suggestion.

"Of course, he's more than welcome to come," she said. "I'll just clean myself up a little, and straighten some around the place." She sounded a little giddy. Remembering my last conversation with Bubba, I couldn't help wondering what kind of game Chloe was playing and if she still thought she had a chance with Jim.

Trees, shrubs and grass had all succumbed to the merciless September heat as Jim and I drove to the Two Bell Ranch that afternoon. We didn't talk much. When we did, we kept to impersonal topics, as if we each were determined to avoid any volatile exchanges—in our highly charged state—that we might regret.

We had discussed Bubba's statements about Chloe's interest in Jim as a potential spouse. We hadn't been able to decide if what he said was Bubba's interpretation of something Chloe had mentioned or if it were her idea.

Broad ways of dry clay outlined pitiful puddles that once had been brimming man-made ponds strategically located about the ranch. When I pointed them out, Jim didn't seem concerned. "They'll be full again by spring."

"But I won't be here to see them then."

Jim withheld comment.

I had forgotten to ask Chloe if she was living in the main house, but assumed that the anticipated move had taken place as we pulled up in front of the sprawling old ranch house where I had met G.C. Gideon that wintry evening that seemed like such a long, long time ago.

This time, the situation was entirely different. Not only was G.C. gone, this time I was physically neither as alone nor as vulnerable as I had felt then. This time I had brought back-up. Jim was with me.

Because of Jim, I knew I had changed, was more confident and, at the same time, more emotionally unstable than I had been before. I couldn't help smiling when I remembered how he had startled me when we first met at a homicide scene nearly a year ago.

"What are you thinking about?" he asked.

"How gruff you were the first time we met." He smiled, remembering, as I continued. "Since then you've really helped me grow and I appreciate that, Jim. I really do thank you for . . . well . . . for everything."

"You sound like I'm already part of your past."

"I didn't mean it like that." I realized it would be better not to say any more.

Chloe greeted us cordially and invited us inside, coquettishly reminding Agent Wills they had never actually met. Chloe wore a pale green scooped-neck blouse that emphasized her cleavage nicely, and crisp, snug white shorts that called attention to her full hips and made her brown legs seem even longer. Her black hair hung in a shimmering braid down her back and her brown eyes held a glint of green—maybe a reflection from the blouse. I felt pale and dowdy beside her.

Thinking of Bubba, I wondered about Chloe's part in the many deaths linked one way or another to the Gideons; even to Bubba's final attempt on my life. There had been no evidence that Chloe was actually a conspirator in any of the slayings. Chloe herself had mentioned that she and Jim Wills had never met. Again I couldn't help wondering if Bubba's final murderous attempt were a result of his interpretation of some passing comment or an actual directive from his lady love. But then he *had* referred to a promise he'd made to G.C. I wondered if Chloe might know about the promise.

Chloe led us across the porch, the screens of which had been replaced with window panes, and on into the living room that now reeked of the familiar odor of ammonia and diapers and/or litter box, smells that seemed habitually to permeate Chloe's dwellings.

"How's the baby?" I asked.

"See for yourself." Chloe indicated a sleeping form propped in an infant seat in the center of the living room floor. A large cat slunk by, stopped to sniff the sleeping baby's mouth, then proceeded into the next room.

Staring at the infant, I was struck dumb. The baby looked like a clone of Bubba Valentine. A passing, idle thought: I hoped he would outgrow the resemblance. When I looked at Jim, he nodded slightly as if he were, as usual, reading my thoughts.

"He certainly looks like his daddy." I shot a pointed look at Chloe.

She smiled. "Yes, he does." Chloe's teeth were white but the canines pointed forward, overlapping their neighbors and I suddenly realized I had never seen Chloe smile before. The smile was not for my benefit, of course. The woman focused shamelessly on Jim. "And he has his daddy's disposition, too. He's a sweet, sweet baby. Hardly ever cries."

I attempted a smile, wondering if Chloe thought to impress us by recalling G.C. or Bubba the finer human being. "Do you see the Valentines?" I asked. "Do they know about him?"

Chloe sobered. "Probably, which is really why I called you." She breathed a heavy sigh—maybe for effect—as she rolled her eyes reluctantly back to me.

"Bubba guessed but I never told him it was his baby, mainly because I didn't want Mr. and Mrs. Gideon to know. But something has happened and it scares me for him, for the baby, I mean." Realizing there was no place for her guests to sit, Chloe suddenly cleared toys to make space for us on the faded flower-upholstered divan, then indicated we should sit. Jim and I sat at opposite ends of the sofa as Chloe gracefully folded herself cross-legged onto the floor beside the baby.

"Little over a month ago, a man came to see Mr. and Mrs. Gideon, but he didn't know they were in the back house now, so he stopped here first. He kind of looked familiar. I'd seen him but couldn't remember exactly where or when it was.

"Then it came to me. He was out here late one night when I still lived in the little house. Mrs. Gideon brought him out the back door of this house to talk by the swimming pool. I guess she didn't want Mr. Gideon to get upset. He sometimes did . . . does . . . since G.C. died, when strangers come around, especially at night.

"Anyway, the man was looking for Mrs. Gideon again. I told

him they'd moved out to the back. He thanked me and went around there. She shooed him backwards out the door and they sat down by the swimming pool again."

I couldn't tell if Chloe was reeling out this spiel in an attempt to exonerate herself or if she honestly didn't realize the game had already been played to its conclusion. Surely she had read the news accounts, but maybe not, or maybe she didn't recognize the names of the players.

"The kids were down for the night." It seemed as if Chloe were basking in the spotlight of our undivided attention. "I slipped out my front door and around through the hedges to listen.

"First, she handed him an envelope, one of those big brown ones. They were talking about Bubba. I couldn't hear their words until I heard the guy say Bubba told them Jesse Chase had paid him for doing G.C. Mrs. Gideon did not act surprised, just nodded for him to go on. Then, he told her something I couldn't hear, which *did* surprise her and she started fidgeting, sliding her rings up and down her finger and squirming in her chair.

"They talked a while after that, but the wind changed and I couldn't hear their words anymore.

"The next morning she came to the house. She wanted to feed the baby his cereal, but he kept fussing because she just sat there staring at him instead of giving him bites. Then she came in where I was folding clothes and talked about G.C. and what a cute baby he had been and how none of my children looked anything like him, especially this new one. I told her I thought all fat little bald babies looked alike, boys and girls both. She mumbled something.

"She asked me if I knew how important it was to be the mother of G.C.'s kids, like that was something special. I don't know who she was kidding. I lived with G.C. He was not good-looking or smart or talented at anything. He was not brave or strong or any of the things you think would make a person important. All he really had going for him was his daddy's money.

"But after she left, I got to thinking, she might have meant something else."

Chloe looked squarely at me. "Maybe Bubba told you, he wanted to kill G.C. for beating up on me. I had to talk him out of it." Chloe flashed a coy look at Jim. "I'm not that kind of person. But someone might have gotten the idea that Bubba had a teeny bit of a personal motive for killing G.C., other than being G.C.'s best friend and him saying G.C. had asked him to do it, and like that.

"I got to thinking, what if Bubba had told lies to this guy who visited Mrs. Gideon, lies like that I asked Bubba to kill G.C. for me? And what if that's what the guy told Mrs. Gideon that surprised her? What then?"

Neither Jim nor I attempted to answer what seemed to be Chloe's rhetorical questions, so she went on.

"What if she meant that it was important to me to be the mother of G.C.'s kids because that was the only thing keeping me alive?"

Jim shifted position on the couch and glanced at me, but I wasn't about to take a step into that pile. When I didn't say anything, he did.

"Why do you think their conversations might have had anything to do with the killings?" he asked.

"Because of the envelope Mrs. Gideon gave him. I started thinking: What if she hired him to kill Mr. Chase for hiring someone to murder G.C.? And what if he was hoping to get paid again by telling her that there was another person who asked Bubba to kill G.C.? And what if he told her it was me, which was really a lie. And what if he told her I didn't have cash money to pay Bubba for the killing so I had to pay him with what I did have that Bubba wanted? And what if he told her to check out the new baby and maybe notice that he didn't look much like G.C.?"

Jim nodded solemnly. Encouraged by the nod, Chloe continued. "And what if she's paid him or someone else to kill me? Who's going to protect me?"

"Chloe, how old is Mrs. Gideon?" Jim asked the question quietly.

"Eighty-four."

"Do you think she wants to go to prison or to raise three small children?"

"No, but if something happens to me, the ranch and the cash all goes to the kids. They would have to have a guardian. Who else would anyone choose, but the grandparents who live right here on the place and who the kids know?"

Chloe hesitated, pretending to be thinking. "But it wouldn't be like that if I got a new daddy for my kids." She looked hard at Jim. "The man I marry would be rich quick, richer than he's probably ever dreamed of bein' in his whole life."

Oh-ho. I was finally catching on. "Chloe," I said, "this man that came to see Mrs. Gideon, can you describe him?"

Chloe stole her eyes from Jim for only a moment. I suspected that glance reflected Chloe's appreciation that she thought my question gave her narrative some credibility.

"Tallish, not fat, not thin. He wore a business suit, had acne bad, and kept picking at his face the whole time they were talking. He was nasty. He scared me to death." She gave Jim another one of those Pauline-in-Peril looks. "Really. He made me afraid for my safety . . . mine and the kids', I mean."

I nodded. Oh, yes, I got it. I didn't look at Jim. I figured we all three knew that the acne-faced Jose Torres was already in custody and that we were playing out this scene for an altogether

341

different reason.

"What do you think you ought to do?" I asked, playing it straight. I was curious about how far she would go with this. "Do you think you should report this to the authorities or do you think you should run—disappear—or what?"

Chloe's expression went dark. "No. I don't think I should run away. Why would I run from them? I'm not afraid of G.C.'s mom and dad. The old man's primed for the old folks' home now and her too. I've got money to burn and I've been told I'm still a nice-looking woman." She looked at Jim as if he were one of the people who thought her nice-looking. "I think I've got what it takes to catch myself the best lookin' guy in town. All I have to do is decide who I want."

I noticed she didn't say the best looking *available* man.

She then turned her face directly to Jim and, bold as brass, winked at him. There was nothing subtle about Chloe. I wondered exactly how dumb Chloe thought he was. I then made the mistake of glancing at Jim. He wore a silly smile. I did a double take and began to wonder if male intellect ever controlled his animal instinct.

Suddenly feeling out of place and really angry, I lashed out. "So, you're thinking of kicking the Gideons out?"

Chloe pursed her lips, kept her eyes on Jim and shook her head. "I couldn't do something like that. What would people think?"

I shook my head and gestured helplessly. "They might think you had your hands full with two old people and three little kids. Besides, what do you care what people think?"

"I have a reputation."

Gee, she certainly had a better opinion of herself than I had. I lowered my eyes and bit both lips to keep from barking a laugh. I hoped it looked like I was trying to think of solutions for Chloe's dilemma.

Jim stood abruptly. "Jancy, I think we should go."

I looked at him, then stood as he stepped over to offer Chloe a hand up from the floor.

"I still don't know what I should do." There was a whine or plea in her voice when Chloe looked into his face. She held onto his hand after she was on her feet as if she needed his strength, his advice . . . him.

I thought I was going to throw up when Jim smiled into Chloe's face and gave her hand a sympathetic pat. "The nursing home's probably not a bad idea. But that would leave you all the way out here alone with your children. That presents problems too."

"You're a very wise man."

I had the distinct impression Chloe had been waiting for one of us to make exactly that suggestion.

"I guess I really should live in town," she said, as if it were a brand new idea, "for the kids' sakes, closer to doctors and schools and all. I suppose I could hire someone to come look after the Gideons out here and the kids and I could move to town.

"You know," Chloe continued, as if following this new line of thinking, "that's a real good idea." She looked wistfully into Jim's dark eyes. "What tribe are you?"

"Italian." He slipped his hand free of hers.

"Well, they're probably the same thing, only one bunch started over there in Europe and the other in this country. But our skin's the same. You are every bit as dark as I am, don't you think?" She turned wide eyes on me like she was expecting me to make the comparison. I nodded as I looked from one set of striking dark, handsome features to the other. Chloe turned back to Jim. "You like kids, don't you? I'll bet you're super good with 'em, too."

"Yeah, I like 'em a lot."

"You're obviously real smart. I like that in a man. We think alike. Maybe I'll cook your supper some night. You could get to know my children." Chloe hesitated meaningfully, before she added, "And me."

Jim smiled again. "That sounds fine. We'll see what works out." He looked at me and indicated he was waiting for me to start toward the door.

In the car, I didn't know how to calm the eruption boiling in my gut. My hesitation allowed Jim to open. "I wonder if she'll be willing to testify against Torres."

I narrowed my eyes and gave him my meanest glare but spoke in a controlled singsong. "She probably will, if you ask her. You're sooo smart and sooo wise and sooo good-looking. What do you think?"

He grinned mischievously, looking smug. "Probably." He cast me a sidelong look, all innocence. "If I ask her nicely."

I shot visual darts at him, but he didn't notice. He was too busy grinning out at the road.

CHAPTER THIRTY-THREE

Jim was exonerated in the death of Bubba Valentine who was killed, the investigation showed, in self-defense.

Daniel Johnson and Jose Torres faced a preliminary hearing as co-defendants in the murder of Jesse Chase. Gary Lido made a deal to help the prosecution in exchange for a reduced sentence. Reese Mabry signed on as prosecutor.

Jim and I went to Mabry after our trip to the Two Bell and suggested he interview Chloe Conklin as a possible witness regarding who had paid for the various killings.

The D.A. delayed prosecution on the assault charges for the attack on me, hoping to nail the perps for the murder. If they missed on that, they would pursue the assault.

Riley Wedge didn't identify himself when I answered the phone at my desk Friday morning, October sixth. He didn't have to. "Have you changed your mind?" he asked right off the bat.

"No, sir."

"Have they got your replacement yet?"

"Yes. He just got out of the Army. He doesn't talk much. His clips are great. He's actually had combat experience so Sheriff Roundtree likes him already. Roundtree can make this job a piece of cake."

"Are you packed and ready?"

"Just about. I've got my airplane ticket. I fly out of Dominion Sunday, October fifteenth, take a cab to the Chestnut Hotel, get settled in my room and report to the bureau at straight up eight a.m. Monday, October sixteenth."

Wedge chuckled. "I imagine Mallory will get there closer to nine-thirty or ten, but there'll be other people around. Don't be bashful. Introduce yourself." There was a pause. "How's the boyfriend?"

"Fine."

"He planning to visit you in California?"

"He hasn't mentioned it."

"You haven't invited him?"

"No. Why?"

"I just wondered if we'd have your undivided attention."

"Definitely."

"Well, sounds like we're all set. I've told them great things about you. Work hard. Make me look good."

"I'll try." I thanked him again for the opportunity and hung up.

I had not thought about it, but neither Jim nor I had mentioned when we might see each other again. Nor had he asked when or if I would be coming back.

It was a troubling new thought. I planned to meet him at Bailey's at six. I would have to think of a way to broach the subject without making it appear that I cared more than he did about any future proximity.

I got to Bailey's on time, as usual, took the only available booth the hostess had, and ordered a drink and an hors d'oeuvre plate, counting on Jim's usual tardiness. Then I leaned back to enjoy the ambiance, the white tablecloths and real napkins, the candlelight assisted by indirect track lighting along the ceiling.

Jim arrived at six-ten.

Watching him wind his way through the room, my breath caught and my heart fluttered. A gray and white shirt freshened his fading tan, the geometric necktie pulling the navy blazer and gray slacks to a G.Q. casual look.

"Good table." He slid into the wall seating beside me, which had both of us facing the room. Looking at him, I didn't know how I could leave him. "What?" he asked, catching the look.

"Nothing." I averted my eyes as the waiter brought the appetizers.

"Buffalo wings. Your favorites." Jim grinned and I pretended to be annoyed at his teasing about my perpetually walking away from a meal with evidence of it on my shirt. The red sauce on the wings would be terribly noticeable.

He offered me the plate and I took a wing cautiously, careful to hold the cocktail napkin directly beneath it. I took one bite, then a second. No problem. Gaining confidence, I put the delicacy down, blotted my mouth and picked up my Tom Collins.

Jim was talking about his day, researching, helping lay the groundwork for the preliminary hearing for Johnson and Torres. My drink was overly full and, listening to Jim, I tipped it just slightly before it reached my mouth. The orange slice garnish perched on the side of the glass grazed my chin as it dropped, skimming the front of my blouse and leaving a bright orange smudge in its wake.

I groaned and clouded up, devastated, intent on short-circuiting Jim's reaction as he grinned and shook his head. I wanted to strike first.

"Why don't you ever do stuff like this?" The words spewed angrily. "Why aren't any of these other people wearing their food on their chests like giant medallions?"

Jim smiled indulgently. "Your mistake is putting your napkin in your lap, like everyone else. When the rest of us spill, it falls onto our napkins in our laps and gets wadded up and tossed. Hardly noticeable. Your spills get intercepted by your shelf." He arched his eyebrows devilishly. "It's the price you pay for being so well endowed."

I picked up my napkin, which lay unscathed in my lap, and swiped at the smudge. With his napkin, Jim brushed a tiny piece of orange pulp from my chin.

My face and stomach knotted. "I hate being a slob."

Jim smiled, his white teeth almost iridescent in the candle-light, his twinkling eyes on my face.

I groaned as I tried to figure out the look on his face, then launched. "Look at you. Not a wrinkle or a pencil mark on you after a whole day. How can you stand me?" When he didn't answer, I shut up.

He lost the mocking grin and studied me seriously for several heartbeats. "I love everything about you." His voice had a matter-of-fact tone. "I love the way you change the subject in a blink, the way you pry into people's most personal thoughts and report their foibles gently, and how you are so quick to find fault with yourself and equally quick to overlook the faults of others."

I didn't know what to say, so I babbled my next unmonitored thought. "Wills, you are a sick man, do you know that? There is no way you can love me. It's like you're blinded to the forest by the tree or something. We need to make a list of our strengths and weaknesses, so we can look it over. One list for you and one for me."

"Okay. Why don't we jot both lists on your napkin, since it's still relatively clean."

"Stop it." I wailed, but I couldn't help smiling. "I'm serious. You're cool, disciplined, funny, smart. You have great taste and remarkable judgment. Your clothes, your hair, your body, your whole person . . . you're gorgeous and always perfectly groomed. You always say the right thing at the right time or you keep quiet.

"I talk too much, don't think before I speak, ask too many

questions, don't pay enough attention to the answers, to my clothes, my make-up, my hair or any personal appearance stuff."

Jim's indulgent smile returned. "All of that may be so, but my interpretation is different. I see you as spontaneous, not bound by shallow, sometimes phony, conventions. You say exactly what you mean. Sometimes it's not tactful, but it's always honest, and it's often refreshing, which makes it funny and unexpected, which is why I think people respond to you like they do. I've seen people tell you everything, from details of their sex lives to their deepest fears. You have a remarkable ability to burrow into people, which is why you are good at what you do.

"It doesn't matter how a person is wrapped, what they wear, how fussy they are about their make-up, their clothes or their persons. What comes through crystal clear about you is the part that really matters: what's inside the package."

He hesitated, staring at me oddly. "I can break a sweat just remembering glimpses I've had of you under your wrappings. But I'm not talking about your physical body here, although I happen to find yours drop-dead gorgeous.

"People who are motivated by anger or greed or jealousy or vengeance, by the dark side of their natures, are ugly, no matter how much money or time they spend trying to camouflage it.

"People who look for the good, the lovely, the virtuous, the strengths in their fellow man, and who act and talk in ways that encourage the best in us, are beautiful."

I tried to cover my embarrassment at his generous assessment. "You make me sound like the distaff side of *The Man of LaMancha*."

Jim fingered his spoon. "I don't recognize myself in your descriptions of me either." He obviously was not to be deterred. "I like who you think I am. It makes me want to be that man. Consequently, I've gotten braver and stronger and more reverent and more cheerful and . . ."

"I'm the woman from LaMancha and you're a boy scout." I laughed grudgingly. "We are an awesome pair, Wills, that's for sure."

"But a pair we are." He looked squarely into my face. "Which brings us to the point of our little meeting here this evening. Today is Friday, October the sixth."

"So?"

"We have been nearly inseparable for a year and a day." Suddenly catching his meaning, I smiled as he plunged on. "And you haven't wrung me out yet, have you?"

"True," I agreed. "You have proved to be neither a washcloth nor a sponge. If you were a stick of gum, you'd definitely have flavor left. I most assuredly am not finished with you yet."

"Nor I with you." He cocked an eyebrow evilly. "So I bought you a little present to mark the occasion."

With that, he took a small, square black velvet box from his coat pocket and handed it to me. Regarding it with some apprehension, my mouth quivered nervously. Finally, I caught it securely and opened the lid.

The diamond solitaire seemed to float, anchored by delicate gold fingerlets. Dozens of facets sparkled, reflecting the dancing candlelight.

I couldn't come up with words to express my kaleidoscope of feelings. I just sat there staring at it, unable to force my eyes away from it. My first demonstrated reaction, finally, was to shake my head. The movement became more pronounced as I eventually was able to force my eyes from the ring to Jim's face. It was a defining, significant moment and I didn't know what to say.

"It's yours, regardless." His voice was quiet, carefully modulated, non-threatening. "You can wear it or not. I want you to have it for two reasons.

"First, it represents me. Like me, it will be there when you want it, if you want it. Remember the old James Taylor song, 'winter, spring, summer or fall, all you have to do is call.'

"Secondly, it's a token, a tiny, insignificant symbol of the priceless treasure you are to me. It's a reminder for you to be smart, take care of yourself, for my sake."

I batted my eyes, blinking hard, but I could not see. Nor would I release either hand from death grips on the ring box to wipe the tears welling in my eyes. Finally I wrapped my right hand around the ring, gripped it in that fist, put the box aside and, turning, groped blindly for Jim with my left hand.

Finding his hand folded on the table, I traced his arm to his face as he leaned toward me. It was a wet kiss, as rivulets of my tears converged at our mouths. Struggling, but not quite able to regain control, I bumped my forehead against his near shoulder and whispered, "Please let me go. Give me this chance. Let me try."

He eased his arm around me. "I want you to go." He hesitated then continued softly. "Every time I say that, I feel like a fool, sending you to your imaginary lover, giving personal success a chance to lure you away from me, but I am about convinced that when you actually get a close look at it, you'll want to come back and when you do, you'll be content. Either way, you'll know exactly what your options look like, close up and personal, and you'll be able to make an informed decision."

I examined the ring but I did not put it on. Instead, I shifted it from one fist to the other through dinner, sneaking a look at it from time to time. The empty ring box remained open on the table. The waiter was careful to work around it without making any mention of it.

Finally, when the plates were cleared and Jim had a last cup of coffee, he brought the subject up again. "The ring doesn't mean no dating. It's not intended to hobble you. If you want to go out with someone, it's your option."

I didn't quite understand. "Are you going to date?"

"I doubt it, but that will be my option. You don't get to carry any guilt around on my account. I'll probably let you know if I do. But, Jancy, if you decide to wear the ring as an engagement ring, let me know. If you put it on thinking commitment, then there will be no dating allowed on either end. Okay?"

I nodded tentatively. After a moment to bring my volatile emotions to heel, I began recovering. "Right. How about hanky pankying?"

Jim grinned. "With me or someone else?"

"Does it make a difference?"

"Oh yeah. Big difference." He didn't smile.

Although Jim and I spent most of our waking hours that weekend together, he did not press his case. Neither of us even mentioned the ring, despite the fact that it dominated all my private thoughts, as I suspected it did his.

I sold most of my furniture at the house to my replacement housemate. Jim loaded my car on Tuesday, October tenth, under my close scrutiny and the occasional kibitzing from my housemates. I left for Carson's Summit before daylight Wednesday the eleventh.

Naturally, I showed my mom the ring and we talked well into the night and most of the next few days, she listening and asking questions and withholding her opinion in what appeared to be an attempt to help me come up with answers of my own.

My whole family went when they drove me to the Dominion airport on the fifteenth for my flight.

The clerk called for loading twice but I stalled, hoping Jim's habitual tardiness would not prevent our last kiss good-bye. I was giving Mom a final squeeze when Jim appeared, his arms full: a new best seller, a bouquet, a sack of hard candy, gum and aspirin and a pair of Oakley sunglasses he claimed were part of the California dress code. He handed me the items one at a time, fitting the sunglasses on my face last.

When the attendant called the flight for the third time, Jim wrapped his arms around me and held me tightly. I got teary again and was reluctant to let him go until he patted the top of my head, annoying the fire out of me. Seeing he had me ruffled, he grinned, a taunting smirk that made me laugh. I hated that he could manipulate me so easily.

"May the Lord watch between me and thee," he said in a hushed voice. I smiled at him, then my parents and brothers, and glanced once more at Jim. With new resolve I turned, handed the attendant my boarding pass and marched into the tunnel.

Jim and the Dewhursts all stood watching, making polite small talk, as Jancy's plane taxied and took off.

"She's going to miss you terribly, I'm afraid." Lucy Dewhurst turned her concerned face to Jim.

"I sure hope so." Jim smiled and gave Jancy's mother a reassuring hug. She clung to him a long moment. He grinned. "You haven't seen the last of me, Mrs. D." He gave her shoulder a comforting pat. She backed away from him and smiled uncertainly, looking much like her daughter.

Jim slipped an envelope into the pocket of his blazer as he waved them good-bye.

CHAPTER THIRTY-FOUR

Jancy had been gone for more than a month.

Jim kept busy with routine work and helping Reese Mabry prepare for the trials of Jose Torres and Daniel Johnson, whose lawyers had asked that the cases be severed, tried separately. Mabry and Jim thought the defendants planned to blame each other for the murders, each claiming he was only a reluctant witness to the other's wrongdoing.

Daniel Johnson was convicted of manslaughter and sentenced to fifteen years. Jose Torres was convicted of being an accessory after the fact and drew a seven-year sentence.

Mabry did not proceed against Mrs. Gideon, who had fallen and broken a hip late in October. Both she and Tyrone Gideon were relegated to a nursing home in Dominion. Chloe Conklin paid their bills, but rarely on time.

Chloe called Jim several times before she tired of his lack of response and gave it up.

With elections looming, Jim threw himself into Democratic party politics as officeholders geared up for campaigns. Although he did not date, per se, Jim spent time with several ladies, most of whom were business associates and/or were acquainted with Jancy.

"Beth, how's it going?" Jim said, taking his sister's telephone call in his office the brisk Friday morning before Thanksgiving.

"How are you, Jimbo?"

"I'm fine." Propping elbows on his desk, he thumbed through

a file. "How's Amanda?"

"She loves school."

"I knew she would. She'll probably be substitute teaching by spring. How about that rowdy boy?"

"He's up to eighteen pounds."

"What are you feeding him, hardware?"

"Listen, Jim," Beth said, her voice serious, "I'm calling to carry tales about something that's none of my business."

"Okay. What?"

"I picked up the kids at Mom's last night. The phone rang. I answered in the den and she picked up in the kitchen. It was Paul."

"And?" He pushed the file aside. His chair creaked as he leaned back to give Beth his full attention.

"Did you know he was in California?"

"Yes, setting up a new production line or something, isn't he?"

"Yes. Well, he's in San Diego."

"That's right."

"I didn't know you knew. Jim, he's been more than a little interested in you and Jancy. He was really smitten when he met her at the house last Thanksgiving. I knew he really liked her when he stayed at the cabin after you left for that school last summer. Did you know about that?"

"I knew they got along."

"It's more than that, Jim. He raves about her, thinks she's a real dolly."

"He's right."

"Jim, he talks about her constantly. He bought season tickets for the university's home games just so he could see her in Bishop. He didn't know she wouldn't be there. He kept asking Mom and Dad if you were still seeing each other."

"Well, not since she left."

"It turns out, he volunteered for the California job, had to pay a guy to get it. He knew Jancy was in San Diego and he knew you weren't. Mom asked him last night if he had seen Jancy. He said he was seeing her every night. Did you know that?"

"Jancy told me Paul had moved to the hotel she's in and that they hung out with some of the same people. You know how it is. They're all single, away from home. Temporary. It's only natural they'd enjoy each other's company."

"So you're not worried?"

"No, but I'll be there to see firsthand tonight. I fly out of here at four-thirty. I bought the ticket the day she left."

"Does she know you're coming?"

"No."

"Maybe you'd better not surprise her."

"Maybe. Maybe not. Anyway, it's not something you need to worry about, although I do appreciate the heads up. How's John?"

"He's fine. He'll be madder than hops that I butted into your business."

"I'm glad you did. It's better to be forewarned about some things."

"Jim, I hope it turns out okay. I don't want you and Paul to have trouble."

"I'm sure things will be fine. I'll call you when I get back Sunday. Thanks, babe."

Jim had a hard time concentrating on work after the call. Jancy wrote to him two or three times a week and called nearly as often. She liked Duke Mallory, joking that he was not exactly the kind of royalty she had anticipated meeting but that he had taken her under his wing and was teaching her the ins and outs of the wire service. She was happy working long hours, saying it helped her not miss him so much.

Jim was concerned about Paul's obvious interest in Jancy but did not realize Paul's business in San Diego was more than a pleasant coincidence. He told Jancy once that people often called him and Paul by each other's names, maybe because of the resemblance. Jim couldn't help wondering if Jancy was confusing them with one another.

He'd longed to see her every one of the thirty-four days she'd been gone. Letters and hearing her voice weren't enough. He hadn't realized before how much her facial expressions clarified the meaning of her words until he tried to hear, not just what she said but what she meant, without seeing her. Today he would see her face before he slept and that thought preempted all others. He was confident of one thing. He would know when he saw her if the magic survived.

Jim's flight was on time. The November twilight in California was balmy compared to the freezing rain that had pelted him as he'd dashed from long-term parking to the terminal in Dominion.

He took a shuttle to the Chestnut Hotel, arrived shortly before seven and went directly to the registration desk. Jancy had not yet returned from work, the clerk said, and Paul had gone out for dinner. Jim identified himself—there the resemblance helped—got a key to Paul's room, paid for a second person in the room for two nights, and took his bag up. He showered, shaved, and put on fresh clothes.

His stomach churned.

He was too nervous to eat but went downstairs to the bar where he situated himself on a barstool in front of a massive mirror that provided a full view of the elevator bank, the front entrance and much of the lobby. He ordered a club soda.

He thought watching people going in and out would relax him. It didn't. He ordered a bourbon and water, keeping a close eye on the front door reflected in the bar mirror.

He had been there twenty minutes when commotion signaled the arrival of a group of revelers as they wheeled themselves through the revolving door.

Jim swore his heart stopped when he saw her face reflected in the mirror, one of the rowdies. She looked tanned in light slacks and a pullover sweater and she was laughing.

Paul spilled out of the next section of the revolving door and draped himself over Jancy's shoulders. Paul had always done a good imitation of a drunk.

Jim squinted, studying Jancy's face in the mirror.

She didn't seem to mind as one of the two other women in the group, which appeared to include Paul and five or six other men, tried to take one of Paul's arms to guide him toward the elevators. Paul was obviously more alert than the girl thought, as he withdrew the captured appendage and reattached himself to Jancy.

Jancy turned and, reaching around Paul, motioned to an older, black bellman who seemed to read her signal. He started forward with a hanging bar luggage rack; then, seeing her frown and shake her head slightly, he grabbed the upright luggage dolly instead. Jancy smiled, indicating he should place the dolly behind Paul, who was oblivious to the signaling.

Jim couldn't help smiling as Jancy's plan became clear.

She stepped in front of Paul, placed her hands on his stomach and then inched forward, easing him back one step at a time until his feet were on the dolly and his back against the tall handle. She stepped away as the bellman tipped the dolly backward.

"I feel the earth move under my feet . . ." Paul sang loudly as his body leaned with the dolly. Out of balance, he sank to a squat, his expression one of genuine bewilderment.

Jancy handed money to the grinning bellman, who was already en route to the freight elevators.

The revelers, who had been only halfway paying attention, applauded Paul's ignoble exit as a victorious Jancy turned to rejoin them.

Jim swiveled on the bar stool to look at her rather than the reflection.

Not twenty feet away, she glanced at him and did a double take as a startled look replaced the laughter on her face.

"Hello?" She spoke uncertainly, the word more of an inquiry than a greeting, and she didn't move.

Jim regarded her solemnly. "Hello." He nodded pleasantly, as if addressing a stranger.

"Hello!" She repeated the word more eagerly, certainty replacing uncertainty, and began walking toward him.

Jim smiled and, without taking his eyes off of her, set his glass on the bar. "Hello." He stood.

At that moment Jancy's expression, a torrid mix of emotions, revealed all Jim wanted to know.

Repeating, "Hello, hello, hello," grinning broadly, she launched into his arms.

Jim laughed out loud as Jancy kissed his throat and his chin, standing on tiptoes trying to reach his mouth. He toyed with her a moment, dodging her attack, until she faltered and he detected the pout, then he lowered his mouth to consume hers. Bystanders watched, astonished.

One of the men in her group gawked. "That guy has got to have the world's best opening line."

"Damned effective. Easy to learn. Only the one word."

Several of the men in Jancy's group discussed it round robin. "I think I've figured out my problem. I say too much. I need to get one word like that, then practice it 'til I get it right."

The men laughed boisterously, clapping each other on the back and consoling one another.

I turned and gave those clowns the evil eye for laughing at me.

"I hope that's Jim Wills," Jason said, sobering and eying me suspiciously.

It was my turn to pretend. I acted surprised and shrugged. "No. I've never seen this guy before. I just like the cut of his jib."

"Sure you do," Aaron muttered as the bunch ambled toward the elevators.

"Come on." I looped my arm through Jim's and enjoyed subtly groping his marvelous biceps, "let's go to my room."

He balked. "I'd rather sit down here and talk for a few minutes, if you don't mind."

That surprised me and the little warning hairs on the back of my neck went on alert, but I nodded and tried to act like I didn't imagine anything was wrong. "Okay."

Jim guided me to a darkened booth he probably had spotted earlier, in a far corner of the bar. He motioned me to sit, then slid in beside me. It had been so long since so much of him had stimulated so much of me, I couldn't help myself. I snuggled under his arm and kissed the side of his face. His response was entirely satisfactory and we went after it for a couple of minutes, quick little kisses spelling long breathless ones.

I came up for air first, barely aware of where we were, then deciding we should go someplace more private. "Why did we stay down here? What do you want to talk about?"

He signaled the waitress. "Do you want something to drink?"

I had a feeling I might need to keep my mental faculties sharp, so I shook my head, all the while trying to read his face. When he turned his attention to the waitress to order another bourbon and water, I slipped the ring off my finger and dropped it into my pocket.

Jim turned his attention back to me. "I was watching when you came in. I saw you give Paul the bum's rush. Smooth. You look like an expert at beating back the hordes. Has he been pestering you?"

Was that jealousy? Well, we'd nip that right in the bud. I laughed lightly. "He's only one of many."

"Paul fancies himself quite the ladies' man."

"I know, but I wouldn't follow this too far, Jim, if I were you. Rosie tattled. She tells me I'm not the only one drawing attention from the opposite sex. She says you've had your hands full of women willing 'to help you in your time of despair.' "

"That's different."

"Yeah, right. How many are we talking about?"

He grimaced. "I went out to Roper's one night to reminisce and watch the dancers. Angie was there. She had an argument with her date and asked for a ride home. I gave her a lift to the house. That's all."

"How much had you had to drink?" I watched his face, reading every change in his expression, listening for every nuance.

He grinned. "Not nearly enough."

"And good old Marilyn Maddox on the election board?"

"How'd you hear about that?"

"You know I don't reveal my sources." I arched my eyebrows. " 'Fess up."

"The Tuesday night after the city elections, I was at the courthouse. Denman invited us over to his place for a victory party. Marilyn rode with me. Ben and Liz were in front of us and jumped to a hasty conclusion. When we got there, I couldn't very well explain how we happened to be there together without it sounding like a disclaimer. I didn't want to hurt Marilyn's feelings."

"Rosie said Marilyn got to her goal weight and looks good."

"True. She looks real good."

"And Ben said she's awfully sweet."

"Very sweet." Jim flashed a playful grin.

I braced myself. "Are you interested in Marilyn?"

"No, baby. Sweet's not my type. You know that. I like my women sassy, like you."

Suddenly I remembered another troubling report and my confidence deflated. "And there was someone else."

Jim looked as if he genuinely had no idea who that might be.

"My source said the girl was short with dark hair, gorgeous, young, a great dancer, hung all over you at Bailey's on Halloween."

His face brightened. "She is a sweet thing. That was Evie, my baby sister."

"Oh." I felt crestfallen and relieved at the same time. Then I remembered my earlier concern and stiffened. "Why are we down here? Did you come all the way out to California to tell me face to face something I don't want to hear?"

"I hope not." He lifted my hand and kissed the inside, then turned it over. "What's this?" He tapped the white line around the otherwise tanned ring finger of my left hand. "You didn't tell me you were wearing the ring."

I pulled my hand out of his grasp. "Jim, are you trying to let me down easy?"

"What about the ring?"

He was avoiding my questions and making me mad. "That's got nothing to do with you."

"It's my ring."

"It doesn't mean you own me."

"An engagement ring usually means somebody does."

My head was beginning to hurt and I hated the tenor of this whole conversation. "A ring doesn't do all that much good around here anyway."

"You mean they just keep coming?"

I scowled down at the table. "This is not the way this conversation should be going, is it?"

Jim drew a deep breath. "I only want to know if you're dating anyone."

"No, I'm not, but I don't think you're supposed to ask. Wasn't that our deal?"

He nodded, but didn't speak.

"I hang out with those people I was with tonight, if I go out at all. How about you?"

He chuckled under his breath. "No. But you're right, we agreed dating was allowed. Now, why aren't you?"

I gave him a wry smile, surrendering. "It wouldn't be any fun. I don't really laugh without you. I couldn't even smile the first week I was here. It was no fun seeing the ocean or the canyons or even Balboa Park Zoo without you. Watching the monkeys, I started crying because I wanted to tell you something and you weren't here.

"When I want to treat myself, I sit in my room and stare at the calendar, counting the days to December nineteenth."

"Is that when you're through here?"

"Yes. Riley's letting me go home for fifteen days." I lowered my voice. "It's a furlough before I fly to London on January third." I saw his jaw flinch but when he spoke, his words sounded kind.

"Good for you. Congratulations."

I had no control over the tears that puddled in my eyes. Watching me closely, Jim said, "That is what you want, isn't it?"

I didn't speak for several seconds, struggling for control.

"Aren't you happy?" he asked.

Mutely, I shook my head no and my lips puckered into a pout. I smashed my mouth to his shoulder, wrapped my hands tightly around his arm and sat for a dozen heartbeats before I made another attempt at conversation. "I want to spend every minute of my time off with you." My voice was husky, resigned, and revealed all my doubts and fear. "Will you take some vacation days, come to Carson's Summit for Christmas?"

Jim studied me quietly a long time before he answered. "No, I don't want to spend Christmas in Carson's Summit."

I looked up, blinking back tears and trying to read his face. "Okay, I'll ask Rosie if I can stay at the house in Bishop for a few days."

"I don't want to spend Christmas in Bishop either." He stared directly into my face.

Was he trying to tell me something? I was wracked with doubt and confusion, but I plowed on in spite of it. "Okay, I'll go to Dominion or wherever you say. I only know I have to be with you."

He shook his head again, looking terribly grim. Then, very softly, he said, "We can't be together over the holidays."

I waited, too stunned to throw up any defenses. When his eyes met mine, however, I saw a glimmer. "Unless. . . ."

"What?" My voice sounded almost as frantic as I felt. "How can we be together?"

"There is only one way."

"Okay. I'll take it. How?"

"We can get married."

If he had slapped me, I don't think I would have been more startled. I slumped a shoulder against the booth's back, too stunned to say a word. He didn't press it, only waited until I got myself together enough to respond. "What do you mean?"

His expression was set. "The only way we can be together this Christmas is if we are married."

I unwrapped my hands from his arm, slouched in the booth and frowned straight ahead at a dark, blank wall. "But what about . . . ?"

Jim shrugged. "We'll work it out."

I sat quietly, studying the room but struggling not to contemplate the question at hand. The waitress brought Jim's drink, which he downed in a series of swigs. Then, I got sort of an idea.

"Can I have some time to think about it?" I didn't look at him, trying not to let him read my thoughts, which might be projected on my face. Instead of waiting for him to think out an answer, I just plunged ahead. "I'd better go up now. Oh," I asked, pretending the thought was incidental, as we slid out of the booth, "where are you staying?"

"With Paul."

"He's. . . ." I hesitated.

"Drunk? Yeah, I know, I saw you come in, remember? He may not know I'm there. I picked up a key earlier."

We walked to the elevators in silence. I rang for a car, then turned to Jim. "Are you ready to go up now?"

"Yes. I've been drinking, as I'm sure you noticed. I need a designated driver."

I chuckled. "To drive the elevator?"

He grinned back.

We stepped into the elevator and I returned his kind expression patronizingly. As the car climbed, I kept my eyes locked on the monitor. When I finally looked at him, his eyes widened as if he wanted to and couldn't read the expression on my face. That was probably best.

We stepped off together on the ninth floor. Paul's room was on eleven but, as I knew he would, Jim walked me all the way to my door.

I produced the key and unlocked, then turned and raised my face for a goodnight kiss. His eyes narrowed suspiciously, but he obliged me. He acted surprised when I pressed my body close to his and opened my mouth to invite his tongue without any prodding.

Locked in that intense embrace, I could feel him warming nicely. Moving slowly, proceeding with my plan, I backed into the room and tugged him along. Grabbing both sides of the doorjamb, abruptly, he abandoned the kiss. The puzzled expression on his face had cleared.

"Not a chance." He smiled through narrowed, seeing eyes. "A team of horses couldn't drag me through this door tonight."

I gave him my wide-eyed innocent look. "Whatever do you mean?"

"I know you. I remember our little discussion about 'if you can have the milk free . . . ?' "

I shrugged, pretending not to understand.

"That cuts both ways, Jance. I've set my stud fee for you, darlin'. Full price, full service only. No free samples. No one-night adventures. I want two whole weeks of honeymoon, leisurely lovemaking, just you and me, no interruptions, no diversions."

"Please," I whispered, drawing an index finger to his belt buckle before he stopped it. "Just this once."

Jim glanced in at the bed dominating the room behind me and gritted his teeth. "No. With you and me, sugar, it's all or nothin'." With one more longing look at the bed, he snorted, shook his head, turned and trotted double-time down the hall toward the elevators.

Paul was reading but laid his book aside when Jim entered Room Eleven twenty-one.

"Hey, bro. Saw your bag. Couldn't get a foot in the door, could you? Don't feel bad, Jimbo, she's bounced the best. Even me. But I'm making progress."

Mumbling a non-answer, Jim hung up his clothes, doused

the lamp on his side, and got into bed. He propped his hands behind his head and stared at the ceiling. Ordinarily he wasn't much of a gambler. He'd just put down what was probably the biggest bet of his life. Now all he needed was the fortitude to bluff it through.

CHAPTER THIRTY-FIVE

When I called at four-thirty a.m., Jim picked up the phone on the first ring. "Hello."

"Okay." My voice sounded hollow as it echoed around my room.

"When?"

I gulped back a throat full of nerves. "My flight goes home Tuesday the nineteenth. My folks will meet me. I've talked to my mom several times. We can have the St. George Chapel at my church at seven p.m. on Friday December twenty-second."

There was definite relief, maybe even a smile in his voice. "December twenty-second?"

"Is that significant?"

He chuckled. "The twenty-first is the longest night of the year."

I took a deep breath. "It can't be any longer than this one has been. Now will you come to my room?"

"No, but I'll meet you in the coffee shop. They open at five. Unless you want to sleep."

"I can't. I've tried. I look awful."

"Not to me."

Jim looked perfectly groomed standing at the door of the coffee shop when the morning manager unlocked it at four-fifty-four a.m. I got off the elevator feeling rumpled in the same tan slacks and sweater I'd worn earlier. I was pleasantly surprised to find him there already, not late for once.

Wordlessly, he put a consoling arm around my shoulders, guided me to a booth and held up two fingers to the waitress, who grabbed a coffee pot on her way to our table.

When she had gone, I wriggled a hand into the pocket of my slacks and produced the ring, which I handed to Jim. He slid it onto my finger, then gave me a businesslike kiss on either side of my face, like one Russian dignitary greeting another.

Feeling a little out-of-sync, I just sat there admiring the many-faceted ring. "I don't know if we're doing the right thing or not."

"It's the rightest thing you've ever done in your life," he said.

"Are you sure?"

"Yes."

"Are you sure enough for both of us?"

"Yes. In most marriages, Jance, one of the parties loves the other a little bit more. When it's the man, when he's the moving force, the marriage seems to have a better chance. If that theory's true, we're a cinch."

"Is that the way it was with your parents?"

"And even more significantly, that's the way it was with yours."

Already disoriented, I gave him a hard look. "You mean you've talked to them about this?"

"Certainly. You didn't think I'd take such a monumental step without consulting the father of the bride, did you?"

"When?"

"I took some papers to Carson's Summit a couple of weeks ago, on a Wednesday. He invited me out for lunch."

"Lions Club?"

Jim nodded ruefully, which made me laugh in spite of the solemn circumstances. "We got along great until the Tail Twister asked your dad to identify me. He had one hell of a time trying to explain exactly who I was. He finally just said, 'I think of him as a third son.' "

We both laughed before I sobered again. "You're saying Daddy thinks it'll work?"

Jim pretended to be offended. "Does his opinion mean more to you than mine?"

I smiled sheepishly, which seemed to please him.

"There's another little irony. Your mother was right. I will be married before Christmas."

Suddenly things seemed better, my future brighter, some of the anticipated obstacles hurdled and behind us. Jim was right there, looking and smelling marvelously familiar and so sexy. I got onto my knees in the booth and began kissing the side of his marvelous face, his ear and his neck until he was forced to defend himself, which he did vigorously.

ABOUT THE AUTHOR

A former newspaper reporter, **Sharon Ervin** has a degree in journalism from the University of Oklahoma. She is married, lives in McAlester, Oklahoma, and has four grown children.

Sharon's published novels include *The Ribbon Murders* (first of the Jancy Dewhurst series), 2006; *Chick Lit for Foxy Hens*, 2006; *Weekend Wife*, 2005; *Counterfeit Cowboy*, 2005; *Bodacious*, 2002; and *Jusu and Mother Earth*, 2000.

Her short work has appeared in *Newsweek, The Harvard Review, Whispers From Heaven, Pray!, True Love, The PEO Record, Arabella*, and other national publications.

Sharon is active in Romance Writers of America and Tulsa affiliate Romance Writers Ink, Sisters in Crime, the Oklahoma Writers Federation, the Lesser North Texas Writers and McAlester's McSherry Writers. Visit Sharon's Web site at www.sharonervin.com.